From Grandeville, A Tale.
Tale Two - Second Edition

LAIR

Being A Place

Where Things Chose To Live.

George R. Mead

E-Cat Worlds Press

Questions, or, comments -> gmead01@gmail.com

LAIR

LCCN 2015913144

Mead, George R.
Portal /George R. Mead.
p. cm.

ISBN-13 978-0-9890927-5-3
1. Portal. Series. From Grandeville – A Tale.

E-Cat Worlds Press, 57744 Foothill Road, La Grande OR 97850
www.ecatworldspress.com
SAN 255-6383

Second Edition: September 2017
Printed in the United States of America

Nonfiction

A History of Union County
The Ethnobotany of the California Indians, 2nd Edition
A History of The Chinese in The West: 1848-1880
Yachats. The Town Called "Dark Water at the Foot of the Mountains."

Fiction

From Grandeville – A Tale.
Portal (revised)
Lair (2nd Edition - revised)
Search
Not Again
And Again.
Magiwitch
Rebirth
Offspring
Holiday
Treasure
E'Nilt
Braidna
Chyndra and Seemna

A Tale of The Feyra
Jonathon and Dee
Dee Of The Fontala
Dee and The People
Dee and The Golden Cartouche

The Seven Lands
(With Zakke L. Zacog)
Seventeen Siblings

Stream
Special Investigator
Dark Souls

To Eastyn.

Just Because.

Tell me a story!

Sure. How's this?

The story always old, and always new.
Robt Browning, *The Ring and the Book,* 1868.

There's only one length for a story and that's the right length.
J. J. Connington, *Four Defenses,* 1940.

This is the tale, as it is told.
Herodotus, *History,* Ca. 445 B.C.

I know all that, just tell me the story!

O. K., here is the tale.

>>>> 2 <<<<

Grandeville Anecdotes

Grandeville. Doc's Home. Mid-Afternoon.

"Well, John, it is good to have you back with us again. It has been almost a year, umm, more or less"

Dr. Kappa Heckmann (called *Doc* by one and all) was addressing his guest at one of his, Doc's, usual, small, late afternoon/early evening gatherings. This one had been hastily called together, earlier than usual, shortly after their "guest" had arrived on Doc's doorsteps, just around noon. The small group was now seated around the large, oak table, leaning back in various postures of slump, very relaxed, sipping their coffee.

Doc smiled at his guest.

"J. C. told me that he hadn't related our little adventure of this past summer to you yet. Too bad you weren't around, you could have joined us in all the fun."

J. C. winced at Doc's usage of the term *fun*.

Doc beamed at his assistant, helper, and associate, J. C. Smith.

The rest of the folk around the table were Old John, and Alandale Frederico Hardcastle IV, known to his friends as *Hard* and The Membrane, as he preferred to be called, one of two of Doc's assistants (as he chose to call them), was a great hulk of a man who had to duck and twist to get through all standard doorways, the other assistant was a small man of slight build, just a wee bit taller than Doc, who was quite short, called Badnews, not a nickname, his given name. He was a very quiet person who seemed to watch everything and nothing, at the same time, with soft brown eyes.

Hard, the somewhat confused looking young man, was a close friend of J. C. and Tinker, and was the only son of the wealthiest family in the local area, if not in the entire state. Old John, John Nerald, was the owner and operator of the local weekly newspaper, *The Mountain View*. It was a newspaper that he had bought some time ago, a kind of working retirement, as he explained it.

As you can tell, the group tended to address each other mostly by their acknowledged nicknames. The group had been meeting, randomly, for a number of years for good food and conversation. But today was an occasion. They were celebrating the return to Grandeville of John Tinker, who had left, suddenly, just about a year ago, more or less.

Tinker smiled at his host and shrugged.

"I was otherwise engaged," he sorta explained, "but, it really is good to be back. I can't stay long, should be getting to my place soon. See what has happened, things like that. Although I imagine that Master Chen has pretty much kept everything in running order."

Doc joined the rest in good humored laughter.

"I dare say, John" he said, " I dare say. Chen has no doubt kept it better than ever you did. Let's head for the living room, shall we? It is a better place for sitting and talking. I've been hearing the most astonishing things from Old John." He winked at Tinker.

As Doc waved them down the hallway. J.C. began to quickly clean the table. Hard helped him.

"We'll wait, J.C." Doc jabbed a thumb over his shoulder. "It seems that in greater downtown Grandeville strange things have been happening. But I'll let our newspaper wizard tell all. He got it straight from the horse's mouth, so to speak."

As they entered the living room and took their customary seats, Old John guffawed at Doc's comments.

"He means that I just heard these things from Quick Draw."

The Chief of Police of the Grandeville Police Department had acquired his nickname a few years back when he had participated in the annual "Wild West" carnival as part of the Downtown Merchants Association planned festivities designed to attract people to visit downtown and hopefully to shop locally.

It seems that his trigger finger was faster than his quick-draw. And as it turned out, it seemed that he had forgotten to load his gun with blanks. So he shot a hole in one foot, gained a very slight limb, and earned an interesting nickname. Which he had learned to hate. None of his immediate employees, that is, members of The Grandeville Police Department, would dare use that nickname within his hearing.

J. C. hurried in, poured everyone a liberal portion of one of Doc's fine brandies, and sat down. Hard followed him in, tripped over the threshold and took his place. No one paid any attention to this. Hard tripped over almost anything, or perhaps, everything. Even things that weren't really there. Everyone settled in their chairs and waited.

Tinker looked at the newspaperman. "O.K., Old John, what's been happening downtown?"

"Well, Young John, some pretty funny things. Even for our fair city. At least the way I hear them they seem to be some pretty funny things."

"What sort of funny things?"

"The kind that pour from the mouth of a bottle."

"Bottle?"

Doc smiled in anticipation.

"As it was told to me," began Old John, "this happened about a two weeks ago. Red and Green, LPD's two-man riot squad, were cruising the gut around 2:15 or 2:30 A.M., after the bars had closed, and they spotted Blind Staggers running pell-mell right down the center line of the main drag." He waved one hand.

"Now as you know, at that hour of the morning, in our fair city, that would be a perfectly safe thing to do, running down the middle of Main Street at that time of night. But, none-the-less, they drove up alongside the hard charging Blind Staggers, popped on their flashing lights, and asked him to pull over to the curb. As Blind Staggers was running out of gas anyway, metaphorically speaking, he lurched to the nearest lamppost, wrapped himself around it, and waited for the usual grilling." Old John smiled at the image he was painting.

"Red asked him what he thought he was doing running down the middle of the street at this time in the morning. Blind Staggers said that he was trying to get away from the rock that had bitten him. Green said, get in the back, and they took him to the station.

"And left him in charge of Beer Belly Berry, the sheriff's deputy, the only man on duty in the city and county shared pokie, and then went back on patrol.

"Now, as you know, Beer Belly is more than a little acquainted with Blind Staggers, they both being inhabitants of many of the same establishments, especially The Railroad Bar and Grill. So he was able to get a coherent, well, at least as coherent a story as anyone can ever get, from Blind Staggers. And this is what Blind Staggers told his old drinking buddy."

When the Railroad Bar and Grill had closed down, he, Blind Staggers, had headed for home in the company of another of our well-known denizens, Choo-Choo. They had headed straight across the railroad tracks, taking their usual shortcut. Their path took them across all three of the main lines and then diagonally through the switchyard.

As they were crossing the switch yard, Choo-Choo decided that it was time to have a little conversation with another old friend of his, the switch engine. So Blind Staggers went on alone. He had almost made it across the last stretch when he thought he saw something moving off to one side. At first he thought it was the large racoon that was bothering his place, so he ran right up to it and gave it a boot. He swears that if his vision had been clearer and his aim truer, he would have broken his foot. It was a large boulder.

He sat down, took off his shoe, and began to massage his foot, the one that he had kicked the rock with, when up it came. This great, big rock, it just sort of sauntered right up to him. Paused. And bit him on the bare foot. It scared him so badly, he ran the wrong way, clear across the tracks and back into downtown.

He thought that he heard it coming after him, and so there he was, ripping right down the center line of Main Street, when he was pulled over by Red and Green. And a good thing it was too. His bare foot was wearing thin.

Beer Belly put him in an empty cell and told him he would be perfectly safe. In the morning, they would go take a look. Of course, in the morning they couldn't find a thing.

"Nothing at all?"

"Nope, John, nothing at all. Other than his boot which he had abandoned during his flight toward the safety of greater downtown Grandeville. They even had a hard time figuring out the exact place where this alleged assault happened. There weren't any large rocks to be found. They did roust out Choo-Choo, who was taking a snooze on the turntable but he claimed that he hadn't heard a thing."

"And that's the news from downtown?"

Old John shook his head, and smiled at his audience. "There is more."

"Really?" Tinker smiled, marveling, once again, at what passed for excitement in this isolated rural valley in the northeast corner of Oregon.

Doc started giggling. J.C. decided everyone needed another hit of brandy. All waited for the next thrilling episode as J. C. poured.

Old John took an appreciative sip, smiled, and nodded.

"Yes, there is certainly more. In fact, if there is

much more news of this nature, the Chief is threatening to get the Health Department to run a quick check on the liquid refreshments that are being sold locally. It seems something is affecting the denizens of the local pubs in the most remarkable way."

Tinker rolled his eyes at Doc who was beginning to snort and gurgle.

"What else have you heard?"

"Weeeeeeelllll, this next story happened just about a week ago. This time it was Choo-Choo's turn."

Choo-Choo had been making a cycle between the back door of B.D's, down the alley, around the corner, and then into the Rail. Well, there he was, just chugging along. Hauling freight right down the alley, taking it easy because there is a slight down grade in that area.

He could see the crossing ahead, so he gave a whistle. Just to warn anyone who might be coming along the sidewalk, and then he saw it.

"Now, you have to realize that this is yet another second-hand story. I also got this one from Beer Belly, who was also on duty at the time. In fact, it was the monster cops, Red and Green, who grabbed Choo-Choo as he was making his second lap around the block screeching his emergency whistle at full volume.

"Anyhow, it seems, as he explained to Red and Green, that when he gave his warning blast, as he neared the crossing, sidewalk and alley, that a great black shape leapt straight up the wall of one of the buildings abutting the alley. And disappeared over the top of the roof. Now, as you know, they are all two-story buildings in that section of town.

"In that alley, it is just a flat, brick surface walls,

all the way. No windows, no doors on the alley. Choo-Choo swears that what he saw was a werewolf. And that he wasn't going to haul any more freight along that route ever again."

Old John paused dramatically. "Like those stories?" He smiled at Tinker.

Tinker laughed. "Yep, they're nice. I can see that life in beautiful, downtown Grandeville has kept its flavor and character while I was gone. But, it does make one wonder what sort of potion they are selling the good folk."

Old John nodded in agreement.

"Certainly does. As a matter of fact, The Chief was getting rather suspicious of the downtown establishments serving those two. I told him, just as a favor, that I would ask around. Figured that the press might be able to do a better job. Well, as far as I able to find out, they were all drinking the usual stuff. Although there is an interesting switch to these stories. Both these two nighthawks had worked a few, small jobs, and were, in both cases, spending their hard won earnings on better than average, regulation, over-the-counter hooch, served by old what's-his-face at the Railroad Bar and Grill and Big Darlene at Big Darlene's. So, I rather suspect, their adventures, as amusing as they were, have more to do with the state of the pickling of their brains than anything being served and consumed locally."

Doc had finally regained control. "Quite so, Old John, quite so. And here's to ingesting a little of the old stuff." He raised his brandy snifter, swirled around the liquid therein, and took an appreciative swallow. He smiled. "And it is quite good, too."

Tinker rose, stretched, and yawned. "Well Doc, it's good to be back, but I ought to go. It's been a long day's drive from the coast. Thanks for the meal, and the updates, always a pleasure." He turned slightly. "Thanks for your stories, John."

Then he waved at J.C. and the rest. "The hour is getting on. And Chen doesn't take kindly to being surprised, by me. J. C., Badnews, in a couple of days, perhaps, we can get together and practice?"

Badnews nodded his head. J.C. jumped to his feet, strode over and clapped Tinker on one shoulder. "It would be great, just great. I need all the practice I can get. Unlike Badnews."

J.C. stopped Tinker as they headed down the hall for the kitchen door. "You have a little more time?"

"Huh?"

J.C. smiled."Thought that I'd tell you what I did on my summer vacation." He laughed. "Our last summer's fun as Doc likes to call it. Seeing as we are telling stories of events in the recent past."

"Sure." Tinker shrugged. "It's a short drive."

"Fine. Let's go up to my rooms. It's not too long a story."

And once they were there, J.C. fished a slip of paper from a shelf and handed it to his friend. "Read this. Dr. Ben gave it to me. Sorta. Then I will tell you my tale of adventure."

Tinker took the paper and looked at it. It was a short note. Written on the back of a sales slip from Ah Fong's Chocolate Delights, Karachi, India.

Gray, Herbert Louis (1917. THE MYTHOLOGY OF ALL RACES. VOL. IV: INDIA AND IRANIAN.)

The Rakshasa are of a particularly terrible aspect: the red hair and eyes and a mouth stretching from ear to ear, the later being pointed like spears. Large and strong, they wander in the darkness and are unconquerable at midnight, and they are skilled sorcerers and wizards, changing shape at will. They haunt the woods and lonely mountains, but they also lie in wait for the pious at places of pilgrim and worship. They delight in destroying the sacrifice and are cannibals, desiring human flesh; yet they can appear in beautiful form when they wish to deceive the unwary.

Tinker looked up.

"Sometimes," began J.C., settling back into a comfortable slump, "life's little adventures start in more malevolent ways. In other places."

Beginnings

Jerusalem.

Yuri ben David Hafas, Ph.D. - Anthropology, bent over his work bench, elbows propped in the carefully organized clutter. He paused and sighed and thought about the heat outside and the noise and dust of Jerusalem. And then he thanked the powers-that-be for understanding the reason for the air-conditioned laboratory.

Studying the relics, he mumbled to himself. Hafas was his own best audience and critic. His focus, as always, was intense and total. He didn't notice that hot day had long since grown into warm night, that the university had been abandoned to the solitary scholar. Even if he had noticed, he would have merely shrugged a shoulder and then continued on with his work.

Hafas made careful notes in his lab book with his right hand as he turned over in his left hand one of the many artifacts recovered from this past season's "dig." There was something about these new bits and pieces, recovered around the newly discovered interior structure, that did not seem quite right. What ever was wrong about them, he did not know. But what he did know was that sooner or later he would figure it out. After all, he was one of the best in his field. Ummmmmm, well, maybe the best.

But there was something here, something about

the shape or the form that was just not proper. His feelings about this were very strong, feelings based upon the intuitive skills that thirty years of study and hard work had developed. There was some minor detail that didn't fit the normal pattern, a small anomaly. A few quick notes and then he picked up the next specimen.

The clock on the wall, stark white face outlined in black metal, every room had one just like it, indicated that it was midnight. Hafas worked on, driven by the need, the desire to know. As he worked his own internal clock told him that by the dawn's breaking that he would have this little puzzle worked out. He would add one more bit of information to the total analysis of the archaeological site, one more piece to be shared with his colleagues working in their laboratories in Rome, Paris, and London.

Hafas sat and worked. The overhead lamp illuminating the scholar sitting in center stage covered by a cone of light edged by dark shadow. The dark shadow breathed softly.

The minute hand on the clock eased its way past vertical.

A dense odor tickled Hafas' nose. It interrupted his concentration. Turning around, he pushed his glasses to the top of his head and peered vaguely toward the back of the room, into the dim reaches of the laboratory, searching for the cause.

One of the sorting tables lurched and toppled over, spilling artifacts and labels. Hafas leaped to his feet. "Who's there?"

A filing cabinet crashed to its side, one drawer

sliding opening coughing papers onto the floor. Hafas jumped sideways as the papers slid to his feet. "Who's there? What do you think you're doing?"

Sudden pain ripped his chest. Hafas gasped and staggered back and fell, a slow twisting spiral down. His vision blurred, his ears rung. He could barely hear another sorting table topple or barely feel with numbing legs the weight pinning him in place.

Books and papers showered down upon him, tumbling clouds of notes, loose sheets of paper swirled from shelves and bookcases, covering Hafas in a drift of knowledge. One arm crawled out and wiggled feeble fingers toward the distant door. A fire began to smoulder at the outskirts of the three year's accumulation of ideas and concepts.

Rome.

Annmarie Corruccini, Ph.D. – Archaeology, carefully studied the large statue, just taken from the Robsen-Brown excavation this past field season. A life size representation of what? Surprisingly heavy.

Annmarie had hoisted it up and set it on top of a pedestal. Now she could walk around it and study the lower portions without crawling on the floor or standing bent over like a market crone. It had taken several hours and her overhead hoist to set him just so. Now, finally freed of all the ropes and thick padding, he was ready for study, close scrutiny.

She had been working all day long on some of the smaller and minor figurines taken from the site this past season and finally finished her preliminary workup early in the evening. Then, Annmarie had decided to start studying this magnificent piece right away rather than waiting until tomorrow. This very large, very puzzling piece.

So she had returned to her loft, after a late dinner, head full of new ideas that she had visualized while she ate. She walked around it, stared up at his face. The figure was obviously male, thick set, powerful, legs slightly bent, seeming ready to spring. She dragged her aluminum step-ladder over and clambered up. Circling his head, much like a crown, was an intertwined mass of cording with a curious blotted appearance. Around his neck he wore a thin cord of some type.

Annmarie peered at his hair with a small magnifying glass. There were still flecks of yellow paint deep in the pores of the stone. She stepped down two rungs.

He appeared to be gnawing on a human head, fresh enough to have discernable features. In his other hand he held a skull, bottom up. Or perhaps it was just a chalice that had the appearance of a skull. She stepped to the floor and dragged the step-ladder out of the way, turned and stared. Other than the two cords, a bulging loincloth was his only other apparel.

She peered here and there with her glass. At some time in the past this being had been painted black. Putting the glass in her smock, she bent forward. Encircling both feet were clusters of small creatures, vultures, ravens, dogs, and a strange hoofed thing, partially human and partially something else, warped and bent. This jumble of beings obscured the feet although she could just make out a couple of claw-tipped toes protruding from beneath the throng.

Annmarie stepped back again and looked up. It was interesting, that face. It almost reminded her of someone. Somehow the sculpture had designed it so that it always seemed to be watching you. The being, some type of deity perhaps, scowled down at her, with just the hint of a smile as the sharp teeth bit into the flesh of the severed head it held.

She smiled back and thought it to be, overall, a rather interesting statue when judged in terms of the sculptor's treatment, the long ago artist approach. Then she shook her head, none-the-less what it represented was a rather unpleasant personage. It seemed to be to be an evil thing. Leaning forward. Anticipating what?

Then she leaned forward to stare at some small detail of the loincloth, some sort of woven pattern, face almost brushing the strange stone. She wrinkled her nose. There seemed to be some sort of unpleasant odor seeping from the statue.

She shrugged her shoulder as she straightened up. The odor, no doubt, had been something that transferred from whatever packing material they had used during the crating back in India.

Annmarie took a quick glance, her last glance, over at her mantel clock, out of place in her workshop, at her treasure. Her clock was ticking away in the midst of boards and jars and other paraphernalia used at some time or another. The clock started a soft, melodic song, telling the hour.

Midnight.

Her head snapped around. She had just heard a soft crushing sound. She gasped, her eyes widening as the statue toppled forward.

Annmarie didn't hear the other figurines being smashed. Or see her papers and notes, books, and files being scattered over the fragments and herself. She couldn't smell the smoke as small flames began to eat their way into the papers demurely covering her, arms and legs flung wide.

The stone face smiled over her shoulder as the figure held her crushed in his rock shattered embrace.

Once upon a Time

Grandeville. Doc's Home. Morning

The monster walked into the library at exactly 9:47 a.m. I knew what time it was, I had glanced up at the clock. But it was all right. He was one of our's.

I had been up since six, my usual time for rising. Then the usual fast breakfast and I had secluded myself in the library, to work and to recover. It had been quite a weekend.

Two and half days of wedding celebration. My best girl friend and ex-fiancee, Shannon, had tied the knot with Deke Morgan, recently arrived to our valley to establish his corporate headquarters here, on their newly acquired ranch. And I had given her away.

Then yesterday, late, I had dragged myself home and to bed. Completely wrecked. For me.

But I recover fast.
    It's all in the genes.
So there I was. In the library.
    Working.
        Just like I was supposed to be.

The library is a nice place to work. It has book shelves from floor to ceiling, covering most of the walls, broken only by the two tall, narrow windows in the east wall, and by the protective heat shield behind the small wood-burning stove which crackles so pleasantly on cold winter days.

But, it being summer, the stove just sat there, waiting, patiently, gathering dust.

Diagonally across the room from my desk there is a spiral staircase. That's my room, up there. Fairly handy, at times.

Well, as I said, there I was. Working away. Same as many other days or nights. But, my stomach had interrupted my chain of thought. I take a lot of food during recuperation.

So I took a sip of coffee and glanced up at the clock. It occupied one part of a book shelf. Served as a sort of book-end.

It was 9:47 a.m.

Exactly.

Almost time for doughnuts.

A soft knock caressed the door.

"Yeah, come on in, you won't be disturbing anything. I'm almost finished." I was just putting the finishing touches to Doc's article for one of the anthropological journals.

The door swung inward and the Membrane stepped in, ducking and twisting. His real name is Reginald Percival Habsling. In an irrational moment I had called him *The Swollen Membrane.* Which soon was shorten to *Membrane* and the nickname had stuck.

He didn't mind. Which had been a great relief for me.

The Membrane, once known as *The Terror of Oakland* stands about 7′ 6″ by roughly 41″ wide at the shoulders, his widest part. And he weighs in the general vicinity of 300 pounds of muscle, give or take a bunch.

As Doc tells it, he found him, so to speak, while Doc was doing what he referred to as "a little fieldwork" in the bay area, that is, San Francisco and environs.

The fieldwork had been taking place in a certain restaurant-bar, *Biker's Heaven,* when the denizens of said place decided to convert our errant anthropologist into an ornament for one of their bikes. As they converged on him, Doc thought he saw an enraged grizzly bear charge through the door from the adjoining pool room. The ensuing rumpus wrecked much of *Biker's Haven,* an even dozen Harley-Davidsons of various shapes and forms, and severely damaged a large number of the bike's owners.

Doc came out of it unscathed. The Membrane with minor scrapes and bruises.

Later, in the courtroom, and then in the judge's chambers, Doc, somehow, manage to convince the judge, a very understanding lady, that he could remove the chaos from Oakland by hiring *The Terror* to oversee some stores that he was opening and by relocating the rather large problem to Grandeville, Oregon. And all's well that ends well. The lie materialized, Doc opened the stores, forced into it by his conscious, I suppose. You've probably seen one, *Cactus Spine,* specializing in cactus and succulents (stores in Washington, Oregon, California, and Idaho). The Membrane became an amateur authority on the Cactaceae in the process.

But enough of that. I put the materials that I was working on into their proper file folder, dropped that in the small filing cabinet.

"What's up?"

He sighed, rumble, rumble. A log truck at idle.

"Doc wants to see you. The mail just arrived and some letter from England has got him worked up. You know what that means."

Did I ever. Doc was headed into some new "adventure" as he chose to call his activities. It was my time to sigh. So, I did. The Membrane smiled.

I asked, "Where's Doc?" It always pays to ask. This house tends to sprawl.

"Said to catch him in the kitchen, perking coffee. Bring a note-pad. I'll be in greenhouse two, new shipment of seed just arrived from Germany." He gazed down at his acres of mid-section. "Going to make breakfast soon?"

"Sure. I'll call you."

He turned and ducked out the door. I grabbed a note-pad and followed.

When I got to the kitchen, a short walk from the library, Doc and Badnews were sitting there, drinking Doc's coffee. They're the only two that can. Doc claims it's authentic Greek.

Doc was saying, ". . . and so make contact with some of your colleagues in London, and bring the car around, we will be leaving shortly. My bag is already outside."

Badnews slipped silently away. I took his chair, nicely warmed and pushed his cup away. I'd make another and different pot later on.

Doc beamed in my direction. He does that a lot. "Ah, J.C., complete with note-pad. Ready? Phone the airport and get us, Badnews and I, tickets for London on whatever the first available flight might be. We're leaving in just a moment or two, as you heard. Just leave a message at the information desk." Doc waved a negligent hand. "And get a hold of Dr. David Ben at Columbia and get him out here. Let's see today is Monday, so I should be back by Friday or Saturday. Of course I could be quicker, maybe Thursday. Of course one never knows, does one? Might be later. Right, have him by Friday or Saturday. Now let's see, how to insure that David will come."

Doc's eyes focused elsewhere. Then he laughed at some private joke, he has many, and fidgeted in his chair. And giggled, eyes returning to this world. "Tell him, Rakshasa. Spell it the way it sounds. He will come. OH! And make sure he understands that we are paying all his expenses." His hand waved in my direction now, dismissing my complaint before I could utter it. "I know, I know, we are going to go over this month's allowance, or next month's, or what ever. Not to worry, J.C., jolly Old England ought to catch us up a pound or two."

Doc set both hands on the table, palms down and started to rise. "AH, ah, ah. It will work out. Always does. Doesn't it? Of course it does." Then he plopped down again and began to play with a knife and fork, stopped and pushed a piece of paper at me. "This is the hotel where we will be staying, I think. Badnews and I will hit the bank on the way out of town. Soooooooooo, what else?" He started up again. Plop. Back into his seat.

"Give David the guest room. Ask our friend downtown to look into the deaths of Dr. Yuri ben David

Hafas, late of Jerusalem, and Dr. Annmarie Corruccini, late of Rome. See if he can find out some little tidbits of interest, hum? Then put together an overview of the Harrapan Civilization and antecedents, mostly west of the Indus Valley. Then I want to know what is going on, in terms of prehistory, that is, in and around the region. O.K.? OH, and see if you can have it done by the time we return."

My jaw dropped open. Doc smiled. He reached over the table and patted my arm. And winked. "I know you can do it, J.C. For you, it is just a small thing. Besides, it will keep you out of trouble, I think." He looked up through his eyebrows at me. "You will keep out of trouble, won't you?" He stood. "Oh, well, do at least a preliminary sketch. And entertain David after he arrives. How was the wedding? Saw you come in. You seem to have recovered all right."

He spun around and headed for the door. Then spun around again. "Ah, in case I forgot to mention it, I will probably return Friday. Or maybe later. Questions? No? Then. I am off. Keep busy, stay out of trouble. Make no mischief."

Doc turned, gave a quick wave and popped out the door, down the balcony stairs, into the car and was waving happily from the passenger side as they drove up and around the driveway.

It wasn't exactly a normal happening. But almost. A sort of indication of things to come.

I cleared up the dishes, made a new pot of coffee, breakfast, and called the Membrane.

Then it was back to the library. I cleared a shelf preparatory for the stuff Doc had suggested and labeled it, Rakshasa. The magic word. And sat at the desk.

Pulling the phone over, I did my little chores.

First the airport. By the time Doc and his constant companion get there they'll only have a half an hour to wait. I talked to a friendly voice at the Information Desk and got that settled.

Next item on the list, David Ben at Columbia.

First check the *Guide to Departments of Anthropology* and give it a fast flip, straight to the C-section. Little medical humor there. Perhaps. So, let us see, ummm, ummmm, urn, ah, ha, there it is. Columbia University. And who works there?

Alland . . . Attinsai . . . Ben.

Bingo, there he is. And everything you would ever want to know:

> David Q. Ben (PhD, Chicago 1954; Prof) Mythology and folklore and magic and ritual, psychological anthropology; India, Mesopotamia.

And here at the bottom, the rest:

> Dept of Anth, Columbia U, New York, NY
> Tel. (212) 280-4552,-4553.

Now to see whether David Q can be fetched or not. Dura, dum, te de, dum da. . . "Hello, hello. Is this the Department of Anthropology?. . . Good. Could I please speak to Dr. David Q. Ben, please?. . . Oh, he's not? Could you tell me when he is expected back? Would you tell him that I called?. . . Yes? Good. Tell him

that Dr. Kappa Heckmann called and that I will try and phone back when he is in his office . . . Yes, he could if he
wishes to do so." So I gave the secretary our phone number and hung up.

Well, that takes care of that. Time to go down to the local newspaper and talk with Old John, the sole owner and operator, so to speak, of the weekly. Old John having had worked on some of the major papers here and there. He still has the ability, and the connections, to find out things, if he wants to, that is. My job, convince him to want to.

So off I went to spend the afternoon talking with Old John. I decided to take *The Tank*. It was my van. An honest 85,000 miles on the odometer. The second time around.

It was a very old friend, tried and true, a leftover from my mis-spent student days, many moons ago. The van still runs, moderately well, and does what is needed, most of the time.

The two of us rattle-banged up and around the driveway, waved goodbye to the Membrane, and zipped, so to speak, into town. It wasn't much of a zip. We live on the edge of Grandeville. Not much of a town, either. But what the heck, that's Grandeville.

8,000 souls living out in the rural back country, say backwater, of northeastern Oregon. The town is about 120 years old. The residents aren't sure. Good ideas here are usually twenty years out of date. Those of us who discuss such things call it "The 20-Year Time Warp." We tend to be in the minority.

When you look around at the local decision

making process, the city government, the county government, and the only movie house, you realize you've just categorized the total entertainment in the area. If you throw in the Byzantine machinations of the faculty at the local college you get the overpowering urge to write TV soaps. Or maybe, the Saturday morning cartoons.

I parked my rig in front of *The Green Front,* the local term of endearment for the state-controlled liqueur store. It is painted a state-agency bilious green. Now that was a shock when I first ventured forth, and north, from sunny southern California to begin my long-term student career in Oregon. A state-controlled liqueur store. Whatever on earth! Imagine that!

The *Green Front* is sandwiched between the pool hall and *Chen's Chinese Restaurant*.

I went in.

"Hi, Thomas."

"Hi, J. C. Something for Doc?"

"Nope, Old John."

"Oh." Thomas turned, snatched a jug from the shelf and shoved it into a plain brown wrapper. "Here you are."

I grabbed the package by its neck. "Thanks, Thomas. Bill Doc. See ya."

"Right J. C. Take care."

Reeling from the dazzling repartee, I drove down the street a bit and parked it in the loading zone in front of the office of *The Mountain View*, Old John's pride and joy, *The Weekly*, as it is called locally, has articles in it written by various of the local folk from various of the small towns in and around the valley telling one and all who came to dinner with whom, who went where, that sort of thing. The front page has local news, the second page editorials, the back page questions and comments. The rest is advertisements and the local columns, each appropriately town titled.

Well, there we were, Old John and I, hard at work. Both pair of feet propped up on his desk, one pair from either side, both pair of bodies (don't think about it) tilted back at precarious angles in swivel chairs. Both of us holding coffee cups within which rested a bit of Wild Turkey, Old John's favorite, just captured at the Green Front.

The office was its usual mess. Of course it is really not large enough to be a big mess, just a small controlled mess. In here there is just enough room for the desk, the swivel chairs, two filing cabinets, two layout tables, and the coffeepot. Directly behind Old John was the washroom. That was my view. His view was out through the large plate glass window into the outer office. His two-man crew sat and worked out there.

Past them was a low counter, the old store front, and finally and really "out there," the main street of Grandeville, named, of course, Main Street.

In the display window lurked faded posters and other relics advertising civic functions long since sifted into the dust of ancient memory.

The home of *The Mountain View* was a Salvation Army discard pile. Three desks, three telephones. Each marked a distinct period in history. All the walls were decorated with clip boards, each clutching in spring-loaded mouths a sheaf of yellowed clippings.

Overall, it was a most comfortable and pleasant place to while away an afternoon.

"Well, John," I never called him Old John to his face, only Doc or Tinker can get away with that, "do you think that you can find out what we want to know? I'd like to get it as soon as possible. Doc gets back Friday. Or there abouts."

Old John edged his feet from the edge of his desk and slowly rotated to a near vertical position. He propped his elbows on the edge of the desk, hands carefully encircling his coffee cup. He didn't want his captive to get away.

"J. C., I'll see what I can do. But, no promises. And I expect Doc to pay for the phone calls and to tell Guz over at the boozeria to set aside a jug of his finest."

"John, no problem, not none at all. I will just give you our credit card number and you can just charge, what you need. And as for Guz (John called him Guz, his name was Thomas, Thomas didn't mind), why I'll just stop over there on my way home and leave a little word in his ear. So when do you think I can hear something?"

If I sounded eager, I was. The amount of work that Doc expected to have completed before his return didn't leave me much slack time.

Old John sighed and took a little sip, then he gave me a half lidded look. "Slow down and relax a little, J. C. These things often take time. Just like any other research. They just come along at their own rate. I think the best thing for us to do is just plan on getting together tomorrow over at the Elk's for lunch, say around 1:30. By that time the business types will have straggled back to work and the mid-afternoon break types won't have started yet. So we can eat, and talk, at our leisure, privately. Won't have eager ears leaning out all over the place. You'll pay, of course?"

"Of course, of course. Well, John, I've got to go." I stood up. "There's a phone call I'm expecting in about twenty minutes or so. Sooooooo. . . I will see you tomorrow about 1:30. Bye." With that I left and watched as Old John rotate back to the horizontal plane again, one hand dragging the telephone to a perch on his stomach, the other hand carefully placing his coffee cup within easy reach.

I waved goodbye to his two assistants, one of whom had a phone on his ear, and headed for home.

Along the way I stopped at *The Green Front* and told Thomas to let Old John take a bottle of whatever he might fancy and to charge it to Doc. Back outside, on the sidewalk, I ran into Fredrico Alandale Hardcastle IV.

He was his usual well-dressed self.
Tall.
Handsome.
Wealthy.
Confused.

"Hi Hard, what's up?"

"Sorry J. C., I didn't see you coming. Not much."

"Then why the frown and furrowed brow? Girls giving you trouble, chasing you down the Street, trying to pull you into dark alleys?"

"Come on, J.C." Hard blushed. Actually he

didn't have any trouble with the young ladies. He was a very eligible bachelor.

"So then . . . ?"

"It's Tinker, J.C. I'm worried."

"Well, he did leave the area all of a sudden."

"Yes. And in the dead of winter. And Master Chen says he hasn't heard from him at all. And doesn't know why he left other than he looked pretty shocked about something. Have you heard anything?"

"Nope. But I'm sure Tinker can take care of himself."

"Me too. But I'm still worried."

"Well, that won't do much good. You need anything from Portland? I am headed that way."

"Not really."

"Well then, I've got to rush. Doc's got me loaded up again. See you later."

"Later." Hard headed toward *Chen's Chinese.* I jumped back into *The Tank.*

As we rattled through town I admired what a nice warm, pleasant day it was. Too bad I wasn't going to see much of the next several. It was my turn to sigh. So I did. That is the way it goes with Doc. Feast or famine. I haven't figured out which I like more.

Back in the library and ready for business. I set up files and in general just diddled around waiting for the phone to ring. And debated whether I ought to phone Dr. Ben instead.

There was only one item to file. The overseas letter that kicked everything into action. It was one of those tissue-thin things, postmarked London. Might as well read it.

Nothing better to do.

So, who signed it? Well, well, well. And well, well, indeed. Sir Winifred Rogers Smyth Robsen-Brown. Doc certainly knows all the right people. Robsen-Brown! Top man in the prehistory of the area Doc wants me to research. But why me, I ask myself? Doc was headed overseas. He could ask Robsen-Brown anything he wanted to and get his answers from the horse's mouth, so to speak. Rather strange that, as the Brits would say.

I shook out the folds in the letter. Humpf, pretty short to start so much commotion.

So read it, J. C. . . . read it.

So, O.K., I will.

I did.

My Dear Heckmann.

As you know, we have been engaged in a long-term expedition, really a series of expeditions, to a small side-valley that leads down onto the main flood plain of the Indus Valley. As we had been working at this site for the past three field seasons, we had decided to spend the next two years in a detailed analysis of our findings before preceding further with the excavations.

Hafas returned to Jerusalem, Corruccini to Rome and Boyer to Paris. Each of us was to work up their respective portions of the final report and to follow up their own interests with the data. We were to be back together again, here in London, after six months time to integrate all the findings, swap ideas, etc. We would edit the report, return to our respective facilities and continue on. Every six months or so we would do it all over again, until, at the end of the two years, or so we hoped, we would be able to issue the final complete report. As we felt that the final report was going to set the world of prehistory back upon its collective heels, we decided to merely hint at our discovery with short papers, but not divulge much until the big, final report.

As you can well image, we were all shocked to hear of Hafas' heart attack in his laboratory in Jerusalem. You can also imagine the further dismay when the news of Corruccini's terrible accident was made known.

I talked to Boyer on the phone and he was extremely agitated, you know how he gets, screaming that he told her over and over again not to place large statuary on pedestals for study.

So now we had lost not only two dear friends but two colleagues as well, colleagues who were absolutely critical to the project.

When I finally got him calmed down, he agreed that we should continue on with the analysis. In addition, each of us was to come up with a list of potential replacements. I sent James Finn, my assistant, to see about securing the materials from Jerusalem and Rome and making all necessary arrangements to have it all shipped here to London.

I reread the inclosed letter from Rasha Roy, the Hindi foreman of our project, who lives in the nearby village, the same village from where our workers come and reside. He was, as you can see, babbling on about the Rakshasa. When I had first received the letter, I had pushed it aside as the normal superstitious nonsense one always hears from the villagers in that partof the world. But now, I am not so sure.

So, dear friend and colleague, read it over and, if you would, come to London and look over our field data.

There were, in addition to the letter, several photographs and some notes on glyphs taken by Roy but I have kept them aside as I don't wish to lose them in the mails. We can discuss them here. I am asking for your help in this matter both as an old friend and as, at the moment, I don't think that I can hand this over to the authorities as I don't believe that they would treat it seriously.

By the by, don't worry about the expense. I will put you on a retainer as a Special Consultant to the project.

So, I remain
yrs

Winnie
Sir Winifred R.S. Robsen-Brown

Humpf!

Again.

That letter certainly doesn't say much to explain what all the excitement is about.

Well, at least not very much. Two prehistorians die while working on the same project.

One has a heart attack and the other is a klutz when working around heavy stone objects.

Well, that's the breaks, no pun intended. Although, as Doc is so fond of saying, 'The long arm of coincidence can only be stretched so far.' Wonder where the inclosed letter from Rasha Roy got to?

At least now I know why Doc wasn't worried about the cost of his trip. Sly devil knew that I'd read the letter

OOPs, there goes the telephone.

"Hello, Dr. Heckmann's residence . . . No, he isn't here at the moment. He'll be back in about three days or so. Could I take a message?. . . Oh, Dr. Ben. This is J. C. Smith, Dr. Heckmann's secretary. I was the one that called earlier. Dr. Heckmann would like you to come out here by this coming Thursday or Friday and maybe stay for a week or so. We will pay all your expenses, of course . . . You can't make it? Ah, Doc . . . that is . . . Dr. Heckmann said to tell you Rakshasa . . .

Yes, that's what I said, Rakshasa. No, I don't. Nope, can't say. But it does seem to be mixed up with some dead prehistorians. Yup. Correct, dead, as in D. E. A. D., dead. Nope, Doc's in London visiting with Sir Winifred R.S. Robsen-Brown . . . Yes, that's it exactly,

Dr. Heckmann said to tell you Rakshasa. What? Say again, please . . . You're coming right out? Now?. . .

Sure, O.K., O.K. Yes, I will meet you at the airport. Tomorrow's flight. That will be fine. Absolutely, I will pick you up at the airport. Oh, by the way, Doc said you should give me a list of whatever books you might want . . . Oh, you'll bring whatever you will need. That's good . . . What? Oh, nothing . . . Yes, I'll see you tomorrow. Bye."

It certainly looks like Doc knew that magic word all right.

Welp, it's time to head for the kitchen. Stomach is telling me something. Check that wrist-o-watcho for the time. Yep, right as rain, time to eat. Past time to eat, almost 5:00-o-clock. p.m. My how time flies when you're having fun. And are we having fun, boys and girls? Right, we're not.

OOOOPS! And double OOPS! Never heard from Doc and Badnews. Well, just have to assume that they got off all right.

Might as well make dinner before hitting the books. And might as well see if the gigantic appetite will join me. Idiot, of course he will. After dinner, I can read whatever we have handy here before I charge off tomorrow to fetch the good, or bad, one never knows about things like that, Dr. Ben. But I can get some work done tonight. If I hurry and stop talking to myself.

So I stopped and headed down the hall and towards the kitchen and past the great hall mirror. And of course I stopped.

Peek-a-boo, I see you, J. C. Same old sorry sight, same old Jersey Charles Smith, known far and wide as

J. C., which I prefer, Six feet two, eyes of blue, and oh what those two hundred pounds or so can get into. My, my, what a swatch you cut through the ivy-covered classrooms of academia. But why do you have to look like a "pretty-boy surfer" anyway?

Parents fault. Stop smiling J. C., it is your bizarre sense of humor that gets you into trouble. Well, be honest now, it's not really that, is it? Nope, not at all. It's your rather unfocused interaction with the world. Of course, Doc fixed that, didn't he? Life hasn't been that same since you started working for Dr. Kappa Heckmann, anthropologist extraordinary, and practicing wizard, in a manner of speaking.

Well, bye guy, see you around! Same time, same place? We'll have to stop meeting like this, people will talk. Ho, Ho!

Down the hall, through the kitchen and outside on a Membrane hunt. Where would the inland whale be? In the greenhouse, one of them, of course. Yep! Whistling coming from deep in the wilds of Greenhouse Numba Two!

Once inside I couldn't see much. The Membrane was down at the far end, happy noises drifting back through the jungle that passes for Doc's horticultural enthusiasms.

Pushing through the underbrush I found our resident monster hard at work at his potting bench setting small cactus seedlings into small clay pots. He uses chopsticks to pick up each seedling and set it into one of the already partially filled pots. Then with a deft scoop of potting mix, a slight tapping of pot on bench, it joined its fellows in a flat. Membrane claimed that he had learned all this while working for a Japanese gardener in Gardena, California.

"Hey there! Feel like coming in and helping me devour a stuffed whale. I have one just finishing in the oven. Care to help carve a cetacean."

He nodded. "Sure, J. C., in just a moment, just a few to go. But, how about steaks and fries instead. I had whale the other day and I don't think that they are in season, just yet. Besides, I'm in the mood for a spot of red wine and it doesn't go with whale." A very low rumbling chuckle vibrated out after this last remark. "Heh, heh, heh." A very large kettle drum humming to itself. The last seedlings jumped into their containers, a quick dusting of hands and the Membrane rose up, filling the end of the greenhouse. Well, it always seems that way. "O.K., let's go and eat! So, how'd your day go, half-pint? I saw you head for town after Doc left. What's the latest? Or didn't you stop in and waste the day with Old John?"

"Yeah, I saw Old John and we talked, a little." This response I threw back over my shoulder. We were walking single file down the long aisle of the greenhouse. There was no way you could pass through the jungle side by side with the Membrane.

"I talked to him about trying to get some information from his overseas contacts."

That reminded me. "Oh, by the way, we are going to have a house-guest for a little while, Dr. David Ben from Columbia University, specialist in things magical and mythological mainly dealing with India and Mesopotamia. So, now you know. No surprises, right?"

"Sure, J. C., sure. No surprises. I promise, cross my heart, that I won't pitch this one on top of the garage, like that last fella. But then, I didn't know he was a house-guest. He sure looked like a prowler. He even looked guilty as he was going up. Anyway, now that I know, no sweat G.I. !"

Back in the kitchen I busied myself with the potatoes and steaks while the Membrane washed his hands in the sink.

"Hey there, when you get done splashing in the water why don't you fetch some wine from below?"

The wine cellar was below the kitchen. Another of Doc's ever changing interests. He had gotten enthused about making wine. So we now have gallons and gallons of fruit wine, dandelion wine, rose petal wine, apricot wine, and so on. Also stashed among the group were cases of the standard grape varieties, purchased not homemade.

So I made dinner just for the four of us, me and the Membrane. And then I worked in the library and went to bed.

Actually it went like this.

Membrane grunted an acknowledgment and disappeared down the stairs returning in a moment with a gallon of red, grocery store special. He waved it at me.

"Here, J. C., this ought to do the trick! Vin rouge ordinaire. Good old table wine. Do we have any bread? And maybe a little cheese? I could do with a little snack while you finish dinner."

I nodded. "Yeah, I think we do. Take a look in the closet. If you empty it, mark the list, I can pick up what we need tomorrow. I will shop on the way back from Portland. Dr. Ben can help, get him started on the right foot, so to speak."

Membrane backed out of the closet, clutching his spoils, and headed out the back door to sit on the porch and spread his "snack" on the table. I started frying the french fries and slid the steaks under the broiler. By the time everything would be ready he will have destroyed the loaf, a round of cheese, and half the wine. But, no matter! For him it was just an appetizer.

After dinner, adequately stuffed, I was back in the library, stereo on, Gregorian Chants soaring. I find it best to work with music like this for background. And why not?

It was supposed to be music to help one concentrate.

Or was it?

Well, it doesn't really matter, does it?

Nope! But it certainly helps me.

The Membrane had gone out for his evening stroll before settling down in the living room with some new books. They had come in today's mail from Abbey Garden Press, an outfit in California that specializes in cactus and succulents. How anyone can spend an evening reading his way through something called, "Illustrated Guide on Cacti and Other Succulents," in four volumes, is beyond me. Of course, he said the same thing when I read, "The Battle for North Africa: 1940-43."

Well, anywho, with Gregorian Chants in the background, I started to skim through the materials we had here, in the library, on Indian archaeology, the

Harrapan Civilization, developments in the Indus Valley, their antecedents to the west and stuff like that there.

Zip through Wheeler's, "The Indus Civilization, 3rd edition," dated but good overview.

Whiz through numerous copies of "Ancient India," bulletins issued by the Archaeological Survey of India.

Maul the last twenty years of the "Proceedings of the Prehistoric Society".

Then pounce on "Radiocarbon and Indian Archaeology" by Agrawal and Ghosh. A quick dip in Ehrich's "Chronologies in Old World Archaeology." Some of this stuff might be out of date, but it was a good start. Sketch out a brief outline, build a little chronology, make a list of this and that, things to find elsewhere, sketch a map, diddle and type.

And. . .

And suddenly it's 1:00 in the a.m.

My, how time flies, etc., etc., etc

So what do we have, you may well ask. Not too much to get excited about, although

I think I now know what Robsen-Brown was up to, and why he is so excited. It goes like this.

It appears that the earliest settlements found seem to be mainly in the north, south, and possibly southern Baluchistan. These turn up around 4000-6000 B.C. Sort of upper Neolithic: pottery, chert-blade industry, sheep, goats, cattle. Then around 4000 B.C., more or less, new influences turn up. This is the period of the first stone disk seal and an increase in the use of copper and bronze. Permanent settlements carbon-dated to around 2528 and 2605. The site of Amri has pre-Harrapan cultural material lying under the Harrapan. Now I suspect that was what Robsen-Brown was chasing; what caused the burst of Indian civilization during the closing centuries of the third millenium B.C.? Instead of finding it in the valley bottoms, he thinks he has found it up in the foothills. The valley bottoms are the places where all the authorities put it, yet he has spent his time digging in the foothills up some obscure side canyon.

I slid my stack of papers into a more or less orderly pile. It would have to wait for a day. After I get our guest settled in, then I can take a few days, head back for the coast and rummage through the several university libraries. Should be pretty complete by the time Doc returns. Membrane can entertain Dr. Ben, take him on a tour of the area. If he is from back East, mountains and pine trees such as we have around here should be entertaining.

Right!

Off to bed, it's a busy day tomorrow.

Correction, today! Oh well, another day, another dollar. After taxes. I climbed the spiral staircase to my room. And fell into bed, clothes and all.

A Visiting Professor

Grandeville. Doc's Home. Morning.

Humpf, mumpf, and various and sundry other waking up noises. For me it was quite late to be rising.

It was 8:00 o'clock in the morning and time to get moving.

But!

First things first.

A cup of coffee and a quiet spot to sit and to sip.

Welp, down the hall, stairs, and into the kitchen, and hope that the Membrane has made a pot of coffee. He usually does.

Early riser.

I could smell it, the friendly odor of freshly made coffee with the undertones of bacon and eggs that had already been eaten. Through the kitchen, grab the pot, a cup and then head for the back porch to enjoy the early morning and the coffee. Not too bad. A mildly warm breeze, birds singing, body waking up. In the distance there were a few chickens making chicken noises with a Greek chorus of cattle sounds. Far distant, happy whistling from one of the greenhouses. The only way to greet the day.

From here, one could look down the gentle slope, across the lower field, and see the edge of town as it sprawled across the line of vision, mostly hidden by masses of trees.

And over the tops of the trees?

Why from here one could look across the valley and see, way over there, another small town crawling up the adjacent lower slopes of the mountain range rearing up in their almost backyards. Clean air, clean water, the stuff of the rural outback. It does have something to offer, doesn't it?

BONG!

Echoing from the main hail came the pronouncement of the grandfather clock that Doc had acquired some time ago. It was 8:30 and time to get moving. Lots of miles to travel.

However there was time to shower, shave, and grab a quick nibble. And then it's off to the big city, to the airport, and to pick up one Dr. David Q. Ben, Doc's choice of wizard to import for whatever was going on this time. And, of course, there was a certain restaurant beckoning as well. Ah, it was a pleasant day for a drive up and down the river.

Portland, prepare thyself!

Guess who just chimed nine times. But here we are, in the garage, pondering, not to deeply, which of the few to take. Jeep, pickup, or The Tank? What the heck, take the pickup. Gas tank is full, so no need to stop right away. Besides, I might as well introduce D. Q. B. to the rural lifestyles as practiced hereabouts, pickup truck and all.

Portland. At the Airport.

"Dr. David Ben?" He looked like he must be my man. Sorta small wearing sorta big glasses. Book tucked under one arm with ragged slips of paper poking out from here and there. Scholar. "Are you Dr. Ben from Columbia?"

My target gave me a startled look and a quick nod. "Why yes, I am. Are you J. C. Smith?"

I nodded back. Just being friendly. "Yep, that's me. But you can call me J. C. Do you have any other luggage" I reached for the small bag he was carrying, one of those things that fit under seats. He handed it to me.

"Yes, I do. It should be coming up in the baggage area, if they haven't lost it somewhere. I had to change planes. Twice! Area No.2, that's where they said my luggage is supposed to be." He peered around, "Do you know where that is?"

"Sure do. It is just down these stairs and around the corner. How many bags did you bring?"

"Oh, just one more bag." Dr. Ben started down the stairs and then spoke over his shoulder, "But there are two boxes." He stumbled, caught himself and added, "I'm afraid that I cost you a little extra for the over-weight."

I smiled and bent over and picked up a piece of paper that had fallen from his book and poked it into a pocket meaning to give it back to him later.

"That's O. K., Dr. Ben. Doc won't mind, not at all." Of course he wouldn't. That was one of my departments, worrying about the budget. Of course, it sounded like Doc was going to be getting a bundle, well maybe a small bundle, from his English buddy.

At the bottom of the stairs, I pointed. "Well, here we are. Look's like you won't have to wait. Just tell me which ones are your's." The luggage was starting to come up and spill out onto the luggage carousel. "All part of the service."

He stared at me, that puzzled, stereotypical scholar puzzled look. And nodded. "Yes. All right." And stared at the stuff riding around and around. "But I don't see . . . ah, there, that grey bag just coming up, the one with the dent on the side. That's mine! And those two boxes just behind. That's my luggage."

So I trundled off, around to a clear spot, and snatched up the grey one as it sidled past and set it between my feet. Then I waited for the other two to come strolling past. So I waited ever so patiently. Poised. Alert. A strange predator waiting for a strange prey.

And there they came, the two innocents. I grabbed box one by the twine wrapping.

And was almost yanked onto the luggage passing by. A little over-weight!

Massaging my fingers, I scanned the luggage bay.

"PORTER! PORTER! OVER HERE!" He headed my way guided by my frantic gestures. "Those two boxes and this grey bag."

The porter popped everything onto his cart and followed us out into the parking lot.

"Dr. Ben, what's in those boxes. I nearly yanked my arm from its socket."

He ducked his head. "OH! I'm sorry, J.C. I should have mentioned that they were rather heavy. They're full of books. From what you said on the phone I thought that I ought to bring whatever material should be needed, guessing of course what might be required. I wanted to be able to answer any question Dr. Heckmann might have. Can you tell me anything more than what you said on the phone?"

We were now well into the parking lot and I had finally spotted the pickup.

Glancing at the porter, I replied to Dr. Ben. "I'll tell what little I know once we are on the road. Are you hungry? If you are, I know this little place that will just tickle your tummy, so to speak. Good food, amazing sandwiches, outstanding chocolate cake. It makes strong men weep."

So I get a wee bit overblown, but it really is good food. And I do like to share the place with others. Besides my stomach was making hungry sounds. Reminding me that I hadn't really eaten much for breakfast. Besides, I was going to go there whether Dr. Ben was hungry or not. Chocolate cake, here we come! Right?

Dr. Ben smiled, a small smile. "I could stand lunch, J.C. The flight did serve some sort of food, but that was some time ago. Besides, you make that place sound rather special. Chocolate cake, did you say?"

I could tell from the gleam in his eyes as he said

"chocolate cake" that I had found a kindred spirit. It was a good start.

"Right!" I gestured dramatically. "Chocolate cake, this high. Wait until you see it."

We arrived and I pointed. "Porter, everything in this truck, right here. Just stick it all in the bed, up front. Right! That's just fine. Here you go." I handed him a couple of bills. It was worth it not to have to carry that load way out here.

"Well, Dr. Ben, jump in and we will be off. And do lunch, as the business types are oft wont to say."

He did.
And we were.
And we did.
And a good time was had by all.

Paris.

M. Anatole Boyer, Ph.D. - Linguistics, sat deep within his highly overstuffed, very expensive chair, his small round belly pressing against his belt. He sat and stared. He was pondering the notes and sketches he had of those most interesting inscriptions. They were the ones that had been found along the side wall of the main tunnel, just outside the interior chamber.

Robsen-Brown's assistant, that strange little man, had found them only during the last days of the last week of the expedition. It always seemed to work that way. Hurried sketches, many photographs using different filters and lighting angles. Can't recheck anything once you have left the field until next summer.

So here he was, sitting and staring at these

things. There really was something quite bothersome about the inscriptions. But what was it, eh? What was it? Boyer gave a Gallic shrug of his shoulders, whatever the puzzle was, it would be solved by a slow logical inspection and analysis. It was just a matter of thinking everything through again. And again. Slowly, logically. And then, viola, the answer, it appears!

Earlier in the evening he had sent his assistant out for the rest of his standard snack.

After she had returned with the bread and the vin rouge ordinaire, he had sent her home with a friendly pat. She had smiled, as she always did. Soon he would have a nibble.

Bread, wine, and his own, made by his own hands and recipe, *pate de lievre.*

But as was usual, he had failed to notice that time was passing, his snack sitting unobserved and unappreciated in the adjoining room. He hadn't heard the faint noise made by the opening and soft closing of the outside door.

Finally he glanced up. Almost tomorrow and his stomach was drawing attention away from this interesting puzzle and to itself. He stroked its soft roundness as it grumbled softly. Half aware of his appetite and half immersed in his thoughts, he wandered into the outer room and slowly, studiously, spread a generous layer of the pate on a piece of the thickly sliced bread, poured a glass of wine, and returned to sit at his desk to munch, sip, and think.

Time passed and the puzzle began to unravel. Suddenly, sharp pains in his stomach brought Boyer lurching to his feet. One hand knocked over his wine glass as he staggered toward the door. He grabbed at the door knob in a vain attempt to slow his fall.

M. Anatole Boyer, Ph.D. - Linguistics, did not hear the sounds of crashing bookcases and the flutter of papers falling.

Nor did he smell the pungent odor filling the room.

Along the River. Grandeville Bound.

Well, I can tell you that my favorite restaurant was a huge success cause there we were whizzing along the highway, pleasantly overstuffed with pastrami-ham-turkey sandwiches and slices of that unbelievable chocolate cake.

And a good time was had by all.

I said that once already, didn't I?

Much better that putting down the gut-bombs offered by the various and sundry fast food outfits.

Soooo, Dr. Ben and I had enjoyed the restaurant and talked about this and that, and ate, and ate, and talked about this and that, etc., etc. It seems that he is as full of tales about restaurants, the good, the bad, and the ugly, as I am.

But anyhow, there we were rolling along, enjoying the fine, balmy, warm, blue-sky, absolutely fine day, tranquilized to a near stupor.

And I can tell you that if you haven't experienced that cake, then you haven't experienced anything named cake.

But enough of that, back to business.

"Dr. Ben, what is this Rakshasa stuff anyway? Doc seemed absolutely sure that it was an important thing to say to you but he didn't tell me anything about it, not at all. Which is fairly typical for Doc."

"Now I can assume that it has something to do with folklore or mythology somewhere in or around either Mesopotamia or India because that is the way you are listed in The Guide. And further, I would assume that it probably is India as that was where Robsen-Brown was working. And that this, somehow, appears to be related to him. But after that, I run out of guesses. So? What is it? What is this all about? Huh, huh?"

Dr. Ben gave me one of those scholarly smiles. "Yes, you do seem to be getting things clear. But."He held up one finger. "Before I say anything, tell me what Dr. Heckmann is up to, this time? And what prompted him to get me to come out here? Especially on such short notice?"

I shrugged. "Well, Dr. Ben, I don't really know how to answer. At the moment I am pretty much in the dark. About all that I can tell you is this. Yesterday, as I mentioned on the phone, Doc got a letter from Sir Winifred R. S. Robsen-Brown." I gave him a questioning look. He nodded that he recognized who that was.

"The result of that call is that Doc now has me working on a paper on the Harrapan Civilization and all the antecedent cultures in the area as well. I am supposed to check whatever information there is relating to that area and the adjoining neighborhoods. Plus!"

It was my turn to shoot a finger into the air, so I

did. "And on top of that I am supposed to check into the deaths of a couple of prehistorians who had been working with R. B. in India. And s. l. t. t."

"S. l. t. t.?"

"Huh? Oh, Stuff Like That There." I waved the finger pointing hand loosely. "Just a little verbal shorthand." I checked my passenger to see how he accepted that and was startled by the expression on his face. "What's a'matta? We leave something back at the airport? Or in the restaurant? I can turn around as soon as I find a spot."

He shook his head violently. "Nooooooooo, no! Nothing like that, J.C., nothing like that. It is those deaths. Troubling, very troubling. Given Doc's message and all." He grabbed my forearm, gently. "Are you sure that is all you know?"

I nodded. And watched the road. We were swinging through a wide curve. "Yup! That's it, the whole megillah. That is all I know. Just that and nothing more, to quote The Raven. But! I do expect to find out more pretty soon."

Then it came back. That was what I was supposed to be doing this afternoon. Talking with Old John, not eating chocolate cake. Oh well, he would understand. And only hold me, us, up for an extra lunch or so.

We drove on and up the slight grade and out into the dry section of the state. From here it was a very long, rather straight, and very dull piece of road for quite a stretch. So I turned to my passenger. "So! Anyhow! What's a Rakshasa?"

I got frowned at.

Dr. Ben cleared his throat. "J.C., I think, for the moment, all I will say is that Rakshasa are a group of Indian, that is, from India, demons who have as personal attributes the most deplorable passions as defined in the myths of India. These are primarily gluttony, lust, violence, and perjury. Of course, that is only in their relations with the other gods and with us lowly mortals. Among themselves they seem to have all the typical middle class American family virtues."

He cleared his throat. "But Rakshasa are destined to play hostile or malevolent roles in the lives of various people. This, of course, tends to be restricted to India. Rather provincial, in a manner of speaking. But for now, that is all I want to say. Especially as they relate to whatever Doc is now involved in. That is why I brought all those books. I wanted to be prepared for whatever questions he might ask or consider relevant to whatever it is. But it is the linkage of those deaths with the Rakshasa that is something to worry about."

He sighed and slumped down in his seat.

And mumbled, "I have spent years working and studying in both Mesopotamia and in India. And while you might not want to believe in things like demons, I have found that in those cultures such things are quite real and often very deadly." He sighed again.

"I have personally experienced events in some of the more isolated rural villages that quite defy explanation unless you want to accept things like that."

I couldn't help it. I smiled.

"Don't smile, J. C., I am quite serious. And I am beginning to suspect that Doc seems to have gotten himself into some really serious and probably unpleasant business. He must have realized that early on because he asked you to get me to come out here. I doubt very much we are in for just a scholarly discourse on the subject. Those things, Rakshasa, are not be taken lightly. Remember, two people have died. And they were working with Robsen-Brown. In India."

He nodded again, mostly to himself. "Now this seems to indicate that something over there started all this. Whatever it was that they were digging up. I am going to have to do quite a bit of review through my materials. I need some time by myself, for the next three days or so."

He reached over and patted my arm. "I hope you don't mind."

I almost laughed. But I controlled it. Just shook my head. "Oh no, that will be fine, just fine. I have to go back to the coast and visit several libraries and bookstores. I was wondering how to keep you entertained while I was gone. You just solved that problem."

And with this last comment we drove down the highway. Each thinking their own thoughts.

Grandeville. Doc's Home.

Well, there we were. Back home again, in a manner of speaking. I whistled up the Membrane and asked him to tote the book boxes to the library and then Dr. Ben's luggage to the guest room. And received a small smile from the monster when Dr. Ben first caught sight of him.

It was in the twilight's last gleaming. And the Membrane had loomed up out of the shadows by way of answering my call. Dr. Ben looked like one of his Rakshasa had just shown up.

Membrane gathered everything up and strolled off. As I turned to follow, I aimed our guest toward the house. "I'll tell you about him later."

We stopped in the kitchen. I told him where to find his room.

"Make yourself comfortable. I have some phone calls to make. You can shower or soak in the tub. Then come back, I'll start making something to eat. Afterwards we can relax in the living room, or whatever you might wish. Our house is your house, as the saying goes."

Then I phoned Old John and got him settled down. He gets wonderfully worked up when people do not keep appointments. All it cost was a bottle of the best and two lunches at The Elks. But he did have some news but insisted that we could talk about that over lunch. Then he said in a rather strange tone of voice that he had found some old newspaper clippings in a seldom used file cabinet and that I might find them interesting. But, it would also wait until lunch. Old John loves a mystery, even if he has to create one.

I was deep inside making a quick and dirty spaghetti sauce when the Membrane wandered in and peered over my shoulder. "I put his books in the library and showed him to his room. But you are going to have to clean up that desk if he is going to use it. It is a mess."

I thumped him on the gut. It made a hollow sound. "That is not a mess. That is the beginning of a very concise report on the antecedents of the Harrapan Civilization in India. I hope you didn't disturb anything."

"Of course not. But."

I nodded. "I know. It is a mess. I'll get to it directly after we eat. Care to join us? I can make twice as much?"

He squinted at the stuff in the pot. "Welllll, I suppose I could. Just to be sociable. I trust that you stopped for groceries."

I started increasing everything. "Bring some wine up, would you? And make garlic bread while I do everything else."

And it wasn't too bad. We have lots of garlic and lots of bread. And we made lots of salad to go along with everything else. So, it wasn't a bad meal after all.

Revelations.

Bits And Pieces.

Grandeville. The Elk's Club. Greater Downtown.

"Well, Old John, what did you find out?"

It was the next afternoon and there we were, sitting in the Elk's and finishing up our lunch. One of the three that I owed him. It was almost a quarter-to-one and most of the regulars had returned to work and to business. And it was still too early for the late-afternoon break crowd. A quiet time, and a private time, to sit and talk.

Old John leaned slightly forward. "Not much J.C., not much! Although there does seem to be much more here than meets the eye."

He frowned at the thought and leaned back. "In fact there does appear to be much too much that is not being said." Then he settled back in his chair. "From what I've learned so far, it appears that in each of the cases that vandals broke into the laboratories and made real messes of the places. In each case, papers were strewn all over the place, tables tipped over, filing cabinets emptied out, and that sort of thing. Fires started. And not only that, but who ever made the mess spilled something that left a terrible stench. Pretty strange, don't you think?"

Then Old John leaned forward again. "But you know what I find interesting. I find it interesting that who ever it was knew when to break in. But that's not the only thing. You know what else I find interesting?" He peered at me. A prosecutor's stare.

I shook my head. Hostile witness. "Nope. What else do you find interesting in the behavior of these vandals?" I was playing my part. He was on a roll, no way to be stopped.

Old John thumped on the table with one knuckle. "It's not the vandals that are interesting, J. C., not at all. It's the prehistorians. You see, each of them had the same thing happen to them. Now that is interesting, don't you think?" He nodded his head. "Sure you do! In Rome, Corruccini's laboratory, was messed up. And in Jerusalem, Hafa's, right? Right!"

He paused. For a moment. "Corruccini's laboratory was messed up," he repeated for emphasis. "The statuary all busted up including the figure she was working on. The one that crushed her. Papers everywhere. Tables tipped over. They even tried to start a fire. But for some reason it only smoldered. It was the smoke from this that tipped someone off that all was not right in the laboratory. Smoke seeping from the cracks under the door and that awful odor. So the firemen busted in, found the mess, and called the cops."

Old John reached for his cup, checked the dining room over, and tipped a little something into his coffee from a silver flask that he carried in the inner pocket of his jacket.

After an appreciative sip, he continued.

"Ummmm, good stuff. In Jerusalem it was pretty much the same thing. But in this case Hafas has a heart attack and tries to crawl for help, but dies. Vandals break in and make a mess. Even there! You'd think there would be more reverence for antiquities there, wouldn't you?"

He took another more appreciative sip from his cup, watching my expression all the time. Then he got to the point. Finally.

"Now, the thing that I find extremely interesting about this whole thing, other than what I've already mentioned, is this!" One knuckle rapped the table, hard. Again. "And here is where I can feel that old itch for news and those carefully kept secrets that someone wants to keep secret. And what is that? I find it most interesting in these two cases, both having an extremely coincidental set of actions, that the official accounts, that is, the ones that got into the newspapers don't mention any of the things that I've just told you. Now that is interesting, isn't it?"

Old John was beginning to glare ominously in my direction. "Now you tell me, why are two different sets of officials, in two different countries, so reticent about what appears to be, on the surface, so trivial a thing. What I mean is this, J. C. So what? So what if some vandals break into some prehistorians laboratories and make big messes?"

He flopped violently back into his chair. "SO WHAT? Who really cares, who gives a hoot? Is there a care out there, in the real world? No body, no thing, no one, that's who. I mean, it's interesting when you see the pretty pictures and read about this or that artifact in the "National Geographic" but few of the folk really care about whether these chaps do this sort of thing or not. Soooo, what's the big secret?"

Old John lowered his voice and whispered dramatically, "Or perhaps, were these people working together on something that really was a secret?" He hunched forward, intently watching my face for any change of expression. He didn't see anything. Old Stone Face, that's me. Besides I didn't have anything to say. "I mean secret in the sense those friendly folk in national governments mean. Well, J. C.?"

Now his eyes were boring into the unfriendly witness. Me. Again.

I smiled at him, "Well, as far as I know, John, they weren't." I sucked in a deep breath. "From everything that I know or have found out, so far, which is damn little at the moment, they were just a group of dedicated prehistorians and the like working up a series of preliminary reports for an endeavor in which they had invested three years, more or less, of sweat and labor. They thought they had an earth-shattering statement to make. But, earth-shattering to them doesn't exactly mean much of a shake to anyone else. Especially national governments. No governmental secrets involved. Just a bunch of scholars from different countries working under the general direction of Sir Winifred R. S. Robson-Brown, who is one of the biggest names in Indian prehistory."

I held up one hand, sucked in another deep breath, and raced on before he could interject. "Now if there was a secret it was one that had to do with Indian prehistory. But nothing to do with today's politics. The time period that they were interested in was around four or five thousand years ago, B.C.!" I shook my head. "As far as I know, no government has yet worked itself into a lather about events that long ago much less whether someone rips off some of their antiquities or not."

Old John started to speak. I sailed on. "I know, I know, one or two do, but they are the exception, not the rule." I settled back into my chair. "Anyhow, I don't see how there could be any connection between any governmental suppression of the news, these two deaths, and political secrets, and that sort of thing. Do you?"

PONK!

I lobbed the ball back into his court.

I received a grim smile. "At the moment I don't. But!" He shot one finger into the air, neatly drilling a hole in the ceiling. I smiled. He frowned.

"Something is going on, J. C . Something that someone doesn't want spread around. And I certainly would like to knew what that is, now that you got me started looking into it. And why?" I received another heavy stare. Time to leave.

So I stood up, looked around for the check, found it, and reached for it. A large, manila envelope dropped over my outstretched hand.

"You might want to read these old clippings, J. C. I found them in some old, very old files, stuffed in the back of one of the drawers. I found them very interesting. Thought you might, too."

So I sat back down. Old John slid the thing

toward me and waved for the waiter to bring more coffee. After both cups were filled and the waiter had left, I opened the envelope and shook out four small, yellowing newspaper clippings. The standard, crummy looking stuff that all old newspapers turn into. "No dates on them, John."

He nodded. "Yes, I noticed that. Must have been some time ago though, before you started working for Doc." He pointed that loaded finger at the clippings. "Read them."

Then he quickly scanned the room, noticed that no-one was watching us, slipped the small flask from his pocket, again, and poured a dollop into his cup. "A little sweetener for your coffee, J.C.?"

"Ummmmm, no, John." I had started reading the articles.

Slowly.

Carefully.

One at a time.

Curiosity at full volume.

ANTHROPOLOGIST SAVES ASSAULT VICTIM

PARIS (UPI) -- An American Anthropologist saved the life of an assault victim in the early morning hours today.

Dr. Kappa Heckmann, on tour, accidently came upon the scene just as the man, still unidentified, was shot through the throat by his assailant.

Dr. Heckmann said that he had just turned into the alley as the shooting took place.

Hospital authorities state that it was only the quick thinking of Dr. Heckmann that saved the man's life. The injured man is reported to be in stable but critical condition.

ASSAULT VICTIM MAJOR CRIME FIGURE

PARIS (UPI) -- The shooting victim saved yesterday, by the American Anthropologist Dr. Kappa Heckmann, has been identified by authorities today as a major crime figure.

The wounded man, still listed as in stable but critical condition, has identified as an American Indian, Badnews Treefalls, known within the Union Corse as "The Iron Dove." Interpol has been tracing Treefalls for years but has never been able to directly link him to a crime.

Anonymous informants state that Treefalls is known throughout the world by the underworld as an enforcer who worked directly for major crime bosses in both the United States and elsewhere.

AUTHORITIES GRILL HOOD

PARIS (UP!) -- Police today were given permission to interrogate the crime figure Badnews Treefalls, known as "The Iron Dove," by hospital authorities.

Due to the throat injury sustained during the shooting which injured him, Treefalls answered all questions in writing.

During the questioning he held up one of two cards which he had prepared beforehand. One stated, "No comment." The other read "It was an accident."

Authorities feel that he knew his assailant but Treefalls probably following the well-know "code of silence" refused to respond to all questions other than with his two cards.

The same authorities have stated that the sooner they can send him out of the country the happier they will be. The American Embassy has acknowledged that papers are being prepared to send Treefalls back to the United States.

TREEFALLS PAROLED TO ANTHROPOLOGIST

PARIS (UPI) -- Badnews Treefalls, also know as The Iron Dove among the criminal elements along the Mediterranean, has been permanently paroled to the man that saved his life. Dr. Kappa Heckmann, American anthropologist, who rescued Treefalls, has refused to comment as to why he has involved himself in this novel situation.

"Perhaps, like the Chinese," he stated, "I feel responsible for him in as much as I saved his life.

It has been found that Dr. Heckmann is a close friend of the American Ambassador here.

It has also been learned the Dr. Heckmann has just had a paper accepted for presentation in the International Anthropological meetings to be held in Toronto, Canada, titled, "Atavistic Tribal Behaviors Among Criminal Organizations With the Union Corse As A Special Case."

Dr Heckmann denies that there is any linkage between his studies and his actions two weeks ago.

I looked up and smiled at Old John. "Well, what do you know about that! The things you find out about your employer." I slid the clippings back into the envelope and sat back. "And associates."

"What are you going to do with them J. C.?"

"Keep them for my memoirs, John." I finished my coffee and started to rise.

"Ah, J. C., I still want to know what's going on!"

"John, when I know you will know." And with that pronouncement I picked up the check and headed for the door. It was time to leave.

For some reason I had decided not to tell Old John about Dr. Ben's ideas. Perhaps it was just my natural reticence. Perhaps something else. The things Old John had mentioned had struck a responsive chord, deep down somewhere, down where all the odds and ends that clutter up the mind swim and float.

Well, one thing for sure, there did certainly appear to be something going on. Maybe even two or three somethings. Oh yes indeedy!

As I strolled down the street toward *The Tank*, it struck me as just that same old problem, appearances and realities. One just never knew how much reality would be lurking beneath some appearance. Just like this sudden revelation between Doc and Badnews. Pretty interesting, that. Doc has certainly gotten himself into some strange situations all right. Umph, almost time to head for the coast. Again. And the several campus libraries. And, just maybe, some old acquaintances. Again. Well, not too old. And my favorite restaurant. Again. Visions of chocolate cake, not sugar plums, danced in my head. Probably spend 3-4 days in all doing the research, maybe less. And I wondered whether these Rakshasa behaved like vandals.

London.

Darkness swirled and eddied in the light evening fog. The fog lay entwined around the large townhouse, and its neighbor. A black form, drifted silently through the fog and stopped. And watched the house. It knew that the last one lived inside. But something had changed. He was no longer the last one. Another was coming. Another was traveling great distances to come here. To join this one.

The dark form blurred into a tree shadow. It could wait until they were together.

It had already spent eternities waiting.

Doc's Tale -- Part 1

Grandeville. Doc's Home.

A week, more or less, later, I pulled back into the garage and put the pickup back into its place. I could see that Doc and Badnews had returned. Their car was in place, next to the jeep. So I walked around to the side of the truck, leaned over and lifted out my box of treasures. Wait 'till Doc sees what sorts of goodies I brought back from the coast. I had copied and scribbled from dawn to dusk, metaphorically speaking.

But, regardless of that, I had pretty much cleaned out the combined knowledge on my chosen topic from the three university libraries. Which either doesn't say much for my chosen topic or doesn't say much for the state of the holdings in the three university libraries. Take your pick. Probably the latter. Nobody was in the kitchen as I trundled through. So I headed for the library to dump the load, thinking to zip upstairs, clean up a little and then check the living room, a logical spot to find Doc.

I'd made it as far as the grandfather clock when I ran into Dr. Ben.

"Hi, Dr. Ben, where's everybody?"

"Oh, hi, J.C. We're all in the living room. Doc thought he heard the truck coming around the driveway. Said to tell you that there was no big rush, just dump your stuff in the library, go upstairs and clean up a little, if you wish, make a snack, and then join us. Doc said that he would wait telling about his little adventure in London until you got there."

"O.K., see you in a bit." I started to pass.

"I must admit it must be quite a tale."

I paused. "Oh, why's that?"

"Well, Doc did get a little battered, you see."

"Battered?" I set my suitcase down and turned to Dr. Ben.

"Well, I assumed that. What with the bandages and all."

"What bandages? What happened anyway?" The box thudded to the floor as I headed for the living room. It wasn't exact a run, more like an extremely fast walk. I popped the doors open and shot into the room. Doc was sitting in his usual place, one leg dangling over one arm-rest.

Membrane was filling up his chair, the one no-one else ever sat in. I didn't see Badnews.

"Doc, where's Badnews? And what are you doing with bandages on half your face and your arm in a sling? Where is Badnews? And what happened in London anyway? And where is Badnews?" Yah, I was upset. Especially now that I really knew about Badnews. How could anyone get close enough to Doc to do that with him around?

Doc smiled and waved one hand. "Oh, hi there, J.C. Get everything that I asked for? How was Portland?"

This approach, as Doc knew, and as I knew, would only serve to irritate me. And as per usual it worked. I got irritated. "Yes, got everything. Portland was fine. The chocolate cake was fine. I'm fine. Everyone over there is fine. Everything here is fine. The cows are fine. The grass is fine! The chickens are fine! Where's Badnews?"

Doc just sat there, drink in hand, swinging one leg idly, smiling that don't get upset and calm down smile. It only worked in reverse.

"DOC!"

"Calm down, J.C., calm down. Don't get so agitated." He beamed at me. "Like you and the cows and the grass, I'm fine. Badnews is fine. But I'll explain shortly. But first, you go fix something to eat. Then come back and I'll relate what happened during my visit in jolly old Londontown. And then? Why then you can see what we have facing us, perhaps. And that will explain why I asked David to join us. O.K.?"

I nodded

"Good!" Doc made shooing motions. "And get something to eat. Oh, and as long as you're at it, make a large pot of coffee and bring it with you when you return. Then, when we're all comfortable, I'll spin my little tale. Go!"

More shooing motions. So I shooed.

Just as I made the door, Doc called after me, "Oh, and bring some cookies, too. Membrane would probably enjoy a little snack."

So I hit the kitchen. And attacked it like a crazed graduate student late for a final exam. I was done eating by the time the coffee was done perking. And then we, the coffee pot, a two-pound bag of cookies, and I, headed back to the living room.

"O. K., here I am. Who wants coffee?" I pitched

the cookie bag to the Membrane.

Everyone did except Dr. Ben. He had brandy. Doc and the Membrane took a lot of that in their coffee. I just settled for coffee. Then I settled as well. Stretched out on the couch, a heap of pillows behind me. From this position I could give all my attention to Doc, drink my coffee, and recline, all at the same time.

Doc chuckled in my general direction. "I see J.C. is ready. So I guess it is time to begin my little tale."

Doc looked around the room. checked his audience, and took his usual dramatic pause. "As you know, Badnews and I flew over to London a few days ago because of a letter I had received from Robsen-Brown. I won't bother to describe the flight over. It was the same as any other flight. Same food, same in-flight movies. Same smiling stewardesses. Same traveling companions. Etc., etc., etc., etc."

He nodded. "When we got through customs, Badnews and I separated. He had several things that needed doing with some of his friends. I haven't seen him since. Although I did talk to him. Once."

"Of course, I don't feel there is any reason to worry, not with a gentleman of Badnews' caliber." Doc flicked a brief smile, on and off. "I rather expect that he will be phoning in the next day or so with his report. So until then, we'll just have to wait, won't we?"

I remembered those newspaper clippings and winced, inwardly. Doc waved one hand casually, waving the incident away.

"Anyway, we separated at the airport to go our different ways. As I was collecting my bags, a chauffeur came up, addressed me by name, said that my car was waiting, picked up my bags, and said would I follow him please. So, of course, I did. And when we got outside there sat Winnie in one of his Rolls, parked in a no-parking zone, waiting patiently. So I smiled and got in."

"Now you know what a Rolls is like. It's just wonderful, just wonderful! This one had one of those fold-down bars built into the front seat. A neat brandy was waiting for me. And it was quiet, just absolutely so quiet. Wonderful car, we should get one." Doc winked at me.

"Don't look so startled, J.C., I was just kidding. I know we can't afford one, but it certainly would be nice. Hmmmm, have to think about that."

Doc popped back to the subject. "Well! I got in, as I said, got settled down nicely while his chauffeur put my bags in the trunk, took a sip of brandy and turned to Winnie."

London.

"Hello Winnie, it's been a long time. Sorry to hear about your friends' deaths. Could you drop me off at my hotel, I'll just freshen up a bit. Then we can go out for dinner and have a nice long talk. And you can tell me what is so upsetting about this latest project of yours."

Winnie smiled a weak smile. "Ah yes, well, I'm afraid that I have a bit more unpleasant news. Quite disturbing in fact. Boyer's dead. Same as the others. Must have happened while you were in route."

"Boyer! Oh I'm terribly sorry, Winnie. But what's going on? And I mean really going on, Winnie. What were you four up to?"

"Hummmm, yes." Winnie shook his head. "Well, you certainly haven't changed a bit since last we worked together. Nice of you to come by on such short notice. But of course I shan't be dropping you off at your hotel. You shall be staying with me, at my London townhouse. It is, was, the center of the expeditions activities, a sort of command post, as it were. Much more convenient you being there. Can show you our field notes, artifacts and all that, all the stuff that came back with us from India, had the devil's own time talking the government officials into letting me take some of the stuff out of the country, didn't want to let us have it, you know. Stuffy buggers, those."

He patted me on the arm. "Besides, we can have dinner there and talk without anyone overhearing what we have to say. Or if you'd rather, we could have dinner at the club, you know. No? Good. Rogers. Take us home!"

"Winnie?"

"Not now, Doc, not now. We'll talk later. At dinner, if you wish. You see, I Just now received the news about poor old Boyer. Just as I started to come out here to get you. The official explanation is food poisoning. Correct or not, I don't believe it. Bit of a shock, you know. This puts the whole expedition into a right bloody, damn shambles. Something is tracking us, you know. And I'm next, you see. The last one. So, let's just let it rest a bit."

Winnie flopped back and stared out the window all the way back to London.

It gave me a chance to look him over. It had been

a long time since last we had worked together. He had put on a bit more weight, token on more of that ruddy, robust complexion people of his type get from being outside great periods of time. But it seemed that he had aged more than his age indicated. Well, it wasn't exactly aging as much as sagging. The sort of thing were intense worry wears one down. The face sags, the shoulders draw down, small creases turn up alongside the eyes and mouth.

Winnie had that kind of physical weariness, that sort of thing. So I left him alone, all the way in from the airport to his place. Deep, deadly silence.

And it is a long drive. So I looked out and inspected all the changes that had occurred since the last time I had made this trip. There were were quite a few. And if anything, the view was more depressing.

Once we got to his place, he had one of his servants take me and my luggage to my room, phone the hotel and cancel my reservations. As soon as I came back down, dinner was served.

And over dinner what did we talk about? Nothing! We just engaged in small talk, the sort of thing old colleagues talk about after long passages of time. What had happened to who, which person had moved to what university, have you read the article by such-as-such, what do you think about this-or-that, that sort of thing.

It was obvious that Winnie wasn't ready to talk about whatever it was that was bothering him. So I just coasted along and waited until he was ready. Then, over some excellent brandy in his study, after closing the doors, he finally got to it.

I settled into a large overstuffed chair. And waited.

"Doc, I am not quite sure where to begin. So please put up with a bit of wandering about while I sketch in some background. And no questions. As I go along I think you will see what it is that is bothering me."

Winnie began to pace as he talked.

"Four years ago I bumped into a piece of information that I, at first, wrote off as shear nonsense. But then, some time later, at one of the meetings I ran into Hafas and over coffee during a break between sessions he mentioned something that he had read and it reminded me of that piece of information. So, of course, I told him about it. Only, as I told him about it, it dawned on me that perhaps it wasn't necessarily nonsense. It might be a piece of information, that if we could verify it, would certainly turn the prehistory of India on its head, so to speak. Well, you know that's heady stuff for people in our profession."

He smiled at the recollection.

Then started again. "As I explained this to Hafas, he got as excited as I was becoming. By the time the meetings had ended we had rounded up Coruccini and Boyer, Krebbs had turned us down, and we began to set up tentative plans for what was to become the last three year's work. One important thing we all agreed on, Doc. We all agreed, right then and there, to keep what we were up to secret and that premature announcements would be counter-productive. We didn't want to be seen as being too over-eager to rush into publication without very heavy documentation."

It seemed like the right place to interject. "Ah, Winnie, what was this big secret that you three, ah, four, were concealing from the profession at large?"

"Doc, we were about to demonstrate that there had been an earlier civilization with a capital 'C', than the Harrapan or any other of the stuff found down in the Indus Valley."

Winnie took a sip of his brandy and smiled. "Terribly exciting, don't you see, civilization up there, not down in the flood plains. Turn over most of the heart-felt theories about why civilizations spring up and all that."

He turned and stared into the fire place, watched the flames. "You see, we were digging into this site which indicated that there had been an earlier civilization that was every bit as advanced as the Harrapan. And we had, in a manner of speaking, a corner on the market, ah, for the moment. Of course, once we released our final report then the rush would be on." He cleared his throat.

"As this was the first site of this type, you can see why we didn't want premature announcements being made. Every specialist in the region would have jumped on our backs arguing that we were wrong, or confused, or had done a poor job of excavation or analysis, and so forth and so on." He shrugged. "You know how that goes."

Winnie turned, blushing. "Oh, your pardon, Doc. I didn't mean that to come out the way it sounded, what with your experiences and all." I winked at him. He turned back to the fire.

"So, we wished to be very cautious and to make

absolutely sure of our facts, to take great pains at what we were doing before anything, either in print or at meetings, came out. I'm sure you understand."

I laughed. "Oh yes, Winnie, quite well. It would upset a large number of individuals who have built their reputations on their knowledge of the area. And they wouldn't like you pointing out how wrong they had been over the past years."

Winnie set down the empty glass and circled the room. "Quite so, Doc, quite so. We were very reticent. But we were sure of what we were doing, right from the very beginning. The past three years have proven that to our satisfaction, that we were correct."

I nodded. "The three deaths, then, are upsetting not only because they were friends, but because of what you were working on?"

Winnie fetched the brandy bottle and recharged our glasses. "Righto. A great, bloody, triple disaster. Personal and professional! It will set back the project by several years, in the very least. It will take that long for new personnel to become familiar with our notes, approach, etc. And that's before they can begin to pick up where the others left off."

He began it to thump around the room. "But that's not why I asked you to come all this way. Not just to listen to me run on about our problems. That, in a sense, is all beside the point. It wasn't just the deaths, coming all at once, in a manner of speaking. It was other matters that I didn't mention in my letter. Vandals! They broke into all the laboratories coincidently with the deaths and messed up the places. Emptied filing cabinets, turned over work tables, broke artifacts, tried to start fires, that sort of thing."

I sat up. Winnie had certainly gotten my attention. "And you don't think that all this destruction is merely some sort of extreme form of coincidence?"

"HA!" Winnie spun around, sloshing brandy on his hand. He paid no attention. "NO! Not at all I don't. Not in the least, that is really too much for coincidence. But the question that I'm trying to answer is why? Why would someone or some group want to do such a thing? You see, what bothers me is that I think that something else deliberately killed my three friends. And then tried to destroy what we were all working on. I don't see any other explanation, do you?"

I really couldn't answer his questions. "Well Winnie, it does appear rather peculiar. But you did mention vandals, didn't you? So how do you know that they were vandals? Or not vandals, as the case may be."

Winnie refilled led his glass, took a sip, and smiled. It was definitely an upper-class smile. "Doc, I am Sir Winifred etc., etc., etc., after all. And rather wealthy on top of all that. Best schools. Best clubs. And all that, you know. So, I placed a few discreet phone calls. And then I received a few in return. And that's how I know. Rah'ther handy system, if one doesn't overdo it. Everything that I heard pointed to vandals."

I nodded. "Ummmmm, yes, quite handy, quite handy. Then why call me? It seems that you can find out whatever it is you wish without my being here, right?" He wandered a bit, then plopped into a chair like mine and stared at the fireplace.

"Yes, it does seem that way, doesn't it! Yes! Well, you see, it's this way. We both know that you seem to have openings to certain segments of society to which I have no entry. And I thought that, perhaps, you could, if you would of course, see if, all these, ah, elements, that is, would have some ideas as to what has been going on, you see, that is, if they would tell you. And why? So you see, I really do believe that those were deliberate murders. But why, who, or by what I am quite confused. Have to eliminate something, you see. I feel that the vandals aspect to all this is some sort of side effect."

Well, by this time I was really getting confused, what with Winnie's dancing all over the place in his story. So I tried to get him aimed straight at what ever he thought that the problem was. "But why not have your contacts check on this for you?"

He turned and peered, a very squinty eyed look. The brandy had by this time really put a flush to his face. He nodded sagely. "Aye, there's the rub. I have already asked a few, very close friends to look into what I have just suggested, very delicately. And they, very delicately, suggested that I might be getting just a bit overwrought. And seeing things that aren't really there, and that sort of thing. So you see, I can't do any more asking. That's why I wrote you. And bout this Rakshasa nonsense. Although I'm not so sure, anymore, that it is, nonsense, that is, you see."

It was time for bluntness.

"Winnie! Will you stop beating about the bushes and spit it out. You keep coming back to Rakshasa. Your letter mentioned it. But that's all. You seem to have gotten several things all tangled together."

"Yes, quite so." He nodded his head in

agreement. "That's the quandary. I do believe that these were murders. But by who or by what, I am not so sure. Not any more." He nodded again. "Yes, yes. I know that I've already said that. But that is the problem. I know, I know. In the car I said it was doing the killing and that I thought that I was next. Well, you see, that's it. I am afraid! I'm afraid that I am right. And that I am next."

I smiled at Winnie over the top of my brandy sniffer. "Oh surely you're not going to suggest that old bogeyman from the movies, archaeologist opens tomb and releases monster. Some sort of thing from Indian mythology. Some hob-goblin lumbering across the landscape, killing people. Are you?" He nodded. I gasped. "You are?"

"Doc, let me show you a map and some figures. Then you can make up your own mind."

I set the glass down. "O.K., lead on, Winnie. Take me where ever you wish to go. Then I'll decide what ever it is that I'm willing to believe."

"Fine, fine." Winnie got up and rummaged around in his desk, top drawer, and pulled out a map which encompassed all the territory from India to Great Britain. He pointed at figures marked on it, here and there.

I walked over to take a better look.

"See here?" He jabbed at several of the notations. "I've penciled in the dates of the several deaths including the ones in India mentioned by Roy. What do you see?"

"Ah, turn the map around so that I can read it right side up. Ummmmmm, yes, much better.

Hummmmnmun. umm, ummmmmm, most interesting, most interesting."

Winnie smiled. "Yes, I thought that you would say that! Ho, ho. But you can see it, can't you? The dates progress from India to Jerusalem to Rome, and now, to Paris. Each is later than the one before. Forming a sequence. And pointed straight toward here. It wasn't until I recalled that letter from Roy that I did this. And that's what decided me to write to you. And Boyer's death just added to the pattern."

He straightened up. "So, that's it, you see. That's the problem and there's the pattern. I've looked into this Rakshasa stuff, Indian mythology and all that. Unpleasant chaps. Demons, in fact."

I smiled and turned to find my brandy glass.

"Now don't you smile at me, Doc. That's what they're called. Demons! Its all in the books. Anyway, that's the problem!" He humpfed at me and started to pace the room again.

I regained my chair and my glass, having added a bit more to the glass first.

"Someone, or some thing, is killing people, including innocent villagers. You see, that's the problem. If it was some poor bugger that hates us for taking things from India, why pick on the natives? And if it was antiquity thieves, robbery of some sort, why break everything, make a mess, and all that? Damn puzzling. BUT !"

He stopped pacing. "If we may assume a demon, if only for a postulate, then it all makes sense, in a kind of ghastly way. Of course, if we assume that, then we have to assume that, somehow, Hafas, Corruccini,

Boyer, and myself, have all broken some version of whatever passes for the Pharaoh's Curse in India, or some such thing."

Winnie shook his head. "Although I must say that I have never heard such a thing in conjunction with India." He gave me a weak smile. "Of course that doesn't mean that it's not there. Frankly, I'm at a loss as to what is really going on, too many hanging threads, you see. And, of course, there is the rather interesting proposition that the map is correct. And that I am next on the list. Rather frightening that."

He circled around and collapsed back into his chair and stared into the fire. "If there had been such curse, or whatever, Boyer should have spotted it, being the one working on inscriptions. Have to recheck his notes when they arrive."

I watched him carefully and noticed how totally worn out he really was.

"Winnie, you do ramble on. What am I supposed to do? Surely not exorcize some sort of demon from India? That is quite a bit out of my line, even for one of my eclectic tastes. I still can't figure out why you asked me to fly halfway around the world. Surely not just for a visit? Or is that it, you just needed company?"

Winnie straightened up and frowned, a bit, in my direction. "Well, Doc, it's just this plain. If it was robbery for antiquities, we should know soon enough. I sent my chief assistant, James Finn, I believe I mentioned him in my letter, to visit each laboratory and see to the packing and shipping of all notes and artifacts relating to the project back here to London. He is due back tomorrow. And then we'll see if anything, has been taken. If some are missing from each place, why then we'll know. won't we? Ummmm, someone was looking for, so to speak"

He ran his hand over his face. "Of course, now Finn will have to turn right around and head to Paris to see to Boyer's effects. Finn must be in transit, I couldn't contact him."

I sighed. "Yes, O.K., then what? Suppose that you find that nothing is missing."

He looked up, saw that I was staring at him, and said in a tone of voice that was almost a command. "Why then, I want you to do two things. First, I want you to check through your contacts, um, resources and see if you can find out if there was some sort of illegal activity going on that I didn't know about or haven't been able to find out about!"

He waggled one finger in my direction. "Ah, ah, no denials! Suffice it to say that I know of your, ah, research in Marseilles, and of certain, ah, friends, shall we say, that you made there, ah, during your stay. Umnmmm, anyway, I don't really believe that there was any such hanky-panky going on. But, you see, I still have to know for certain, really know, don't you see. If there was, then that would well explain everything, wouldn't it."

He gave a great sigh. "Ah well. Second, if that doesn't pan out, then all you have to do, and you can draw from any resource you might wish, of any kind, anywhere within my power to grant, is to find out what is really going on, be it demon or whatever! I'll pay for it all, of course. And then some. Cost, as you might suspect, is no factor in all this." He smiled shyly, and nodded. "Although I would expect you be reasonable, none the less."

Winnie leaned forward, both hands on his knees. "So there you are, old chap. What do you say?" He looked expectant, and half afraid that I would turn him down. So what could I do?

"Aaaah, Winnie." I smiled, and nodded back at him. "O.K., it's a deal. But I hope you won't be too shocked if we find out the worst. It does strike me that it could have been some sort of international smuggling deal of some sort. Thieves falling out and all that. In fact, that was my first thought when I read your letter. After all, three world famous prehistorians, in close cooperation with the locals, traveling back and forth over a number of years, could have removed a considerable amount of contraband from one place to another. Especially if it was something small in volume and high in price like cocaine, for example"

And I laughed at his expression. "And I know what poor salaries people in our professions make, don't I? So it would not be altogether surprising if that was not the fact in this case, wouldn't it? Of course, if that is what was going on, it will really raise the roof when it becomes known. Do you really want to do that? Give a black-eye to the profession. It really would, wouldn't it? But we shall have to see, won't we?"

"Doc, do what you think best. And let the pieces fall where they may. However terrible the result."

And with that weary thought we broke off for the evening. Winnie stayed in his study to work and to ponder for awhile and to start trying to untangle the mess that the project had become.

I went to my room. From there I phoned Badnews and told him to start checking with various of his old contacts, just to see what he might chase up along the lines of international smuggling. Or the illegal antiquities trade. We made arrangements to meet the next day in one of the parks.

Badnews and I both felt that if it was an international smuggling effort then it would have had to have been initiated from the other side. It just didn't seem likely that the typical prehistorian would have had the slightest idea of how to go about contacting the right people without ending up in the hands of the police or blowing bubbles in some river or bay.

So we figured that given enough time and enough money to spread around and enough money to spread into the right hands that Badnews would be able to locate the right individuals and get from them the answers to our questions.

Having decided all this we hung up. I went to bed and lay there awhile wondering about the other choices. Perhaps Winnie's friends had merely gotten in the way of some very determined antiquity thieves. Well, that question should be answered on the morrow when James Finn brings back the answer.

And that left that last question -- demons! Well, I figured there was no worry there, so I rolled over and went to sleep.

Doc's Tale -- Part 2

The next morning, after breakfast, I met James Finn.

Now there was an interesting person. Rather short. An almost stocky person with largish features on an oversized head. Full beard and moustache with rather a large amount of grey. He was wearing those big, round glasses of the affected kind. With pink lens! Staring blue eyes. He was dressed in a windbreaker over a turtleneck sweater with blue jeans and some sort of running shoes.

After awhile he let you know right away that he thought he was an athlete. He did this mainly by bounding up and down on his toes, or stretching and twisting in the most affected way, All this motion went on as he talked at you. And I wish to stress that, talked at you! Truely amazing. A real performer. He could lecture at me and pander to Winnie in the same sentence. And Winnie never noticed what was going on. If ever there was a gold metal event in the Olympics for pandering, Finn would bring home the gold. And it wasn't what he said. If you closed your eyes and just paid attention to the words, they were all the right sort. He did it all with tone. Really quite schizophrenic. He would be vocally professing one thing and emotionally indicating absolutely the contrary. I'll have to check with Tommy and see what he has to say about someone like that.

Well, anyway, there we were. Finn was rather pleasant at first. He smiled and laughed.

But when you paid attention, it was a robot laugh. Ha. . . ha. . . ha. . . After some time I felt as if I was being addressed by my superior who was letting me know, oh so ever subtly, how dumb I really was.

So he discoursed in his rather heavy, dogmatic way, on what he called, rather frequently, his area of so-called 'special expertise.'

Later I asked Winnie about his creature, about Finn's educational background.

Winnie said that Finn was the equivalent of an educational drop-out. There was a hint of him being thrown out of a graduate program. Winnie suggested that I must have heard of Finn as he was known in the local area as quite an expert who had done major research projects there. It seems that Finn used to teach at one of the small colleges not too far from Grandeville. According to Winnie, Finn was the hub of the universe at that place and had a rather impressive string of publications to back it up. Seems Hafas had met him there.

And it was only later that Finn came into Winnie's employ.

To borrow a term from J.C., Finn was an instant creep as far as I was concerned. Mostly self-taught with all the intellectual problems that brings. Extremely pedantic. You know the type. He doesn't converse; he proclaims. Suggests that he is in full control of the literature, yet is misquoting half the time. Enough of Finn. You see how he affects people. You get so annoyed at the effrontery you can't stop talking about it.

So Finn was back and he had brought with him all the field notes of Hafas and Corruccini as well as selected portions of the artifactual material they were studying. The rest would come along later in a number of shipping creates. And, as far as Finn was able to tell, nothing had been taken by these so-called vandals.

Or to put it more correctly, Finn announced, "If that stands up, and Sir Winifred will let me know when the final accounting is finished, it will eliminate any linkage between vandals killing the prehistorians and the theft of artifacts." He shrugged his shoulders. "So it appears, for the moment, that robbery is ruled out! Neither Sir Winifred nor I could see any reason at all why antiquity thieves would go through so much trouble to fake the causes of two deaths when they would appear either to be natural or accidental."

With that Finn left to go off and work on the materials in the lab. He had to sort them out and get everything in order so that the new members of the team, after they had been selected, would be able to get into it right away. Of course, Finn gave the impression that he was the only one that could do this and that he was probably more well qualified than anyone else that might come along but that he was perfectly willing to help them get started on the right foot and all that.

Cliches and nonsense! Professional obligation this, theoretical archaeology that! A complete bore! I asked Winnie how he could put up with so much drivel all the time.

Winnie suggested that I was over-reacting and

that Finn was really quite good at his job.

And so, I let it drop. After all, he had known him much longer that I. So Finn left. And we settled back to finish our breakfast. Just sitting there admiring the way the sunlight streamed through the windows. It was a rather a nice looking day.

Well, as it turned out, Finn was the first sour note. The next was about to arrive.

So, there we sat, sipping our coffee, admiring the view, as I've said, and Winnie had just suggested that perhaps we ought to move off to the laboratory when the doors burst open. Bang!

Winnie's butler, yes, yes, he has one, came back-peddling into the room. He was being shoved along by a very angry customer.

The butler was protesting and this fellow was shouting. The butler trying to keep him out. This chap was equally determined to get in.

Then they were into the room, the butler slammed back flat against the wall; this other chap just standing there, red-faced, eyes bugging out, hair going every which way, fists clenched.

He didn't even see me as he began shouting at Winnie.

"Sir Winifred, it is time that you stopped this charade and stopped trying to con the profession with your phoney operation. I've heard about those deaths and you should well know that I'm not going to allow you to use these unfortunate circumstances to gain a false sympathy for your shoddy game, not at all. That site you have been working, if you can honestly call it that, is a phoney and know it! Your whole operation stinks to high heaven and I am going to prove it. And neither you nor your minions will be able to stop me either. I don't care how much money you have or how well connected you might be! And tell your toad here to get out of my way! Or I'll bust his nose for him."

"Um, yes." Winnie waved one hand casually. "That will be all Fields, just stand over there by the door." He gave me a slight smile. "Dr. Kappa Heckmann, may I introduce Dr. Theodore Krebbs. Dr. Kebbs, Dr. Heckmann." He bobbed his head toward the other. "Dr. Krebbs, as you may have gathered, does not exactly agree with my, our, ideas about that site we have been working on, do you Theodore?"

This triggered another explosion.

"DAMN RIGHT! Dr. Heckmann, heh? So, you're bringing some kraut on board to help you now, is that it? Well it won't help." Krebbs' glare flamed in my direction. "Herr Doctor Heckmann, if you are very smart, you will disassociate yourself from this entire operation before you find your reputation as ruined as his will soon be. A fraud! And I am on the verge of proving it. In print! So buzz off, if you know what is good for you."

"Ah, Dr. Krebbs, that was the name, was it not?"

"Damn'd right. K-R-E-B-B-S, Krebbs!"

I nodded pleasantly at him. And even smiled.

"Well O.K., K-R-E-B-B-S, Krebbs, listen carefully. I am not a kraut as you so delicately put it. I am an American, third generation. I am also an anthropologist. I am also a Ph.D. AND, I am also an old friend of Sir Winifred. AND I have gathered, from your big mouth and your extremely unpleasant manner and manners, that you do not agree with what Sir Winifred, and his colleagues, are doing. So, I ask you, what, other than childish behavior and overbearing statements, can you offer, in terms of sound data, if you know what that means, that would clearly, I repeat, CLEARLY demonstrate that all your noise is something other than bluster and bullshit!"

He drew himself up into a more rigid stance. "Dr. Heckmann, if you were familiar with the prehistory of India, you would recognize my name and understand that what I am saying is based upon sound fact!"

So I gave him another nod. "Dr. Krebbs, I do recognize your name. SO WHAT? Ah, ah! No more outburst, bad for the blood pressure. Would you care to enlighten me as to why this operation, as you labeled it, is a phoney?"

Both arms flew wide, a gesture of sheer frustration. "Heckmann, I don't have time to go into all that right now. The article which I shall shortly submit to *Antiquity* will tell you, and everyone who reads it, of the full absurdity. Sir Winifred may attempt to refute it if he wishes, but the plain fact is that the game is up! So, it would be best for you to put as much distance between his project and yourself as possible." He dropped his voice to a low, serious whisper. "Otherwise you will certainly see your reputation go down the drain right along with all the others."

"Well Krebbs, it is hard for dead men to refute your allegations, isn't it. Rather convenient, I would say."

He frowned and shrugged his shoulders. "They

had their chances when they were alive, you know." And in a swift gesture he turned toward Winnie. "Good riddance to bad rubbish, as the saying goes!" It was all malice and anger.

Winnie leaped to his feet, face purpling. "OUT! If. . . you. . .don't. . . get. . . out. At this very. . . moment. . . else I shall have you locked up. GET OUT OF MY HOUSE! NOW!"

"You can't threatened me, Sir Winifred! I'm going, I'm going. You!" He shoved Fields further back. "Get out of my way." Then he stared at Winnie. "And do not send your dog, Finn, to my home lurking about the place anymore either. If I catch that weasel sneaking about again I'll put a bullet between his eyes and end his misery, the psychotic creep, and make the world a cleaner place at the same time!" These last comments came roaring over his shoulder as he slammed his way out the front door.

I turned toward Winnie, who stood sadly shaking his head. He nodded to Fields who silently left, closing the door gently as he did.

"Well Winnie, just exactly what was that all about?"

Winnie sat and poured himself another cup of coffee and began to absent-mindedly shovel sugar into it. "Doc, I really am frightfully sorry that had to happen. Especially now. But, you see, that is part of why I am frightened. You saw Krebbs. Totally convinced, righteously convinced, angrily convinced, that the four of us are, or were, part of some deep, dark plot. Krebbs, as you probably know, is, perhaps now, was, one the top men in the field. But he appears to have gone completely around the bend. He writes letters and articles, give speeches, of the most horrible type, one step from slander. Some of his letters even were printed in *The Times.* He is ruining his reputation, not mine! Funny though. I am sort of responsible for it all, I suppose."

I reached over and put my hand over his coffee cup. And got a load of sugar dumped on it.

"Oh! Sorry Doc, not paying attention."

"How responsible, Winnie?"

"Well, he was the first person I contacted. Turned me down, cold! Said it wasn't possible for such a culture to exist. Wouldn't even consider the possibility. Said my data was fallacious. Later I talked to Hafas and the others, as I said, I think, and off we went." He sighed deeply. "And Krebbs has been on our backs ever since. Lately he has become much more antagonistic and violent. He would be quite capable of giving Hafas a heart attack. And he is quite strong. And didn't like Boyer at all, even before all this."

He started to stir his coffee, glanced down and was momentarily confused by what he saw.

"Oh surely Winnie, you're not suggesting that Krebbs is responsible for the deaths, are you?"

He pushed his coffee cup to one side and began to fiddle with his spoon. "Doc, at the moment I really don't know what I want to suggest. Or wish to suggest. Right now I don't know what is happening. So there you are! That's why you are here. And that's why I need your help, even if you think it's all stuff and nonsense."

"Ummmm, yes, all right, let's get on with it. Let's

look at the stuff in your laboratory, obvious place to start."

Winnie popped to his feet. "Right! One moment, I've got to give Fields some instructions for lunch, then we can go. Be right back."

Now during all that commotion, Krebbs had been waving a fist-full of rather crumpled sheets of paper in the air. His article I had supposed. As Winnie left the room and closed the door I noticed one sheet lying on the floor. It must have shaken loose. So I picked it up and put it in my pocket intending to look it over a bit later. Winnie returned and off we went to his laboratory which was located in another section of the house.

The laboratory was a large room with a ten foot ceiling. The entire north wall was glass, immense windows rising from floor to ceiling. The two side walls were cabinets and glass-faced specimen cases. Four rows of work tables occupied most of the space. Artifacts were neatly lined up in rows. Here and there labels stuck with tape to the table tops.

Rumpled paper bags, showing the dirt and damage produced by field use, were jumbled among them. Pencils, pens, ink bottles, paint brushes and all the other paraphernalia of an archaeological laboratory strewn all over the place.

To one side a drafting table and a small bench with a binocular microscope.

On the last wall, the one through which we entered, a large bulletin board with sketches, artifact drawings, a site map, notes, memos and what have you sticking here and there.

And finally, in a corner, that most necessary piece of equipment of all, a pot of hot water, cups, sugar, spoons and all the makings.

Winnie waved an arm. "Well, there you are Doc. That's it! Three years accumulation with the exception of the larger stuff. Doesn't look like much of anything for three people to die over, does it? I'll have to expand into the next room when the other collections arrive from the other labs. I'll just leave you here. Finn will be popping in and out. I'm quite sure he can answer any questions you might have. But, do whatever you wish. I'll pop in just before lunch."

Winnie left and there I was, surrounded with the remains of another culture and another time. This room was a classic example of ordered chaos. Pieces of statuary here, stone objects of another sort over there. Piles of pot shards, sorted by color and texture.

Beads. Soapstone fragments of something. Piles of photographs, sketches and notes. Field stained maps with notes. Field books. Artifact bags still to be unloaded.

Finn came in and took a place in a far corner and began painting numbers on a series of small objects and trying to watch me without being obvious. So I just wandered around, a professional tourist, not knowing what to look for or at, not even sure that I would recognize whatever it was, if I saw it. Just browsing, thank you.

I found a pile of photographs that the police had taken of all three of the ruined laboratories. I wondered how Winnie had managed to get them. They were obviously taken before anything had been removed including the bodies.

I stared carefully at them searching for clues. Then I went through the artifact catalogs and the field catalogs. Figured I might spot some discrepancy if someone were taking artifacts on the sly. Didn't find anything.

Well, that's how the morning went. Just before lunch Fields came in, plugged in a telephone and announced that I had a phone call.

It was Badnews reminding me to meet him in one of the parks later in the day. He said that he would rather talk there than have me come to the house where he was staying rather spend the time on the phone. I said that I would meet him there, naming the park to make sure that I had the right one. I would just walk about and he could contact me.

Finn left saying he was off to Paris. Then Winnie came in, it being almost noon and off we went to his club for lunch.

Over lunch it was obvious that he was waiting for me to say something. Finally he burst out. "Well Doc, what do you think?"

"Not much Winnie, not much,"

"Not much?" His eyebrows shot up in surprise.

I nodded. "Quite right. I looked through your records and it doesn't seem to me that there was any pilfering of artifacts. Of course that assumes that the records haven't been fiddled with. I looked at those photographs you had of the other laboratories and I didn't see anything in them either. Of course, there is always Krebbs, isn't there? But I can't really see him charging from country to country getting rid of your colleagues. Do you?"

He sighed. "No, actually I don't. Feel quite sorry for him though, poor chap." His expression softened and he stared into space.

So I continued. "So there you are. Theft by your own expedition members appears to be ruled out. It appears that these so-called vandals haven't taken anything, no theft there. We both rule Krebbs out. Haven't made much progress, have we? But we have ruled out some of the possibilities. Now what does that leave us with?"

Winnie frowned. "Quite right, what does that leave us with? Rakshasa?"

I stared at his expression. "Well, Winnie, I do not think that I am quite ready for that possibility not just yet. After all we haven't fully considered the possibility of smuggling. The deaths and destruction does smack of a certain kind of criminal syndicate mentality. A kind of warning to others not to step out of line. Especially if drugs were involved."

One heavy fist pounded down, rattling the dishes and turning heads. "NO! Bloody hell! Surely your not suggesting that Hafas, Corruccini, or Boyer, or all three together, were some sort of drug ring. Now that possibility, Doc, I cannot and will not accept. Not at all!"

I leaned forward. "Oh for heaven's sake Winnie, of course not! Settle down will you, we don't want to be thrown out of your club, do we? And you already suggested it."

He looked around at the staring faces and then leaned toward me. "Well then, what are you suggesting?" At best his voice was a very loud stage whisper.

I took a sip of coffee. "Only raising the possibility, that's all. Besides, having that matter looked into, as you suggested, I am quite confident that we can clear up that point very soon. But after that, then what's left, huh?"

Winnie shook his head. "Haven't the foggiest, you know."

"Well, that's where we are, for the moment. Don't worry Winnie, I'm sure that we'll figure it out, sooner or later." After all, what else could I say?

So, for the rest of the meal, we talked about the food and this and that. And I told him that I would just walk around London for awhile and think over everything that we had talked about and that I had seen and that, hopefully, by evening I would have a new idea or something more to offer. Winnie wasn't very happy with that, but there wasn't much either one of us could do. Besides, I figured Badnews had something but I didn't think this was the time to tell Winnie about that.

I spent a most pleasant afternoon. Wandered about the British Museum. Took tea, at tea-time of course, in a small shop on one of the side streets, browsed through several bookstores. Even thought that I saw Finn but then I wasn't sure that I did.

Doc paused. "By the way, J.C., here's a bill from Blackwell's. They're sending a few things, by air"

Then he regained the thread of his story.

When I left that store I had a small snack at one of the nicer spots figuring to eat dinner with Winnie later on. And before you know it, it was time to meet

Badnews in the park.

Once there I just strolled around trying to see whether I could spot him. Of course you never can, not unless he wishes you to. Way across the grass I could see this large, black dog. He was just sort of standing there. It felt as if he was staring at me. Then he just sort of faded into the bushes.

In the middle space there was a large group of children playing some sort of ring-around game. I watched for a bit and then walked on waiting for Badnews to materialize.

Suddenly there was all this screaming and yelling coming from the children. I turned to see what was going on and there was that dog charging straight through the kiddies, bowling them this way and that. He looked to be running straight at me so I turned to speak to his master who I assumed must be right behind me. There was no-one there. One of the nurses, she was with the children you see, started yelling, "Look out, look out!"

I swung around and there he was, all teeth and snarl, leaping right at me. Somehow, and I don't really recall how, just as he leapt I swung my arm in front of my face and he clamped down on my forearm rather than my face or throat. Of course, I don't know which he was actually aiming for but it doesn't really matter, does it?

Anyway, as he grabbed my arm I twisted around, spinning hard and managed to lift him from his feet. About this time I thought that if I could swing him into a handy tree I might get lucky and break his back. However, he was rather heavy, and I was rather out of balance, and I misjudged just where the tree was. So instead of smashing him across a tree trunk I spun right into one with my face instead. The blow knocked me down and there we were, the two of us, in a heap.

From what people said afterwards, at this point the dog jumped up and ran away before anyone could get their hands on him. Several of the witnesses did say that they thought they saw a smallish individual running after the dog. But in the confusion they weren't too sure. The only thing that I really remember about that animal, other than his color of course, was his smell. It was terrible. I don't what he had been rolling in but whatever it was it was pretty rank.

So people crowded about doing all the normal dithering one expects. Helping me to my feet. Brushing off the leaves. Offering handkerchiefs to stop the blood. Then up ran a policeman tweeting on his whistle and the next thing I knew, there we were, in an ambulance with some attendants patching me up.

You can imagine the look on Winnie's face when we drove up to his place and I walked in trailing apologizing cops. I had told them who I was and that I was staying with Winnie. I wasn't in any mood to stand around and talk so I left it to Winnie to straighten out anything that needed straightening out and went to bed. Winnie's personal physician shortly turned up, checked everything, said that I was fine, and talked to the cops as well.

The next morning I got up, somewhat stiffly, and made a phone call to Badnews. I didn't mention what had happened. He sounded a bit different so I asked him if he had caught a cold. He said no, he had not caught a cold, and that he would start taking care of things today and hung up.

So I went downstairs for breakfast. Winnie's conversation mostly revolved around me and that blasted dog with little mention of the things that I had come to look into. I made my escape and spent the rest of the day in the laboratory. Then the next day or so until it was time to catch my flight back. Winnie had Fields pack my bags and load them in the car. Then off we went, Winnie and I, in the Rolls, to the airport. Everything was well timed. We arrived, said our farewells, promised to keep in contact, and I boarded.

"And here I am. Never did get my report from Badnews. Just have to wait for it."

Doc smiled at every one in the room.

"And so there you are. That's my big trip to London, class. And none the worse for wear, ah, in a manner of speaking." He looked around and beamed at us.

So I jumped right in. "Doc, it seems that for all the travel that you haven't learned much about what ever it is that is going on."

"Ah no, J.C., we really haven't learned much. Although we did eliminate a few things, didn't we?" He began to rummage in his pockets. "Of course I did bring a few, ah, souvenirs, a few small things, back with me." Then he looked up.

"Ah, if you would fetch my overcoat J.C., and bring it here, I'll show you. Of course I was just a bit worried about customs. Would have been a bit of trouble as I didn't bother to declare anything. And for that matter, I didn't exactly tell Winnie, or that odious assistant of his either, that I was borrowing them. Just our little secret."

Doc held up one finger. "Membrane, if you would, break out a new bottle of brandy while J. C. is moving about. We can all use a good snort before anything else."

So I fetched the overcoat and was sorely tempted to take a leetle peek in the pockets to see what it was that Doc had smuggled back. But then I decided that Doc would be too bent out of shape if I spoiled his surprise. So I didn't peek. I felt the pockets from the outside. Couldn't tell much though. By the time I got back the Membrane had poured four generous glasses. Three were taken so I claimed the left-overs and sat down.

Doc lifted his glass. "Well gentlemen, cheers! Ahhhhhhhhh, good stuff. Now J. C.. if you would just reach into the outside left hand pocket and retrieve what's in there. Good! Give those things to David, please. Good, good!"

I handed the things to Dr. Ben who looked at Doc questioningly, brows furrowing, full of questions, no doubt.

"David, that folded piece of paper is the inscription that Rasha Roy copied from an inner chamber at the site. See whether you can make anything out of it, say in the next day or two. Same thing for the cylinder seals in the box."

Doc swivelled his gaze in my direction. "Now J. C., if you would take the pot-shards from the right hand pocket. Right!" He reached into his shirt pocket and pulled out a filing card and handed it to me. "Ship one-third of them to the first address, one-third to the second, and keep the rest in some safe place. Perhaps the library."

Then he handed me a badly crumpled, now sort of flattened out, piece of paper.

"Take this and see whether you can track down any of these articles and get copies of them. I want the one circled in red. Go where ever you have to. Just get them. I think that it is extremely important that we get a look at them."

So I looked at my treasures. One three-by-five card with two addresses. A bunch of pot-shards. One very crumpled piece of paper which looked like someone's bibliography with several entries circled in smudged red pencil.

"Doc, is this the paper that Krebbs dropped?"

"Very good, J. C., you are quite right. Must have something to do with that article he claimed he was writing. It seemed to me that we might be able to get some idea as to what is agitating him so badly if we could read the same references that he circled in red. They might be, after all, the keys to the puzzle we have been handed. Might even solve the whole thing and wouldn't that be nice?"

I sat down, sipped a little brandy, top of the line it was indeed, and started wondering where I was going to find these little babies. And wondering who I could phone tomorrow to check them out for me. And wondering which library was the most likely place to start. And wondering about stopping in Portland for a piece of chocolate cake.

Suddenly all three of our heads were snapped around by the loud gasp that came from Dr. Ben.

He was sitting bolt upright in his chair, brandy glass on the table next to him. His eyes were wide, staring, and slightly bugged-out, aimed at the three cylinder seals that he held nestled carefully in the hand on his lap. His other hand tightly gripped the arm of the chair, fingers digging into the material, It looked like a seizure of some kind the way the cords on his neck were standing out.

Doc called softly. "David, David! What's the matter? Have you taken a swallow of brandy down the wrong tube?"

Dr. Ben gave a quick shake of his head. "No."

"Well then, take a drink of it and restore your circulation and tell me what the problem is."

Dr. Ben released the chair, grabbed his glass, gulped down a sizeable portion, shuddered and looked at Doc. "Doc, it's these cylinder seals. They're, they're, ah, where did you get them? Where did you get them. WHERE DID THEY COME FROM?"

Doc shot from his chair, motioning the Membrane to stay where he was and took the seals from Dr. Ben's hand. Then he lifted Dr. Ben's other hand, still holding the brandy glass and pushed it up under his nose. "Here David, take another sip. It won't hurt, not at all."

Dr. Ben took a swallow, this time the wrong way, coughed and visibly began to relax. I heard a slow release of breath as the Membrane followed suit.

Apparently the second dose did the trick. Dr. Ben began to regain his color.

Doc turned and resettled himself, one leg kicked over one arm of his chair. "O.K. David, now take a deep breath, exhale slowly and then tell me. What did you see?"

Dr. Ben followed instruction, leaned forward. "Doc, where did you get these seals. Where? Where did they come from?"

Doc smiled at him. "Ah yes, same old question, huh? Well, if you promise not to get so agitated, I'll tell you. O.K.? Promise?"

Dr. Ben nodded.

"Good! But first, another sip of brandy like a good fellow. There. Good, good! Now sit back. And relax. Right!"

Doc held his hand out, palm up. The three cylinder seals laid side by side. "These came from the laboratories of Hafas, Corruccini, and Boyer. Hafas was clenching one in his fist when he died. Corruccini had one in her smock pocket rapped in tissue. The third was found sitting next to a partially eaten open-faced sandwich on Boyer's work bench, a work bench rather stoutly fastened to the wall. So, now you know. Tell me! What. . . did . . . you see?"

Dr. Ben reached out and gently picked up the seals and began to turn them over and over, one at a time. "Doc, as you no doubt know, each of these has a series of incised symbols carved into them. All cylinder seals do. If you rolled them across soft clay or wax they will leave a raised picture. A sort of ownership label. A way of marking certain kinds of property or messages. Now while I can't totally make out all the symbols on them, just by inspection, they do appear to be identical.

If J. C. could find a bit of clay I'll check them more closely in more detail. But what startled me was this. Each has one set of symbols identical to the other cylinders. In this set I recognized one immediately. That symbol stands for Rakshasa!"

Doc nodded his head. "Ummmmm, I see, I see. But so what?"

"This! For two days I have been reviewing all my materials on the Rakshasa. And taking that into consideration, plus what you have just told us about your trip to London, plus the events that have taken place relative to Boyer, Corruccini, and Hafas, I can truly say that I now know what is responsible for all these things. Not only do I know it, I believe it!"

The intensity of his voice had us all leaning forward.

"Rakshasa!" It was almost a whisper. "They are responsible. Villagers, Hafas, Corruccini, Boyer. Soon Robsen-Brown. You're included too, Doc. That dog wasn't a dog, it was a Rakshasa. You see, it is all coming together. Types of deaths, smells, destruction. Typical behavior for Rakshasa. Cylinder seals. Inner chamber inscription. Everything!"

Dr. Ben swivelled his head around, looking at each of us in turn. "I think Robsen- Brown had better be told and warned of the danger."

He stared at Doc intently. "You will have to convince him that it is true. Otherwise it will be four deaths!"

He stabbed one finger at Doc. "And one final point, Doc. You've brought these things home. And that means, you, we, all of us here, are now in as much danger as Robsen-Brown in London. Of course we have more time before they turn up here."

By this time the skin on my arms was going all goose bumps. I don't normally hold stock in ghosties and hob-goblins and things that go "bump" in the night, but it was beginning to get to me. The fear, shock, or what ever Dr. Ben was feeling, was beginning to communicate itself to me on all channels. And I didn't like the message that I was receiving, not even a little bit. Nope, not at all.

Doc was humming to himself. Finally he spoke. "Ah, David, what you have said is most interesting, most interesting, indeed. But perhaps you might elaborate a little bit. Give us some supporting data. Things like that."

Dr. Ben nodded, a dutiful student. "O.K. Doc, it's like this. Rakshasa are demons that live in India, well noted in the mythology of the sub-continent. They are particularly nasty vicious and are destined to play a brutalizing part in their interactions with humanity. They interfere in the affairs of men, mainly in the most malevolent manner possible. They can change their shape and appearance."

Dr. Ben gave a heavy sigh. "It would appear the Sir Winifred and his crew have put an excavation where they shouldn't have. My best guess is that they uncovered or opened up a tomb or some sort of chamber of a dread nature that had been sealed for many centuries. And this place had a guardian waiting patiently through the millennia, watching over something placed there."

He paused, looked at his empty glass. I snatched

the bottle and hurriedly gave him a refill, and after a slow sip he continued. "They removed this thing and woke the guardian from its slumber. A Rakshasa! This action caused their destinies to become intertwined. And it followed its own destiny. Down the canyon, through the village and westward. Jerusalem, Rome, Paris. Soon London."

He stopped, a great sadness pulling his features down. "And now! Doc, you've visited the lab in London, handled the artifacts and been attacked." Dr. Ben's eyes began twitching around the room. He lurched to his feet. "Soon it comes here!"

"Well," said Doc, standing and stretching, not looking all that concerned. "I think that it is time for everyone to hit the sack. David, you have given us all something to think about. And I think that if we all get a good nights sleep that in the light of day we will be able to gain a better perspective on everything. SO!" He popped his hands together. "J. C., in the morning I want to look over whatever you have compiled on those matters that I asked you to look into to. Well?" Doc scanned the room. "Good night all!"

And with that we all headed for bed and a good nights sleep. Although from the look on Dr. Ben's face I very much doubted whether he was going to get much sleeping done at all. For that matter, neither did I.

Several things managed to keep me awake. One was that Doc had managed to not mention anything at all about where Badnews was or what he was up to or why he wasn't with Doc as he was supposed to be. It was sort of like knowing that someone has launched a nuclear tipped missile but they didn't tell you where the thing is coming down, exactly.

Then there was Dr. Ben and that Rakshasa stuff.

So, insomnia poked its boney finger into my bedroom and beckoned. I worked through a good part of the night in the library and finally trudged up the spiral stairs to fall bleary-eyed into bed and to sleep.

But I kept waking up. And each time I was sure that there was something standing there. In my room! Black and amorphous. Of course, every time I clicked on the light there wasn't anything there. Just an overactive imagination, right?

Krebbs

London.

Dr. Theodore V. Krebbs mumbled to himself as he worked in his office and laboratory. It was a new habit, one that had developed since the time that Robsen-Brown had first approached him about working on the "new" project, wanting him to work on that dig in India. Of course he had refused as soon as he had heard what was being proposed. Nonsense, total nonsense!

"Just wait until this article appears in *Antiquity*, that will show them, it will all right, yes. And serve them right too, the whole ruddy lot of them especially that damned ugly chap, Finn, bloody colonial anyway . . . thinks that he knows about everything, damn provincial American anyway, from some speck in the middle of nowhere. What does he know? Nothing, that's what! Coming around here trying to tell me what to do, damn cheeky little toad. That is what he is, a boot-licking toady."

Krebbs heaved himself upright from deep within his chair and stamped over to the tall window and looked out at the darkness and stillness of the late evening. "Huh, moon's past full but stilled damned bright. See every tree and shrub down there in the garden, didn't realize it was so late. Let see . . . huh, midnight. Damned late, all right.

Now what? Something moved down there in the shadows. Bet it's that Finn creature, spying around again. Steady, Krebbs old boy, steady. Nothing there and you know it, nothing at all. Just your imagination, just been working too hard."

"That's it! Been working too hard, much too hard. Must take a vacation when we're done, aye? Back to the article, finish it up. Then a little nip to celebrate the end and put it to bed. Must send Robsen-Brown a copy when I mail it in. Wouldn't do to appear unprofessional when I scuttle his boat full of dreams, misbegotten as they are. Well, he can write his rebuttal, get it ready. If he dares, if he dares. Don't see how he would have the nerve to try and answer. His career is finished either way. Too bad in a way. Decent enough chap before all this started. But! Serves him right, serves him right, with his great bloody fraud, trying to pass it off as real. Why any fool can see that this site is a phoney. Hoax it is, great ruddy hoax. Spent all that time building a hoax when he could have been doing real productive work. Strange the way some folks chose to go. Well, can't stand here all night staring at shadows, imagining lurkers in the garden. Right! Back to work . . . What's that! Something did move down there... Now, now Krebbs, steady on. Just your imagination, huh, said that already you did. Talk to myself too much. All Robsen-Brown's fault, all his fault, him and that damned hoax. Right! Back to work!"

He walked back to his desk, sat down and squared the edges of his manuscript. Then starting at page one, he began to slowly read the document, correcting a word here, a phrase there, editing, burnishing, honing each paragraph until the logic of his argument was so right that no-one could miss the point, no-one could fail to see the clarity of it all. "Oh, that's good Krebbs, that's good. Can't miss that point there. Not unless they are all bloody fools."

"What's that? Noise in the hall! Oh nonsense, working too hard. That's it, working too hard."

He worked on until he reached the section that dealt with the inscriptions. "Damn, that doesn't look right. Better check it Krebbs, better check it. Just see what the chart says."

He lurched to his feet again and walked over to the wall that was covered with charts and graphs. Sheets were hung over sheets, some attached with tape, some stuck on with pins. "Yeesssss, now let's see here, where is it, that section, that section, damned decent of Boyer to loan me copies of his stuff. Too bad he didn't pay any attention to me when I told him that it was a fake. Ot course, he said that he would check. Don't suppose he got that chance though, too bad. Now he'll be tarred with the same brush as Robsen- Brown. Now let's see, where is that piece? Around here somewhere." He lifted a sheet and then another and another. "Ahhhhhh, ha! Yes, that looks like it. Yes. Right about here. Ah, there it is, now let's see how that translation goes. Hummmmmmmmm."

Behind him the door silently swung open, open onto the darkness of the hallway.

It waited and watched, a vague blackness that stood, waiting, waiting.

"Yes, there it is Krebbs. You did it, you know, you really did it!" He walked back to his desk reading over the page snatched from the wall and plopped down in his chair and sat hunched over his manuscript, pushing it here and there as he rummaged for the page that he had in mind. Quickly he made corrections, adding a new page, finishing his final statement, the cornerstone of his career.

No-one would ever read it. The strong odor brought his head up with a snap. It was the last thing he would ever know as darkness fell upon him through the open door. Manuscript pages flew in the air to be joined by other papers and books being swept from shelves.

Then it was quiet, broken only by the ticking of the clock in the corner. A shaft of moonlight had inched its way up the wall and now shown on the clock's face. It was 12:15 and a single chime struck.

Good News from Badnews

Grandeville. Doc's Home.

Three days stretched to four days, four days stretched to five days, etc., etc.

I had finally returned with my cargo of notes, photocopied material and boxes of books. Even so it meant having to drive during all hours of the day and night just to get from one place to the other and back again. Anyhow, I made it back in time for dinner. This time I had returned from the south and had driven northeast across the several mountain ranges to get back to good old Grandeville, U.S.A. What that meant was that I had to miss the traditional stop in Portland for a wee bit o' chocolate cake and what-have-you.

Oh well, that's the sacrifices one has to make at times. Shows how dedicated I am when I really put my heart into it.

I got the Membrane to help me unload my "treasures," which we then piled in one place making a rather impressive pile, sitting there on the floor, in the library, next to the desk. I figured that after dinner I had plenty of time to start organizing the stuff. Besides I had noticed with my eagle eye that there was also a sizeable pile of newspaper clippings and what-not which meant that Old John had, in the interim, been a busy little beaver, too. It appeared to me as if there was enough stuff sitting there to keep me occupied for the next couple days or so. Unless, of course, Doc had switched direction by now and had something else planned for you-know-who.

After dinner, there we were, all of us, in the front room, enjoying a little of the best, from the liquor cabinet.

"Well Doc, what's new? Learned anything else since I left and journeyed over to civilization to return bearing priceless gifts and other rare treasures such as only I can find in the far reaches of fair Cathy, and other likewise exotic places?"

Doc shook his head. "J. C., J. C. There are times when your linguistic hodge-podge is amazing and, of a time, amusing, sort of. But! However, yes. We have several new pieces of information to add to our puzzle, none good, some interesting and some disturbing."

He shot one finger into the air.

"IL PRIMO! As you have no doubt seen, Old John has done his usual excellent job of sending us more newspaper clippings than we could possible need, all relating to the rather unusual demise of three prehistorians. However well these things fill in minor additional details there is essentially nothing new in them and they do little to help us understand this mystery of ours."

A second finger joined the first.

"IL SECONDO! Dr. Theodore Krebbs, you remember that I mentioned him in telling you of my stay in London, well, it seems that he has died, rather suddenly and under much the same circumstances as the other three. I find this most disturbing and rather puzzling. After all, he had no direct connection with Sir

Winifred's activities, did he? In fact he was very much opposed to them. Yet there he is, dead! And under what appears to be much the same state of affairs. If Rakshasa, rather strange don't you think?"

Three fingers wiggled, fetchingly, at me.

"IL TERZO! Sir Winifred is coming here, to stay. For a little while. I felt that it would be all that much safer for him to be here than at his house in London. After all, if whatever it is headed in his direction, as all the facts, such as they are, seem to indicate, and in as much as the death of Dr. Krebbs seems to put it in London, then, a little extra distance, in this case, a whole lot of distance, should give us some additional time to work out this puzzle we have and see whether we can figure out something before our unwelcome guest or guests turn up for a brief visit."

Doc winked at me. "Maybe these things don't cross oceans. After all they are indigenous to India. Maybe they're landlocked." He smiled.

I shot to my feet. "WHAT! Come on Doc, surely you don't believe that this thing, whatever it is, is going to turn up here in good old backwoods Grandeville? Do you?"

He motioned me back into my chair, waited until I was resettled arid continued, serenely. "Why, of course I do, J. C., of course I do. This problem, let us call it that for the time being, must come to us, here in Grandeville. After all, what else can it do? Sir Winifred is the last of the series. And now he appears to be the only key to the solution to the puzzle. So, if he is here, does it not seem logical that this thing will have to follow after him? Assuming, of course, that it can cross oceans, heh, heh."

"But," he jumped up, "not to worry. After all." He pointed at the walls. "This is our home ground. In military terms we are in a much stronger position, being on the defensive and all that. We know the territory and it doesn't! Right? Right!"

Doc plopped back into his chair. "Besides, I have sent for reinforcements. In fact, rather sizable reinforcements, heh, heh. Oh dear." He beamed at Membrane. "A rather poor pun, I suppose?"

I looked at the Membrane, who smiled and nodded. "What reinforcements? What are we going to be doing now? Not digging trenches? Stringing barbed wire? Standing guard and all the rest?"

Doc sighed and slumped further into his chair. "Now, now J. C., nothing as dramatic as all that, I assure you! Although dramatic enough, I suppose. I spoke to The Chief of Police and asked him to loan us two of his officers. They should join us soon, mostly likely tomorrow, I should imagine. Yes, most certainly tomorrow. Right!" He nodded his head in total agreement with himself.

"All right, Doc," I hissed. "Which two officers are we borrowing? You really spoke to Quick Draw?"

"Indeed, I did." He smiled at me. "Red and Green. Ummm, they agreed. And, umm, we are paying for their, um, vacation lime."

"Red and Green! Oh for heavens sake, what are we going to do with both of them on hand, recreate Hannibal's elephant corps?"

Doc straightened up and gave me a stern look. "Now, now J. C., that is not kind, not kind at all. I just felt that it would be handy to have the both of them around, on hand as you say, to help us out, that's all. After all it will be just for a short while. And I do think our pantry can stand the gustatory impact. At least for a little while."

I nodded. Red and Green are about the same size as the Membrane. The three of them could eat us out of house and home in short order. I shrugged. Oh well, I like Red and Green.

Doc glanced past me, then at me, and winked. "If you would see to your shopping, instead of messing about all over the place!"

Then he glanced rather pointedly past me. I turned my head to see what was going on. What we all now saw was the outside door knob slowly turning. Membrane nodded his head, made some excuse or another about getting more ice from the kitchen and hurried from the room.

Dr. Ben nodded. "Good idea." He was agreeing with the shopping expedition. Then he finally noticed what Doc was signaling. His eyes sort of bugged out as he pushed himself back into his chair, drink in hand forgotten.

Doc started speaking, about some nonsense that had happened downtown.

The door knob had finished its full rotation. The door started, oh so very slowly, to open.

I was busily checking the room trying to decide what was the most lethal thing I could get my hands upon when we heard a loud bellow from outside. It was The Membrane in full cry.

"**GOTCHA**! All right you little weasel, what the

hell do you think you're doing creeping around through the underbrush like some sort of junior grade CIA agent?"

The door quivered.

"Put me down, or I will break every bone in your massive body and leave the remains in the elephant's graveyard!"

This voice could only be described as the sort of thing that the worst villain you ever heard would sound like. It was coupled with a hoarseness, sort of stage whisper, carrying undertones of such malice, cold death, that it never failed to put, momentarily, goose bumps right on top of my goose bumps. A talking venomous snake. Badnews had arrived.

The door opened gently and he entered followed by the Membrane who was grinning from ear to ear. The two of them had become fast friends almost from the moment they met. I wasn't sure but I had a strong hunch that Badnews probably never had a real friend before. Doc was in a different position, someone to obey and protect.

Badnews and I were just acquaintances, people who worked together and did things together. As for the rest of humanity, well most people, in Badnews' eyes, just didn't seem to exist. John Tinker was one of the exceptions though. Of course he was giving Badnews weekly workouts in the martial arts. They took turns beating upon each others bodies.

Bad news is one of those short, wiry guys with sharp features. However, unlike Doc, he didn't move with the quick darting pace than seems to characterize short, little guys. He flows like a dancer. Smooth, easy.

Dead, dead eyes watched from a face with carved lines for creases. It was a weatherbeaten, outdoor face.

Flat.

Expressionless.

Blank.

He slid into the room, eyes checking everything, hardly pausing on Dr. Ben.

Membrane closed the door behind them. And I thought, well there he is, alive and well, as least as far as it was possible to tell.

Badnews eased across the room and stood and waited for Doc to initiate the conversation. He never spoke to Doc first.

"Welcome home Badnews, it is good to see you back." Doc waved one arm impatiently. "Well, sit down, sit down. And tell me what you learned during your absence. Oh! This is Dr. David Ben, my house guest. He'll be with us for awhile."

Dr. Ben had started to relax. He smiled tentatively. "Pleased to meet you."

Badnews looked through him and whispered, "Yes." Then he pulled a chair over by Doc and sat down facing him.

Doc smiled. "I trust all went well with you?"

And this chilling stage whisper voice started as Badnews leaned forward, hands on his knees, speaking to Doc.

"I did as you wished. I looked into those matters you listed. But I did not start right away. There were other things to do first."

Badnews looked at the floor. "I was too far away

there in the park. I was late. A terrible fault. I did not see the dog move until it was too late. And I was too far away. You were unprotected. I should have been closer. I should have been there earlier. It was my fault."

Doc patted on of his hands. "Now, now, it wasn't really, you know. I just got there too soon, that's all. Not your fault at all. But if it was, I forgive you."

Badnews looked up through his eyebrows. "The dog is dead. It will bite no more people. I . . . spoke. . . with.. . the. . . owner. He promised that he would never let one of his dogs run loose again. Ever. He promised."

I felt sorry for the dog's owner.

Doc merely nodded his head. He knew discussion over this point would be useless.

Badnews continued his report, head held up again. "After finishing with the necessary business in London, I went to Paris, then to Rome, then to Jerusalem. Then I checked with Marseilles. Everywhere they said the same thing."

It was the usual abbreviated account. Badnews only told the part that was necessary to carry the message. No elaborations, never the rest, none of the details. I had always wondered what he did in the past, pre-Doc. I had a feeling Doc knew more than he was willing to say. Now, after reading those clippings I was beginning to catch a glimmer. I knew that I really didn't want to know what lay in between the spaces in his narrative. But still I was kinda curious.

". . . The dog is dead, It will bite no more people. I . . . spoke . . . with . . . the . . . owner. He promised that he would never let one of his dogs run loose again. Ever. He promised."

Henry Higgins was a large man with a florid face. He didn't like jokes being made about his name and he didn't like that bloody, daft stage play and that even worse, bloody, daft movie either. After that last dust-up with that loud mouthed bloke at the foundry, jokes had finally stopped. He couldn't do anything about their smiles behind his back but they wouldn't be doing any smiling to his face, that was for sure, chappy!

Henry was in a foul mood. Today had been a bad day. And pity the person who got in his way now. Dinner hadn't been what he had wanted when he stomped angrily into the house. Now the old woman was at the neighbors for some mutual back patting, discussing what rotten men they had married. Old wind bags! And she had let the dog get out again and it hadn't returned home yet. Another reason to curse the day.

Nothing worth watching on the telly, if it worked, and the beer didn't taste as good as it should! Everything was going downhill these days.

AND NOW, some sorry sot was ringing the front bell. Probably some bloody salesman. Henry lurched up from his chair and threw the empty bottle into a corner of the room. Well he would be sorry all right, when he received the full-bore blast of Mr. Henry Higgins at his red-faced best. The poor sot!

Henry charged, threw open the door, the knob slamming into its usual depression in the wall. Henry stared down his long nose and thought, it's some bloody damn wog looking for a handout.

He roared, "Well, what do you want?"

The small man stood there, left hand held behind his back, right hand just dropping from the doorbell and asked in a strange whispering voice with undertones that should have warned Henry if he hadn't been so enjoying his own self-righteous anger.

"Are you the owner of a large black dog which used to enjoy running in the park?"

"That's right! What's it to you? And what'cha mean, used to?"

"Your dog, then. It attacked a . . . friend. I have brought it home."

The left hand slowly swung around and held out the limp form dangling from a hand tightly clenched around its throat. It was dropped on Henry's feet.

"Your dog was ill-mannered."

Some of the red color drained from Henry's face. "Wha . . . wha.. . what is the meaning of this, you . . . you bastard. Just who the bloody hell do you think you are?"

He made a grab for the wog's shirt front, just to teach him a lesson.

A wave of pain shot up his arm that almost brought him to his knees. His right hand was tightly held, the flesh between the thumb and forefinger pinched by the fingers of his visitor. A sharp blow just below the sternum thrust him back into the hallway where he slowly slid down the wall gasping for breath. The slight figure leaned over him and with a sharp rap with his knuckle numbed the other arm from shoulder to finger tips.

"Now," whispered the harsh voice in his ear. "Let me tell you what will happen to you if you should ever get another dog and if you do not raise it to be more well-mannered."

Henry Higgins' wife came home some time later feeling much better after having commiserated with her friend and after having a few nips from the friend's gin bottle.

She found him sitting in the hallway softly crying to himself, the body of his dog cradled in his lap.

She never learned what had happened or why he became such a considerate husband. Or why he never got another dog. She just counted her blessings.

"After finishing the necessary business in London, I went to Paris . . ."

On the ferry crossing the channel, Badnews thought back to his youth, growing up on the reservation. It was a life on barren, rocky land, land thrown away by the white-eyes, land given to the Indians to try and survive on, as best as they could.

His father had taught him all his skills; running, hunting, stalking, killing, silence, patience. He had not grown as tall as his father but stayed small and slight like his mother. He had inherited her wiry strength.

She had been a war-bride from Sicily. His father had been attracted to her, her village and their tribal customs. She was from a small village high in the hills. Her father and her brothers had been impressed with this American's skills. So they had agreed that she could marry him and go to live in America. They didn't know where her husband had come from and he didn't tell them.

Badnews was his parents only child, named by his father. He was an amalgamation of his parents: brown hair, brown eyes, dusky skin. He grew up a taciturn Indian with a devious mind. He spoke Italian, various Indian dialects as well as a number of other languages which he had picked up much later in his travels.

Badnews had left the reservation when his father died. His mother had returned to her village. Before going she had left him in care of some of his "cousins" in New York City and across the river in New Jersey. With them as eager teachers he had learned new skills. Where ever he had gone, he had learned new skills. He always learned new skills.

It was how he had earned his living, utilizing those skills. And he had earned his pay in that tribal society, too. It was a world of warring tribes, his home until recently.

Soon he would be in Paris.

Chi Chi le Duc was a successful, small-time, but very busy Parisian businessman who happened to operate on the wrong side of the law. He frequently did small favors for the police, which favors mostly accounted for his success, such as it was, for staying out of jail. He was a small-time businessman because his close friends knew about his favors and tended to keep their business secrets to themselves and hence their ability to make money and also stay out of jail. Le Duc never read the newspapers.

It was a most pleasant evening as he, le Duc, casually strolled along the streets of Montmartre admiring the very bad art of the street artists as they sold and stole from the tourists. It was more than a pleasant evening. It was a successful evening!

One of his "favors" had netted him a nice profit, a full pocket of francs. Truly, it was good to be alive and living in Paris.

The first part of that statement he would shortly question. The second he would change forever as within a few hours he would flee Paris never to return.

Chi Chi le Duc stepped from the curb, circled around one of the artist's easels and the artist, smiled at the artist, dodged through a cluster of tourists, and started down the other side of the street. He crossed in front of one of the many small alleys and headed for his favorite café for a well-earned, to his mind at least, reward.

He didn't make it.

A figure slipped from the alley as he passed, walked in step with him, sliding his right arm up under le Duc's left.

A soft voice whispered harshly into his ear. "A nice pleasant Paris evening, is it not, Chi Chi le ferret of the flics? Come! Stroll with me. And answer a few questions."

Le Duc shot a glance to his left, startled. Who would grab him so? The shock would have brought him to his knees if he had not been held up by a tight grip. As it was, he staggered a few steps before he could recover his composure. "You! I . . . saw . . . you . . . die!"

"It appears that you were wrong, my Little Fountain of Information."

"But your voice, what is wrong with your voice?"

"Ahhhh, that! A surprise, eh? Well you see, it is just this way. A small caliber bullet which is really a lady's weapon, in the throat doesn't always do what it is supposed to do, does it, mon petit businessman? Especially if one isn't really very good at that business and is scared at the same time, eh? You should stick to knives in the back. But, enough of these small reminiscences! I have some questions to ask. And if I feel that the information that you impart to me is of sufficient value, why then, all is forgiven and you may live to a

ripe old age elsewhere. Now! Tell me . . ."

Chi Chi le Duc's neighbors had never seen him move so fast before. It was a wonder! They always marveled at it. It was a subject of conversation for months. So was the subject of where he had gone.

No one ever heard.

" . . . then to Rome . . ."

On the airplane, Badnews thought about his new position in life and working for The Doctor. It was much less hazardous than before. He absentmindedly touched the scar on his neck.

The stewardess noticed this gesture and stopped to ask the distinguished, grey-haired gentleman in the elegant silk suit with the jaunty touch of red at jacket pocket and throat scarf whether he would care for a drink.

He answered in Italian.

Movie producer, she thought.

As he sipped his wine and looked out the window, Badnews smiled to himself. So far the trip hadn't cost his boss a dime. Le Duc had been only too happy to reimburse for any out-of-pocket expenses so far incurred. It was something that the Doctor would certainly frown upon. But then, how was he ever to know?

He thought, if he had time he would stop in Sicily and visit with his mother's relatives. They always welcomed him. He was a son relatives could be proud of. A success in a field of endeavor they understood quite well.

At the airport he strode quickly through customs, an important man on business, sunglasses covering his eyes, a cigar tucked in one corner of his mouth, passport well worn and heavily stamped.

No luggage, no need, just a quick trip, out and back home again, eh?

The guard furrowed his brow for a moment. And then waved him on.

Badnews rented a car, striding impatiently up and down until it arrived, and then hurried off. The girl behind the counter knew she had just missed a golden opportunity for stardom. But he had waved good-bye.

At one of the more tourist laden hotels, Badnews checked in his car, strolled through the hotel lobby and out into the street. Leisurely he strolled to a small penzione that he was well acquainted with, a place where he could acquire things, change clothes. Wash the grey from his hair. It wouldn't cost much. He knew the proper words to whisper in the ear of the owner.

Soon he was again strolling down the street, just one more local pedestrian.

Badnews headed for a small neighborhood spot where he could get answers to his questions.

Benito "Chicken" Cacciatorini sold, and enjoyed, the good, solid, red wines of Italy. Everything about his person spoke of that enjoyment. In many ways he was his own best customer as well as his own best advertisement. His mother had named him after a hero of hers who had once run the trains of Italy on time. "Chicken" had been bestowed upon him by some of his visiting "cousins" from New York City, U.S.A. They had thought that it was pretty funny, but he didn't. Still, he found their patronizing humor useful, in fact very useful at times.

So he sat there, in his "office" in the café, taking care of the buying and selling of his favorite product, and from time to time a stranger would sit down and speak to him in a peculiar New York City, U.S.A., accented Italian and ask for The Chicken. Then, after the usual bargaining, he would see to it that they were introduced to certain other individuals and receive a certain sum of money for his knowledge and services rendered.

Then he would depart to look after the affairs of his red, and sometimes white, treasures carefully forgetting the faces and places that he had seen and been. All-in-all it was a very good arrangement, although sometimes it was hard on the nerves.

A face that he hadn't seen in a long, long time sat down across the table from him, poured a generous amount of red wine into a not altogether spotless tumbler, took a large mouthful, held it there, savored it to the full measure, swallowed, let out a soft sigh and spoke to him in an accent that he never was able to place.

"Well Chicken, I see that the wine is still as good as always. Pardon the coarseness of my voice, a small accident, of no matter. Tell me, do you still talk to some of the 'friends?' I have some questions to which I need answers, and I need to get those answers rather quickly. Then I must be on my way. But first, let us fully appreciate the rest of the bottle, no?"

Benito "Chicken" Cacciatorini quickly nodded his head in agreement. After all, his nickname also spoke eloquently of the level of his personal courage. Here was one "friend" that he would be glad to see on his way. As quickly as possible! He would be delighted to help this one, for free. A magnanimous gesture of goodwill on his part. A gesture comprised partially of a burning zeal to stay alive and from an equally burning zeal to obtain certain favors from certain individuals that he had only heard certain rumors about. But he had heard that they could be very generous to the right lucky person who was called upon to provide aid to another certain individual at the correct time and place.

And now, there he sat, that certain individual across the table, watching him, drinking his wine.

The "Chicken" felt that this was the correct time and place. So he spoke honestly and softly to the "client" as the client asked his questions.

Some time later The Chicken's friends didn't believe him when he said that the money was an inheritance from a rich Aunt that had lived in Naples. Never before had he mentioned such an Aunt living in Naples. And such an Aunt would surely have been mentioned and talked about, more than once.

But, that is all Benito "Chicken" Cacciatorini ever told them.

". . . then to Jerusalem . . ."

A bent-backed, old man hobbled aboard the airplane. His wispy beard blew in the light breeze. He was so arched over that he mostly spoke to the floor. Few questions were directed toward him. He mumbled and bumbled his way to his seat and with a heavy sigh collapsed into it. After a certain amount of tussling, aided in his struggles by the steward, he managed to get his seat belt fastened and his cane neatly stowed next to his knee, against the wall. He slowly turned his head to look out the window as the airplane rolled down the runway and took to the air.

He thought about the trip he was making. So, he was returning to the land of constant turmoil. Such a land he didn't need to visit! But, there was a person he had to see. One who would know the answers to questions that needed to be asked.

A deal could be made. It wouldn't be a problem. It hadn't been in the past. No problem as long as the one he was seeking was still alive. That shouldn't be a problem either. That one had a positive knack for survival. He had seen it at work. Up close. And they had both survived. A number of their adversaries hadn't. It had been a sight to see!

He dozed.

When he woke, the steward asked him if he would like something to drink. He nodded, a glass of water would be fine, thank you. He sipped his water and massaged his knees. And wiggled and adjusted his pillows. Soon they would land.

Because he was so slow, he waited until everyone else had embarked. Then he inched his way down the boarding stairs and out and into the airport. Maybe his one piece of shabby luggage would be ready to pick up by the time he got there. Perhaps he wouldn't have to wait very long.

He was lucky. His luggage was waiting for him. He picked it up, clutched it to himself and at the front desk asked a pretty, young lady to get him a cab.

Once in the cab he sighed again. Soon he would be at his destination. Once inside his room he could straighten up again. It would be a pleasure.

Dimitri Nozanovsky wondered how he had talked himself into coming to Israel after enjoying the good life along Fairfax Avenue in Los Angeles. It had been even more pleasant there than it had been in Chicago. So, he asked himself that old joke as he had on numerous times before. So what's a nice Jewish boy like you doing in a place like this?

Oy, yoi, yoi! Meshuggener arabs trying to kill everyone in sight and here you are, right in the middle, as always. The original klutz waiting to trip over someone's misplaced hand-grenade and blow bits of yourself all over the place.

But then he answered himself as he always did, although at times it seemed to him that the voice that answered was the voice of his mother. *Don't be a schmuck, be a mensch, fight for your people!* His mother had been rowdy and coarse when she felt like it.

So he had listened to the reply and did what it said, as always. And here he was.

In Jerusalem!

At first glance Dimitri thought that it was a rich arab businessman in a $1,000 suit that was beckoning to him from across the street. It was how this "little deals" usually started.

Halfway across the street he recognized the face. He felt his lunch, recently eaten, start to congeal in his well-developed stomach. Oh my, oh my, a badnews friend like that I need like a hole in the head! He thought about running but he knew that with his pear-shaped physique that it would be a waste of time.

He smiled, and waved, and hurried the rest of the way to see what the deal was to be.

"Shalom Aleichem, Dimitri."

"Aleichem Shalom, Badnews."

"So Dimitri, how's by you?"

"Eh, by me, things could be better. Of course, it could be worse, nu?"

"So, so. But! Have I got a deal for you!"

"Badnews, deal me no deals! That last deal was so good that it almost got us both killed. Such a deal!"

"Aaaaaaaaaaaaah! But think of the profits!"

"Profits, schmofits! I should wish a profit like that on my mother-in-law, if I was married. But!

Enough of this schmaltz, what's up?"

"First we find a place that is fit for a little nosh and then having snacked well we can have a little schmooz. Just that, a little talk, nothing else. No action. No deals. Just talk."

"A favor for a favor, eh?"

Dimitri stepped back and looked Badnews over, slowly, from head to toe. It was the same Badnews, the same give away nothingness that he knew, from past experience, hid sudden death. Nothing had changed since the last time, just the voice. It was a strange voice, a peculiar whisper that made the faintness of the voice all the more threatening.

He stopped his inspection and with a shrug of his shoulders set off down the sidewalk. Oh well, the last time they were on the same side. Hopefully this time they still were.

They were.

Three terrorists and their car and their supply of explosives had an accident and scattered bits and pieces of themselves and their belongings up and down and all over a small side street. At the time of the explosion the street was empty. Little damage was done to the buildings. Everyone said it was amazing.

They had been on their way to set up a car-bomb in front of one of the favorite tourist hotels. The fourth member of the team somehow "miraculously" survived the explosion and was found, unconscious, propped up against a nearby building. In his pockets the investigating agents found a list of their safe houses, names of the other members of their gang and lists of places where they had made caches of guns, ammunition and explosives.

" . . . and finally to Marseilles."

A dapper figure tied his dingy to the dock. He was dressed in the latest, most fashionable, yachting togs. He slung his designer duffle-bag over his shoulder and ambled up the dock and down the street, His deck shoes were new and unscuffed. He stopped and peered into shop windows and admired the latest things for the boating crowd. The sun glinted off the jewel in the ring on his little finger. Shop-keepers wondered which of the big yachts anchored in the harbor was his and made quiet prayers that he would grace their store.

Entering the fashionable café, he plunked his bag under a table and walked to the rear, looking for the mens. Hours later the owner questioned his help about that bag still sitting there. They shrugged their shoulders. Someone had left it. But so many had come and gone. No one remembered whose it was, for sure. The owner took the bag to his office and opened it. Just to see whether he could find a name, of course. All he found were balled-up newspapers. A whole designer bag full. He tossed the bag in his closet and had the help throw away the paper. Strange people came off the yachts. Perhaps, one of these days, the owner would return, looking for his bag.

A small, slight figure dressed in black, black turtle-necked sweater and black pants, slipped down an unnamed alley in a certain run-down section of town near the waterfront. He slipped into a deep shadow and stood quietly, motionless, watching one of the dim lit doorways across the way. After a long time, his curiosity satisfied, he darted from the shadows and entered the doorway adjacent to the one he had been so carefully watching.

Inside the dilapidated structure he ran silently through a series of interconnecting hallways until he passed into the building he had been watching. He bypassed the several men who were loitering here and there to prevent just such unwanted visitors

Finally, turning a corner, he stepped into the center of the hallway and approached the last of the guards. This one was standing directly in front of the door that was his destination.

The guard carefully hid his surprise at the sudden appearance of an unknown visitor and waited for him to make the first move.

A voice whispered to him. "Tell The Boss that the Iron Dove wishes to see him!"

The guard looked the black-clad figure over very slowly and carefully and then settled himself more solidly in front of the door.

Again the whisper. "Listen carefully, dog-meat. Please carry my message inside. Please."

"Little man." The guard had an easy foot in height advantage as well as a good100 pounds in weight. "Go away! Leave! You have obviously wandered into the wrong building for the wrong reasons and are searching for the wrong person. There is no Boss here. Now. . . go away. That way! Down the hall, there! That way is the front door. Now go. Good-bye!"

The little man slipped forward. "O.K., guard, you have done your duty. Now move aside."

The door exploded open with such force that it knocked the guard stumbling forward and then slammed into the wall with a crashing bang. A burly figure burst through, yanked the guard out of the way and bellowed in a roaring basso profundo voice.

"**DON'T TOUCH HIM!**"

He grinned widely. "He's one of my wife's many nephews. He's green! He's young! And besides, if he gets killed my wife would never forgive me!" His face split by a wide grin as he threw both arms around the slight figure before him and pounded his back with ham-sized hands, roaring with laughter.

Stepping back he gestured broadly. "Come inside, come inside, I'll tell him." He jabbed a finger at the startled guard. "About it later. We have much to talk about. It has been some time since we saw you last."

"So! As you can see, the same old place." He slammed the door shut, cutting off the stare of his guard. "With the same old furniture! Well, sit down, sit down."

The Boss flung both arms wide and beamed at his visitor who dutifully sat in the 'guest' chair. He boomed. "The same old faces, almost, and the same old me, maybe a little heavier and a little uglier, perhaps, no?"

Circling around, The Boss settled himself behind the desk and shoved a clutter of papers, telephones and pieces of pistols in various stages of assembly to one side. He leaned forward on thick forearms, a look of concern on his face, and asked gently. "We knew that you had survived your, ah. . . accident, but are you. . . well?"

Badnews nodded. "Yes, well. But as you can hear, the voice has changed somewhat."

The Boss smiled. "Ummmm, yes. I heard this voice in the hall and it took me a moment before I could tell who it was. It was your subtle approach. Another moment and I suppose I would have had a very upset wife, no? No, no, say nothing. I understand. You knew I was listening, as I always do, and you put on a little show just for me, right?"

He paused, sucked in a deep breath, and then continued. "So, you have returned to us? No! Ah well, but you have been missed. You stay with The Dottore now, is this not so? He is a friend."

"A friend. I did not know this."

The Boss chuckled. "Well not a friend in the usual sense of the word but a friend all the same. Few know of this fact. When you worked for me you had no need to know. But now you may know. Once, some time ago, we did him a favor. So he owed us. He is an honorable man. When he saw to your recovery, he repaid his debt. It was fortunate that he was in Paris at the same time, was it not?"

"Yes, fortunate. For me."

The Boss leaned back, his chair creaked loudly. "Well Dove, why are you here? What is it that you wish? Surely, it is not business?"

"Information, nothing more. Let me tell you what I need to know and why I am here. Then we may decide upon the price and whether you wish to provide the answers, if there are any, to the questions that I must ask. O.K.?"

The Boss smiled. "Dove, this has to do with The Dottore, does it not? Yes, I thought so, Proceed."

"Boss, some time ago The Doctor received a letter from a colleague of his in England, Sir Winifred Robsen-Brown. In this letter . . ."

Not long thereafter Badnews was on his way home, flying in a private jet. He had all the answers to all the questions that he asked. However, it appeared that these answers would not be of any help at all.

"They all said the same thing. That there is no connection between Corruccini, Hafas, and Boyer and any kind of illegal activity anywhere in Europe or in the lands surrounding the Mediterranean Basin. None whatever! My sources would not lie."

Badnews sat back and waited for Doc to indicate what he was to do next. He waited, blank-faced, infinitely patient.

Well, that was the trouble with Badnews, he just gave those bare-boned statements. You never knew what he did or how he did it. He just did it.

There were times when I wished that I knew what it was that he did. And then there were times when I thought that it was probably just as well that I didn't know.

Especially after reading those newspaper articles.

Doc stood up, stretched and yawned. "Well troops, I think that it is time for me to go to bed. Thank you Badnews, your report was most helpful." Doc headed for the door. "See you all in the morning, ready for what the morrow brings, what?"

I followed Doc's pattern and headed for bed. Badnews and the Membrane went off to some corner of the house to talk and discuss what ever it was that they talked about. I don't know what Dr. Ben did.

Reminiscences, for the Nonce

You know everyone wonders how I started working for Doc. It is not really much of a story. But, I will tell ya anyway.

Corvallis.

So there I was, one fine day, just prior to the start of the Fall Semester. I had just acquired the next academic year's schedule, tucked it under my arm and was heading for the *Gut-Bomb Heavon,* the students' affectionate term for the campus hamburgeria.

The campus was one of those sprawling places that appears to have crawled all over the slopes on the edge of town. Of course, the town had done its fair share of crawling too. They had eventually run into each other and now the general outline of where the campus or the town started or stopped tended to get rather blurred. One sort of walked along and, willy-nilly, passed into the campus or the town depending upon which way one was headed. It was a joy to live there. Everything was within walking distance and most of the time the weather was nice enough to allow for slow-strolling.

So I had strolled up the gentle grade, into the administration building, grabbed a copy of the schedule and went off to fill my gut.

On the way into the food area I ran into one of my professors, who wasn't exactly startled to see me. I had more time in grade, acquired my M.A. in anthropology this spring, and hadn't decided what to do next. So I smiled, wanna buy a car, waved and passed into the odors of burger grease french fries. I stood in line and eventually got to place my order.

Once I had my tray loaded with fries, two "grease-burgers," and coffee, I headed for a empty table way back in the corner away from all the meeting and greeting. Tucked into this cozy place with my food and with my schedule propped up by the napkin dispenser, I began the process of deciding what field to assail next, carefully drooling grease into my plate and wiping my chin. I wasn't really paying any attention to anyone else although I had noticed that someone had sat down at my table.

I had begun to approach making a decision. I was debating the merits of either taking up something in business or perhaps physical education, becoming a coach you see, when this voice interrupted my deep thinking.

"Good afternoon J.C. Would you mind passing the napkins, please?"

I looked up at this stranger not all that surprised that he knew my name. After all I had been here longer than many of the newer professors.

He was a little guy dressed all in brown. I resettled my schedule against the sugar jar and catsup container and handed him the napkins. Another guy sat next to him.

This other guy was about the same size. One glance was enough to wake up my warning system with a loud metaphoric clang and when that happens it suggests to my mind that it is time to go.

My first though was "hood." My second thought was "nonsense." There is nothing that the mafia would want from me. I don't gamble. Nor do I do anything that is in their field of endeavor. So I shrugged, mentally, and went back to my schedule and started checking class times, class conflicts, and all that sort of student thing.

I had brought along the full college catalog and opened it to my new choice. Business! Carefully checking the requirements I saw that there wasn't all that much that I had to take, not after all the course work I had already completed. Just the business courses to do. The more I thought about it the more I liked the idea. Business was looking good! Might even find a way to make a living out there in the real world. That was a novel thought. Stop being a student and move out into the real world of struggle and conflict. Ah, but that was in the future!

I figured that it would take no more than a year-and-a-half to get my M.B.A. Worry about the real world later. I was roughing out my fall schedule when this little guy busted into my train of thought again.

"You are J.C. Smith, aren't you?"

I looked up. "Yep, that's me all right." And went back to figuring.

He leaned forward, having moved into a chair opposite me, reached over and lightly touched my sleeve. "Pardon me J.C., but do you mind if I ask you a question?"

Sighing the sigh of the put-upon, I folded all my materials together, made a neat stack and gave him my frosty look. The other guy sorta glanced in my direction with that look that just sort of looked right through people. With that, I figured that it was time for me to leave.

"All right, just one question. Then I have to go to the library." It was the standard excuse for getting away.

This little guy in brown smiled. "Ah. . . what do you think you want to be when you grow up?"

Now I was then, and still am, in fine physical shape and made about two of this joker. So I thought maybe just a small tap ought to do it. But there was something about his partner that made me change my mind. So I just stood up and started to leave. Wisdom before valor.

The question asker plucked at my sleeve. "Please, just five minutes of your time. Please?"

The other one looked like he was ready to spring.

"Please?"

How could I refuse. He still had my sleeve tethered by his fingers. I shrugged and sat down. What the heck, maybe it was some new approach to selling life insurance. As I was now going into the business profession, it might be nice to know.

"O.K., sport, what are you selling?"

A small smile flickered on and off his face. "Adventure, travel, romance!" He paused.

I thought, well that was certainly a way to get your attention. But how will he link that to life insurance?

"I want to give you a chance to put to use all that knowledge that you have been storing up there in your head."

He turned to his companion. "Badnews, would you get us a pot of coffee, please. I think that J.C. and I will be perfectly fine until you return."

The other one headed off on his errand. I thought that he certainly looked like his name. And, how was I going to get away from this pair? Well, first drink their coffee and be polite.

He cleared his throat. "From what I have been able to find out, you have had a most remarkable career. You have cut a swath through chemistry, physics, engineering, ornamental horticulture, art, music, history, with advanced courses in psychology, sociology, and anthropology, earning a 4.0 all the time. What with the athletics, you have become a true legend. Did I miss anything?"

Then he gazed around the room and back and smiled at me.

I smiled back and thought, my what a busy little bugger this guy has been.

"Nope. What do you want?"

He cleared this throat, again, and spoke in a very low tone so that only I could hear his next words. "Ah J. C., what I would like to do is make you an offer that you can't refuse." He giggled.

The blood drained from my face. Badnews, indeed! Why me? What did I ever do? There was only one solution. Agree to anything, abandon my future plans for a business career and get out of town. I was being forced into the real world prematurely. Well, maybe it was about time that I saw some of the rest of the world. Tahiti might be nice at this time of the year.

He patted my arm. I didn't move an inch.

"Please don't take my words unkindly J. C. It is just that I think that you have so much potential and that it is being wasted. It is time that you stop burying yourself in academia. I want you to work for me. I could use your help."

I just stared at him A career in crime wasn't exactly what I had been looking forward to. It wasn't the type of business that I had in mind.

"Here! Let me give you my card."

He fished around in one of his pockets, found one and passed it over.

His helper returned and gave us all a fresh cup of coffee and sat down. And watched me and everything else in the room.

I looked down at the card. How novel! Now the mob, or whatever he was, handed out business cards. It was the standard kind, the kind that businessmen passed to each other.

KAPPA HECKMANN, PH.D.

ANTHROPOLOGICAL ENTERPRISES

GRANDEVILLE, OREGON

"You are Dr. Heckmann, I take it?"

"Yes, J. C., I am." He nodded his head and waved one hand.

"This is my, ah, driver, Badnews Treefalls."

I looked at that one again." Pleased to meet you."

He didn't say a word. Just looked.

Doc cleared his throat, I didn't call him that, not then. "Ah, J. C., this job offer is quite serious, you know. I would pay a decent wage plus room and board. I really do need an assistant. And from what I have heard about you, you would be just the ticket, just the sort of person that I have been looking for. Especially when considering your rather, ah, broad academic background. And, of course, your athletic prowess and, ah, um, natural, um, mental abilities."

"Yah." I wasn't exactly enthused. Nor was I really feeling very happy about someone poking around in my background.

"Yes. I think that it is time for you to come out of here." He smiled and waved one arm at our student cluttered surroundings.

I smiled back. "I like it here. I am happy. I am content. I do not need your job!"

He nodded and smiled a return volley. "True, true, true, true! Economically you are well taken care off. But I really do think that it is time for you to start putting all your talents to better use, something new and different. Stop being an academic hat-rack, as it were!"

"Well." I shook my head in wonderment. "For a potential employer trying to recruit, you certainly have a novel approach." Maybe I could use this in business after all.

He frowned. "Yes, I suppose so." Then he turned very serious. "Work for me, J. C"

"Why?"

He laughed loudly, turning heads. "Why for the

adventure, travel, and romance that I mentioned, of course. I am leaving in two days for North Africa. I assume you can be ready on such short notice. After that I have to go to Copenhagen. Then from there we go to Nice. Thence to New Delhi. And finally home again. Of course, as my assistant, you would come along."

Well that certainly sounded like quite an itinerary. Travel would be interesting. I nodded at his friend. "What about him?"

"Badnews? Oh he goes everywhere that I do. It is a kind of a, um, ah, contract which I honor, so to speak." He looked at me expectantly. "Well?"

"O. K., Dr. Heckmann, if I took the job what exactly would I be doing?" I was getting hooked. And we both knew it.

"Well J. C., first you can call me Doc. Now let's see, your duties would be rather varied, I'm afraid. I need a research assistant who knows how to find answers. All your ex-professors tell me that this is one of your major strong points. Then, I would need someone to take care of my household accounts, Ah, you wouldn't have to study business to do that!" He had noticed what I had underlined in the course schedule.

He smiled at his little joke. "Then I need a cook and bottle washer. Again, I understand that you are quite good in that department. I need someone who has a strong independent streak, one who can follow my train of thought, help me prepare professional articles, papers, and all that. You fit the bill. Perhaps you don't like to travel?"

I shook my head. "Nope, ah, Doc, it is not that at

all. It is just that have to think about it, that's all."

He stood up. "I understand J. C. Here." He wrote a number on my class schedule. "Phone me this evening and let me know." And he walked off. With his shadow.

So I wandered around town, had dinner, thought about everything he had said.

I phoned.

"Hello. Doc?"

"Yes. That you, J. C.?"

"Yep! O.K., I'll take the job."

"Good, good! Meet me here tomorrow morning at eight sharp with one packed bag. I like to travel light. We have a plane to catch in Portland. When we get back we can take care of getting you moved."

"You can get another ticket that quickly?"

"Oh, well, ahem, I made these reservations some time ago. Three. First class seats. See you in the morning J. C. Good night."

So that's how I got started with Doc. And a whirlwind tour it was. By the end, Badnews had accepted me as Doc's assistant. And I found out that he even talked. A little.

Rakshasa Interlude

Grandeville. Doc's Place.

The next morning I was up and moving, around 7:15, give or take a little. Well, it isn't a bad time to get up. Especially if one just wakes up without an alarm clock blasting your mind loose. I always felt that it didn't really matter when you woke up but how you woke up. Right? Right!

Stumbling along in the normal dawn's early light stupor, I headed down to the kitchen. The stupor was somewhat enhanced by the lack of sleep.

From the sounds of silence it seemed that the others didn't have any problem snoozing on. Not a mouse was stirring. Humf, humf, slug-a-beds! Although I figured the Membrane was probably already up and out, having eaten and left a pot of coffee on the stove.

Oozing into the kitchen I saw that I was right, once again!

There waiting for my friendly face, was the coffee pot on warm.

And dirty dishes in the sink. Ignoring those, I launched into the day.

Cup in one hand, coffee pot in the other, I went outside to sit on the porch, enjoy the slight cool of the starting day and slowly let all my senses realize that it was time to get going again.

Each of us have our own rituals, don't we?

Well, there I was, seeping into yet another day of mad-cap adventure and excitement and beginning to realize that all my parts had decided, once again, to come fully awake when the monster hall clock went off, clanging and banging its way through the full repertoire of hourly celebration, announcing to one and all that, sho 'nuff, it was eight-o-clock in the morning. Bong, bong, etc!

Just as all that finished, Doc slid out the door with his cup. Now while I gladly will admit that I am a slow riser, that is, slow to come fully awake, at least under normal circumstances, Doc is a good approximation of the walking dead going from horizontal asleep to vertical asleep in some magical way.

He grunted an acknowledgement of my presense, slumped into his chair, poured a cup of coffee, another dose for me and began sipping at his.

Doc was his usual study in brown, his favorite color choice. He gets dressed while apparently sound asleep. But there he was, all decked out, this small person in brown. Five feet six or so, one twenty pounds, brown hair, brown eyes, bushy brown mustache, dressed in a light brown shirt, dark brown slacks, brown corduroy jacket, brown tie, brown shoes with brown socks. Standard attire.

I slipped back into the house to shower, shave and dress, knowing full well that nothing would be awake out there for at least an hour. That would give me plenty time to get all that stuff he had wanted into some sort of order and still eat breakfast.

I wondered if Dr. Ben was up. I bet myself, no loser there, that he didn't sleep any too well, not with what he thinks is going on. So I got ready for the day.

And soon.

I was ready!

"Morning Doc," I said cheerfully. He was still sitting in the same place. But I could see that he was now fully awake. So I figure that I might as well start the day off on good footing. After all, you never know where it is going to go after that. So why not? Right? Right! "Breakfast?"

"Morning J. C. Sure! Three eggs, four-five slices of bacon, three slices of toast, a few fried potatoes and make another pot of coffee. While I am eating you can give me the rundown on what you have managed to gather together, so far. Then we can go into the den and look it over in detail."

"O. K. Doc, coming right up." With an order like that I knew we were in for a long day, working straight through, skipping lunch. But we would take a break for afternoon tea. So I set to, broiling bacon, slicing potatoes, etc., etc.

"And that's about all that I could get, so far." I was just finishing my explanation of what I had been doing for the past few days when Dr. Ben joined us. Doc nodded and finished eating, looking quite satisfied at my report and the breakfast.

Dr. Ben looked a disaster area. Poor guy. He didn't appear as one who had slept the sleep of the innocent. Probably expected a Rakshasa to slip into his bed at any moment.

Well, last night was last night, but today is today. And in the bright light of day it didn't seem near as creepy as it had last night. Although, from the way Dr. Ben's eyes kept shifting around he didn't appear to share my view, no pun intended. 'Course I didn't really share it with him either.

Doc nodded at him. "Ah, good morning David. How would you like your eggs fixed? J.C. is one of the best short order cooks for miles around. And that includes most of the slop chutes in our fair city." He gestured vaguely in the direction of town. "Just name it and he will have it out here in jig time. Sit down, sit down! Have a cup of coffee." Doc shoved a full cup over to Dr. Ben. It was Doc's cup.

Dr. Ben sat and took it. "Thanks Doc. I'll probably need quiet a few cups of coffee today. I didn't really sleep very well last night. I just couldn't get my mind off of everything you said and that J. C. had mentioned earlier. I still have a bit of checking to do and, I'm afraid, several long distance phone calls to make."

"No problem, David." Doc reached over and patted the back of his hand. "Just use the phone in the library. You'll find the credit card number taped to the top of the receiver. Just phone where ever you wish. Now, how would you like your eggs?"

"Eggs? Oh sure, eggs! J. C., could you make two poached with two slices of whole wheat toast?"

I winced. It wasn't the egg order. It was Doc's offer of the phone. There went the phone bill, again!

Dr. Ben looked worried. "Something the matter, J. C.? I could always have scrambled if you would prefer."

"No! No problem, Dr. Ben. Scrambled, ah, poached it is! What ever you want, Dr. Ben, what ever you want." I headed for the kitchen and was stopped in mid-flight by Doc,

"Oh, one more thing to add to your data collection J. C. I found out that Corruccini had also worked on the same dig that Hafas had been running not too far from here. That's the same one that Finn had assisted on near where he used to teach. Interesting, huh?"

"Sure." It didn't seem all the wonderfully interesting to me. Into the kitchen, And then there I was, back on the range again. I also sang it, 'Home On The Range.' Poaching eggs. Pretty exciting, all right. That's me, hard at it. The "Super-Gofer." Ah well, that's what the man pays me for. So who am I to complain. Although I did mumble to myself a bit about the offer to use the credit card.

"J. C.!" Doc was shouting from the back porch, "Get everything into the den for a going over at 11:00. O.K.?"

"Right, Doc! 11:00 it is!" Plenty of time to go out and visit with the Membrane and the animals in the barn. An activity I always enjoyed, especially as I didn't have to clean up that area. So I did this and that and visited here and there. And then it was time.

11:00 and we were in the den, Doc and I, with all the material that I had gathered piled at one end of the conference table.

"O.K., J. C. Let's see what we have so far, hummmmmmmmm. But first, tell me what Old John has been able to find out. That will be a good place to start."

So I told him. I had the entire conversation neatly typed up and in a folder, correctly labeled. Can't beat efficiency. I didn't tell him about those old clippings though.

Doc beamed. "That is fine, J. C., just fine. Yes, I agree. It does seem strange and it does appear as if there is some sort of coverup going on. But I also completely agree with you. I doubt that there is any kind of governmental secret activity involved in all this. After all, none of them were Americans. And it is only American anthropologists that get accused of working for the CIA, not foreign nationals. Besides I can't imagine the secret agencies of four different national governments having the capability of getting along with each other, none that I've ever heard about so far. I just kept mulling it over and over and over, and I can't think of anything, or anyone, that would be able to do something like this."

He frowned. "However, the three of them could have been involved in smuggling contraband. That might explain the news blackout. Wouldn't want to tip off their contacts that they were about to be caught, hummmmmm. So! What else?"

Doc began to riffle through the various orderly piles which he was rapidly scrambling together. "Ahhhhhh, your rough draft on the prehistory of India." He hefted the paper in one hand, a weighing gesture.

"Wellllll, you did get quite a bit done in a short period of time, didn't you?" Then he started to thumb through it. "Ah, ha! Ah, ah, ha! Yes, most interesting. And I see that you cited Krebbs quite a bit as well. He is quite an authority, isn't he? Most interesting. Ah, ha! Ah! Ha!"

Doc continued flipping through my report, stopping here and there to read something. Then he carefully read the references cited.

There was a soft knock at the door.

"Come in, Membrane, come in." The Membrane entered with duck and a twist, carrying a bundle under one arm that looked like more books. "Here's what you were looking for, Doc, your parcel from England."

England! How did he manage to get that thing sent here so fast?

Doc beamed. "Good, good! Just give it to J.C. See you at lunch."

The Membrane made his exit. And I stood there with this very heavy bundle in my hands.

"Well J. C., don't just stand there. Open it, open it!"

So I did. And I got the bill, too! Well there went the old book budget, again. Doc had bought a large segment of the *British Archaeological Abstracts.* And weighty tomes they were too. I set them on the table.

Doc rapped one knuckle on the pile. "Well, there you are J. C.! Pretty nice, eh? Yes, yes, quite a find. So! Check through these abstracts before you head out to find those references that I gave you last night. It might save you a little time in your search, ummmmm?" He popped his hands together. "So! Let's see, what's next, eh? Oh yes. Tell me, what do you think of this idea of David's about the Rakshasa? Do you think that we might have a monstrous problem on our hands? Some sort of visit by the supernatural and all that?" He beamed at me, professor to student.

I had to smile. "Doc, no slight to Dr. Ben and all, but I put the Rakshasa in the same category as the Abominable Snowman, Sasquatch, and all the rest of that crowd. If we ever catch one and put him, her or it, in a cage so that we can examine it at our leisure then maybe I'll buy it. But not until then! Although I will admit that last night when Dr. Ben turned white that for awhile there I was pretty well convinced. But! That was last night and this is this morning."

I shrugged one shoulder at him. "So, in spite of popular beliefs to the contrary, I just can't swallow the idea. For me it is a matter of function. I don't see the functional place in reality for such things, not even a little bit. Of course, I'm not denying that people believe in such things. And that in those cultures where they do hold such beliefs that such things do exist, at least in the sense that the belief seems to cause certain events to occur. But, in this culture, at this time, they do not exist, they do not affect people or events. They are not real! If people elsewhere wish to believe in voodoo or whatever and then lie down and die, that is their cultural problem, not mine. Therefore, no matter how many hexes or curses someone wishes to place on me, I don't think that I will believe in their effectiveness and cooperate by lying down and dying at their command." It was quite a speech, for me!

Doc smiled and nodded. "Yes, quite so J.C., quite so. But we still do have the indisputable fact that a number of people are dead and that David does feel rather strongly that they were killed by Rakshasa. What about that?"

"Look Doc, Dr. Ben may choose to believe whatever he wishes. And those villagers in India may do the same thing!" If I was sounding exasperated, it was because I was. "But I do not! And I don't believe Boyer or Hafas or Corruccini were done in by any demon from India. Nor some dumb mutt in England. Not killed. The dog I mean!"

Doc stood silent for about two beats. "Ummmmmmmm, I suppose you are right. But we shall just have to see what we shall see, eh, J. C.?"

I nodded my head in agreement. "Yeah Doc, I suppose so."

Doc aimlessly wandered around the den, back to the table, and shuffled through my report, again. "Now let's see . . . what else is there to do? Apparently nothing. So! Off with you then. I do need those references as soon as possible, so you might as well get right on that . . . ah, I almost forgot! See if David is done with breakfast or whatever he might be up to. Then round up the Membrane and meet me in the library. We might as well get the full story on the Rakshasa, all together and all at once. Right? Right!"

Off I went, telling myself that I had heard all that I wanted to hear about that subject. I collected the Membrane from out back by the cattle sheds, a nice relaxing ten minute round trip. Then I disconnected Dr. Ben from the phone in the kitchen where he was just finishing up another long-distance call which was, no doubt, going to be very expensive. Then there we were, all in the library.

While I had been on my herding trip, Doc had made a fresh pot of coffee and collected the necessary cups, spoons, etc., and was waiting, patiently, for our return. As we entered he waved us to our chairs.

"Sit down, class, sit down. Coffee anyone?" He got up and poured, regained his seat, and nodded at Dr. Ben, ready to start our seminar.

"Now David, if you would. Tell us everything we need to know about Rakshasa. What they are, how they operate, why they do what they do, etc., etc. And most importantly, why would we, if we should, have to worry about their presence? O.K. David, it's all your's. Feel free to use the blackboard. I know how it is with you professorial types, can't talk without one. Speaking from experience, of course, ha, ha."

So we settled back with Doc's professorial humor not exactly ringing in our ears. He had scattered note pads and pencils around the table apparently under the impression that someone might feel so moved as to want to take notes. I always favored doodling.

However, in as much as one of my many duties was also to be secretary for such gatherings, I grabbed a pad, quickly scratched the date at the top and sat back wondering whether there would be anything else on the paper by the time Dr. Ben finished speaking.

Notes, that is. The doodles had already begun.

Dr. Ben stood up, placed his coffee cup within easy reach, picked up a piece of chalk and printed on the board in neat capital letters . . . RAKSHASA - DEMON. Well here we go, I said to myself, a real lecture. It had been quite a while since I had sat in on the last one. I hoped that I wouldn't fall asleep. Old student syndrome, you know.

"Doc, that," Dr. Ben tapped the blackboard, "as you know, is what got me to come here in the first place. You had J. C. tell me Rakshasa over the phone with no details. As you knew my particular speciality and areas of interest, you knew that would be enough to get me out here. Now, however, I am not so sure that I wish to be here. To explain, the Rakshasa were the subject of my Master's Thesis and Doc had sat on that committee. My

dissertation explored various occult matters in certain villages in India. There I learned about certain things which I took an oath never to reveal. Doc helped me over that hurtle with my committee."

He took a quick sip of coffee. "So when I received that phone call, I assumed that what Doc had was additional data, new information, on the subject. What I didn't think then, but realize now, is how intimately involved with the subject I would become. As we all are. None the less, as you are all now aware, the Rakshasa are a type of demon noted in the mythology of India."

I stifled a yawn.

Dr. Ben paused and took a deep breath.

"In Indian mythology the line that separates the gods from the demons is not very clear. Both are gifted with remarkable and mysterious powers which are manifested simultaneously by their moral and physical attributes. In this mythological world there are three classes of evil beings: The Asuras, The Pisakas, and The Rakshasa. The Asuras are only opposed to the gods, the Pisakas are opposed to the dead, but the Rakshasa are the enemies of man."

He sucked in a deep breath."The Rakshasa are great magicians and have the power to assume any shape they wish. They are fierce, blood-drinking, flesh-eating, man-eating creatures who are especially powerful during twilight and at nightfall. They can move faster than the wind. They have associated with them the Yatu. The Yatu take the form of vultures, ravens, hoofed spirits, and dogs! They devour the remnants left behind by the Rakshasa."

He pointed at Doc. "Remember the black dog. It could have been either one. The witnesses stated that they saw a small figure running after it when it left the park. It may well be that it was a Yatu that attacked you and that figure was its master, a Rakshasa!" Dr. Ben paused to let that sink in. My doodle was growing nicely. He took another sip of coffee.

"Now, in general, the Rakshasa are not, by nature, evil beings. But they are creatures destined by inescapable fate, Dharma, to play a hostile or malevolent part in the life of various individuals in various situations. And I think we know that we are now in such a situation." Dr. Ben looked inside his coffee cup, walked over to the pot, refilled it and returned to center stage.

"What do they look like? The Rakshasa are black as soot with yellow hair, often described in the mythologies as looking like a thunder cloud. The few pictures show them wearing a wreath of entrails with a sacrificial cord of hair around the neck, gnawing a man's head and drinking blood out of a skull. Because of their attire and habits their smell is rank and extremely strong and overall quite unpleasant. They are probably pre-Arayan."

Dr. Ben looked around the room. Nobody asked a question. Standard class.

He cleared his throat. "That about does it in a Reader's Digest sort of way. What else? Oh, yes! The Rakshasa are also known as The Injurious and as That Which Is To Be Guarded Against. Of course there is one saving grace in all this gloom, so to speak, if I can figure out a way to use it. Ummmmmm, ummmmmmm, ha! Perhaps there is, hum, I wonder, ahhhhhh, ah yes! Of course, of course!"

He refocused his eyes on us and blushed. "Oh sorry. It's Agni. Agni, the Fire, is often sought out to drive them away and to destroy them. Agni often goes by the name, Slayer of Rakshasa. Any questions? No? Then, that's that! Doc?" Dr. Ben sat down.

"A fine presentation, David, a fine presentation." Doc bobbled his head. "One question, not directly related to your presentation however. Have you been able to make head or tail out of that inscription from the inner chamber that I gave you?"

Dr. Ben shook his head. "No Doc, not at all. It is most strange, I looked at it this morning, briefly. I think it will take a few days to even begin to make sense out of it, if I can."

He fished around in his pocket and handed me a folded piece of paper. "J. C., here's a list of books that I will need. Can you bring them back with you when you return."

Then he looked back at Doc. "There is really something bothersome about this whole thing, inscription and cylinder seals and all, but I can't quite put my finger on it. Yet! Perhaps in a day or two." He frowned at the thought.

"Ah, no hints, David?"

Dr. Ben shook his head, again. "No hints Doc, no hints. I really don't want to say anything yet. Not until I've gotten more work done. So far all I have is just a feeling, one of those gut level things that hasn't really formed up yet. So, if we are finished here, and you'll excuse me, I've got a few more phone calls to make."

He smiled a weak one in Doc's direction. "Hope your phone bill isn't too much of a shock." Then it was my turn. "You won't forget those books will you J. C.?"

It was my turn to shake my head, so I did. "Have no fear Dr. Ben. When searching for the goods I bring 'em back alive."

Doc chuckled at the pronouncement. I knew he would.

He walked over and patted Dr. Ben on the arm. "Don't worry David, if those things are available on the West Coast, J. C. will find them. If he can't, we can always order them from elsewhere."

"Well then let's hope they're available out here. I do not think we have all that much time to search for them. If you'll excuse me I had best get back to work."

Dr. Ben turned and headed out the door. I could hear him mumbling to himself as he went down the hall, "Yes, Agni might be the right way. . ."

"Well Doc, anything else? If not, I'll be off as soon as I finished looking through those abstracts."

Doc had started to drift off. "Ummmmmmp. Oh! Yes, ah, sure J. C., do that! See you in two-three days,

O.K.?"

"I hope so, Doc, I hope so." I wasn't so sure that he even heard me. His eyes were staring at something, or nothing, out the window but his mind was somewhere else.

I left a note pinned to the Membranes chair in the living room telling him where I had gone off to, carrying the bundle of abstracts with me. I figured that I could look them over at my leisure after I got to Portland, over a piece of chocolate cake.

So there I was. Once again. On the road again! Ah well, such is the life of an academically inclined gofer.

Here Comes Sherlock Holmes' Buddy

Grandeville. Doc's Home.

It was a bright sunny morning here in Grandeville. I was hard at work, back from my hunting and gathering trip, doing nothing, when I heard the approaching noise.

The rental lemo bounced around the curve and roared to a halt in the driveway giving the nearby bushes and shrubs another light coating of dust. They were used to it.

Anyway, the Membrane gave them a bath every day with the hose.

So I sat there, admiring the morning, the view, and the dust cloud billowing around the plants and asking myself the burning question of the moment, now what?

The door swung open and this caricature of an Englishman got out of the driver's seat, walked over to where I was sprawling on the grass, out of the dust cloud range, enjoying the beginning of yet another day and pondering the events of the past two weeks. He was dressed in tweeds, had one of those curved pipes in his mouth, and came equipped with a bushy, sandy-brown mustache. The only things that were missing were the gumboots and the shotgun casually draped under one arm.

It spoke to me.

"I say, my good man, can you tell me whether this is the Doctor Heckmann residence?"

It took all my carefully trained self-control to keep from bursting out into rolling peals of laughter. For a moment I was sorely tempted to send him on an aimless trip back into the wilds of Grandeville, but I didn't. Get thee behind me, Satan!

This had to be the one and only Sir Winifred Rogers Smyth Robsen-Brown, archaeologist extraordinary, friend of Doc and the cause of everything that had happened so far. Oh well, appearances are deceiving as they say, whoever they might be. I gave him my very best lower-class look and said, "At's royt gov'nor, this be the 'eckmann residence. If you'll just pop yurself through that door there, you'll find himself in the kitchen messin' abot."

I stood up. "Well gov, I've got to pop meself off to the barns and see to the ruddy sheep and cattle . . . ta, ta!"

I headed down the road to see if I could find the Membrane and Badnews before they pounced upon our guest. Didn't want any unforeseen accidents happening. I didn't start giggling until I got into the greenhouse and out of sight.

But I didn't get to stay out of sight for long. Doc buzzed me on the intercom and called me back into the house, to the study to meet our new guest and to plot grand strategy and all that.

Back in the house I could hear them talking as I ambled down the hail toward the study.

"Really Doc, you do have some strange people working for you! I had the most amazing response from some chap that was lounging out back."

So I entered the room, stamped both my feet, hard, snapped to a rigid position of attention, gave Doc a limey salute and said in my best parade ground voice, "SAH!"

"Oh, by George, that's the one!"

Doc managed to suppress his smile. "All right J. C., I think that is quite enough. I believe that you have already met Winnie. Winnie, this is my assistant, J. C. Smith. I believe that I told you about him. J. C., this is Winnie."

I turned to Sir Winifred, gave him my best used-car salesman smile and shook his hand. He really had a firm grip. But he never batted an eye, just shook my hand and gave me a smile that said that he knew what the game was all about. Then he burst out laughing.

"Oh, ho, ho, ho, ho! Yes I do suppose that I make the picture of a perfect Colonel Blimp. Quite right! Ho, ho, ho, ho! Yes, quite right! But, I am very pleased to meet you J. C., quite pleased indeed."

It wasn't until Sir Winifred started to laugh that I knew where I had seen him before. In the movies! He was a perfect carbon-copy of Basil Rathbone's sidekick in the old Sherlock Holmes movies as played by Nigel Bruce. He was Doctor Watson right down to the slightly startled expression. Doc stood next to him, the top of his head level with Sir Winifred's shoulder, a diminutive Sherlock.

"J. C., would you get us a pot of tea. Then we can

settle down and see what information Winnie has brought us from jolly old England."

So I did and we did and the news was not all that great. I had dragged Dr. Ben along and after the necessary round of introductions, Doc spoke.

"Well Winnie, suppose you start. Tell us anything that you think might be of interest since last we spoke."

Sir Winifred took a sip of tea. "Righto, Doc. First, you remember that I told you of Krebb's death over the phone. Good. Ah, well I meant about the information, not about the death. Ummmm, rather good too! I did give you the details, didn't I?"

Doc shook his head.

"No? I didn't? Well, didn't really have much of that when we talked. Not much to say. Krebbs was found in his laboratory-office by the cleaning lady he employed. He had been dead for some time. Place was a bloody mess, papers and artifacts strewn all over the place. Terrible stench in the air. So the cleaning lady said. By the time the police had arrived she had pretty much aired out the room. All-in-all it sounds much the same as all the others. This was found lying next to the door."

Sir Winifred held out his hand. Nestled in it was another cylinder seal.

Dr. Ben jumped up, grabbed it, and hurried over to a window to give it a good look. Sir Winifred gave him a startled Nigel Bruce look and began to rummage in a coat pocket.

"Then there is the matter of the letter from Rasha Roy. It should have been enclosed in that letter that I sent you. But somehow my assistant, James Finn, managed to drop it behind a work bench and then forget to retrieve it, and send it along. Rather strange that. Finn is usually much better organized than that. Probably all these deaths and confusion. Enough to put anyone off their feed, what?"

He pulled out a folded letter and gave it to Doc. Doc passed to me. So I read it.

> Sir Winifred:
>
> The most terrible thing has happened in our village that I must hasten to tell you about it so you may arm vourself against the horror of it all. Four nights past we were all waken from our sleep by terrified screams from the house of Gupta Pan, the stone cutter, who you may remember from his duties in the main shaft. When we rushed to his presence all was quiet. The village headman banged loudly on his door but no sound came from within, only an odor of the most terrible kind.
>
> Terrified we entered Gupta Pan's house and were struck miserably in the eye by the sight we did see. Gupta Pan and his three sons were all dead, scattered about the room as if thrown by terrible force. The next morning we could see large footprints leading away from the house although none could be

found coming in. Two day's later, Old Raj, the wood cutter, came screaming down from the hills where the diggings had been working, shouting Rakshasa, Rakshasa. As I was your foreman, I went to the site. And when I came upon it the most terrible odor is smelled and to startled my eyes I saw coming from the entry tunnel a set of footprints the same as those of Gupta Pan house. I entered the entry tunnel and found way in the back in chamber C, a wall pushed out and fallen into the walk space behind which was a small chamber. This one is unknown to me. Inclosed are photographs made by the wondrous camera you left with us, also your film, and a copy by hand I made of the glyphs of the inner wall. It is a most ancient script as you can see. The wise old one of the village says that it means Rakshasa is loose. Everyone is afraid and boarding themselves in their homes. Please to warn your esteemed friends to have care.

Humbly,

Rasha Roy

I gave the letter to Dr. Ben. As he read it his complexion changed from this shade to that. He sat down, slowly, in one of the wing-back chairs and stared at the cylinder seal and then at the letter and back and forth. Finally he looked at Doc.

"Doc, this is horrible, simply horrible."

Doc nodded. "Yes David, I think you can say that."

"It's horrible, all those people dying, everything points to Rakshasa, right?"

"Yes, quite correct David."

"Wrong, wrong, wrong! Doc, something is terribly wrong, all wrong, cylinder seals, inscriptions, letter, evidence, all wrong!"

"How? What's wrong with all these things?"

Dr. Ben gave Doc a very wan smile. "I don't know Doc, but they are wrong none-the-less you see, all wrong, all wrong!"

He jumped to his feet, eyes wide, staring. "I've got to get back to work. Something is wrong, inscriptions, evidence, doesn't make sense. I got to find out what it is before anyone else dies. Rakshasa and death, the answer lies there. But these damned inscriptions aren't right!" He ran from the room.

"Doc?"

"Yes, J. C.?"

"That's what he said some time ago, the inscriptions are all wrong. He keeps saying that, but nothing comes of it."

"It will, J. C., it will." Doc turned to Sir Winifred who was sputtering to himself.

"Yes Winnie?"

Sir Winifred puffed out his cheeks and bobbed his head toward the door, blowing out a breath as he did so. "Really Doc, a very strange fellow! Are you sure he is all right." He tapped his right temple.

"And what does he mean that those inscriptions are all wrong? Boyer was one of the best in the field, he would have spotted any errors in them, if there were any. Wrong indeed!"

Doc threw a leg over one arm of his chair. "Winnie, that strange chap is Dr. David Ben, Chicago, now at Columbia. You have heard of him, haven't you? Or perhaps the introduction didn't register?"

Sir Winifred did his startled look. "Introduction? Oh dear me no, it didn't! You hadn't mentioned Chicago, not at all. David Ben! Oh, quite right. Heard he was a rather brilliant chap but rather unorthodox. But he does seem a bit strange even given that sort of reputation. What is wrong with him?"

Doc smiled. "Well Winnie, I'd say that he is suffering a bit of a shock. He studied in India, as you know. Lived in the rural, isolated villages and all that. Apparently while he was working there, he saw and experienced things that he never wrote about but which gave him a unique, deep insight into the mythology there. Well, east is east and west is west and never the twain shall meet."

Doc began to swing his leg. "I think that he compartmentalized his knowledge. Now here he is in Grandeville, U.S.A., not in whatever India, and his mythology seems to have come back alive, here, out of context, and he doesn't know quite what to make of it or do about it. But tell me, did you see anything wrong in the inscriptions that Boyer was studying, anything at all?"

Sir Winifred slowly shook his head. "Fraid not Doc. Didn't really look at them too much, you see, left it all to Boyer, his specialty and all that."

"Ummmmm yes, well David will find it, whatever it is."

Doc frowned in my direction. "J. C., you have been getting him whatever he needs, haven't you?"

I nodded my head violently. "Sure, whatever he wants, Dr. Ben gets." I almost sang the line. "Right now he's got charts and papers strewn and pinned to the walls. He even has a sheet with some sort complicated design tacked to the ceiling. There is going to be a lot of patching to do after he leaves. And, he is burning incense incessantly."

Got a smile from Doc on that one.

"Those long sticks! Dr. Ben's got them stuck in little bowls of sand, had to buy the entire supply at the grocery store, all over the room. At the rate that he is going there won't be a stick left in town."

Doc mumbled. "Urm, ah yes, oh well." And redirected the conversation. "So Winnie, what else do you have for us?"

"Not much. But I did manage to retrieve these from the police." And out of his jacket pocket came several sheets of paper folded over. He handed them to Doc. "These were found taped underneath the desk in Krebb's laboratory. They are copies of the inscriptions that Boyer was working on when he died. How Krebbs got them I really do not know." Sir Winifred leaned forward and pointed at something that I couldn't see from where I was sitting. "But see here, Krebbs was making some kind of notes in the margins, just there.

Notice that he has written in a slightly different inscription. Praps we should give this to Dr. Ben as well. Maybe he can make sense out of what ever Krebbs was doing or thinking?"

Doc refolded the sheets and shoved them into one of his pockets. "Ah yes, Winnie. Ummmmmm, leave these with me and I'll get them to David in a bit. I think we have enough time."

"Time for what, Doc?" I asked the obvious question.

He smiled at me. "Why time to build our Rakshasa trap of course."

"Huh?"

"Rakshasa trap! Ummm, yes, I think that it is going to he even more interesting than a Sasquatch hunt, don't you?" He nodded, more to himself than to anyone in the room. "Well, I think that I had better go and talk with David for awhile."

Doc got up and left the room, leaving me to entertain our guest.

So what else could I do? I took him on a tour of the place, first visit and all that. Beside he wanted to see the Irish Dexter cattle.

Outside we strolled down the path. "Well, what do you think of Doc's place, Sir Winifred?"

"Quite nice, J. C., quite nice, although it does tend to sprawl about some. But please, call me Winnie! Outside of certain segments of society the Sir Winifred is a bit much, don't you know. Winnie will do rather nicely."

"Oh, I say!" Winnie jolted to a halt and stared. I almost stepped on his heels. I was just crossing behind him. He pointed down the path toward the greenhouse. I couldn't see anything exciting down there, just the Membrane working. Then I realized that was what Winnie was staring at.

So I whispered in my most terrified voice. "It's one of the Rakshasa, we've got to get away before it sees us!" I pulled on his arm, but he was rooted to the spot.

"J. C., let go of my arm. Rakshasa indeed! I am going over there and take a look. Come along!"

It was not a suggestion, it was a command. Off he started. I tagged along.

When we arrived the Membrane straightened up and stretched, bigger and bigger and bigger.

"Morning, J. C. Who's your friend?"

So I introduced them, receiving a rather cross look from Winnie who didn't seem to appreciate my joke, such as it had been.

Just then two large hands grabbed me under the armpits and I soared into the air.

The Stoplight Twins had arrived. Red and Green "loaned" to us by the Grandeville P. D.

Winnie's eyes popped wide for a moment. "Oh my word, there is more of them!" He blushed a bright red. "Pardon me gentlemen, that was quite rude of me. Please accept my apologies."

"That's all right, Doctor Watson," the Membrane rumbled. "Think nothing of it." He had made the same connection that I had. Green just smiled over my shoulder at Winnie as he set me back on the ground.

Red rasped, "Be gentle with him, partner. He's just a little guy. Hi, Membrane."

For a moment Winnie looked confused, then he chuckled. And winked at the Membrane. "Doctor Watson? Oh, I see! Ho, ho! Yes, there is some resemblance. Asked mother about it one time. She said as far as she knew there was no family connection, none at all with Nigel Bruce. Didn't seem to think that there ought to be! Just one of those things, you know."

Winnie and I headed back to the house for lunch. Followed by the herd of three.

Lunch was the usual amazing thing, only more so. Winnie sat in astonishment all through the proceedings, not quite believing what he was seeing. And it was amazing too. Even for me. And I was used to seeing the Membrane demolish everything in sight.

But now, there were three of them! Red and Green were just about the same size as the Membrane, the three largest people in this part of the state.

Did I mention, by the by, that the Membrane has a twin still living down south. Astounding, isn't? How their mother managed them is one of those mysteries of life that only mother's understand. She is only four feet five inches or so in her stocking feet. But neither of these two hulks will give her as much as a crossword glance. When she said jump, they both left the floor and all you could hear was thump, thump! Just like that.

Anyway, after lunch we had a strategy session. Doc outlined what we were supposed to do when, or I should say if, the Rakshasa actually turned up, having followed Winnie halfway across the world and crossing one or another of the oceans.

Doc felt that they would turn up. I didn't. Dr. Ben looked as if he would be happy to talk about something else. The Membrane, the gigantic cops, and Badnews just sat and waited for whatever was to come, become, or whatever. Judging by their reactions we might as well have been planning a picnic in the woods or an outing in the park, with George.

So we sat and hatched out 'The Great Plan.' It was simplicity itself. We would do nothing! Just sit and let the Rakshasa come to us. And then? Why then, we would trap it, or them. Quite simple, huh?

Well, we didn't actually do nothing. For the next two days I was busy, stringing outdoor lights all over the place. Some of these were the old standbys from Christmas, others were newly purchased. I was helped in this endeavor by the Red and Green who operated as a kind of walking stepladder. The Membrane was off doing something else.

While we were busy, Doc, Dr. Ben, and Winnie talked and muttered in the library about this and that. Finally in the twilight's last gleaming of the second day, I was done.

Then I waited for it to get good and dark outside. Standing on an upstairs balcony I threw 'The Master Switch', took a quick look around for Igor and admired the view. The outside was, as they say, lit up as if by day, with one exception.

One side of the house was rather dark. Shadows flowed out and down across the lawn, through the pasture and across a half mile of pitch to the far edge toward where the main driveway wandered along from its way at the edge of town on its trip up the slope to our home.

Therein was laid the big plan. It was a deliberate

corridor of darkness. Doc and Dr. Ben had decided that the Rakshasa would have to come through there, where the darkness lay. Right up to the house, the side of the house with the outside door opening directly into the living room. It was the very same door Badnews had passed through.

So the Rakshasa would have access to the house from the outside and they would come through the door that we chose. Now, "The Big Plan," such as it was, was to somehow either keep them from entering the house at all or do something about it after one or more of them did. How we were to do either of these things Doc wasn't telling, at least not to me. But he was working out something with The Big Three and Badnews.

Whatever it was, I hoped that it would be effective. Otherwise the local community would have the biggest happening to talk about since the Indian raids of the 1860's.

Now all we could do was to wait and hope!

Trains, Passing Strange in the Night

Grandeville. Here and There.

Choo-Choo and Two Bottle, two of the more notable characters among the small handful that inhabited the lower reaches of Grandeville society, were celebrating their good fortune. Earlier during the day, they had both managed to acquire employment of the only type that either one of them would deem to take. Short! And non-permanent!

They had worked at their chores, finished and had been paid. Happy and contented with their lot, they, unlike many of their brethren, had gone off together, to slowly savor the good feelings that are engendered by noble toil, the feel of honest sweat upon their somewhat grimy brows.

In the early hours of the evening they had enjoyed a complete and nourishing meal, another rare treat, at the Railroad Bar and Grill, one of their favorite hangouts.

Then satiated, stomachs bulging pleasantly, they had ambled over to the nearby grocery store and had purchased two gallons of their favorite beverage. It was the cheapest thing on the shelves. Because of the earlier good fortune they even had a few dollars left.

Now here they were, deep in the evening,

reclined in regal splendor against the ancient ash piles, in the furthest corner of the railroad freight yard, admiring the song of the crickets, the stars above, the soft rumble of the passing freights, all the nocturnal sounds of their part of the world.

Having fully attained that wonderful glow they had so often sought but infrequently found, they decided that it was time for adventure, travel, time to seek out the quaint and curious! Stashing the untouched gallon in a place that they knew to be safe, they set out.

To explore the far frontier!

To go where no man had gone before!

They lurched easily through downtown and started up the long grade, the gentle slope that the town was built upon. This was a region of terra incognita. A land as exotic to them as the furthest reaches of the Orient were to the early explorers. Their world, the backside of downtown and the freight yards, was soon left behind. They stared about them. This was a passing strange land indeed!

They wobbled their way through alleys and front yards, up the grade, Choo-Choo in the lead, huffing quietly. All he had this wonderful evening was a single caboose. So he just idled up the slope. The track ahead was clear. Overhead the trees blocked out much of the evening sky. Here and there a street lamp cast its isolated circle of day. As they approached the upper edges of town, they could see a stretch of darkness. They were approaching the very edge of civilization as they knew it.

Choo-Choo gave one long, low howl of his whistle, just to wake up the crew in the caboose. And then they entered the darkness and drew to a shuddering halt, air brakes hissing.

Behind them the town, ahead the darkness. They peered into the gloom.

But hark! What light through yon darkness shines?

Tis Doc's place.

With a finger of darkness that stretched forth and beckoned to them. From the look of the lights hung here and there it must be Christmas!

Unseasonably warm for this time of the year.

How could they resist? Giving two short hoots of his whistle, Choo-Choo chugged forward and slipped under the fence. His faithful caboose trailed along behind.

They worked their way slowly upward, slipping over the rough ground with the easy grace of those who had spent a considerable part of their life weaving from point to point through the alcoholic groundswells of the sidewalks.

Suddenly a foul stench penetrated even the nostrils of Choo-Choo. Ahead, across the tracks, loomed something unformed. A blackness! With a screech of his whistle, Choo-Choo slammed on his emergency brakes and shoved the whole works into reverse. The caboose slammed into his rear-end.

Then they were in full flight, down grade, clattering through the tree-lined streets and down short-cut alleys, back to the freight yard. One of the city police on patrol saw them fly past, eyes wide and staring. Apparitions in their own right.

He shrugged his shoulders and drove on.

Rakshasa Peek-a-boo

Grandeville. Doc's Home.

So, we waited. One day. Two days. Then on the twentieth day, counting from the arrival of Winnie's letter, it began, rather quietly, like most disasters.

I was up at six as usual and was getting my cup of coffee in the kitchen ready to head into the great outdoors and admire the day when Doc poked his head in through the outside door.

Now that was certainly a surprise. But hardly was disaster spelled Doc-up-very-early-in-the-morning!

"J. C., come outside here and tell me what you think!" So I followed him out. He was going my way, anyhow.

I stood next to the railing and took a sip. "Ummm, think about what, Doc?"

"Just take a deep breath of this clean, clear, fresh mountain air, then answer the question."

So I did. "AhhhhHHHHH, YUCK! What is that? Did we trap a skunk in the greenhouse again? Damn, it will take days to get the smell out of there. Wait till the Membrane finds out. Boy, will he be pissed!"

"Ahhhhhhh, J. C.?"

I looked at Doc.

He winked. "Not skunk . . . Rakshasa!"

My cup took one bounce off the porch railing

and tumbled through the rose bushes, drops of coffee adding their twinkle to the dew still on the petals.

"Rakshasa! Here! Now!"

Doc peered down at my coffee cup. "One moment, J.C., one moment. First! Yes, Rakshasa. Second! Yes, here. Third! No, not now, last night. It would appear that the visit is over for the moment but the memory lingers on, as it were." He giggled at this last bit of levity. It didn't really strike me as all that funny. Not a bit, in fact.

Up to now the whole idea of monsters from India had struck me as a bit of a joke being on the same level as hobgoblins and all the rest of that Halloween crowd. But now, after couple more sniffs, it was apparent that this odor certainly wasn't skunk. It didn't smell like anything that I had ever encountered before.

So, one of these things was real after all. Now that took some getting used to. I plopped down in a chair. Doc fetched another cup and poured it full from the ever handy pot. I sipped and pondered what we thought we were doing.

Doc was planning on catching it. But how does one catch a demon? And keeping the thing caught? So far all we were planning on doing was letting him, her or it walk right up to the house and come on in. Then what?

At this point I knew we had a disaster on our hands. Unwanted dread had just become a companion. In spite of the sharp rays of sunshine hitting the landscape I could feel the waves of menace washing over the house.

Doc leaned on the porch railing, staring out. "Yes

J. C., it is a bit unsettling, isn't it? Now that one of these things is actually here. It didn't take long, did it?"

He pointed vaguely. "Badnews is looking around to see whether he can find signs of our visitor or visitors. I do hope we only have one of them to face. Several might be more than we can handle."

I nodded my head in agreement and wondered whether these things might run in herds.

Doc turned and patted my shoulder. "However, I think that this whole matter will be resolved tonight. I think that whatever was prowling around was looking for a way in. Yes! I do believe that tonight we will actually see what a Rakshasa looks like."

He leaned back against the railing and rubbed his hands together. It was an eager gesture. "As an anthropologist you should be looking forward to it. After all, we have legends and folk descriptions, such as those given to us by David, but what do we really know? Nothing! But now we will see, really see, if the tales and all that, tally with reality. I wonder if they photograph. Have to try. Many of these kind of phenomena don't seem to. Did you know that?"

I nodded my head again. I was fully awake. A new world's record. Whoopee!

Then I had the thought that must have occurred to all the heros of old. If this was going to be the last day of the last brawl, then let's make it a good one! I jumped over the railing, retrieved my coffee cup and went back into the kitchen and made a heroic breakfast: heuvos rancheros, using three eggs, with a side of ham, sliced thick, and lots of toast and butter and blueberry jam. The condemned man ate a hearty meal.

Then I decided to scout the territory. So I walked through the living room to the outside through the planned Rakshasa entry way. The first thing that caught my eye were two large mounds of hay parked just beyond the lawn in the pasture, sitting about twenty feet apart. Badnews was walking from that direction.

"Hey, Badnews, where did the hay come from?"

"Doc bought it the other day, delivered yesterday. You were to busy to notice."

I hadn't been too busy. I had been downtown shopping. And working on the house, off to one side. So? I didn't notice.

Then I wondered, what project has Doc started this time? Then I thought, what difference does it make? Tonight we come face to face with demon.

I went back into the house and headed for Dr. Ben's room. Maybe he would know what kind of weapon would be proper to use against one of these things. I met him in the hall headed for the kitchen.

"Hi, Dr. Ben. Had breakfast yet?"

"No J. C., not yet. You?"

"Sure did. If you like heuvos rancheros, I can cook you some."

"O.K., I'll try it, whatever it is."

So I busied myself at the stove and waited until he was at least halfway through his breakfast before I asked him.

"Say Dr. Ben, what sort of weapon would one use against an Indian demon anyway? Just thought that it might be interesting to know." I was going to sort of sneak up our last night's visitor on him.

Dr. Ben took a big bite of toast. "Well J. C., there

doesn't seem to be one, not in the sense of what you are asking. At least I haven't been able to find anything in the literature that would suggest that there is. Of course there are types of spells, chants as it were, that are protective and are alleged to ward them off."

Another piece of toast followed the first. "However it really does seem to me that the only thing we can do, and we should do that as soon as possible, is to put back or restore to its original condition whatever it was that Sir Winifred and crew upset in the first place. Because whatever they did released the Rakshasa. So once things are put back together again it should return. We will have to go to India, visit the site and try to figure out right there on the ground what to do. Of course that will be quite hazardous as we will be in close proximity to the tomb. But I don't really see we have much choice in the matter. When Sir Winifred gets up we'll have to ask him to start making the necessary arrangements right away."

Dr. Ben nodded his head and took a swallow of coffee. "I am sure that is the only real thing that we can do. But as I said, there are the special chants, things that the people in the isolated villages believe, chants connected with Agni. Other than that, nothing. Why do you ask?" He piled the rest of the eggs on the remaining piece of toast.

I took a deep breath. "Well Dr. Ben, it is this way. I do no think that we will have time to ask Winnie to arrange all that travel, not right now. It seems to be too late. We had a visitor last night. It appears that one of the Rakshasa was hanging about the house."

The air was filled with the spray of egg particles

and bits of toast as Dr. Ben leaped to his feet. "What? Here? Now?"

I had managed to stay just beyond the splash radius. "My questions exactly. And if I may give you Doc's answers, and they were . . . yes, yes, no! Doc thinks we will have a repeat visit tonight. He thinks that we will finally get to see what a Rakshasa really looks like. Pretty exciting, huh?"

Dr. Ben was shaking his head violently from side to side.

"Doc also feels that we will be able to catch it and in the process of doing so manage to keep ourselves from being killed or maimed or whatever."

Dr. Ben grabbed his cup and took a swift jot of coffee. "But that is not possible J. C., just not possible! Where is he? I have to talk to him right away!" He waved his arms rather wildly and his toast sailed across the room unnoticed by the sender.

"He is out on the dark side of the house doing something or other with Badnews. You should find him there, somewhere. I will be in the barn. If you should need anything, just buzz."

"In the barn?" He looked even more startled. "What are you going to be doing out there?"

I headed for the back door. "Well Dr. Ben I'll tell you. What I am going to be doing, off and on, for the rest of the day, is going through all the martial routines that I ever learned from my friend John Tinker and trying to get my mind in the right frame of mood for facing monsters, demons, or whatever. Been studying for three years and I certainly wish Tinker was still around. We could use his talents at the moment.

Anyhow, that is what I will be doing. Whatever the brawl is to be with, I will be ready. Morituri te salutamus!" I gave him the gladiator salute and headed for the barn.

Then I turned around and cleaned up the kitchen. He had made quite a mess.

By the time afternoon had wended its way into twilight I was ready.

Dinner was a rather subdued affair. Each had been preparing himself in their own way for the coming event. Little was said.

Even Dr. Ben had calmed down. He was wearing saffron robes and had stuff on his face.

Later we sat in the living room and waited for full darkness to descend. Each sipped his favorite beverage, listened to the classic music on the NPR station and waited.

I looked outside and threw the master light switch. The shadowed corridor seemed to have taken on a texture that it didn't have last night. Overhead, clouds had settled in. It was going to be a very dark evening. It felt damp. In the pasture I could barely see the mists forming.

I circled the house in an aimless pattern and finally settled again in the living room. And waited.

The grandfather clock chimed eleven-o-clock. Badnews, the Membrane, and Red and Green slipped from the room and headed for where ever Doc had directed them. Dr. Ben went to his room. Doc, Winnie and I remained in the living room.

And waited.

I thought about and focused my mind on the

soon-to-be confrontation. Then I couldn't stand it any longer and went outside to wait in the darkness.

The clouds had cut off most of the moonlight. A small amount of reflected light from nearby Grandeville touched overhead.

It didn't help!

The ground-fog had developed nicely and lay across the pasture in a low billowing mat. It seemed to be flowing up toward the house.

I waited.

In the black.

Bong!

The grandfather clock announced the first stroke of midnight.

Bong!

The favorite hour for all the bad things to come calling.

Bong!

The Rakshasa are large and strong.

Bong!

They like to wander in the darkness.

Bong!

They are unconquerable at midnight.

Bong!

The ground-fog stirred. And eddied.

Bong!

I could feel the presence of something. Out there!

Bong!

A foul odor drifted up from the pasture.

Bong!

Rustling, soft noises came from the pasture. Up through the grass.

Bong!

I started toward the space between the hay mounds.

Bong!

Low growling sounds.

Bong!

A vague shape.
Moving.
Toward me.
Between the hay mounds.

Silence.

The hay mounds erupted with a rustling, tearing sound.

A voice screamed in terror, rising higher and higher in pitch until the vocal cords could no longer sustain the shock. Rank smell washed over me.

Silence

Not a sound.

Stillness.

Waiting.

Then I heard them. Moving. Rustling. And heavy, heavy footsteps. Coming my way. I was standing between them and the house.

A large misshapen form loomed from the darkness, fog swirling around its legs. Huge. Plodding straight ahead.

I charged and leaped at the right side, going for where the throat ought to be. All my energy was focused, it was a killing blow. I smashed into a large hand which struck my chest, knocking me backward into the grass.

Rolling sideways, gasping for breath, I tried to scrabble out of the way. Thick fingers touched my back, clutching at me. I desperately tried to move. Too late. They dug into my shirt and lifted me off the ground.

"J. C., what do you think you are doing

anyway?"

It was the Membrane!

He set me on my feet. I turned and took a close look into the dimness. Red and Green held something between them. They had it gripped under the armpits, holding the figure off the ground. From all appearances it was dead, the head lolled and hung on its chest.

The Membrane rumbled. "Come on J. C., let's take this thing inside and see what we have caught before the stench overwhelms us all. I'll you one thing, if this is a demon it certainly is a piker. Although for a moment there I thought there was something larger. Come on, let's get inside."

We headed across the lawn toward the door to the living room. The thing they carried certainly smelled bad. As we stepped onto the patio a shadow slipped silently from a darker patch along the wall. I jumped backwards into the Membrane.

"Easy, J. C., easy, it is just Badnews. Go inside and turn on the living room lights so we can see what we have."

I opened the door and stepped in, switching on the lights. Doc and Winnie were still sitting there. Winnie held a cannon of some kind in one hand pointed directly at us.

Seeing who it was he viably relaxed and set the gun in his lap. Doc was in his favorite wingback chair, one leg draped over one armrest, brandy-snifter cradled in his hands, apparently not overly bothered by all the commotion, not at all.

The Membrane and the cops came ducking sideways through the door and heaved their burden, not any too gently, into the middle of the floor and stepped back so we could all take a peek at what ever it was that they had caught.

It was a smallish creature covered in black, shiny skin.

Badnews stepped forward and with one toe of his boot rolled the thing over onto its back. It appeared to be human in spite of the odor.

I bent over to take a closer look. It was a man dressed all in black leather. On his belt were several leather pouches, one leaking some kind of oily fluid. It was the source of the terrible smell. I heard a heavy thump behind me.

I jumped and whirled around. It was Winnie. He had jumped to his feet, the pistol falling to the floor. He stared at the figure and then bent down and brushed some of the dirt and mud from the face.

"**BLOODY HELL!**"

Grand Finale

Grandeville. Doc's Home.

Winnie looked at Doc. "Doc, do you know why he is here? I mean, did you invite him here? He is supposed to be in London working on the site material!"

Doc took a small sample from his glass. "Well Winnie, I propose that we ask Mister Finn these questions as soon as he comes around. I trust the Membrane and Red and Green haven't hurt him too badly. He doesn't appear all that dead to me, just fainted. Take a seat, it should only be a moment or two."

Winnie reseated himself."All right, we will wait for him to wake."

Sir Winifred didn't look all that good to me. Seemed as if the sudden appearance of his helper being dumped on the floor had unnerved him.

I opened the door and peered out. Nothing. Turned back and nodded. "Doc, I hate to interrupt all this agreeing to wait until sleeping beauty wakens but shouldn't we get back outside and look into where that Rakshasa is. The Membrane, Red and Green, Badnews and I could just skip outside and see to it that we aren't taken by surprise. O.K.?"

Doc shook his head. "That matter can wait. Ah there, his eyes are open. Or are they?" He peered down at Finn.

Finn's eyes were open all right but there was something elsewhere that he was seeing. A long, drawn out moan came from him. "Nooooooooooooo, no, nooo, no! Go back! You aren't real! I didn't call you! Nnnnnnnnnnooooooooooooooo!"

Doc stepped lightly over to Finn, leaned down and cracked him across the face hard enough to jolt his head around. It was effective.

Finn's eyes started to focus. Then he saw us and slowly sat up and heaved himself to his feet, swaying slightly from side to side. The color began returning to his face under the mud and dirt. It was obvious that his control was returning as well. He gave an abbreviated bow in Doc's direction.

"Ah, Doctor Heckmann. And Sir Winifred. It is good to see you again. Perhaps I could have a bit of whiskey. I think I need to sit down."

He started to turn, looking for a chair and saw the Membrane and Red and Green leaning against the far wall. Finn's eyes bugged and he began to back-peddle across the room. "Noooooooooo!" The end-table went over, taking the lamp with it. Doc dodged sideways out of his path. "Nooooooooo!" Finn pressed himself flat against the walls, eyes rolling frantically. Doc jumped in front of him, motioning for the big three to leave the room.

Doc smacked him across the face. I winced.

"Finn, stop it, stop it! That is just the Membrane and two local policemen. Stop it!"

Doc had Finn by the shoulders and was shaking him none too gently. I could hear his head thumping against the wall. But however hard it was on Finn, it was effective. He calmed down.

Doc took his arm. "Now come over here and sit down! And tell us what you were doing out there!" Doc thrust him into a chair, grabbed a glass and the whiskey bottle, slopped some into the glass and held it under Finn's nose. Finn grabbed the glass with both hands and managed to get it to his lips. And took a swallow and licked his lips. "Yes, yes, that's what Old Finn should do all right, that is what he should do."

Finn stared around the room but you couldn't tell whether he was seeing it or something else. Then his face took on a sly expression and he started to address no-one in particular in a sly knowing manner. He nodded his head as he spoke.

"Old Finn fixed them didn't he? Oh yes! He had it all set, should have been chairman of the department but they brought in someone else, someone from the outside. BUT it should have been Finn! It was all Finn's doing, all those students. They were all in Finn's classes. Finn saw to that didn't he? All the students had to take Finn's classes. After all, it was his program, it didn't belong to anyone else. FINN'S! But they brought in someone else. And HE pushed Finn out. Didn't understand that Finn was a genius. But the students knew. Finn told them. They were doing all my work."

Finn began to poke his chest with one finger.

"They were working on my research, doing my fieldwork, following my program. I was the leader! And they followed, doing what I told them to do. A good program, a good program. And I published the research!"

He gave Doc a condescending smile. "I should have brought you my vita, Doctor Heckmann. Then you could have seen for yourself. Dozens of publications, all mine! And I was the editor of the journal, too!"

Finn began to move his head slowly from side to side. "But they didn't understand. I designed the program. When Smiley died I should have become the chairman, permanently! But no, they had to bring in someone else, from the outside, and then they pushed me out. Isolated me from my department and my program, said I couldn't get along with the other faculty. But it wasn't true."

He leaned toward Doc. "I was the professional! I was doing the research! I was the genius! I had the students! But they pushed ME out!" Then the sly expression returned and his voice dropped to a crafty stage whisper. "But you know what? I won after all!" Finn stood up and stretched, an exaggerated gesture. He began to pace up and down in a small tight pattern, gesturing. His voice became more animated, projecting.

He was beginning to lecture. To a classroom of unseen students.

"So I left for a better position. I was hired by SIR Winifred R.S. Robsen-Brown to be HIS assistant! Did you know that. I was a much better archaeologist than Sir Winifred? I never told him that, but it is true you know. Much better!" He nodded his head. "Much better!"

Finn paused dramatically and then swept his arms wide. "Then it started again. They tried to get me again, just like before. But this time I knew who they were. They had shown their true colors. Hafas!

Corruccini! Boyer! THEY were out to get me, just like the others, even Krebbs. Out . . . to . . . get . . . Old . . . Finn. Didn't understand his genius. Just like graduate school, trying to throw Finn out. But Finn fixed them this time. Yes, he did!"

He beamed around the room. "Heh, heh, the Rakshasa did it, you know. Came out of the crypt and crept! Right from the tomb, right from the vault. See, it worked like this." He began to draw a diagram on a blackboard only he could see.

As he wrote, he continued his lecture. "It took a few years to work it all out but Sir Winifred never noticed. He wasn't as good an archaeologist as Old Finn. He would never figure it out. He brought in the others. Hafas! Corruccini! Boyer! They tried to get Finn but it didn't work. Now everyone will say that it is another mystery like the Piltdown Man. But you see, I was going to tell, write it all up, after their reports were written. Then they would see the genius of Finn. Then they would know that he was the best. Krebbs had almost figured it out. Krebbs and the rest. So, they had to be removed."

It was an offhand comment. Finn waved his hands gently, shooing away flies.

"Terminated with extreme prejudice, as the saying goes. So they went, heh, heh, heh! They went! Fixed it just right. They went away. Bye-bye," His voice dropped to a conspiratorial level. "And everyone thinks that it is Rakshasa. But it is not, you know."

He suddenly jerked upright and turned toward Doc, giving him a knowing smile and a slow wink.

"Just Finn, just Finn. Not Rakshasa, not at all.

FINN! Fixed them all. You know Doctor Heckmann, I would have fixed you too. Oh yes I would have. But!" He whispered as he peered carefully around the room. "They came, the Rakshasa. They knew and they came. Almost got me, you know, almost they did, almost. But! I was too quick for them, even them, the Rakshasa."

Finn turned away and began writing again. On the invisible blackboard. "Yes, yes, the genius of Finn was even stronger than the Rakshasa. Finn got away. So, that's all there is, you see. Just Old Finn."

He dismissed the class, patting his hands together to get rid of the chalk dust, and gave Doc a quick bow and turned slowly.

"But enough of this, time to get back to work! Ah, Sir Winifred, so nice of you to join us. I brought some reports for you to look over. Oh dear, I seem to have misplaced them." Finn stood patting his pockets, smiling a very bright smile. "But they ought to be here, somewhere." Then he shrugged. "Oh well, must have dropped them outside. No matter! When we return to London we can get additional copies." He popped his hands together. "Right! Back to London and back to work on the project, that's the ticket! Have to plan for the next field season, you know."

Doc walked slowly over to Finn and gently put his arm around his shoulders, softly directing him toward the hallway door.

"I think that it is time that we all went to bed, don't you think so? It has been a long night." Doc gestured with his free hand. "Badnews, put him in the end bedroom, please."

Badnews slipped up, took Finn by the arm and

led him from the room and down the hall. We could hear Finn telling Badnews all about the amount of work that he would have to do to get ready for next year's field season until the sound was suddenly cut off by the closing of the far bedroom door.

Doc nodded toward the outside door. "J.C., poke your head out and ask the Membrane to watch his window tonight and see that he doesn't decide to leave. Tomorrow we can let Red and Green take over. And that should be that!"

I did as I was told and the three house monsters lumbered off and around the corner of the house.

As I popped back in Doc was saying, ". . . and I think that takes care of the Rakshasa business, don't you?"

Winnie nodded.

"J. C .?"

I shook my head. "Not exactly, Doc, not exactly."

Doc looked puzzled. "So what is bothering you then. It seems perfectly clear to me."

"Well Doc, if it is, please explain."

He gave me one of his super smiles. "Well all right J. C., all right."

Doc whirled around and plopped down in his chair and waved for Winnie and me to sit as well. We were still standing. We sat.

Doc cleared his throat. "It goes this way. After I returned from London, I was continually bothered by Finn. There was something about him that just didn't seem right. It was more than just his slimey personality. It was his insistence on his so-called expertise. A truly competent person doesn't need to do that. So I made a few phone calls."

Doc proceeded to tell us how he had talked to people at the last school Finn had been at and a large number of professors who had once also taught there. Doc had talked to Finn's graduate school and his ex-professors there. While in grad school Finn had tried to plagiarize some data and written work and pass it off as his Thesis.

Somehow Finn had managed to get the Thesis through the system before anyone realized what had happened. Everyone had signed off on it. Then they found out. They took back his degree and threw him out. But, somehow, he managed to get a job in a small college where he pandered to chairman in such a way as to be allowed to engineer the curriculum in a manner that fixed it so he wound up with all the graduate students.

Using their talents, he wrote a large number of articles which he published in the house journal which he edited. Then he used this list of publications to build a reputation as the local expert. The school's administration wouldn't, for some reason, pay any attention to what was going on even though, year after year, faculty left and turmoil reigned supreme.

Suddenly the old chairman died and the school brought in someone from the outside. The new chairman managed to push Finn out of the department and away from the students. But he couldn't really touch him, Finn was tenured.

At about this time Hafas was doing a large excavation in the area, with Corruccini and Boyer as Senior Investigators. Finn was hired as a sop to local politics. Finn tried to usurp Hafa's position and Hafas threw him off the dig. Then all three of them wrote blistering letters to his school administration discussing in no uncertain terms Finn's totally unprofessional conduct and disruptive behavior. Finn disappeared.

Then he surfaced and somehow managed to obtain a position with Winnie as an assistant using, I suspect, fake letters of recommendation and credentials.

Then slowly and slowly Finn worked up an elaborate scheme for creating a false operation based upon faulty premises and hand-crafted artifacts. He had hoped to devastate all their reputations and reveal his genius, as he put it. But Winnie's colleagues were all close to figuring it out. So Finn killed them using the Rakshasa myth as a cover. Krebbs seemed to have discovered the same facts that the others were uncovering. So Rakshasa-Finn struck again.

We were next. But Doc had planted the Membrane outside. With Red and Green inside the hay stacks with Badnews as backup. They popped out and grabbed him.

However, the shock apparently pushed Finn over the thin edge he had been walking for years.

Doc frowned. "I rather think that he shall need institutional care from now on, poor chap." He stood up. "Well, now I really do think that that is enough for one evening. Shall we go to bed?"

So, we did.

The next morning, after Finn had been hauled away, the place settled down into a nice peaceful, quiet state of being. It would be up to the numerous nation's political and legal systems to figure out who got Finn first. Doc and I were sitting on the porch, sipping from our coffee cups and watching the day slide by.

Last night I thought I was going to die. Today I am alive. It is truly amazing how that changes the way you see things. It was a beautiful day.

The Membrane and Badnews had departed on a short hike into the foothills for the day. Red and Green went back to work, after Doc thanked the Chief of Police for their "loan." Dr. Ben was upstairs packing, preparing to leave.

Dr. Ben had already apologized about the condition of his room. But I had suggested that a couple days of airing out would probably do it good. He had been burning great gobs of incense and chanting to Agni all through the night.

Winnie had gone out into the greenhouses to "putter about" after announcing that he was a bit of a gardener himself. "Have a greenhouse and all that, you know."

Which left, as I said, just Doc and me admiring the day and enjoying the quiet.

"Doc what else is there? I know that there is more to last night than meets the eye. You know more than you told us."

Doc didn't look at me, just sat and sipped a bit. Then he nodded.

"Yes, you are quite right J. C., there is more. As you might have guessed, but didn't, I wasn't ready to accept the Rakshasa idea, not at all. That is why I asked David to come out. I figured that he would spot any falsity in it. And he did! He knew something was wrong but couldn't quite bring it up. If events had moved slower I sure he would have. When I told him this morning about Finn, then it all clicked together. It was those cylinder seals, all forgeries. Krebbs had gotten one and was going to use it in his article. David saw some subtlety in the carvings, some slight error in style, and was puzzling over this. Of course he was also doing his priestly duty as he had learned to do up in some hill village."

Doc stood, poured us both another dose and leaned his elbows on the railing, cup held in both hands and continued to talk, a kind of amazement in his voice.

"You know that all the people that I talked to about Finn were all of the same opinion, and there was a large number of them! He was universally disliked, in some cases positively hated. I doubt there will be any mourners out there weeping over his sad fate, such as it is."

Doc shrugged his shoulders. "Well anyhow, to me, everything seemed to point toward Finn. Of course I may have been somewhat motivated by the same feelings as seem to have been shared by so many. The information gathered by Badnews cleared those that died of illegal activities and that reinforced my opinion. So I convinced Winnie to come over here. And Finn followed."

He gave a great sigh. "Of course Finn was always a little mad what with his ego-centric world view and all. But it now appears that he was so much a part of the Rakshasa, or rather being a Rakshasa, that when he was grabbed by those two great shapes which he thought were really Rakshasa, over he went."

Doc turned and leaned back against the railing

giving me a gentle smile. "And, as it turns out, all your research was, in one sense, a waste of time. Although I am sure you would have found the same thing that Krebbs did." He laughed, a laugh of no humor.

"It is interesting isn't it, how four highly qualified investigators, four highly qualified professionals in the true meaning of the term, could only see what they wanted to see especially when they thought they were going to turn the world of prehistory on its ears."

Doc set his cup on the railing and pointed. "I will entertain the press, here comes Old John now. I think that he and I shall take a little stroll and talk. Ah, see if you can get the household back into some sort of decent shape, will you. Ta, ta! Have fun!"

Doc jumped lightly over the edge and walked toward the battered heap that was Old John's car to tell him as much of the story as he felt ought to be printed in the local rag, er, newspaper.

I went off to work in the library and see to the household accounts first. I didn't tell Doc about the rather sizable check that Winnie had handed me on the sly, for business expenses you know, herump, herump! Just hide this little economic windfall somewhere, use it for a cushion for the next thing that Doc gets us into.

We were back in the black again, economically speaking.

Well, well, all's well that ends well. Ha, ha.

I passed the hall mirror on my way and took a peek. You know, it did seem as if there were a few more grey hairs there than I remembered.

J. C. leaned back and smiled. "So, that's how I spent my summer vacation." And waggled one hand. "You want to tell what you have been doing?"

Tinker shook his head. "Not right now. I better get home. Chen will be wondering what I am up to."

J. C. walked him out to his car. "Good to have you back in town, buddy." And wiped the thin layer of snow from the car's windshield. The weather had shifted some.

Reassemble: To Bring Together

Tinker drove through Grandeville, down Main Street, admired the small town of the place, including the street naming system in town, and then circled back around and headed along the edge of Doc's place and out of town. Up the valley side to his home. It was just a short drive from town. On a secondary county road.

But far enough. Where he lived was rather isolated and quiet. One could enjoy the silence, open space, and privacy. It had been a long year's absence. He was returning harder and more resilient than when he had left. He turned to his right. Off the county road.

Up the open slope to home.

In the rear-view mirror, he admired the valley below as the road snaked up the steep pitch. It was one of the reasons why he had picked this spot.

For the view.

Grandeville. Tinker's Place.

He swung the car into the final bend of the driveway and coasted snow crunching glide to a halt. As he eased from the car, the outside lights snapped on, the side door flew open, and a small, slightly-built

Chinese gentleman flowed down the porch to stand waiting. Not bothered by the winter wind blowing.

He bowed once. "Welcome home, Nephew. I have a pot of tea sitting on the wood stove. Your room is ready."

Tinker smiled. "Thank you, Master Chen, it is good to be back. Home. Again." He followed Chen into the house, hung his jacket on a wall-peg in the kitchen and strolled through the hallway into the living room. The tea was ready. He sat in his favorite chair, poured a cup, and sat back, sighing happily.

The big room was large enough for two couches, several chairs, a large rug and the wood stove. The wood stove was set near the east wall, flanked by two large windows.

Several windows in the south wall allowed sunlight to pour in during the winter months, helping warm the room.

The stove muttered. The house creaked an answer. Chen took another cup, poured, and sat on the couch, joining Tinker in silent contemplation of the wood stove-house conversation.

Finally Chen broke the silence. "Well, student, you look well. Everything is all right, now?"

Tinker nodded. "Yes, it is. The pain is gone. The anguish is gone. But deep down, there is a small ball of hate."

"But you have control, is that not so?"

Tinker nodded again. "Yes, it is so."

"GOOD! Tomorrow we can start where we left off. A year ago." He looked carefully at Tinker, dark eyes carefully appraising his friend and student.

"Although it appears to me that you have changed in subtle ways. Maybe more than you realize. You practiced much, did you not?"

Tinker nodded, slowly. "Yes, I did. After the first day I could hardly move. But, as the pain and anger burned away, it got better and better. Every day. I also studied with Wa Chang and Hip Wan Do.

"And what did you learn from them, Nephew?" Chen still watched him, ever so carefully.

"I learned that death is easily delivered. And while it is easy to do physically, it is hard to do morally." He poured more tea into his cup. "The weapon that I have become is stronger and sharper."

Chen nodded. "And what else?"

"More restraint and more care."

"Perhaps a little wisdom as well?" asked Chen, smiling gently.

Tinker laughed softly. "Yes, perhaps a little wisdom as well." He peered at Chen over the top of his tea cup. "So, how have you been? Is everything well with you?"

Chen smiled. "I am fine. Your house is fine. My restaurant is fine. Your lands are fine. Your toys," he gestured toward the dining room, "are fine. Although I cannot speak for that thing." He jerked his head toward the far corner of the room. "That lives over there."

Tinker's glance snapped to the corner and back to Chen's face. "You didn't touch it, did you?"

"I DID NOT! It has stayed just there, undusted, untouched. Unwanted. But I have taken care of the rest to the best of my humble abilities." Chen leaned forward and tapped Tinker sharply on the knee with one finger. "You were very sloppy. It took some time to clean this place." He rose and gestured. "Come, I'll show you where I put the toys. They were rather dirty and banged around looking. So I cleaned them and repainted the soldiers." Leading Tinker into the dining room, he pointed. "There they are."

A small case hung on the wall. Inside, on several shelves, standing in rows, were the toys. One shelf held a row of wooden soldiers, twelve in all, painted in bright red and blue. The other shelf held a plastic, windup Toucan and a Goose, two short and squat, wind up robots, a rubber stegosaurus, and a small, fluffy, yellow Easter chicken, the kind one used to find is baskets with candy,

Chen spoke softly. "They are all here." He walked quietly away, back to the living room. Tinker stood and stared at the collection, sharp, painful memories flooding back. He jerked away and hurried back to his chair and tea cup.

"You have done well, Master Chen. I have a great debt to repay. What is your wish?"

Chen smiled, shook his head. "Nothing. But, perhaps, one day, you will tell me how those small things caused such great pain and anguish." He sprang lightly to his feet.

"Your room is ready. Have a good night's sleep."

As Tinker followed him into the hail, Chen said over his shoulder. "We had a strange visitor. But we can discuss that in the morning."

"You expected me tonight?"

Chen nodded.

"How?"

"Oriental secret." Chen laughed, a very sly laugh.

"Oh?"

"Doc called when you arrived. And as soon as you left his place."

Tinker laughed. "Of course. Good night."

"In the morning," stated Chen. "For practice. I want to see what you have learned."

Tinker stepped into his bedroom and carefully hung up his clothes, remembering Chen's comment about sloppy. His pajamas where laid out, ready for use, the bed covers neatly turned down. It was good to be home.

The king-size water bed was warm and comfortable. He stretched and listened to the air bubbles gurgle as the water gently sloshed back and forth. It always lulled him to sleep, to a sleep that came soft and swift.

CRASH!

Tinker's eyes popped open.

It was still dark.

He lay still, waiting.

Was that just a dream?

Or not?

A faint scuffling sound. Voices. Muffled by the intervening walls. Someone. Several someones. In his house.

He rolled fluidly from his bed and silently eased into the hall. Standing in a low crouch, he peered up and down the hall. No light, no movement. The voices seemed to be coming from the dining room. He slipped down the hall and drifted into the kitchen, from shadow to shadow. Light streamed from the dining room. They were in there.

Chen was standing facing into the dining room, a large wooden spoon clenched in his right hand.

A voice snapped at Chen, "STAND AND BE STILL! One false gesture with wooden implement and I will most certainly pierce you through and through. BROTHER! SISTER! Have a care, I do believe this person do mean for to us attack."

Another voice demanded, "STAND VARLET! Cease and desist."

Tinker slipped up alongside Chen and gently touched his arm with one fingertip.

It was a cautionary gesture. "Put your weapons down, group. You are in my house and I don't want a bloody mess made in my dining room."

A flash of yellow hurtled from the dining room and thudded against him, arms wrapping around his chest. A muffled voice sobbed and mumbled against his chest. "My Lord, Oh My Lord, we do know not where we had come nor where thee had gone. And thy servant do appear most threatening."

The figure dressed in black with a white shirt showing under his jacket, straightened up, slamming his sword into its scabbard and peered at Tinker, one eyebrow shooting straight up. "Highness, it do seem we do be together still."

The remaining figure, all in white, danced and giggled, a broad smile splitting his face. "By all that's holy, Sire, we do indeed do still together be." He waved one hand, the sword tip scratched a gouge across the ceiling. "Ooops. Your pardon, Sire. If thee mayhap scrape fondlin' sister from chest praps thee couldst tell us where rest of The Company do be a'lodged?"

Tinker laughed. "All right, all right, everyone relax. Goose, Toucan, Chicken, come into the living room. We'll talk." He started to head that way. "Chen, perhaps a pot of tea would help."

Chen turned back into the kitchen, they went into the living room.

Tinker flopped into his favorite chair. Chicken sat on the floor, leaning against his legs, one arm wrapped around them. Toucan and Goose sat on one of the couches and waited. In a few moments, Chen entered and served the tea.

Tinker cleared his throat. "I am not sure where to start. It has been a year since I left this place. I just returned."

Toucan's eyebrows shot up, Goose lost his smile. Chicken's arms tightened around his legs. She looked up at his face.

"Surprised? Well, you're not half as surprised as I am to find you all back again. Changed back again." He stopped and swallowed heavily. And turned his head to stare out the window.

Toucan finally broke the silence. "Highness, where do be the rest?"

Tinker's head snapped back. "It was The Thought's promise. He said that we would all be returned to our own worlds when we had finished his quest. We were scattered all over the universes of time and place. From what I could tell, there . . . at . . . the . . . end, everyone went back to their homes. The rest came with me. But . . . you were all . . . toys again."

He faced the window again, they could barely hear his whispered words. "I had lost everyone." He frowned and growled, "I think that somehow Dram was responsible for that."

Slowly he turned back and tried a weak smile, blinking away the tears. "It is time for introductions. Master Chen, this is Prince Toucan, Prince Goose, and The Princess Chicken, who, as it turns out, is my Queen, ummmm, my, ah, consort, eh, wife, ummm, so to speak. And, this is Master Adam Liu Chen, my good friend. And my most wise teacher."

Chen refilled their cups and sank gently to the floor, legs tucked underneath, his position one of total attention. He smiled at their three visitors, especially at Chicken.

Tinker looked at him. "Perhaps, I ought to tell you about them. And how they came to be. Then I think we ought to address ourselves to whatever might be going on." He looked at each of them in turn. Each head nodded.

"O.K., it all started this way. There I was, sitting right here, early in the morning, sipping my cup of coffee and then . . ."

Tinker related all his adventures. Chen sat immobile, giving no sign of emotion or excitement as the strange tale unfolded. Goose, Toucan, and Chicken relaxed at the familiar telling of the tale of their past quest, and looked curiously around the room and at Master Chen.

They finished the pot of tea.

". . . so there I was. Back home. Everyone was scattered to the winds. And you were toys again. And I was empty, almost broken."

Then he narrated his past year. And his study of the darker side of the martial arts.

"It kept me sane. And I found that I could finally handle the loss. So, I returned, and here I am. Then, suddenly, there you are." Tinker looked at Chen. "So, now you know."

Then he looked at the others. "Did you know you were toys, again?"

Toucan spoke for them. "No, Highness, we do not. All we do know be that one step in and one step out from some great height into what, as we do know now, do be thy dining room. Untangled we from some bodily heap and thy servant do flash magical light pon one and all, holding wooden implement in most threatening manner. We do have nary idea one, as to place, nor time, nor where all but us had disappeared. One moment we t'were bout to fight free, then thee didst appear. Knowest why we do return so?"

Tinker shook his head. "Not a clue, Toucan. But I don't really care. You are here and that is just fine. Welcome to my world, welcome to my home." His hand held Chicken's shoulder tightly. Her hand reached up and covered his.

Chen rose. "Perhaps it would be best if we placed the rest of them in the dojo. That way, if they should happen to return, they won't destroy the house, especially the stegosaurus."

Tinker grinned. "Right, Chen, let's do it." He looked at his three companions. "I wonder why just you three and not the rest?"

Toucan shook his head. "Tis a puzzlement, Highness. Think thee that strange quest still be on? That we do be not done?"

"I have no idea. And I do not want to know. I am home, you are home. Come on, let's put the rest of them out of harm's way."

He stood, pulling Chicken up with him. "Princess, I thought that I had lost you forever. It has been a long and hard year . . . without you. And Smoke."

Toucan and Chen walked around them, pulling Goose along.

Her fingers traced across his face. "Oh, My Lord, tis true. Deep lines do We see where fore this there were naught. For Us, t'was but most fleeting a'moment. Thee do vanish and we three do then stand in strange place, angered at our loss. Thy year was but a quickly passing thing. Tis most unpleasant knowing that which thou hast just narrated."

Tinker yanked her close, and thought, at least I am two-thirds complete.

Yes, JohnLove, We be that. We do also feel loss of Great Smoke deeply.

"What? That still works, we are still merged? Mind to mind?"

Truly. Smoke's fair gift holds true.

Well, then, give us a welcoming kiss, My Princess. She did. Their minds fusing, sharing, joining, and parting again.

"NEPHEW," commanded Chen, "if you would come in here so we can get on with our business."

"Huh? Oh, right, Chen, be right there." He kissed the end of her nose. "Shall we join the others? When it gets light I'll take you on a tour of the place. It ain't much, but it's all mine. And your's. I wonder what is next, strange things happen in threes, do they not?"

Chicken's brow furrowed. "What strange things, My Lord?"

"Oh, just some crazy stories I heard this afternoon on the way home. About events in town. I'll tell them to you over breakfast." He gave her an exaggerated wink and leer.

"Say, My Dear, have you ever slept on a water bed?" It was Tinker as W.C. Fields.

Chicken leered back. "Nay, Sweet Prince, never have We done so. Water bed? What manner of device do be a bed constructed from water? And tell me true, be that all one do in such a'device, sleep?"

"Not from, filled. I'll show you after we finish

with business. There is so much to show and tell and share." He hugged her tighter and gave her another long, lingering kiss.

"And there are one or two other things we might do beside sleep."

Chicken slipped her hand inside his pajama top.

"NEPHEW!"

"Coming, Chen, coming" Releasing her, he tried to turn away only to find that she had loosened the tie at his waist. Hastily yanking his bottoms up as they started to fall, he retied the string, then threw an arm around her shoulders."Welcome to my world, Princess." She grinned at him, bright blue eyes sparkling, as they walked into the dining room.

Chen had gathered up the rest of the toys and was waiting, patiently, as always. Goose giggled. Toucan's eyebrow shot straight up. He gave a short, stiff bow.

"Ready?"

"You betcha, Chen. But perhaps we ought to leave a note with them. That way if The Guard or any of the rest return they will know where they are, and where we are." Tinker hurried into the hail and started to rummage around in a closet. "Here." He handed Goose a large roll of paper, then popped back into the closet, returning in a moment with a felt-tip pen and a roll of tape.

"O.K., let's go." He grabbed the paper from Goose and headed for the back door.

Once inside the dojo, the large, double-garage sized practice room, Chen set the toys in the middle of the floor while Tinker wrote a very large note and taped it to the walls.

"There. If they return, they can't miss that. We'll leave the lights on. Keep them from breaking up the place, don't you think?"

"The Guard do be most well behaved, Sire."

"I hope so, Goose. Can they read?"

"I do believe me the Sergeant can, Sire. But probably not the rest. Foot soldiers do tend to come from the lower classes, you know. Generally not awfully well educated, and all that."

"Ummmmmmm, I suppose so. Back to the house, there's a few hours left to this evening, or morning, or whatever, and we could all use some sleep. I suspect."

They trooped from dojo to kitchen.

"Chen would you show Goose and Toucan the extra bedroom." He tugged Chicken by the arm. "Come on, Princess, let me show you the wonders of modern technology."

"Thy magical bed of water, My Lord?"

"No magic involved. But, right. It may have been but a moment for you, but it has been a long year for me."

They walked back down the hall and into his bedroom. Chicken was tugging her shirt loose as the door closed behind them.

Chen led the others further down and opened a door.

"Here you are, gentlemen. Twin beds. The bathroom is down the hall and through there. Good morning."

"Good morning, Master Chen?"

"Yes, Prince Toucan, good morning. The sun will

rise in a few hours. I think John was correct in that. After breakfast we should all have a long talk about all this." Chen bowed and backed from the room.

Goose closed the door and sat on one of the beds, facing his brother. "Well, what think thee?"

"I know not. That oriental person do appear both servant, friend, and teacher to Our Lord Tinker. This Master Chen is a most powerful person, do thee feel not to be so?"

"Toucan, old worrier, this do be land minus demons, monsters, and the ilk. Me'thinks that our fair sister shall soon erase terrible deep lines in Lord Tinker's face. Think you we shall see that pair on the morrow?"

"Praps depends on how magical strange bed of his do truly be."

"Rah'ther." Giggling to himself, Goose flopped back. "Oh, I say, these do be quite comfortable. Do extinguish bright light thing."

"Truly brother, I know not how."

"Well, it do seem a'me that Chen did waggle fingers pon wall causing flame to jump up there. Just near that squarish plate. Just there." Goose pointed.

Toucan touched the switch plate and after a bit found that the lever moved up and down, controlling the ceiling light.

"Fair magical time and place, this." He crawled into bed.

In the living room, Chen sat, staring into the dark, fingering a small carved figurine that hung from a fine, golden chain.

Far Away. In Space. In Time.

He stared into the darkness that was his soul, the night, and his thoughts. And smiled.

Off We Go Again

Grandeville. Tinker's Place.

Bright streams of light poured through the living room windows. Outside the sun had just slipped up over the distant ridge line and was beginning to lighten the valley floor with the soft gold of morning.

In the overstuffed chair a figure yawned and stretched.

Master Chen rose, stretched and walked from the room, down the hall. He stopped at a door and knocked sharply upon it with one knuckle. "Prince Toucan, Prince Goose, it is morning. Breakfast will soon be ready." He walked to the last door in the hall and thumped heavily upon it with the ball of his fist. "NEPHEW! MORNING!"

Something mumbled from the far side. "Ummmmpf? Huh? Oh, Chen, sure. See you in a bit."

Chen passed from the hall and into the kitchen and then outside and over to the dojo. He peered inside. The toys were as they had been left the previous evening. He turned and reentered the house. In the pantry he selected the necessary ingredients and began to prepare breakfast.

Tinker sat up, yawned and stretched. Then he poked at a mound in the blankets and comforter next to himself. It took a number of pokes before it moved and began to make waking sounds. He lifted up one edge and looked inside. "Good morning, sleepy head. What do you think of modern technology, the water bed?"

Bright blue eyes twinkled out at him. "My Lord, this bed of water do be really and truly thing most clever. It do itself undulate in most interesting a'manner. What other wonders do there be here in this thy Verra Own kingdom?"

"How about a two-people shower?"

"Prithee, My Lord, what manner of device be this?"

"Just come with me, pretty thing."

"A thing We do be not." Chicken sat up. "Show Us this device."

"My, my," said Tinker. "Definitely pretty."

Chen heard, from the kitchen, over the sounds of gushing water, someone say, "My Lord, indeed this be a wonder. OHHHH."

After awhile, the water and the noise stopped. Chen finished his preparations and set the table. Toucan and Goose walked in and sat at the dining room table, having walked down the hall and through the kitchen.

Goose grinned at Chen and nudged Toucan. "I say, do thee hear some giggling, gurgling noise as we do pass last door?"

Toucan sipped his coffee. And nodded. "A wondrous brew, this."

Chen set breakfast on the table and brought in the coffee pot. As he took his seat, Tinker and Chicken stepped into the room. Each was wearing a bulky white robe. She had her cuffs rolled back to the elbows. Her eyes sparkled. She passed behind her brothers, ruffling their hair as she did, and took a seat facing Tinker.

"Brothers," she announced. "This land do be one of wonders many. Hast thee tried fair shower closet? Tis most like standing in rain. Thee might have most any temperature thee might wish." Noticing that they were listening, not eating, she added, "Come, let's to breakfast go and after, inspect what other magic Our Lord's lands do offer." She began to scoop sizeable portions of several food items onto her plate.

Tinker stared at her. "You going to eat all that, Princess?"

She nodded. "Indeed, My Lord. Warriors have large appetites." She scooped up a heap of scrambled eggs on her fork, peered at it, and ate it.

"Ummm, yes. Pass the eggs, please."

Goose tittered and did.

When they had finished, Goose volunteered to help Chen clean up. Tinker walked with him into the kitchen and showed him how to operate the dishwasher.

"Oh, I say," called Goose. "Brother, peer here. One do set most be'foul'd plates thus, and clever box do them clean. Most magical."

"Not magic, Goose," said Tinker. "Just a machine." He started down the hall, stopped and turned, and looked back into the kitchen. "We'll dress and take a little tour."

Goose straightened up. "Righto, Sire."

Chicken strode through and wrapped one arm around Tinker's waist, her fingers tugging at the belt looped around his waist. "Brothers, do wait thyselves in fair living room. We do be along . . . soon." And tugged Tinker toward the bedroom.

And some time later, dressed properly for the day, and after handing coats and jackets around, Tinker led them outside and took them on a tour, showing them the garage, the barn, the chicken coop, the orchard and the surrounding fields. Standing out in the first pasture, he pointed at the far edges.

"So, that's it. That's all of it, 1,000 acres, more or less. A small kingdom, but large enough for quiet and privacy. Next door, down there over that way, the land belongs to Doc, a friend of mine. Those are his cattle. Well, what do you want to do next?" He looked at Chicken, Goose, and Toucan.

They shrugged their shoulders and looked noncommittal.

Chen said, "Perhaps it is time to tell you of my visitor. Let's go inside, it is starting to snow again."

They straggled back toward the house, following Chen. Goose charged to one side, kicking through small snow drifts and giggling, "Whoop, whoop, whoop." Snow flew in all directions.

"A silly Goose," mumbled Tinker.

Chicken smiled and whispered back, "Indeed, My Lord, all too true."

Back in the kitchen, Chen slid a number of cups, already filled with cocoa into the microwave. When the bell chimed he handed one to each and led them into the living room and waited until all were seated. He also carried a large steaming pot.

"Nephew," said Chen, resting his cup on the arm of his chair, "this visitor appeared early in the day when you returned. It was young man, about twenty years or so, who knocked gently upon the front door. He was rather large, rather heavyset, and dressed from head to toe in clothes of reddish colors."

"Red?"

Chen nodded. "Yes, all shades of red. He said he wished to speak with you, said he was to give you some messages. I told him you were not here. He said he would tell me the messages and I could tell you, as soon as possible." Chen smiled. "This message was in the form of three sayings. Very Chinese."

"So?"

"The messages were thus spoken:

Evil never dies.

Dangers foreseen are the sooner prevented.

The one cruel fact about heros is that they are made of flesh and blood."

Tinker stared at Chen. "Did this stranger give you a name?"

"A most strange name. He said his name was Silly-All-The-Day. He did not appear to be a Native American."

Tinker grunted. "Sounds like Big Red to me. Except for the age and name." He held up the steaming pot. "Anyone for more hot cocoa?"

"Tis named cocoa?" asked Chicken.

"Yep. Want a marshmallow in it?"

Goose held out his cup. "Whatever they do be, let's have at'em, Sire."

Tinker plopped one into the cup held out by Goose. "There you go."

They sat and sipped, pondering the strange set of messages. Chen set his cup down, reached up and lifted a fine, golden chain from around his neck. A small figurine hung from the chain. He handed the jewelry to Tinker.

"Here, Nephew, wear this around your neck."

Tinker took the chain and looked at it, and the figurine hanging from it. "What is it?"

"It is a dragon. Many years ago I was given this by my teacher, Grandmaster Chen. His instructions were plain and straight forward. 'Wear it; it will protect you.' So now, I pass it on to you with the same instructions. Put it around your neck and leave it there. Always."

Chen smiled at Chicken. "Princess, you will see to it that he follows my instructions?"

"Indeed, Master Chen, IT WILL BE as you say. Do put it on, My Lord."

"O. K., O. K." Tinker held the chain up and peered at the small figurine. "It doesn't appear to show any wear."

"No," stated Chen. "It will not wear. It is special. It is an amulet."

"A what?"

"Amulet, Nephew, amulet." Chen nodded his head, one nod. "I see that it is time for a short lesson." He took a sip of his cocoa, and began.

"The word *amulet* comes from the Latin word amuletum, which has variously been considered to mean charm, talisman, or amulet. An amuletum is worn to ward off evil. Often, however, it is a protecting charm against whatever one needs to be protected against." He took the chain from Tinker, held it and slowly swung it back and forth.

"We might consider this a talisman. SIT BACK, NEPHEW! And don't interrupt."

He looked at Chicken. "The virtue of a talisman is derived from four facts: One, the time of its creation; Two, the material from which it is made; Three, the figure which it portrays; and, Four, the inscription written upon it. For this small thing, we can say that it is very, very old; that it is made of silver even though it appears to be made of gold; that the figure is a dragon, the name of one of the original martial arts, and one of the four mythological beasts; and that the inscription stands for strength and wisdom."

Chen held out his cup, Tinker refilled it. "One final point to be made and then this mini-lecture is over. This small thing is a Chinese dragon which is quite different than your European dragons. Chinese dragons tend to be beautiful, friendly, and wise. They have often been described as having the head of a camel, ears like cows, a neck like a snake, belly like a frog, scales like a carp, claws like an eagle, paws like a tiger, and having whiskers on either side of the mouth. They breath clouds rather than fire. Their voices are musical. And, most importantly, they control the forces of nature."

He gestured at Tinker with the hand not holding the cup. The amulet swayed back and forth. "As you know, there is a saying that relates to the dragon style. Now that you will be wearing this dragon, I will repeat it. This way you will remember.

Control yourself, let others do what they will.

This does not mean that you are weak.
Control your heart, obey the principles of life.
This does not mean that others are stronger."

Chen stood, handed the amulet to Tinker, and gestured. "Come. It is time to practice. The others may relax and wait for our visitor to return." He started toward the kitchen and the dojo, and stopped. "One more thing. The dragon has green eyes."

"Green eyes?"

"Yes. Jade green." Chen headed off, Tinker following. Over his shoulder, Tinker said, "See you in a couple hours or so."

Three hours later they returned. Chen appeared unruffled. Tinker's eyes sparkled. One cheek glowed red under a slightly puffy eye. The chain was still around his neck.

Chicken leaped to her feet. "My Lord, thee hast been injured." She glared at Chen.

Tinker smiled. "A slight error on my part. So, what have you been doing while we worked out?"

"Little. Sitting here. Drinking fair beverage with white globes."

"White globes?"

"Marsh mallows, Sire," stated Goose.

"Indeed," said Chicken. "They do be most tasty."

Tasty.

"As I said, My Lord."

"Did you hear that, Princess?"

"Most assuredly. Thee did say tasty. And We did Us so agree."

"I didn't say that."

"We did. Just this past instance."

"It was mindtalk."

T'was?

Yes, Princess, it was. Didn't you hear it?

Oh Aye, Sweet Prince.

Tinker looked at Goose and Toucan, who were watching the two of them stare at each other. "What have you guys been doing?"

"Reading, Highness. I have been reading something called 'The Second World War'."

"Which book?"

"This one, by a chap named Lidell-Hart. Brother Goose and I do discuss maneuver called panzerblitz."

"Aye, Sire. Quite reminds me when mighty Guard do charge." Goose stood and stepped to the window, looking outside. "Wind do be a'blowin' rather strong. Snow do be a'driftin'."

Someone thumped upon the front door. Chen hurried to see who the visitor might be. Then he ushered the someone into the living room. "Nephew, this is the person from before. This is," he waved his visitor forward with a quick jerk of his arm, "Silly-All-The-Day. As you can see, he does not appear to be a Native American."

Their visitor stood and stared from face to face. He knocked some snow from his shoulders. All his clothes were red, various shades of red. Even his hair. He wore an alpine hat with one long feather protruding at a rakish angle. It was red.

Tinker leaped up and gasped. "Big Red, what are you doing here?"

The figure smiled and bowed. "I am not Big Red, John Tinker. I am his son, named as you heard, Silly-All-The-Day. My father sent me and his greeting." He smiled at each of the others in turn. "These must be the noble companions of whom I have heard." He nodded at Master Chen. "We have already met."

Silly looked at Tinker. "Are you ready to go?"

Tinker's jaw dropped. "What?" He pointed at a vacant chair. "Maybe you had better sit down and explain your last statement." He grabbed his chair and pushed it around to face Silly who was sitting down as directed, a puzzled expression on his face.

Chicken walked around and stood behind Tinker, her hands resting lightly upon his shoulders. Toucan and Goose eyed their swords which were leaning in a nearby corner of the room. Chen settled himself on the couch and watched everyone.

Silly leaned forward, his arms on his knees. "Did you not receive my father's messages?"

"Sure. So what?"

"SO WHAT?" Silly bounced back in his chair. Chicken's fingers dug into Tinker's shoulders. "You must be ready to depart." He sighed. "I can tell that you're not. Why aren't you? I am the last of the three messengers."

"No, you're not, you are the first."

"The other's haven't arrived? Yet?"

"Nope." Tinker stared at him. "You really Big Red's son?"

"I am."

"Prove it."

"I cannot do that. I don't have any of his

capabilities. He is unique."

"Then how do we know you are really who you claim to be?"

Silly smiled and relaxed back in his chair. "My father said to say to you this. You are The Chosen One of Legend. And that when you arrive on Paradise he would furnish you a loaf of bread and a jug of wine. You would have to do the singing. Does that answer your question?"

"Yes."

"May I ask a favor?"

"Ask away."

"May I stay here. My magical father neglected to provide me with the means to secure either food or shelter and your land is most uncomfortable to one used to Paradise."

"Where have you been?"

"Outside, just wandering back and forth, waiting to talk to you."

"In this weather?"

"He, ahhhhh, took care of that. Somewhat."

"Stay. We're eating soon. Anything else?"

"Call me Silly, my parents do. And hurry please, we were supposed to be leaving as soon as my message was delivered."

"Relax, Silly, we'll decide about that. If we decide." Tinker turned his head and asked, "Well gang, any ideas? Those messages seem to mean us. I suppose we were the heroes last time. And we are certainly flesh and blood."

Goose shrugged his shoulders. "For this moment, Sire, for this moment."

"Right. Let's hope it's permanent."

"Hear, hear, Sire. Hear, hear." Goose beamed.

"Any ideas? Anyone?"

"My Lord?"

"Princess?"

"First message forebodes no good. We all do see foul Dram blasted down deep crater and disappear. We do fear Us his first message, "evil never dies," do be most clear. Dram, The Evil One, do be still alive."

Toucan nodded. "Indeed, Highness, Dram do live still. Second message, "dangers foreseen are the sooner prevented," do suggest quest do be on again and Big Red do himself summon us forth."

Tinker jumped up and began to pace back and forth. "Damn, damn, damn. So we're to be the pigeons again, is that it?"

"Pigeons, Highness?"

Chen lightly touched Toucan's arm. "What my student wishes to say is that he doesn't want to be treated as a simpleton or a dupe."

Tinker spun around and glared at Silly. "Right. Let's eat, I'm hungry."

Chen stood and nodded. "In one hour. A good meal cannot be rushed." He beckoned with one finger. "Silly will help." He headed for the kitchen, Silly followed.

Goose walked over and grabbed the three swords. "Sire, I do feel me'self there might be a'need such." He buckled on his and handed the others to Chicken and Toucan.

Tinker sighed. "If you wish." He pointed at the far corner. "But I'm leaving that thing where it is." The great black sword hummed softly, just loud enough for them to hear it. The jewel set in the hilt began to pulsate.

"Now what?" Tinker frowned. "I'm beginning to think that Big Red is playing tricks with us. Again. Well, he is in for a big surprise. I am staying home." He threw his arm around Chicken's waist. She could feel his resolve in the tension in his body.

Goose smiled. "As thee do command, Sire. Minus The Guard we do be most sadly manned should most foul demons pounce. Think thee not Brother?"

Toucan nodded. "Quite right, quite right. We do need rest and quiet." He looked at Tinker. "Highness, t'was but a day since we did leave Dram's foul world. We might fair use peace and solitude. Brother Goose do speak true, tis better for to stay in castle a'resting."

He smiled at Chicken. "Mine Noble Sister Queen do quite agree."

Chicken slipped her arm around Tinker's back. "Aye, Brothers, tis so. Enough of Big Red plots." She kissed Tinker's cheek. "My Lord, We would, Ourself, outside go for but some fleeting moment for to weather watch, then to dinner a'go." She turned and hurried outside, her left hand clenching the hilt of her sword.

Tinker flopped into his chair and stared into somewhere. Goose and Toucan exchanged guarded looks. Goose wrapped his arm around Toucan's shoulders and drew him over to face out one of the picture windows. "Tis mighty storm, Brother."

When Tinker stepped into the dining room to set the table, Goose whispered to his brother, "It do pear a'me that our Most Noble and Headstrong Sister do have fair back up pon somethin'. Share you mine suspicion that some other visitor do be a'lurkin' outside and she do just now charge into the fray?"

Toucan nodded. "Indeed, Brother. Mayhap thee might slip through kitchen whilst I do same from here under sly pretense of gathering wood for fire. We might thus check these grounds. Given her mood, silent visitor wilt become sliced meat err she do think for to raise them fair question as to intent. Let us away fore Our Lord do realize what's a'wind."

"Righto." Goose turned and walked into the dining room. "Sire, I do think to pop off to kitchen and see how things be a'doin'."

"What? Oh, sure. But don't get in Chen's way. He gets testy when he's cooking."

Tinker finished setting the table and wandered back into the living room deep in thought.

He didn't notice that Toucan had gone. He stood and looked down at the great black sword resting in one corner of the living room, his face bathed in the flickering yellow light pulsating from the golden jewel set in the hilt. Absentmindedly he began to brush away the dust and cob webs that coated the weaponkin. And began to worry, deep down inside.

"HIST! Toucan, here."

"Ah, there thee be. Whither our Sister?"

"Yonder. See. Boot prints do lead toward dark barn. Might it not be well do we her back for to guard?"

"Indeed."

They drifted silently through the swirling snow toward the barn. Ahead they could see the vague shape of Chicken as she eased herself into the lee side of the structure, sword blade glittering in the moon light. Blackness unfolded from a dense shadow between a snow drift forming along the barn wall and wrapped itself around her. She disappeared without a sound.

"Quickly, Brother." The sword hissed into Goose's hand as he charged forward.

Toucan raced behind him, guarding his back. They ran to the spot where Chicken had been, stared and started searching for some sign of her.

A curt voice froze them in place. "DESIST! Both!" Chicken stepped from a shadow mass and glared at them. "We do believe not that We do gently a'you ask for thy company, Brothers."

"Tis true, Sister Queen, thee do not," answered Goose. "We do feel, we do, that three do be some better than one pon investigatin' whatever do lurk outside. So, here we do be. What do be this stuff?" He waggled one arm loosely at the blackness.

Chicken tapped the pommel of her sword on his chest. "Recognize thee not fair companion of our past?"

"Fraid not, Sister, fraid not? Of what companion do thee speak?"

"Brothers, do take thy selves most wide-eyed a'look. Show thyself, please."

The darkness unwound and a great shape flowed silently over to them. A large dog-like face peered down at them over Chicken's shoulder, great rabbit ears standing vertical. The upper canines, protruding well below the lower jaws, gleamed white.

"Tis The Lady Smoke," gasped Goose.

"Larger than before," observed Toucan drily.

"But how be this possible? Sister, speak."

"Brother, tis strange fact but true that in her place time do pass more than two years since last we do see her. Now she do be most grown, most fully grown. It seems a'us, it do, t'will great fair surprise do be for Our Lord Tinker, think thee not?"

Toucan nodded.

Goose giggled. "A mighty surprise, indeed."

Toucan frowned. "Surprise indeed, but message not pleasing to receive."

She frowned back at him. "How so?"

"Sister Mine, it does pear to me that we do be but reassembled for some purpose yet unexplained. And that strange purpose do be that which Our Lord do not wish and do resist a'doing. Come, let us to hall return, back to warmth and comfort." Toucan spun on his heels and headed back toward the house. Chicken and Goose followed. Behind them padded the silent blackness of Smoke.

"Brother," said Chicken at Toucan's back. "It do seem a'Us t'would be least unsettling do our guest but wait till after this evening's meal err do she present herself. Think you not?"

"Most well bespoke. Good meal, warming libation, then t'will be time enough for surprises. What do Lady Smoke think?"

"She will wait pon front porch," stated Chicken.

Four entered the porch. Three entered the living room. Chen called from the dining room. "Just in time. Sit up, sit up. The meat is quite tender, the vegetables rendered harmless. You won't need your weapons."

Sheepishly smiling, the three unbuckled their

swords and leaned them against the wall. Chicken bowed toward Tinker. "After thee, Me'Lord." They joined Chen and Silly who had already taken places. Chen urged them to help themselves.

"Oh, I say, it do all look most frightfully good." Goose reached out and began to heap his plate. Laughing with him, the rest joined in. Every once in a while, Chen would glance over at the outside window.

Finally Tinker asked. "What's up? That's the fourth or fifth time I've seen you do that."

"I feel something out there. But I haven't seen anything nor have I heard a sound. Perhaps I should just give it a check."

Before Chen could rise, Goose dropped a hand on his shoulder. "Tis but wind's mischief and nothin' more. Eat hearty, Master Chen, fret yourself not!"

Chen glanced at Goose and felt the heavy downward pressure of his hand. He smiled at Tinker. "It is probably as Prince Goose says, Nephew, only the storm. Who is ready for dessert?"

Goose smiled. Chen brought it in. The conversation wandered from topic to topic. Goose had a second serving, complimented Chen on everything served and asked what it was that they had just eaten.

"Prince Goose, this confection is called a *Black Forest Cake.* This is a somewhat different version than the norm as I make more layers, but thinner. There is one, small piece left. Please get rid of it."

Goose rolled his eyes and glanced around the table. Chicken smiled at his obvious desire and shoved the cake plate toward him.

"Eat hardy, Brother." She laughed.

"Indeed. Truly of all great wonders of this your land, Sire, me'thinks this do be one of the greatest." He began to eat the remaining portion of the cake.

Tinker glanced around the table. "As soon as Goose is done, what say we all retire to the living room. We can decide what we're going to do, or not do. O.K.? I'll bring the brandy. After that meal, it is the appropriate thing to have." He rose and went into the living room, fetching the brandy and glasses from a cabinet. Each of them settled in what was becoming their favorite spot. They sat quietly, sipping and listening to the stove mutter to itself. And the house creaking in response.

"My Lord?"

"Princess?"

"We do yet another visitor have."

"We do?"

"Indeed."

Chen flashed a glance at the front porch.

Tinker caught it. "Ahhhhhhhh, and why do we keep this guest on the front porch?"

"We felt, we do, Goose, Toucan, and Ourself, t'would do be best till after we do sup."

"Well, we have."

Chicken rose, strode across the room and threw open the outer door.

Tinker saw Chen set himself as he swung his head toward the door.

MindMate, how have you been?

Tinker sprang to his feet, joy, surprise, and puzzlement racing across his face. "**SMOKE!**"

Yes.

"It was you that I thought I heard earlier."

Yes. I have been searching for you for some time.

"For some lime?"

Yes.

She flowed through the open door, filling the space as she slipped inside. Chicken shut the door behind her, watching that Smoke's tail cleared first.

"You frightened Choo-Choo?"

Yes. A very strange person. I felt sure that he hadn't seen me, but he caught a glimpse.

"Just a shadow. You're larger, aren't you. Come on, into the center of the room where we can all see you."

She padded silently into the space indicated, occupying it. A great, catlike form, covered in soft, black fur that absorbed rather than reflected the light. Her shoulders were now almost even with the top of his head. She dropped her head down, the long rabbit-like ears folding back, avoiding the ceiling.

Speak to me.

Are you still growing?

Not now. Now I am almost fully grown. Before, I was still somewhat of a . . . kitten. It has been what you would call two years since we parted.

"Not for me, it hasn't, only one. And for the rest, no time at all."

Chicken told me of that. You feel well.

"I am now, having you and Chicken back together makes me feel, ummm, complete again. But two years?"

Remember what the red magician said. Time runs at different rates in the various times and places. She gently flowed though his mind, carefully checking.

He sighed. "Right. We were thrown all over the place. Everyone sent home."

Toucan and Goose ignored the strange conversation as they could only hear the parts spoken out loud by Tinker. Chicken listened to everything, glad to still have the ability that had been impressed upon her by Smoke when they were in Dram's world.

The portal appeared one day as we slipped through the forest. I vested my sister, who now heads the Velvetmist again, and stepped through. Here I am. It did take some time to find you.

Hungry?

No, I found some large and tasty things in your forests. Introduce me to Master Chen.

Tinker turned to face Chen who was leaning back in his chair watching the play of emotions on Tinker's and Chicken's faces.

"Master Chen, this is Smoke, of The Velvetmist."

Chen nodded. "She is formidable."

Tinker laughed. "Right, she surely is. Before she was large, now look at her. Smoke, lie down, I can't see anyone with you in the way." He sat in his favorite chair.

Smoke settled and propped her head upon one chair arm rest, her ears rising straight up. Chicken sat on the other arm rest and threw an arm around his shoulders. Smoke's long, prehensile tail rose lazily and curled over his back and over Chicken's shoulders.

Tinker sighed. "It seems Big Red is up to something. He is trying to suck us in again. Last time no-one had a choice, now we do. Silly, say something.

What do you think?"

"I can add little beyond what I have already told you. Smoke is one of the messages. I don't know what the other one is. I didn't even know she was, but she must be."

Tinker stared at the golden eyes, the vertical pupils narrowed in the light of the room. "You are a message?"

I suppose. But all I did was step through the portal. My presence must be the message.

"He is being cryptic as all hell isn't he?" Now he was really beginning to worry,

Something scratched at the front door.

"Now what?" asked Tinker.

Goose jumped up. "I will see to it, Sire." They heard the door open and a startled yell. "**YOWP**! Watch it, Sire, tis headed in thy direction."

A large boulder shot into the living room. In one fluid motion, Smoke rose, batted the thing into the dining room and bounded after it.

Smoke, get out of the way.

"Chen, through the hall, around through the kitchen."

Tinker leaped for the corner and grabbed up his great sword and ran for the dining room.

Behind him he heard swords slithering from scabbards as the others armed themselves and charged after him. Tinker jolted to a halt almost causing a pileup behind himself.

"Watch it, Toucan."

"Do be most careful My Lord," said Chicken at his back.

The boulder sat almost in the doorway to the kitchen. From that side Chen drifted lightly toward it holding a metal tenderizing mallet. Smoke stood in range, one paw lifted, ready to strike, ebony claws out.

The boulder crackled, thin lines appeared on the outside and widened. Four crystal eyes peered at them.

It lifted up and walked toward them.

"Careful, Highness." Toucan was sidling around the dining room table, approaching the creature from the side.

It walked up to Tinker and stopped, just beyond the tip of the great sword he held pointing at it. The sword was humming softly. It was beginning to take control, ready to begin killing things

A crackling voice spoke. "Greetings, Strange Creature. I am Quartzeye. We bear a message from the Gett-tda for The Chosen One, John Tinker, sometimes called Lord. Which of you is that one?"

"You are Quartzeye the Gett who traveled with Mountain?" asked Tinker.

"We are related. Can you give us aid, Strange Creature?"

"Sure. I'm John Tinker. What do you want?"

"To give you a message."

"Give it."

"The message is this.

> From the Gett'tda to the Mountain who was Gettish,
> And to The Chosen One, John Tinker, called Lord.
> Greetings, Strange Creatures.

The Sand Trells are crying.
May your way be clear."

The four eyes snapped shut. With an audible thump the Gett dropped to the floor.

"That's the message? Quartzeye. HEY, Quartzeye." Tinker bent forward, frowning at the Gett.

Toucan nudged it with his foot. Then he bent over and peered at it. He rapped its shell with one knuckle. "Pears to have died, Highness."

"Dead?"

"Seems so."

Sleeping.

"Huh?"

"Pardon, Highness?"

Sleeping, MindMate. Remember what Mountain said. The Gett sleep from sunset to sunrise. Somehow this one managed to stay awake in order to deliver its message. This must be the second messenger.

"Some message, some messenger," grumbled Tinker as he stalked off, into the living room. "Sleeping," he mumbled at Toucan. He leaned his weaponkin back in the corner, and flopped into a chair, listening to the stove mutter. The rest trailed in and settled themselves, watching him.

Tinker glared at Silly. "Your old man has a sense of the dramatic that borders on the grotesque. You know that?"

"Yes. I do." Silly squirmed in his chair. "What shall I tell him?" He wasn't sure what to do.

"Tell him?"

"Yes."

"When are you going to see him?"

"Tomorrow."

"TOMORROW!" Tinker stood up. "How?"

Silly jerked back deeper into his chair. "He told me that the portal would appear in the morning of the day after the last messenger arrived.

He also said to say, 'Welcome to Paradise.' And that a loaf of bread and a jug of wine would await your pleasure. That is the last of the messages, Lord Tinker." Silly sank lower in his chair. "Oh, I already told you that." He blushed.

Tinker scanned the other faces watching him. "Well gang, it seems that it is decision time. I, for one, am not interested in whatever it is that Big Red wants. On that last jaunt, I had no choice, this time I do. So I choose . . . NO!" One hand stroked Smoke's fur as she sat next to him, the other hand had possessively intertwined with Chicken's as she stood by the other side of his chair.

Goose glanced up over the top of the brandy snifter which he had just refilled.

"Where ever you do lead, Sire, where ever. But, this do be most pleasant a'place. Toucan?"

"Brother Goose, as thee do say. Although there might be some obligation toward the Red Magician. He do be, ultimately, responsible for our becoming sapient beings. Yet we do be gift to Our Lord. Still . . . We do be most able for to make choices."

Tinker smiled. "You may always do as you wish, all of you. You are free agents. I, ahhhhh, release you from your obligations." He looked at Goose. "What do you think?"

"Always t'were great worrier t'was Toucan. I do suppose, I do, we ought go. We do have great experience at this sort of thing, you know. Poppin' here and there, slayin' monsters, and all that. Jolly good fun, pip pip, and tally ho."

"So, we should go?"

"If thee do so command, Sire, it will be done. Rather difficult minus The Guard though. Sister, what say thee?"

"Hard question, Brother. The Lady Smoke, My Lord Tinker, and we do be, once again, one mind and one soul. Being pulled asunder do strike Us as most unpleasant. Smoke?"

You know as I know, as we know. One being, three minds. But if that evil is alive, perhaps we have a duty to finish. My adjustment to separation was hard also. She held from them the raw feelings of pain and anguish she had felt and the terror of the struggle to remain sane.

Tinker stood, and sighed, "Settled, we go in the morning."

He looked at Toucan and then at Goose. "O. K. We're off, again. In the morning." He paused in the doorway to the hall. "Back in a bit." And disappeared down the hall. Smoke and Chicken both felt and saw the idea that had suddenly sprung into his mind.

Silence filled the space in the room. Smoke thrummed, deep in her chest, a song of comfort only Chicken could hear.

Master Chen stepped over and brushed an errant strand of hair from Chicken's face and watched a silent tear run a jagged course down her cheek.

"Don't cry for John, daughter. He is far more

capable of surviving than even he understands. And will he not have warriors of strange and wonderful capabilities walking at his side? And did I not give him my amulet? And do you not have an obligation, a duty?"

A dark figure slipped into and across the room. "You're absolutely correct, Chen. Obligation, and duty. Goose, gather up the toys. Chen, do we have a strong sack we can put them into? Big Red will either reconstitute them or we won't budge from Paradise. Shall we pack our gear? This time I want to be well prepared." He told them everything that he wanted taken from the several closets in the hall.

"My Lord, tis thy quest attire. And most great quantity of stuff for to take."

"Right. One always dresses for the occasion." He glanced over at the corner. The sword hummed softly. "Looks like everyone was ready to go, but me." He yanked Chicken against his side. "This time we will be prepared. And this time we are not going to get separated, that's another little thing Big Red will have to fix. You, me, Smoke. Together. Always." He leaned his head against her's and gently stroked her hair, and whispered softly. "And that's a promise." Her arms tightened around his waist. He knew that he couldn't take that wrenching of the soul again.

"Sire?"

"Huh? Oh, what?"

"T'others do leave, sayin' they would prepare all necessary gear for the morrow. As thee do seem . . . most lost in thought, I do remain."

"Time to retire, Goose. The hour is late. Princess,

shall we waterbed? Smoke?"

"Indeed, Sire."

I shall stay here and enjoy the heat from the wood stove. The sensenet is cast, none may approach without my knowing.

"By all means, My Lord . . . Johnlove." She pulled him toward the hall. Tinker caught the wide grim on Goose's face as he turned and waved goodnight. "Goose."

Goose giggled. "Your humble servant, Sire." He made a wide sweeping bow.

"Pleasant dreams, My Lord and Lady." He turned to watch the snow blow past the window, stepping around Smoke as he did.

Chen took the cups and the tea pot back to the kitchen. And then helped Silly fix up one of the couches. Silly would have to sleep there.

Sunrise.

Blankets and comforters rose up and leaned sideways

"Morning, me'love." Chicken leaned over and tickled the tip of his nose.

"Mumpf."

"Tis morning, Sweet prince. Tickle, tickle."

"Huh? Princess, don't do. . . GOTCHA." He grabbed her and rolled her onto her side.

"WHAT? OHHHHH. My Lord. . . tis fair morning.. . ohhhhh, most fair a'morning." Her arms wrapped around his chest."Yesssssssss, it is. Turn about . . . is . . . fair . . . play."

"Ummmmmmmmmm, indeed . . . and . . . fair . . . it . . . is."

The large tangle of blankets and comforters resettled itself.

"Methinks tis truly time to rise, My Lord."

"Do you really think so?"

"Indeed, My Lord. All do be a'waiting pon us."

His hand lightly slid here and there, and held her.

"Sweet Prince, do be thee up to no good?"

"Feels pretty good to me."

"Our Verra Own, We do be thy most willing bed wench, yet We do believe we ought prepare ourselves just now for departure."

He kissed her. "S'pose you're right, Princess." Covers and blankets flew in all directions as Tinker thrashed to the surface.

Somewhere under the mound, a voice spoke. "May we not try shower closet again, Our Own Love?"

"Whatever you wish, Princess. After you." He yanked all the bed clothes to the floor.

In the dining room, Goose turned to his brother. "It do sound a'me that soon we shall be joined." He looked into the kitchen and asked, "Master Chen, be there more of these wondrous concoctions?"

"Beer waffles, Prince. With sour cream, brown sugar, and sliced strawberries."

"RIGHTO! I do think me to have some more. Toucan, be thee finished so soon? Where do that young chap get to?"

"Silly betook himself outside for to watch for

strange portal arrival. The Gett await in living room. Ahhhhh, good morn, Highness, Sister." Toucan rose and made a half bow.

Goose beamed at them. "Mornin'. Do try these. Truly wonderful." He thrust a fork with a skewered morsel at Chicken who took the offered foodstuff.

"MY. Tis most delightful. Fair Morn, Toucan, Master Chen." She took a seat and began to attack breakfast with a gusto. Chen beamed and returned to the kitchen.

Tinker ate in silence and finally looked up and glanced around the table, one hand holding his coffee cup. "We ready?"

"Aye, Highness," replied Toucan. "Packs and supplies, well secured, pon front porch do await. Silly do watch for portal. The Gett await just there." He pointed. "Smoke do be outside, a'prowling. We do be most ready."

"Righto, Sire. Into the fray." Goose bounded to his feet. He pointed to an ornate pouch attached to his belt. "Master Chen hast made fine sack for to hold The Guard, Tai, and Two-Byte." A broad smile split his face.

Tinker returned the smile. "Let's relax in the living room until the portal appears."

They did. Chen came in and sat with them.

"I'll tell you all about J. C.'s adventures this past summer when we return,"said Tinker to Chen. "I don't know how long we will be gone"

Chen held up one hand. "Fret not, Nephew. I shall watch over everything until you return. May it be less than a year, this time."

They sat and waited. Chen brought out a fresh

pot of coffee while they idled.

Chicken nestled against Tinker's side and exchanged thoughts with Smoke.

BONG!

Tinker slipped his arm from around Chicken, stood and stretched. "Well, there it is, still chiming."

The portal. Smoke trotted around the corner of the house from the back lawn and sat near their packs, neatly stacked at the end of the front porch.

Heard it.

They walked outside and grabbed the appropriate back pack as assigned to them by Toucan. The Gett clattered across the wooden planks of the porch.

The portal stood in the middle of the driveway. Flames danced over its surface as the fire snakes twined around the edges, roiling and hissing, snapping at snow flakes.

Tinker looked at it. "Looks the same as before. O.K., here is the sequence we'll follow. Silly goes first. Then Quartzeye, Toucan, Smoke, Chicken, and myself. Goose brings up the rear." He turned. "Goodbye Chen, see you whenever."

Chen bowed deeply, both hands clenched to the front of his chest. "Goodbye, Nephew." He stepped back and bowed again, tucked his hands inside his sleeves and bowed to each of the others. And stood and watched. A small, impassive figure.

"Let's go," said Tinker.

Silly stepped through the portal followed by the

Gett and Toucan. Each stepped into the crackling surface and disappeared.

"Chicken, your hand. Smoke, your, ah, tail. This time, no separation." He grabbed Chicken's wrist lightly and clenched Smoke's tail. The length sticking past his fist wrapped itself firmly around his wrist. "Ready?"

"Yes, My Lord."

Yes. MindMates.

They stepped through. Goose waved to Chen and followed.

Without a sound, the portal vanished.

The wind blew snow across the bare patch caused by the device. Chen brushed a few flakes from his clothes, turned and walked back into the house.

Far Away. In Space. In Time.

He nodded to himself. This time, a small pun he thought, it would be different. He would win. And that other bother would lose. It would be a pleasure to watch that happen. A pleasure to feel it happen. A pleasure to make it happen. Here, at the every end of everything.

Certainly A Surprise All Right

Land's Bright. A Sunny and Cold Day.

It hung there.

It just hung there, six feet in the air, flashing colors. Doing nothing.

Someone stepped out and dropped. "What?"

And sank, waist deep.

Into the snow.

He looked around, eyes wide, unbelieving. And turned quickly to stared up at it, the portal.

A large, round, brownish object sailed into space and fell. He caught it in both hands and was driven backward, sprawling in an explosion of white. And screamed, "GO BACK, GO BACK!" Another figure stepped out, into space. "LOOK OUT!" yelled the one lying down as the other dropped into a controlled crouch next to him.

"Silly, what do be you a'doing?"

"LOOK OUT, LOOK OUT!"

Toucan leaped sideways, dragging Silly by one arm. Tinker and Chicken fell, tumbling, held momentarily by his grip on Smoke's tail. Smoke dropped lightly landing on all fours. The three of them disappeared into the snow. The wave of white washed over Toucan as he was bending over to peer at whatever it was that Silly was clenching so desperately.

Goose spilled out, splashed to a landing, giggling wildly. "By George, tis acres of snow."

"MY LORD," shouted Chicken.

"WHAT?" snapped Tinker. "Watch your feet, Smoke. Get off, get off."

The black form sailed into the air and landed in a huff of white shook, she violently, her black fur now a marked contrast to her surroundings.

Tinker surged to his feet. "Now what?" He brushed snow from his clothes and reached down to yank Chicken to her feet.

"My Lord," she gasped. "Do the mighty magician play some foul jest pon us?"

His head jerked here and there as he searched their surroundings. "I don't see that damned portal anywhere. We've been dumped here and I don't think this is some stupid joke of Big Red's. Where's Silly?"

"Highness, he do be here, a'lying in the snow."

Goose waded over and looked down at the prone figure. "Silly, old boy, what clench you so tightly to stomach?"

"It is the Gett," gasped Silly. "This thing is so heavy I can hardly breathe. Help me."

Goose bent and lifted the rock creature. "Most true. A mighty weight do be this Gett."

Tinker shrugged off his pack and began rummaging through one large side pocket. He tossed the roll of material at Toucan. "Spread this out and set the Gett on that." He lifted the top flap of the pack and yanked out a jacket and handed it to Chicken. "Better get our jackets on, this is no Paradise."

Silly flapped at the snow on his clothes, dropped his pack, and began to search for his jacket. "Certainly not!"

"Where are we?" asked Tinker.

"No idea," said Silly. "Never saw this place before."

"Just wonderful," grumbled Tinker. "Smoke?"

Nothing around that I can feel.

Soon everyone was dressed for the climate.

"Most well planned, My Lord," said Chicken, tugging on heavy gloves.

"Yeah. But I never believed we'd use all this stuff. Well, anyone have any feeling as to which way we should go?"

That way. Smoke was staring at a faint point on a far horizon.

Tinker pointed. "There? What is it?"

Toucan stared in the indicated direction. "A tall spire of rock, Highness."

"Only thing here that isn't snow," mumbled Tinker. "Might as well go take a look." He waved one arm. "Spread out, let's look for firmer snow to walk on. Toucan, Silly, see if you can rig a sling, use the tent poles, to carry the Gett."

Hibernating.

"Just what we need, Smoke."

She just smiled. It was all mental, that smile.

Honbakbar. Late Evening.

Abadoda had felt the pulse and ran to the twice guarded room. She quickly activated the viewing pool.

And stared into the image displayed. And gasped. Then, after roiling the liquid and erasing the image, she spun and hurried away.

Land's Bright. Just Another Day.

Tinker sat up with a jolt. "WHAT? . . . Where? Oh." He stared at the tent walls.

"Coffee?" Toucan pushed a steaming cup into his hand. "Highness?"

'Thanks." Tinker shuddered. Crazy dream. He reached over and ruffled Chicken's hair where it was poking from the sleeping bag. "Morning. Time to wake up."

Her head popped out, two blue eyes peered at him, and blinked.

Smoke gently eased upright, sliding Goose to the floor. Her long tail arched over and gently brushed along one of Chicken's cheeks. *Sleep well, Our Lady Chicken?*

Quite well, Our Lady Smoke. And thee, Our Lord?

Rather sleep in the waterbed. For a fleeting moment he thought he caught a furtive, but highly erotic thought, then it was gone. Chicken smiled at him.

"Anything out there?"

As far as I can see, nothing.

"Let's eat and hit the road, in a manner of speaking."

Toucan was preparing something over the small stove. He ladled a portion onto a tin plate and handed it to Tinker. Silly peered over his shoulder.

"Look's good," said Silly.

"Good as might be expected in such a situation,"

mumbled Tinker.

"Tis edible, t'will suffice," said Goose reaching for a plate.

They all moved carefully in the crowded tent space as they ate their meal, such as it was.

Smoke?

I ate shortly before we left your time and place. For some while I will require nothing.

They finished quickly.

Toucan gestured. "Smoke, t'would lick clean these things t'will assist packing."

She obliged.

"Many thanks," said Toucan. "Silly, pull the sleeping Gett outside."

Silly slipped out the entrance tunnel and yanked the stone creature, still wrapped in sheeting, outside.

In a flurry of activity Goose was moving. "Righto, Brother, Sire, everyone out." He began packing their gear and shoving backpacks out the entrance. They helped finish demolishing the tent and distributed the parts, and swung their packs back into place.

"By George, Sire, tis great mountain of snow do grow next by us. A mighty storm do blow, yet I do hear nary a sound so deep do I sleep."

"Well, if there had been a reason to wake, I'm sure Smoke would have roused us."

Of course, mate of my mind.

And mine, My Lord.

Love you both, Ladies, don't argue.

Of course, MindMate.

Of course, My Lord.

They started for their target, still a dot on the far

horizon, walking on the hard packed snow. Smoke led the way wandering back and forth as she sensed where the surface was the most firm.

Goose and Silly carried the Gett in its sling. Toucan walked alongside Smoke. "No need for a rear guard, you know."

Chicken walked at Tinker's side, engaging him in a mental conversation only Smoke could overhear. They were enclosed in a bubble of warmth that emanated from his clothes.

It was an unexpected aspect of his attire, yet another thing they hadn't know before, another thing that hadn't been explained. The last time.

The sunlight reflected brilliant from the snow. White landscape, azure sky. Tinker stopped them and made everyone don ski goggles.

"Sire, what else do be packed away?"

"Everything that there was, Goose. And then some. I threw in stuff for any climate and condition. And I hoped that the packs wouldn't be too heavy. And that we wouldn't have to carry them too far. So we're prepared. Hopefully." He heaved his pack into a slightly different spot. And wondered how far they would be able to carry these loads.

"Hope so, Sire, hope so. Tis ill luck that great Tai do with us travel not. Great beast would easily carry all without strainin' a muscle." He hitched his pack up, just a little.

"Suppose so, Goose. But I don't know how a dinosaur would do in snow country. She might go to sleep like the Gett. Hate to try and carry her."

"Oh, rah'ther, Sire, rah . . . ther."

"See anything, Toucan?"

"No, Highness. Still most far to yon black spot. Look there." He pointed off to one side.

"Where?"

"Just there."

"What is it?"

"Unknown, Highness. Strange."

They walked out to see what it was that Toucan had spotted. And stared at it. First one way, then the other.

"Wow," said Tinker.

"Most whoppin', bloody great trench." Goose walked to the edge and looked up and down its length.

"Certainly looks like one," said Tinker. "But round bottomed."

"My Lord, this thing do stretch itself eight feet wide and from one horizon to other."

"Heads toward our goal. Or it came from there. What do you think, Toucan?"

Toucan was bent over squinting at the hard packed snow. "Passing strange."

A hunter.

What?

A hunter. I can smell it, here in its track. It went ahead of us. But it is beyond.

"Oh boy, just what we need. Something that hunts and is build like a greyhound bus. Time to take a detour, a large detour. Let's go."

They started off at a sharp angle to the path made by the thing, walking much faster than they had been doing. Finally, Smoke turned them back toward their original direction.

And another day passed. Low conversations passed uneventful hiking, up snow dune and down snow dune. Their footsteps crunched counterpoint to their words. When the sun touched the horizon, they made camp. In the distance the black thing had taken on shape and form. It did not appear to be natural. They made dinner, ate, and wiggled and squirmed into comfortable positions inside the tent.

"Do you see any detail yet, Toucan?"

"Nay, Highness. But tis work of sapient creatures. Of some kind."

"Right," grumbled Tinker. "Of some kind. Silly, I sure hope your father realizes we're missing pretty soon and sends that toy of his to fetch us."

Silly nodded. "I'm sure he will. After all, all he has to do is to decide to do it, and it is done. Ah, once he realizes that there is a problem, of course."

"Then what, Silly me'boy."

"Then, Goose, something will turn up to fetch us. To Paradise."

"Rather anxious to see this paradise of your'n, old chap. We ain't been there, you know. Not since we do become, ah, er, reactivated, so to speak, after that portal do scatter one and all hither and yon."

"Not scattered now, Brother. Nor much might we do err we be, either."

"Too true, too true."

"Let's get some sleep," suggested Tinker. "Tomorrow might prove to be interesting."

Comfortable, Princess?

Indeed, Mine Prince. She wiggled against him.

Purrrrrr, purrrrr.

Nonsense, Smoke.

Sleep well, MindMate.

Right. "Light," said Tinker.

Toucan extinguished the candle lamp.

Silence.

The first glimmer of dawn touching their tent wall woke Toucan. He set out the breakfast and crawled outside, out over the lump that was the Gett. He stood, stretched and stared at the tall spire. It was still too far to see details, even in the first light striking it at such a sharp angle. He crawled back inside, shoved the Gett outside, and started the day for the others.

"Tis morning, Highness." He shoved at an inert form.

"Umpf."

"Morning. Here." And pushed a steaming cup into one hand.

Tinker sat up. "Huh? Oh, thanks. Tastes good. Princess?"

Ummmmm, m'lors?

"Morning. Time to rise and shine."

She sat up. "Oh that we could, My Lord." And peered at him through a swath of soft brown hair.

"What?"

"Why, rise and shine." She grinned at him and tossed her hair back.

"Ohhhhh, yes. Well, who knows what this evening may bring."

"A noble thought that. What do be breakfast?"

"Here," said Toucan.

"Do taste good, Brother. Goose, Silly. Eat." It was a Royal command.

"Dare say we ought, Sister, err thy appetite consumes all." Goose served himself and Silly.

During the meal the light banter continued, but Tinker could feel the tension building. Toucan, Goose, and Chicken were warriors and, somehow, felt that their skills would soon be called into action. He noticed that Smoke's muscles would ripple, then one of her ears would twitch.

What?

Not yet. But soon.

"Let's go," said Tinker. They quickly broke camp and shouldered their packs and the Gett.

"Ready?"

"Righto, Sire."

"Yes, Highness."

"Ready, My Lord."

"All set, John Tinker."

"Lead off, Smoke," said Tinker.

It was a silent party, each watching their surroundings, wondering what was out there. And what it would do. And what they could do about it. Chicken fingered the hilt of her sword and glanced at the great black thing that rode on Tinker's back. It was humming softly.

Toucan walked alongside Silly who was glancing nervously from side to side. Toucan looked sideways and placed one hand lightly on Silly's shoulder. "Relax, m'boy, relax."

"Easy for you to say, Prince. You're armed, I'm not."

Toucan waggled the sword hung on his belt. "Would you know how to use it, if I do it a'you give?"

"Not really. Still."

"Tut, tut, still. In the way and most probably underfoot. A good way for injury. You remain with sleeping Gett if anything do happen. Guard it well. Wouldn't want to lose rocky creature, would we? Relax, tension do impede action. If there do action be."

MindMate.

Smoke?

Beings ahead. A herd.

A herd?

Many many.

Do be they friend or foe, Dark Sister?

Can't say.

Chicken walked away from Tinker's side until she judged she had sufficient room to swing her blade. Goose and Toucan noticed immediately.

"Brother, thee do see?"

"Indeed, Goose, I do. Silly, stay with the Gett. And do try and stay with us. We may be moving rapidly."

"What's happening?"

"I know not, yet. Just do as you do be told. Please."

Toucan strode away from the sling bearers. They began to walk just a bit faster, just a bit more aware.

Then everyone stopped and looked at the thing in front of them. It was black and soared straight up, polished surfaces glistening. It reminded Tinker of an office building he had seen in Hollywood. All flat planes, rising from the street. Sterile. Impersonal.

"No windows."

"Indeed, Highness. There do be no openings for to be seen."

"Is it a structure? Or just a big piece of stone?"

"I know not. Where are the builders, if it do be built, of this thing?"

Smoke?

Under the snow, all around us. Tunnels, Chambers. Warmth.

Warmth?

Yes . . . MindMate, they know we're here. They are coming.

Mood?

Curiosity. They don't know what we are.

"Toucan, Goose, Silly, Smoke says we're surrounded by the owners of this thing. They're under the snow. Seem to be watching us. No sudden moves when they appear."

Tinker yanked off a glove, walked over and placed one hand upon the polished surface. Cold, it was cold. Cold as the snow that surrounded them.

"Now that's very strange."

"What, Highness?"

"This thing."

"Indeed, a most unusual object, what with strange pattern and all."

"NO, no. Touch the surface."

"Ummmmmmm, cold."

"Touch Smoke's fur."

"Ah, most warm."

"Right. And they're both black. It's a bright sunny day. This mass of black stone should be soaking up the sun and getting nice and toasty, but it's cold."

"Well, Highness," said Toucan, "praps the locals will speak upon this strangeness. Ah, when they do chose for to appear of course."

Smoke?

All around. Under the snow . . . Here they come.

Fountains of snow boiled into the air all around them. Large white forms floated to the surface, their shape obscured by the clouds of snow drifting down. As it resettled they could see a line of creatures standing and staring at them. They had barrel-shaped bodies covered with thick white fur. Long tails dragged upon the snow. Their legs, ended in large flat feet. The front pair sported large, hooked claws, claws which curled into the hard packed surface they were standing upon. The round heads were flat faced. Six eyes peered out at them. Each pair a different size.

A voice spoke to them. It issued from the closest of the creatures. "Who and what are you? Why have you come here to Land's Bright?"

Tinker took one step toward it. "I am called John Tinker and these," he waved one arm, "are my companions. "We've come to, ah, Land's Bright, by accident."

"We are," said the creature, "the Snojin. You are not of this world, that we can see. Never has your kind been here before. Yet, there must be some relationship between us."

A small bipedal creature stepped from between the legs, from where the voice had been speaking. IT was covered in fur. The top of its head just brushed against the chest fur of the creature looming above it. It approached Tinker and stopped. And shrugged its shoulders. The hood and face covering fell away. A small, human face peered up at him.

Tinker smiled. "Yes, there must be a relationship. We mean you no harm."

The being nodded. "We see that it is so. For that, you are welcome. Welcome to Land's Bright. Come, follow me. Please."

It turned and walked away, the larger creature walking by its side. In front of them the snow cascaded down and away. It was the mouth of a steep tunnel. Tinker followed, beckoning for the rest of The Company to come along. Toucan and Silly hoisted the sling and trailed after their small party. The remaining Snojin jostled and formed a solid mass crowding the tunnel behind these strange visitors. The last few to enter refilled the entrance. The light faded.

"Do not worry, Johntinker." Their guide spoke to him over its shoulder. "That is to keep out the Dunju. We were surprised to find you on the surface when one is nearby. Little survives. We must talk of this later."

With a slight shrug, the creature increased its pace until Tinker found that he had to be in a near jog just to keep up. They spun down and down and down, a long twisting corridor twirling them deeper and deeper below the surface. Faint light seeming to emanate from the walls. The deeper they went the higher the temperature.

Finally the corridor straightened out and became level and true. One sharp turn and they entered a large chamber carved into the black stone which formed walls, floor and ceiling. As they walked into this vast opening, the large bear-like creatures crowded around them, staring with great, round eyes. From between their front legs emerged small beings, clothed in white fur. With quick motions they shed their outer garments, disappeared back between the front legs and returned.

Tinker watched and waited. He was facing a row of small men and women. They reminded him of Sorrowful Mistidings, the Teller of Tales from the Six Lands, his small companion during the last quest.

"This is our home, Johntinker," stated the one who had led them to this place. "And these," he reached up and gently ruffled the dense fur of the creature standing behind him, "are the Snoju."

"We," he bowed, the others followed suit, "are the Rinjin. Collectively we are the Snojin. Each must have the other to survive. From the similarities between our forms, the Rinjin and you, there must be some relationship. The Snoju are puzzled by the great dark one. Their minds have similarities, but vast differences. A matter of size, perhaps. And color. They are puzzled and curious. We might talk of these things later. I will show you and those with you a place to stay. After The Meal we will discuss. This way."

He walked off accompanied by one of the Snoju. Tinker and the rest followed. The rest of the Snojin wandered off on business of their own.

After traversing a number of twisting and curving corridors they were led into a large chamber having only one entrance.

"This is your dom. There are no seals here. No one will enter unless bidden to do so. I will return to take you to The Meal. I am Tenjin. This is Snoten. Call if you have needs unmet." Their guide spun on his heels and left them.

Tinker gestured at the chamber. "Well gang, here we are, out of the open and in our own little room. Comments? Smoke?"

Interesting beings, MindMate. There is a mild mindlink between the Snoju and the Rinjin, much stronger among the Snoju. But not as well developed as The Velvetmist nor as bright as that between the Princess Chicken and you and me. Perhaps it is because they are plant eaters. Different forms, stomach pouches.

Stomach pouches?

The Rinjin fit in them when they are outside.

Tinker laughed. "Human kangaroos. It seems that there are several parallel branches in the universe of times and places. You and the Snoju, the Rinjin and Sorrowful's folks, and those like myself."

You missed one stream.

"I did?"

The great folk.

"Right, Mountain and his ilk."

Dark Sister?

Princess self?

Why do the Rinjin and the Snoju stay so close, always in pairs?

They are symbiontes.

??

Neither can survive without the other. The Snoju do not have the mental faculties of the Rinjin. The Rinjin cannot see the way the Snoju do nor move across this frozen environment with the same ease. They have become a complex organism of pairs, bonding at an earlier age. Tenjin comes.

Tenjin stood at the doorway. "It is time for The Meal." Snoten peered over his shoulder at them. Tenjin beckoned them to follow. They did.

Outside, the corridor was filled and filling with jostling pairs all headed in the same direction. They surged into a large domed chamber filled with ranks of benches and tables.

"Come Johntinker and company, a special place has been made for you." Tenjin led them to a larger table having mounds of pillows heaped along one side. "We sit on these during The Meal," said Tenjin. He plopped down. Snoten settled next to him making soft whuffling sounds. Everywhere in the hail, Tinker could see similar pairs doing the same thing.

After all were settled, after the last stragglers had arrived, the throng quieted down.

The ceiling darkened to a deep blue. The Rinjin began to chant. As their voices rose in volume, the lights faded, the room grew dark. The chanting swelled and boomed. At one edge a faint glow started and gradually worked its way across the ceiling. The chanting ebbed and stopped. A moment of silence, then conversations burst forth, laughter rang out and the food was served.

Toucan leaned toward Tinker. "It appears, Highness, that they all eat the same thing."

"Seems so, Toucan, seems so. Here comes our food."

Three pairs approached their table, placed large bowls down the center of it, and withdrew.

Tinker tugged one over and peered at it and then around the room. "Communal bowls, gang. And this stuff is three-finger."

Chicken frowned. "Three-finger, My Lord?"

"Yes, Princess, take a look at our hosts."

The Rinjin were swirling three fingers through the gelatinous food and popping them into their mouths. The Snoju lapped at theirs with delicate tongues.

Goose unhesitatingly followed suit and grinned. "By George, Sire, tis rather good."

"That's good, Goose."

"Ummmm, quite so, Sire, quite so, some fishy a'tastin' for vegetables." He scooped up more.

Tinker licked at his fingers. "So it is. Oh well, when in Rome . . ."

"Rome, Sire?"

"Do as the Romans do."

"Oh . . . yes . . . I do suppose so." Goose nodded. And swirled his fingers through his food again.

They ate and watched their hosts who seemed to be taking no notice of the strange people in their midst. Little by little, the pairs drifted from the hall until Tinker and his group were almost by themselves. As he licked the last of the food from his fingers, Tinker saw three pair rise and approach their table.

"It was good, Johntinker?"

"Ah . . . it was good, Tenjin."

"Tral. Would you be more comfortable in your dom? Or may we talk here?"

"Here would be fine. Or, where ever you wish."

"Tral. Here, then." Tenjin bowed. His companions followed suit. "We would talk of Dunju outside."

Tinker nodded his head. "O.K., tell us about it."

"We would first have you talk of yourselves, outside."

"Ourselves? Outside?"

Tenjin bobbled his head. "Tral. You are formed as we, but larger. Your colors are different." He waited.

Tinker smiled. "I see. Ummmmm, this might be rather hard to follow. But here goes. We are from another world, actually other worlds, where we are normal sized and, ah, our colors are normal, for us. We are . . . travelers who have had an, ah, accident which put us here. On your world."

He paused. "Of course, it might not have been an accident. For us, at times, it is unclear. Tell us of this Dunju." From their expressions, Tinker couldn't tell whether their hosts believed what he had said, or were merely wondering what sort of crazies they had brought into their home.

"The Dunju is one of many few." Tenjin gestured wide ."It is a great misfortune that one comes here. They feed on everything, but favor Snoju. They will not leave until satiated. Many, many times a stonord is emptied, laid waste. They are fierce, solitary beasts. Whole Snoju are swallowed in one bite. They fly through the world while we can only run."

Tenjin held his arms wide. "It is many times this wide, and many, many times this in length. Great, unhinging jaws that swallow everything into the tunnels of their insides. On the nose, organs to see warm beings."

Tinker held up one hand to stop the flow of words. "Does this thing move on the surface?"

"Sometimes, they do, when in a hurry. They

leave The Trace of Extinction."

Tinker frowned. "A wide furrow of hard packed snow?"

"Tral, sobit! You saw one of these?"

"Yes."

"Why didn't the eater find you?"

Tinker laughed. "Who knows, just lucky I guess."

He looked at his companions. "What do you think?" From their expressions he knew. Nothing.

Then Toucan cleared his throat. "Ahem, Highness, if I might?"

"Sure."

"It does seem to me, Highness, that this creature, this Snoju, ought be gotten rid of err it starts terrorizing our hosts. I do venture me some guess that this do be very thing why strange portal do place us hither." He glanced sideways. "What say you, Brother Goose?"

Goose beamed. "In the before we do reach time and place to find there evil thing that we must treat err portal would take us ever onward. Thus do it seem foul creature must die. And it do seem to me that foul beasty be rahther nasty." He turned toward Tinker. "Sire, I would say, kill it."

Tinker stood. "Probably right. So what can we do about it? Any suggestions?"

Goose gave a quick shake of his head. Toucan's eyes were focused elsewhere, thinking. Chicken frowned. Smoke sat, the tip of her tail ticking quietly. Silly looked embarrassed.

Chicken rose and stood by his side, one arm sliding through his. "My Lord, praps t'would be matter requiring some long thought, um, in our dom?"

Everyone stood.

"Might as well," agreed Tinker. "Tenjin could you lead us back, we have to think about it. Do you have any suggestions?"

Tenjin and his companions leaped to their feet, startled expressions on their faces.

"NO. We have no ideas. We have never been able to rid ourselves of those things. They come, usually many die." He beckoned. "This way."

They followed their hosts. Behind Tinker and Chicken, Toucan and Goose conversed in low tones. Smoke reached out and felt the presence of the Dunju circling, circling.

As Tenjin ushered them into their dom, he asked, "Is there anything I may do to help?"

Tinker shook his head. "Not that I know of, right now. But we'll ask if there is, rest assured of that."

"Tral." Tenjin turned and left.

Tinker flopped onto a mound of pillows. Chicken kicked a few more in place and settled by his side. He stared at the ceiling. "Anyone have any bright ideas? Silly, how about you, you've been awfully quiet?"

Silly lifted one shoulder and let it drop. "No, nary a one. This sort of thing is all new to me. This is more in your line, ah, your lines of work. I am just a messenger, of a sort, from my father. I don't have any experience in slaying monsters."

He slid down into a heap of cushions. "After all, I was born and raised in Paradise. These sorts of things can't happen there, you know." He sat upright. "Of course I'll be glad to do whatever you want." He flashed a quick smile. "It's just that you'll have to tell me what to do, that's all."

Tinker smiled at the ceiling. "Toucan? Goose? Chicken? Smoke?" He poked one foot at the large black form sprawled there. "How about it, Smoke? Some little thing from your carnivorous time and place? Some little tidbit that the Velvetmist used?"

No, nothing. This time/place is too unlike mine. Your time and place has regions similar to this. Is there something that creatures who dwell there utilize in similar situations?

Tinker rolled, shoved and rose to his feet. And began to pace around the dom, mumbling to himself. "Good idea. That might be the trick. Let's see, who lives in ice and snow? Eskimos and that crowd. Now what do I remember about them? Not much, not much. What do they eat? Fish, seals, whales. No help there."

He flopped back into the pillows and rolled sideways, wrapped one arm around Chicken's waist and leered at her. He was W.C. Fields. "Hello, my dear." Then he spun back and lay with his head on Smoke's side, a great fur-covered pillow.

Be my guest, MindMate.

Me also?

Of course, SisterSelf

Chicken rearranged herself alongside Tinker who was staring blankly at the ceiling. Chicken and Smoke watched his mind racing. He was humming softly to himself.

Goose, Toucan, and Silly withdrew to the far side of the dom where they began talking quietly among themselves.

Chicken blew softly in his ear. "What song do

thee hum, Mine Own?"

Tinker muttered, "Ummmmmmm?"

"What song dost thee sing so sweet, My Lord?"

Tinker turned his head and kissed the tip of her nose. "What song is what song, Princess?"

She kissed him back. "Why fair song that just this moment past thee didst hum to thyself."

"Was I humming a song?"

SmokeSister.

Princess?

Show him.

A flood of music poured through his mind.

"Oh, that song."

Chicken gently poked him in the ribs. "Oh, aye, Me'Lord, that one."

Tinker slipped one arm under her shoulders and yanked her close. "I don't really know the name of it, just the melody and some of the words."

She whispered in his ear. "Speak to Us those words." One hand popped a button loose on his shirt and slipped inside.

Smoke's tail gently tickled the side of his face.

Tell me, also.

Tinker laughed. "Caught between the two of you, how could I refuse. It goes something like this:

Tis a gift to be simple;
Tis a gift to be free.
Tis a gift to come down where you ought to be.
And when we find ourselves in the place just right;

T'will be in the valley of love and delight."

Chicken blinked her eyes. "My Lord, tis most pleasing a song. Yet do We feel most deep sadness there within."

Tinker turned his face and stared into those blue pools so carefully watching him. "It is a yearning for home, for the place just right, Princess. It is why I didn't want to come on this quest, or any other, ever again." He stared back at the ceiling, frustration and anger in his voice. "But here we are. Again. And we are stuck here until we take care of this Dunju thing. Damn, DAMN." He jumped to his feet. "Come on, Princess, walk with me. I need to move. And walk off the frustration and worry."

She rolled to her feet and crashed into him, both arms wrapping around his chest. "Fret not, Sweet Prince" She laughed softly. "Praps we might find ourselves some small, empty dom."

Tinker spoke to the others. "Stay here, we are going for a walk." He emphasized the last word and gave her a slight pinch.

"Smoke, keep track of us, please?"

Of course.

He unwrapped Chicken from himself, took one of her hands and started off down the corridor. "I don't know how I get talked into things like this, I ought to have my head examined."

"Thy koff pears most handsome as tis."

He stomped down this corridor, then that one. Chicken matched him stride for stride, casting wary glances from time to time at his head. He muttered to himself. He wasn't going anywhere, just walking off the frustration. They turned into a dead-end.

As he turned around, Chicken shoved him into a corner.

"**OOOF.**"

"Give Us a kiss, Sweet Prince." She leaned against him.

He obeyed.

"UMMMMMMM," hummed Chicken.

Smoke, can you lead us back?

Certainly, MindMate. Whenever you are done abusing her.

I am not abusing her.

Indeed not, Dark Sister. Most friendly. Chicken smiled at him. "Thy orbs do sparkle, My Lord."

"Must be your fault, Princess."

"Most better be," she growled.

Smoke.

MindMate.

Lead us back, please.

They strolled down the corridors, turning right or left, as directed by Smoke, until they stepped back into their dom.

"Thanks, Smoke."

No charge.

"Ho, ho."

A pair of Snojin passed the doorway. As usual the smaller one was walking in front of the larger.

"You know, Princess, the Snoju look just like polar bears. Wonder what the Eskimo would think if they saw one of those? Big surprise, that's what. Bet they would hesitate to take on one of them one with only a knife. If they were smart they'd use one of those spring coils of bone."

"How so, My Lord?"

He tugged her sideways, she bumped against his hip with one of hers, and replied, "Oh, nothing, just talking, that's all."

The dom lights began to fade.

Goose smiled at them. "In the nick of time, Sire. It do appear dark night do come pon us."

"Seems that way, Goose. Maybe we'll have better ideas in the morning."

Tinker sprawled across pillows and Smoke, who heaved and humped into a more comfortable position. Chicken curled against his side, one arm thrown protectively across his chest. "Night, all."

The rest settled into their spots and drifted into sleep.

Honbakbar. Neither Morning Nor Night.

"What?" gasped Natanada, frowned darkly at her Third Rank Sorcerous.

"Most true," stated Abadoda to the First Sorcerous. "Something has brought that one into the elseplaces again."

"With companions?"

Abadoda nodded. "A strange assortment. The female looks bonded." She waggled one hand. "A warrior consort of some sort. His group appears to have acquired a rather large, black, furred beast pet of some unknown type. Larger than the one he was associated with before."

"Did you smell flowers?"

"NO!" The Third Rank Sorcerous violently shook her head. "It was a swift viewing. Too short for the Wood With to become aware of our gaze."

Natanada nodded. "Wait some while before next viewing. I had thought that one's link to our future severed. Something strong has dragged him back."

"Most true." Abadoda cleared her throat.

"What?"

"Has a new elseplace been selected?"

Natanada smiled and stood. "Come look at the selected few and give me your thoughts. But we have no urgency to relocate. Just yet."

Onward

Land's Bright.

Morning came with the slow brightening of their ceiling. Toucan was awake and moving at the first slight change in the light. The rest slowly roused themselves.

"Morning, Highness," said Toucan. "Sleep well?"

"Umpf? Mumpfs, uh?" Tinker stretched and yawned. "Ahhhhhh, ugh. Morning?"

Goose bounded to his feet. "Righto, Sire. Tis dawn." He giggled and swung his arms vigorously. "Time for us a'bein' up and about, doin' things, doin' in things, such as fell Dunju. GAD, t'will be most pleasurable for to be a'bidden adieu to most cold and icy abode of white pon white."

Tinker crawled across the dom and began to rummage in their gear.

"How about we make a cup of coffee before we charge forth to slay monsters?"

Toucan rushed over to take charge. Tinker suggested that he work on the food while the coffee was being made. Toucan nodded. And did.

Chicken rose and stretched, momentarily diverting Tinker from what he was doing.

She strode over and dropped to her knees next to him. "My Lord Ogle Eyes, hast thee some sly plan for this day?"

Tinker had the camp stove heating water. "Yep. Make some coffee." And grumbled at her, "Wasn't ogling anything."

"Pish tosh, Our Love."

He sat back and waited, staring at the water, daring it to not boil.

Eventually the water boiled. Eventually he sat back, sipping carefully from the hot beverage. "Not too bad." And then, after a period of quiet, he said, "O.K., let me tell you all a tale from our last quest. Remember the Land of the Heuden?"

"Oh, aye, Sire," said Goose. "Lord Tremlor, most vile a'beast."

Toucan and Chicken agreed with that statement.

"Right place, wrong event. Remember our housing arrangement in that first place we stopped?"

"Indeed, My Lord." Chicken frowned. "And poor they do be."

Tinker laughed. "At least that's in the past. Smoke, I'll need some help here."

??

"They need to share an experience Sorrowful and I had when we were in our first room, O.K.?"

They will have to sit quietly.

Tinker explained what was about to happen and waited until they all settled down.

"Silly also," he added, nodding at Smoke.

The dom disappeared.

They were all John Tinker, in the Land of the Heuden, in the room he had shared with Sorrowful.

Tinker sat bolt upright in his bed, screams of terror and panic tearing at his eardrums. He saw Sorrowful rolling from his bed, dagger clenched in his hand. He grabbed for Slayer. It was gone. The lights were still on.

In the middle of the room were five figures, five mis-shapen creatures struggling with something and with each other. They were screaming and howling in terror. In their midst a sixth jerked about. The five were struggling with this cental figure, trying desperately to wrest Tinker's sword from it and trying equally hard to get away from the slashing weapon. The being in the middle, hand clenching the sword, screeched as he tried to throw it away.

As the struggling mass staggered back and forth, arms, bits and pieces, dead bodies began to fall. The sword was jumping here and there, whistling through the air.

Tinker and Sorrowful stood and stared, unsure of what to do.

Five dead bodies lay at the feet of the sixth creature. The sword twisted, twitched and with a final jerk plunged deep into the last creature. As it crumpled into the pile, the sword slid free and fell with a dull clang to the gore puddled floor. The room was quiet.

Tinker walked over and reclaimed his weaponkin. He could feel a slight tremor in the hilt. "Now what was that all about, do you suppose?"

"John Tinker, it would appear that those things were in the act of stealing your sword."

"Yes, apparently so. But if so, why didn't they just take it and run? Instead they just squabbled about it here in the room. Dumb?" He prodded one of the bodies with his toe.

"Certainly ugly things. Wonder how we'll find a clean room. I don't think I want to sleep in here with this pile. Wonder what happened?"

"Ah, John Tinker, something I learned that I have not found time to tell you about."

"Yes, Sorrowful, and what might that be?" He sat heavily on the bed.

"Well, it is this way. When Smoke and I were on Growing Deep we spoke to each other utilizing the golden eye set in the hilt of my dagger. You remember my telling you about that, right?"

"So?"

"Well, you know how the contact between minds also produces a kind of merging between individuals. You know, you learn more than you had intended to know, things like that?"

"Yes, yes."

"Well, it seems that with long usage of the golden eye, such as Smoke and I were engaged in, I learned something about another being as well."

"Another being? But there was only Smoke and you. What other being?"

"The dagger, John Tinker, the dagger." He waved it in the air. "My weaponkin. The clue was there all the time but no one saw it. Or rather, heard it. It was all in the name. Weapon kin."

"Weaponkin. Yah, so what?"

"Kin, John Tinker, kin. The term implies a blood relationship. Remember the binding back in the hall with The Thought when we were first given these things, the weaponkin?"

"Yes. The Thought cut our palms and then we grasped the hilts and were bound with our weapons. And so?"

"SO! These things, the weaponkin, are sentient beings permanently linked in a bond of being to that person whose blood they first taste. That is us. You, me, Mountain. Each of us has one of these. These weapons have the ability to take control. You may have noticed how easily they are wielded. How every cut and slash is correct and in the right place. How they fairly dance through combat. Well, that is why. They know what they are doing. In some ways, during combat, you are an extension of them rather than the other way around. The other thing is this. No one can handle them other than their kin. Because of the binding, first blood and all that. They only have one kin, one person, their owner. This pile of carrion is the result."

Tinker jumped up and began to pace. "I almost handed this thing to Princess Chicken so she could look at the jewel in the hilt." He could feel the slight tingling in the hilt, a familiar feel that now took on new meaning.

The dom faded back into existence.

Chicken grasped his arm tightly. "My Lord, tis a most fearful and bewitched thing thee do possess."

"Yes, it is that. But that is how we're going to get rid of the Dunju."

Toucan stood and looked down at Tinker, a very grave look on his face. "Highness, thee hast some plan clever for thy monstrous thing?"

Tinker stood and began to pace back and forth "Not all that monstrous." He patted Toucan on the shoulder as he passed. "But monstrous enough." He nodded his head. "Yep, I have a plan. It came to me this morning as I was waking up. It really was something that I mentioned to Chicken last night but I hadn't got the facts quite right, that's all." He stopped and smiled at them.

"It was as Smoke suggested. How do folk who live in similar environments cope with things. I merely borrowed an idea, that's all. The Eskimo use coiled springs of bone inside balls of fat. The balls freeze solid keeping the coils tight. They let these things be found by hungry wolves, who swallow them whole. Then when the heat from their stomachs softens the fat, the coils spring open and pierce the stomachs, killing the wolves."

He laughed. "That's what we're going to do to the Dunju, attack from the inside. We'll get the Snojin to make a dummy Snoju, put my weaponkin inside, and wait for the Dunju to swallow it whole. And when it does, swish. One dead beastie. Pretty neat, huh?"

Goose bounded to his feet, sloshing coffee every which way. "Oh rahther, Sire, rahther."

Tinker smiled, and wiped some drops from his face. "I think so. Toucan, see if you can gather up our hosts? We'll see what they think of our plan."

Toucan strode out the door, a mixed expression on his face.

"Huh," said Tinker. "He doesn't seem all that pleased."

Goose clapped his free hand on Tinker's shoulder. "Brother Toucan do be most great a'worrier, Sire."

Soon, Toucan returned, trailed by Tenjin and Snoten.

"Quick trip, Brother," observed Goose.

"They do be a'headed this a'way when we do meet."

"Thanks, Toucan." Tinker turned toward their hosts. "Did Toucan tell you what we have thought about doing?"

"We are going to need your help."

Tenjin stared at him. His eyes blinked. "In what ever way we may, Johntinker." His voice dropped to a low, harsh whisper. "You will rid us of this Dunju?"

"Yep, that's the plan," said Tinker. Then he told them the entire idea.

Tenjin bobbed up and down on his toes. "Tral, tral, we can do that. It will be done in less than one period. We leave to start now." He backed from the doorway and ran down the corridor, his large companion clumping at his side.

Tinker beamed. "Well, that's that. Let's eat breakfast, I'm starved. Whatever they fed us last night didn't seem to stick."

So they ate breakfast. And then lolled about, waiting.

It was late in the afternoon when Tenjin reappeared at their doorway. He had several others with him. Tinker beckoned them to come in.

"Johntinker," announced Tenjin, "we are

finished. Would you care to inspect our craft?" He gestured toward the corridor.

Everyone crowded outside the dom and stopped. Facing them was a crowd of Snoju, all staring at their doorway.

Tenjin pointed at the group. "There it is."

Tinker looked at the crowd and then at Tenjin."Where?"

Tenjin gave a wave of his hand. All but one of the Snoju bobbed their heads. "There, that one."

Tinker laughed. "It's perfect. I couldn't tell it from a real one. Now all we have to do is to move it to the surface, put it where you think the Dunju will find it, and stuff it with the proper medicine. Shall we go?"

Toucan dropped a restraining hand on Tinker's shoulder. "One moment, Highness, I do now fear me some small point do be overlooken."

"Oh, what's that?"

Toucan looked steadily at Tinker. "Who do animate thy most fearful weaponkin, Highness?"

Tinker was puzzled. "Animate? What do you mean?"

Toucan hesitated, then spoke. "It do seem to me, Highness, it do, when thee do show of thy adventure in the Land of the Heuden, that in that place some loathsome creature do unwilling supply required animating force for fearful weapon for to do most gory work."

"Ummmm, well, ho." Tinker stood lost in thought. "Ha, I don't know the answer to that. We've never had an occasion to find out before. I suppose we'll find out shortly."

"Ah, Highness, one further point, um, if I may?"

"Sure. What?"

"If these things do be self-animating not, how do we retrieve thy blade, ah, after Dunju does it swallow?"

Tinker slumped against the wall. "Right. Good point . . ." He straightened up. "Well, only one way to do it. I'll hide inside the mockup with Slayer. We'll cut our way out." He whirled around. "Tenjin, you'll have to make that thing capable of holding me inside."

"MY LORD!" Chicken grabbed his arm.

Tenjin looked apologetic. "We can not do that, Johntinker, you are much too large. Even if we could fit you, it still would not work. You do not smell correct. The Dunju would refuse the bait. For all their fierceness they are quite cautious."

Tinker frowned and started back toward their dom. "That takes the cake, then. Back to the drawing board." He turned back and smiled at Tenjin. "Thanks anyway, we'll just have to figure out something else." He spun on his heels and stepped toward the doorway. A small hand touched his hand and stopped him. It was Tenjin.

"There is one other way, Johntinker. We could place one of ourselves inside the bait. We smell correct. And the individual inside would provide this animating force of which you speak."

"NAY!" gasped Chicken.

"Steady, Princess." Tinker looked down at Tenjin. "We can't allow you to do that. As far as we know, the weaponkin doesn't distinguish friend from foe. Anyone who tries to handle it will be killed alongside the Dunju. I don't think we want that to happen." Tinker shrugged.

"We'll just have to figure something else out, that's all." He turned once again toward the dom.

Tenjin's grip still held him. "Johntinker, there is still a way. We will send the lostdead to handle this weapon."

Tinker turned slowly around. "What? What's lostdead?"

Tenjin shook his head sadly. "It is a terrible affliction that sometimes strikes one of our people." He beckoned and spoke softly. "Grynjin, step forward, please."

A young woman with great staring sad eyes stepped forward and looked at Tinker.

Tenjin placed one arm around her shoulders protectively.

"This is Grynjin. She is one of the lostdead. Snogryn was of her. Not many periods ago, a Dunju attacked one outside far off gathering party. Snogryn threw herself between the beast and Grynjin. Grynjin's companions pulled her to safety but Snogryn died. Uneaten. Strangely so. Now the bond is broken. Grynjin is alone. And lostdead. She is alive, but not alive. Her life has no purpose. We knew that for the nonSnoju to be correct one of us would have to be inside. She volunteered. It is her wish to do so. To aid her people. To join Snogryn in the Great Whiteness. To give her life purpose. You may not refuse, Johntinker. No moral creature may refuse her request. IT IS SO! TRAL!" He held her tightly, arms wrapped around her shoulders, and watched Tinker's face.

Smoke?

It seems so, MindMate. When such a bond is broken, usually the other dies. She was too strong. All the pairs watch you. They feel your sadness, our sadness at this. They all silently weep for Grynjin and Snogryn.

For a brief moment Tinker felt their collective sorrow, then Smoke held it away. His shoulders sagged.

"I see. Well then. . . let it be so." Tinker stepped forward and gently tilted Grynjin's face up so he could look into her eyes. "We will do as you wish. But you must do exactly as I say if we are to be successful. Understand?"

Gryjin nodded her head. It seemed to Tinker that some of the misty sadness faded from her eyes.

Tinker turned to his companions. "All right, let's get everything to the surface. Toucan, Goose, Silly, gather up everything, sling the Gett, and head upstairs. Princess, stay with me. Smoke, watch everything."

"Sire, why carry all?"

"Based upon past experience, if we're successful, the portal will appear. We don't want to miss our ride from here, do we?"

"NO, SIRE." Goose clicked his heals together, bowed, trotted away and urged the others to hurry.

Outside, on the hard-packed snow, far from the exit they located the track of the Dunju. After settling the fake Snoju next to the hard packed snow trough, Tinker slid his weaponkin down the throat, hilt first. Next to him, Grynjin prepared to scramble through the stomach pouch into the hollow interior. Tinker placed a restraining hand on her shoulder.

"Remember what I told you. You can't grab that

thing until the Dunju swallows everything whole. At least don't grab it until the Dunju grabs you. Then use both hands and hang on tight."

The small fur clad figure nodded and ducked inside. From the interior he heard a muffled, "Tral."

"Tenjin, we are set. Now what?"

Tenjin pointed back toward the black spire. "We join the others."

As the small group hurried back, Tinker asked, "How will we escape detection? I thought you said that the Dunju has heat-seeking capabilities."

Tenjin rummaged inside one of his outer pockets and produced a grapefruit-sized object. It was colored flat white. It looked like a white grapefruit.

"We will use this. It is a Heatdrain. They are rare and hard to find." He handed the object to Tinker.

Tinker took it, turned it around, noticing that it seemed somewhat cool to the touch, and handed it back. "How does it work?"

Tenjin shrugged. "We do not know that, only that if you possess one the heat from your bodies does not attract the Dunju as long as there are not too many to hide. It all seems to drain into the Heatdrain. But it never gets warmer. Never. It is a treasure. Tral."

They trotted up to the others waiting near the entrance. Chicken, Goose, Toucan and Silly formed a sub-grouping. All their gear was stacked in a neat pile.

"Guess we're ready," said Tinker. They all picked up their packs and slung them on their backs.

Goose and Silly stood at either end of the Gett's sling. Tinker turned toward Tenjin.

"How long before the Dunju appears?"

"Not long, the Snoju feel it approaching." Tenjin placed a comforting hand against his constant companion who was shuffing his feet nervously. Then Tenjin walked a few paces toward their distant lure and placed the Heatdrain on the hard packed snow. He returned and crouched down. Everyone did the same.

Far away they could hear it. A rustling, crunching sound. Then they saw a gout of snow erupting toward them. A head whipped high, held on the end of a long, thin neck.

The mouth opened wide, rows of teeth glistened in the clear air. It turned this way and that way, seeking the prey it felt was near, seeking the warmth of food.

Tenjin chanted. "Came the Dunju. Coming along, it came."

"It looks like a nightmare version of a sea serpent," said Tinker.

"A most bad a'vision that, My Lord." Chicken grabbed Tinker's arm.

Smoke bumped his side. *An evil thing.* Her ears were laid back along her neck, coiled tight, as she stared at the monster slithering along, approaching their decoy.

It flashed forward dipping its great head, jaws flying winder and wider. A fountain of snow erupted, it disappeared.

Another explosion of white and the head towered high, the neck stretched out. In the throat they could see a lump moving downward, propelled by ripples of neck muscle.

The Dunju twisted its head, searching for more, hungering for more.

Suddenly it lurched, shuddered, and began to whip its head from side to side, muscle spasms retching upward, trying to dislodge the thing in its throat. Blood gushed from between the snapping jaws. It screeched, a high-pitched, whistling cry.

A spot in the neck blew open in a geyser of blood which rapidly encircled it in a crimson fountain.

The head tumbled one way, the neck and body flailed and thrashed. A bloody lump flew through the air.

They could hear the teeth clattering in the final death throes of the head.

Tinker started to run forward. "She did it."

"HOLD!" It was a command from Tenjin. Tinker jolted to a halt.

"What?"

"You stay, Johntinker, we go." The pairs of Snojin started toward the gore covered patch of snow. It was a long file, walking with measured step.

An arm slipped around Tinker's waist. "My Lord, think thee she do survive ordeal most fierce?"

He turned and looked into blue eyes glistening with tears. "I don't know, Princess.

"We'll have to wait and see." His voice sounded husky to his ears. "Smoke? How is she?"

I can not tell, her mind was, is, strangely closed. Faint life signs. They will not last.

They watched the Snojin moving around, doing something. Then they turned and began to make the slow journey back. As they approached, they could see that Tenjin carried a slight, limp figure cradled in his arms. He stopped in front of Tinker as the rest but one pair filed down into the deep corridor leading below.

Grynjin had only a few red splotches on her otherwise white furs. Her eyes fluttered and opened to look at Tinker as a faint smile crossed her face. Then they closed.

Tenjin's companion took the slack body from Tenjin and trudged slowly away.

Tenjin reached down and untied a fine cord from around his waist. It trailed out across the snow.

"This is tied to your thing, Johntinker, we would not touch it." He handed the cord to Tinker.

Tinker began to wind in the line. He could feel a weight dragging across the hard snow surface. Then the black sword came sliding into view. He picked it up, detached the cord, and handed the line to Tenjin and flapped the blade up and over. It settled in its usual place, nestled across his back, under the pack, the hilt poking up over his left shoulder.

Tenjin looked up into Tinker's face. "You are truly not of my world. This domic is forever in your debt. Now we must part, for Grynjin is rapidly hurtling toward the Great Whiteness and we must aid her in her passage. Your thing did not touch her."

He trust his hand deep into a outside pocket and shoved a small white object at Tinker.

"A gift for a gift."

Tinker looked at the gift. "I can't take that. How will you survive?"

Tenjin gestured back across the snow. "You have already seen to that. We shall survive until another will be found. A gift may not be denied, Johntinker." He thrust it into Tinker's hand, turned and hurried into the waiting corridor. It closed behind him in a gush of snow.

They stood alone in the quiet of white silence. The black spire towered over them.

Tinker dropped the Heatdrain into a pocket and zipped it shut. "Now we wait."

"Nay, Highness." Toucan pointed back past Tinker's shoulder. Tinker turned.

The portal waited. It began to crackle and buzz as the flames danced over its surface. The fire snakes roiled and hissed around the edges. Spots of color danced across the snow surface.

Tinker laughed. "Prettiest sight I've seen in a while. Let's go. Princess, your hand. Smoke, watch our backs. Everyone ready?" He grabbed Chicken's left wrist. "We're not going to be separated."

As they stepped through, they heard Goose call at their back. "Pray for warmth and sunshine, Sire."

Smoke waited and watched, then stepped after Silly, her tail flicking from side to side.

The portal winked out.

A slight breeze ruffled the light dusting of powder snow sifting over the hard packed surface. Eddy and drift covered their tracks and slowly obscured the stiff carcass and gory patches further out.

It delicately ruffled the fur covering the decoy, the empty husk that had been Snogryn.

The Koran Allots At Least A Third of Paradise To Well-Behaved Women

Surprise, Surprise.

Tinker stepped forth, Chicken at his side. They hastily stepped to one side and looked around.

As he released her wrist, she stepped away and drew her sword.

"Most strange and feral looking a'place this, My Lord."

Toucan appeared, followed by Goose and Silly.

Toucan hurried over, calling, "What Ho, Sister Queen, drawn sword?"

She waggled it at their surroundings.

"Tis most foul and drear a'place do we now a'journey, Brother Mine."

Goose dropped his end of the sling and bounded over, his sword flashing in the air as it passed through the thin shafts of sunlight piercing the dense foliage overhead.

"By George, Sire, this do be most savage a'woods. Still, tis warmer. That do be a boon!" He giggled.

"Stony Gett ought rise and walk unaided soon."

Smoke slid from the portal, flickering her tail forward as the device winked away.

MindMate, something approaches, from up that narrow way. It feels most evil. And it senses our presence.

They were standing in a narrow draw, in a very small but clear space. The ravine twisted away in both directions. The trees, thin trunks but heavily leafed, soared straight up enclosing their space.

Tinker stared in the direction that Smoke had indicated. All he could see was a tangle of trees and shrubs. But now he could hear something coming.

Something large was coming, something large and heavy was coming, crashing through the brush, toward them.

Goose walked in the direction of the noise and peered into the dense shadow.

"Do be not much visible yonder, Sire. Below, Brother?"

Toucan walked back to them, shaking his head.

"Much the same. We do seem for to be a'standing in only open space. We may flee but t'will entangled be in great rough brush and vine becomen. Here we must stand, Highness."

Tinker nodded and looked from one to the other.

"As you say, Counselor. Goose, deploy your troops, such as we are."

"Righto, Sire!"

He pointed. "Toucan and I do be standin' just there, t'either side of more narrow a'draw as it do debouche into fair clearin'. What comes must pass us first. Thee do stand just there, at the bottom, just there do be fine. Our Noble Warrior Sister do stand with thee.

Smoke, overhead. We might just dark surprise drop pon what do come this a'way. Silly, stand over yonder with still deep slumberin' Gett."

Goose took his position and jammed his blade into the soft forest duff covered ground and rubbed his hands together. "And thus do wait we."

The crashing grew louder. Some thing was breathing heavily, heavy blowing coming in short, sharp puffs. Intermixed with the puffing, it made low, gurgling sounds. It sounded like water splashing over rocks.

"Sire," hissed Goose from the shadows where he stood. "Tis just upon us for I do see some motion a'comin'." He yanked his sword free and wiped it on one pant leg.

Tinker heard the metallic hiss, seeming louder than it was, as Toucan yanked his weapon from its scabbard. The air whistled next to him as Chicken slashed her blade back and forth, warming up. Tinker reached up and over his left shoulder and swung the great, black sword down and out. His hand and arm tingled with the faint vibration of the weaponkin becoming ready for combat.

A great shape bounded into their small clearing, two huge bat wings almost scraping the canopy overhead as they fluttered. Two large hands, fingers as long as a standing man twitched at the ends of short arms. The head waggled at the end of a long, snake-like neck. Great incisors snapped and clashed together. A long tail trailed behind the beast, off into the gloom. It stood on two large, three-toed feet. Its eyes glowed red in the twilight of the clearing. It seemed to Tinker that the thing was wearing a bright yellow vest held closed by three, brightly polished brass buttons.

"NOW SIRE!"

Goose and Toucan leaped from their hiding places and attacked, swords flashing.

Chicken slipped forward, ducking under one clenching hand as the monster darted its head toward her, neck stretching out.

Tinker leaped, this weaponkin whirling through the air. It was a great, overhand, down stroke with both hands and full body weight behind it.

SNICKER-SNACK!

The blade buried itself deep in the soft ground. The creature's head rolled to the base of the clearing and came to rest against a tree bole. The body slowly collapsed as the combatants leaped away, out from under the toppling creature.

Chicken sheathed her blade and looked questioningly at Tinker, a slight frown on her face.

"My Lord, didst hear thee most strange sound thy weaponkin do be just now did a'maken?"

"When?"

"Just pon instant past." She pointed at the heap in the clearing.

"When foul head t'was a'severed from snake neck," she added.

Tinker frowned, yanked his sword free and wiped the soil and mud off using the thick grass.

"It made a noise? Just now?"

She nodded.

"Most true. It do sing, snicker snack, it do. Just the once." She repeated the sound, carefully. "Snicker snack. As you do swing most mighty a'blow."

Tinker laughed.

"Come on, snicker snack?"

Goose bounded close. "Tis most true, Sire, for I do, m'self, hear self same sound over yonder. Do you not, Toucan?"

Toucan walked over and joined them, and nodded.

"Oh aye, Highness, tis nought but as mine own Brother Goose and thy fair and Noble Lady, Our Sister, thy very own Queen Chicken do just now profess most strongly. Thy blade, so mightily wielded, do sing most strange song, and this song do seem to these ears to say most clear, snicker snack."

Tinker looked from one serious face to the next, and smiled at them, and shrugged.

"O.K., gang, if you insist. But I didn't hear anything."

He walked away and kicked the crumpled beast and stared at it.

"There is something vaguely familiar about this thing. It seems like have seen it some place before."

Smoke thumped to the forest floor, stretched and yawned.

There is something floating in your memory, but deep beyond my reach. Shall I probe?

Tinker gave the thing another push with one boot toe.

It began to fade. As it disappeared, the trees and gloom faded with it. Now they stood on an open, grass covered plain, in the bright sunshine. Across one horizon stretched a vast forest. Off to one side they could see the sunken track of a pathway wending its way down the slope.

A figure came hiking over the distant crest, moving hurriedly toward them.

Tinker walked over to inspect the pathway. Then he started to laugh. The others hurried to his side. He pointed at the path, still laughing.

Chicken gasped. She knelt and ran a finger over the paving.

"These do be gold bricks. Who hast such wealth for to surface their trails with gold?"

"Guess where we are, gang?"

Tinker was wiping tears from his cheeks.

A great voice boomed from the distance, the sound echoing back and forth from the forests on either side.

"**WELCOME TO PARADISE, JOHN TINKER!**"

Then a large hand clapped him on the shoulder, spun him around, and wrapped him in a bear-like hug.

As he was released, Chicken, Goose, and Toucan danced away, swords slithering out, flashing in the sunlight.

Smoke walked toward them from one side.

Silly dropped his end of the sling and started forward, smiling.

"Father, it is so good to be back home."

Toucan and Goose slid their weapons back into their sheaths and waited for instructions from Tinker.

Chicken stalked closer, sword held dangerously low in front, the tip just flicking slightly, her eyes blazing in anger.

Tinker hastily stepped between her and this person dressed all in red.

"Stay your hand, Princess. This," he pointed, "is someone you should meet."

Tinker smiled at her. "Besides, you could never have touched him no matter how hard you tried."

Chicken glared at this stranger and slowly slipped her weapon into its scabbard and stood, legs astraddle, left hand clenching her sword's hilt, face blank, watching him carefully, ever so carefully.

The large man laughed boisterously and smiled at them and then at Tinker.

"My goodness, John, she is certainly a fierce person. Well, introduce us, quickly, before she decides to do me in." He stepped up to Tinker's side.

Tinker gestured to his companions.

"My pleasure." He pointed from one to the next.

"This is the Prince Toucan, his brother Prince Goose. This one," he winked at her, "is the Warrior Queen, Princess Chicken, their sister. You know Smoke, of course. Over there is the Gett, Quartzeye."

He threw one arm around the massive shoulders of the man in red and announced, "Lady and Gentlemen, this is your host and the one that is responsible for your being, and your being with me. This is Big Red. And we are in Paradise."

Toucan and Goose fell to one knee, heads bowed.

Chicken's face registered shock, flushed and turned red, as she stammered, "My. . . my most humble apologies, Terrible Wizard, for We do not know."

Big Red laughed.

"Terrible wizard? On your feet warriors, no apology necessary, Lady. John, tell them to relax, we are all friends here." He waved one arm grandly.

"Come, to Nutcrack, let us go."

He clapped his hands together, once.

Bang!

Paradise. Nutcrack.

They were standing in front of a large Tudor-style structure. Big Red gestured them toward the front door.

"Come, inside. Food awaits. Dancing-All-The-Day is both anxious to see her son and to hear from you-all the tales of adventures that only you can tell."

As they pushed their way through the front door, Big Red leaned over and whispered softly into one of Tinker's ears. "And I am also very interested to hear how my little box of toys turned out. They're amazing. I didn't really know how they would be, you know. She is very pretty."

Then he pushed them down the hall. "Come, noble companions, let us eat."

Goose giggled and beamed. "Most right jolly good idea, that. I do be most sorely famished."

They followed Big Red down the hall and into a baronial dining hall. Arms and armor hung on all the walls. Tattered battle flags draped from the ceiling beams. Big Red smiled sheepishly at Tinker.

"Ah, um, just a little thing I added since last you were here. Sit, sit." He plopped down in the chair upholstered in deep red. "As soon as my wife arrives we may eat."

Goose looked blankly at the empty table. It was bare, polished wood.

Chicken sat next to Tinker and placed one hand protectively on his arm and began to look around the room. Tinker smiled to himself.

A far door opened and the beauty that was Dancing-All-The-Day greeted them, "Good evening everyone. Welcome. It is good to see you again, son, healthy and safe." She shot a hard look at her husband.

Big Red leaped to his feet. "Madame, we have waited table for you." He made a round of introductions. As soon as his wife took a seat, Big Red flopped happily back into his chair, beaming at them.

"Ready to eat?" He clapped his hands together.

The table was covered with a heavy damask cloth, place settings of creamy-white china and gleaming crystal for all.

Big Red winked at John. Then he clapped once again.

Now the table was littered with bowls and pots, steam and mouth-watering odors drifted from the many containers.

Big Red looked down the table. "We don't sit on formality, dig in." He reached for the nearest platter and began to heap his plate and then handed a great flagon to Tinker.

"Some red wine, John?"

That was the end of conversation for a while.

Over desert, "flaming something-or-other," as

Big Red called it as he mumbled in Tinker's direction and then asked them of their adventures.

Dancing-All-The-Day spoke to him, softly. "Please dear, not with your mouth full."

Sheepishly, he swallowed. "Yes m'dear. Ah, there." Then, he beamed at Tinker.

"JOHN, what did you think of the Jabberwock? Did it with eyes of flame, come whiffling through the tilgey wood? And did it properly burble? And did you, with your vorpal blade, my son, go snicker-snack, and leave it dead?"

Tinker laughed. "Snicker snack. I didn't recognize it. One of those Big Red jests."

"JEST!" Chicken spat the word at Big Red and lurched to her feet, hand flying to sword hilt. "That jest mayhap thee most gravely injured, My Lord." She glared at Big Red, obviously judging the distance between them.

Big Red hung his head and looked up at her through his eyebrows and smiled a wan smile. It was the same look that he had given to his wife.

"Oh no, Princess, you are quite mistaken in that, quite mistaken." He raised his head and smiled at her, a warm beaming smile.

"It could not have harmed John, or anyone else, or anything else, here in Paradise. This is MY PLACE. It was merely a small jest, some small diversion, quite harmless. See."

He held out one hand, palm up. A small Jabberwock, the size of a baby kitten jumped to the table and stalked across the table. It stopped in front of Chicken and hissed at her. A soft *poof* and it disappeared.

"You see," intoned Big Red. "Just that, and nothing more, my fair Lenore." He waggled his eyebrows. Chicken sat down.

Tinker laughed gently and bumped her playfully with one shoulder, and said, "I'd try to explain his behavior, but it would take some time."

Chicken gave Big Red a tentative smile and spoke to Tinker.

He is a good friend, just a trifle playful.

He do be a mighty wizard. This do be the very one that do gift us a'thee, when we do be but mere toys?

Yes.

We do fear Us still most confused be.

Big Red smiled at Chicken and turned toward Smoke. "Show her, please."

The room faded away as Smoke began to feed her the memory trace from Tinker's memories of his first meeting with the being who called himself Big Red.

Big Red was speaking . . .

"Well, that about does that. Oh yes, one other small item that almost slipped my mind." He winked at Tinker. "I do enjoy a joke. Some small pun. Might as well enjoy life."

Dancing-All-The-Day entered the room carrying a large serving tray and handled each of them a glass, serving Big Red last, except for Smoke of course. Setting the tray on the floor next to his chair she sat on its arm and laid one hand on his shoulder.

Tinker straightened up and leaned toward them,

shaking his head.

"Not good enough. That explanation didn't explain anything. What you told us, we already knew, more or less. How about explaining the yellow brick road, the 100 Acker Wood, and that stuff? Ah, if you would?"

"Ah yes, John Tinker, ah yes." Big Red sounded exactly like W.C. Fields, as Tinker had heard him in an old movie that Tinker had watched, as Big Red sat up from the soft confines of his chair.

"You see, it is really quite simple, it has to do with how I came to be." He paused dramatically and looked from face to face. A master story teller.

"I was created in the imagination of a young girl with a most unusual, but very pretty name. She was six or seven at the time she did this. I was her imaginary playmate, a gigantic Rhode Island Red chicken whom she named Big Red, who lived in this place called Nutcrack."

Big Red looked over at Tinker. "She is a neighbor of your's, John, lives just over aways, at the next place, name of CatAshleigh." He paused, smiled to himself, then continued.

"Anyway, she had this imaginary friend as many children do. But then, one day, through some process that even I do not understand, suddenly, all of a sudden, there. . . I . . . was. Just sitting there. Perched right in the middle of nowhere. Just sitting there, feet firmly placed upon nothing. Just floating there right in the middle of time and space, admiring the darkness all around me and the stars and stuff like that there. I was human, no longer an oversized chicken." He sat up and plopped his hands on both of his knees.

"Weellll, luckily for me, she made me magic. So I created Paradise." Frowning deeply, Big Red stated, "After all, it is rather dull just hanging about in the emptiness of space with nothing particular under your feet. Now the really interesting part of all this is that this young lady also created my wife, who, by the by, is not magic. As soon as I created Paradise, puff, there she was, standing there, smiling at me. For this I am most grateful. Just think how dull life would have been otherwise." Big Red waved one hand and answered their unspoken question.

"Of course I could have created my own companion. But then there would have been no mystery to them at all. All predictable. No mystery, none. Not a bit. Also rather dull." He smiled, and waggled his fingers at Tinker. "So there you are, John. Welcome to Paradise." He laughed.

"And that explains all the allusions to the various tales and stuff. As you ought to realize by now, we have the very same cultural background, you and I, John."

Tinker nodded and leaned back in his chair.

"O.K., that explains that. Some of that. What do you mean, you are magic?"

"Quite simple, elementary my Dear Watson. I am magic. I don't do magic. I am. Magic. You see?" He squinted his eyes and peered around the room at the several kinds of blank stares.

"Hummmmm, I see, you do not. See. Maybe this way. I am magic personified. I am that quantity often referred to as magic. I am not merely a being such as you-all are, I am a stuff, a particular kind of stuff.

Magic. That makes me unique. Nowhere, no how, no time, not here, there or elsewhere, not in any other place or universe, is there another. Not even my wife." He sighed deeply.

"It is my fate, as it were. In some way, it has to do with how I was created. How I came into being, not as an oversized chicken, but as a human being. However . . . I can, if I wish . . . lay eggs. See."

Big Red held out his hands, cupped together, palms up. In this nest an egg slowly materialized. It was large. It turned a golden color. He opened his hands. The egg hit the floor with a solid thump.

"I could be that goose, too."

The room faded back into existence . . .

Then Smoke grabbed another memory trace.

Big Red was speaking to Tinker . . .

"It is these same forces that make it necessary for you and the others to do the hard work of cleaning house, so to speak. You may, and probably will, receive aid from many places. It is on your backs that the burden lies. Only the intermediaries may meet, never the absolute forces, not directly. You are our's. You will meet his. Doom was only one. There are others, much worse. Enough of this, here, a small gift."

A large table materialized. Big Red stepped over and shoved a small wooden box from the table center toward Tinker.

"It doesn't look like much, but it is all your's."

Tinker reached out and pulled it over. Then he unhooked the lid and dumped out the contents. He smiled and poked at the things with one finger. Small toys. A white, plastic wind-up goose with orange feet and bill. A wind-up toucan. Two wind-up robots, one red, one blue. There was a small yellow chicken made of fuzzy material straight from some child's Easter basket. Jumbled around were an even dozen wooden soldiers painted to look similar to British Grenadier Guards. The last toy seemed out of character. It was a large rubber stegosaurus colored an outlandish purple-red. On its belly was impressed *Made in Taiwan.*

Big Red walked around the table and began to put the toys back into the box.

"This is part of the aid that I just mentioned. Do keep this box with you at all times. Do not lose it."

Tinker latched the box top as Big Red spun away.

"Let's stroll back to the house, John. It is almost time for dinner."

Tinker grabbed the box with one hand and followed him.

The dining hall reappeared.

Tinker was holding one of Chicken's hands.

Big Red smiled gently. "So, now you know."

She returned his smile. "Indeed. Many thanks for you do Us give more than you do realize."

Big Red chucked to himself. "Indeed, Princess, indeed." She received a Grandfatherly wink.

"SIRE!" Goose had leaped to his feet and was waving an ornate pouch.

"Toss it here, Goose." Tinker caught it and

shoved it across the table top toward Big Red.

"What is this?" He picked up the pouch and emptied it upon the now clean and empty wood surface, and smiled.

"Well bless my soul, it is the toy soldiers."

"Right," said Tinker. "Something happened to the portal, again. When we started from Dram's time and place, that happened. To them all." His voice cracked and faltered.

"It happened to us all, all scattered, all lost." His voice was a mere whisper, laden with pain and anguish. He was staring fixedly at the table's surface, seeing bad memories.

Chicken grabbed his arm and spoke gently, "My Lord, My Lord, dwell not pon those thoughts, do dwell not."

"John," said Big Red, gently. "I am truly sorry for all that has happened but it was Dram. He somehow jiggered the portal more than I saw or realized. That is what happened to The Princess and the rest of them. Smoke, Mountain, Sorrowful, and yourself were sent home because that is what The Thought promised. All would go home after you had finished with The Evil One. It has taken me quite some time but I have finally repaired the portal, cleaned it out, so to speak." He sighed heavily. "I wish I could undo pain and anguish but I cannot do that."

Tinker slowly looked up. His eyes seemed to have aged and grown cold.

"Why are we here? Why have we been dragged back?"

Big Red leaned forward. "That basta . . ." He shot

a quick glance at his wife. "Ah, that unpleasant person has started up again, worse than before. Before he only wanted to rule everything. Forever. Now he wants to end it. Forever. I am trying to gather together the right troops. You. All of you. You must help, you must."

"And if we do not?"

Big Red's voice sank even lower. "Then evil will triumph." He smiled a sly smile at Tinker.

"And we can't have that, can we?" Big Red bounded from his chair, the chair sliding backward until it stopped against the wall. "OF COURSE NOT!" He looked from face to face.

"It is now time for sleep, not for talk. We will speak of this in the morning. As the Chinese are wont to say: "Sleep is a priceless treasure; the more one has of it, the better it is. I bid you adieu." He began to fade from sight until only a faint wisp of ruby color glowed in the air.

They were alone in the great hall. During the last of the conversation Dancing-All-The-Day and Silly had withdrawn.

Tinker rose to his feet. "To bed, then." He pointed at the floor. "Just follow the winking lights. They'll take you to your rooms." He slipped an arm around Chicken's waist. "This way, Princess, we have the green glow, they have the blue. Smoke?"

I shall enjoy the luxury of a warm night. She slipped toward the outside.

The others followed their guide lights.

Murklan Obscuratan. A Place Never Visited.

In a forest black as shadow the palace sprawled

casting no reflection from the few points of light that penetrated the dense vegetation over and around it. One narrow path wound a sinuous trail to a distant open meadow, startling green in all that midnight growth.

In the center of the meadow a dark spot formed. And she stepped out, a tall figure dressed in a forest green robe almost as black as the surrounding forest. She clenched a short gold staff in one hand. Turning, she strolled across the meadow and into the near tunnel of the only path. And soon stepped through the dark smudge that was the entrance to the large structure. Blood red flame cast flickering light on the polished stone of floor, walls, and ceiling.

She strode the remembered corridors and finally arrived at her destination and announced herself as she walked into the main temple. The great open space was dominated by the altar stretching across and in front of the feet of the stature of The Lady of Death.

Peering up at the shadow hidden features, she stated, clearly, firmly, "Lady Fairdeath returned from the Lands Beyond. I beg release!"

She waited, patient as the death she asked for.

After the appropriate amount of time had passed, she turned and spoke to the silent figure sitting on the stone throne of Thantos, set just adjacent and slightly to the front of the statue, "This one has heard tales told of one dark as death. That one brings The Release even to The Final Darkness that opposes The Light of Life."

Another strode into the temple, stopped and peered up at the hidden face of The Lady of Death.

"Lady Dawnmort returned from the Lands Beyond. I beg release."

She waited, patient as the death she asked for.

After the appropriate amount of time had passed, she turned and joined the pair standing so still and silent, and spoke to them.

"This one felt a pull from that one. Perhaps this is the living consort of The Lady, Lord Shadow Wraith, the Dual Bringer of Death and Destruction?"

Lady Grimtouch, Glimmer of The Divineal of Thantala, looked from one to the other. "We have heard similar from the last four that returned from the Lands Beyond. When two more return then shall we all gather in The Chamber of Thantos and open The Book of Death and look deep into that container."

She bowed to the statue and said to the pair waiting ever so patiently in the soft whisper of warning, "It may be so for we do feel some strange force emerging."

And all went to their small rooms to speak to The Lady in private.

Paradise.

Dawn tinged the horizon with a faint pink line that slowly turned a deep crimson.

The sun nudged the clouds and came crackling into the deep blue sky flashing warm everywhere.

The sound woke Tinker who poked his head out from under a blanket. It had sounded as if a gigantic bowl of breakfast cereal had just been drenched with gallons of milk. A figure turned from viewing the landscape outside their window. It was Big Red.

"Pretty nice, huh?"

"Nope. Sounded just like breakfast food. Back to the drawing board."

"Well, it is better than all that thunder we had last time. I ran that for awhile after you left, you know, the dawn coming up like thunder, and all that. But it was not satisfactory. Kept cracking the plaster which I got tired of fixing. So I thought maybe something a bit more muted." He frowned at Tinker.

"You don't like it, huh?"

"Nope. Who ever heard of the dawn coming up like crackle. It doesn't sound right: crackle, crackle, crackle." He lifted the covers and sang, "Crackle, crackle, crackle."

Chicken's head popped into view.

"Fair morn, Our Own. Why dust thee crackle for so a'Us?" Then she saw Big Red standing there, beaming, and frowned at him.

"Do be this some magical voyeurism, Wizard?"

Big Red laughed. "Certainly not, Princess, I was just getting John's opinion about how the dawn was coming up. Remain where you are, I am leaving. Breakfast will be ready when ever you are."

He disappeared.

"That wasn't nice," grumbled Tinker.

She rolled sideways and wrapped herself around him, and said, "Pish tosh."

"After all, he is your father."

She looked indignant. "Hardly Our own sire, Sir Liege JohnLove Lord."

Tinker grumbled, mainly at the extended title structure she had decided to use, "O.K. But still a sort of father of a sort so to speak."

"As you wish, Lord of My Heart." She smiled. "Sides, me'thinks he do require most rough a'handling for to behave." She rolled back pulling him with her.

He tostled her hair. "I'll leave that up to you ladies."

"Most Fair Prince Grumble, do that be some pun?"

"Ummmmmm, sort of."

She was sitting on his stomach smiling happily.

He was smiling back.

"We will be the last down for breakfast."

"Thee hast some pressing business, My Lord?"

"Is that some pun?"

"Nay, Our Own." Chicken smiled at him.

"Yet, My Lord, if it We thy business do be, then tis true, for hast thee not been most a'pressing pon Us as We, thy noble scabbard, do most happily sheath thy mighty sword." She slowly leaned forward until her nose touched his. "And art thou now most well engaged pon some pressing a'business? Me'Love?"

He slid his hands lightly along her ribs.

"We Are already late. Might as well be good and late."

She sighed. "Indeed."

Some time later, she announced, "We do Ourself do be rather hungry." And tickled his ribs.

"I am not surprised. Ah, I do have some hard bargaining to do with Big Red so if we disappear for long periods of time don't get worried, all right?"

"Indeed." Chicken leaped to her feet, throwing bed clothes in all directions, then she jumped to the floor.

"We wilt make Ourself ready as soon as We might discover in what far comer thee didst scatter Our own rainments when attacking Us as fiercely as thee do."

"Hump," answered Tinker, looking under the bed for his clothes.

She laughed.

He finished first.

As she tucked her pant legs into boot tops and started for the door, she swung her sword belt in place and fastened it. "Well, let's to breakfast go!"

Tinker threw open the door and made a courtly bow. To him, it was courtly, and intoned, "After you, My Lady."

Smoke was waiting for them.

Good morning, MindMates.

Morning Smoke, pleasant dreams?

As pleasant as both of your's.

Tinker reached up and ruffled the fur behind one of her ears. "Right. Shall we join the others?"

"Yes, My Lord."

They wait for us.

"Then let's go eat."

Eat much, you need to keep your strength up.

Chicken laughed.

They hurried down the corridor and into the dining hall. It had been revised into something all chrome and shining plastic.

Big Red jumped to his feet, smiling broadly.

"Good morning to one and all. What will you have?" He waved one arm. "We have already eaten."

"Eggs over, toast, hash browns, bacon, coffee, raspberry jelly, and, ummm, a cinnamon roll," replied Tinker.

"Done."

In front of Tinker's chair appeared his breakfast. Chicken cast an eye at it and grinned.

"Princess?" asked Big Red.

She pointed. "Do be most fine a'Us."

"And done again."

She sat next to Tinker and pulled her dishes over.

Big Red started for the door beckoning for the rest to come with him.

"Goose, your troops are waiting outside. John, when you have finished, I think we should have a little talk. I will be outside in the patio. Ah, I just added it, um, for our little talk."

He left, Toucan and Goose on his heels.

Smoke's tail lightly caressed across Tinker's back and Chicken's neck as she padded silently outside.

As the door slipped shut, they could hear Goose calling, "Sergeant, Sergeant, to me. Hurry, man, hurry!"

Chicken nudged Tinker lightly.

"How now, Me'Love?"

He sat back and sipped his coffee.

"Now, we finish our breakfast in a leisurely manner. Then, I go outside and see what kinds of information I can pry out of Big Red about whatever he thinks we ought to be doing. And then, when he finally thinks that I have decided to do what ever it is that he wants us to do, I drop the bomb."

"Thee do bring fierce infernal machine?" She shook her head. "Me'thinks t'will ruffle nary hair pon red head."

He quickly suppressed the laughter bubbling up his throat.

"Not what I meant. What I meant is that I am going to layout MY conditions before we take on any job that he thinks we should do."

"Most hard a'bargain?"

He nodded. "All he can do is send us home." Tinker spread jelly on his toast and smiled at her.

"Princess, how did you manage to get egg yoke on the tip of your nose?" He dabbed at it with her napkin.

"Our hooter do poke forward some." She rubbed the tip of her nose. "And what will thee for Us for to be a'doing?"

"You? Oh, just wander around and relax. I suspect we will only be in Paradise for a short while. If this excursion is anything like that last one, we probably won't have too many places for rest and relaxation."

She nodded, her eyes sliding sideways to glance at him, one corner of her mouth smiling.

He set down his cup and shoved his chair back.

"I'll see you later. Time to push Big Red and see what happens." She grabbed his hand.

"Be thee ever most careful, My Lord, anger him not."

"I won't do that. I think."

She released him and watched him leave the room.

Then she called to Smoke.

Outside, Tinker circled the house and finally located Big Red lounging in a lawn chair, staring out at the view. They were on the edge of a vast rolling plain of knee high grass, sea green, gently waving in the breeze.

"Ah, there you are, John."

"Yep. Here I am." He sat down in the chair that appeared next to Big Red.

Big Red stood.

"Join me on the reviewing platform first. As Commander-In-Chief of this jolly band, it is your duty, you know."

A small platform materialized at the edge of the patio, facing away from the view.

Big Red climbed the stairs, beckoned to Tinker and pointed. "Stand right here." As soon as Tinker did, Big Red asked, "Ready?"

"Sure."

"O. K., . . . here we go."

Big Red pointed to one side. A brass band appeared and began to roar out a rousing, marching tune. It was *The Stars and Stripes Forever*. Big Red smiled.

"One of my favorites." He pointed to their left.

"Here they come."

Tinker followed the pointing finger. He could see a figure in gleaming white marching toward them followed by two rows of soldiers. As they approached, Tinker could see that it was Goose, sword held straight out in front of himself. Tinker laughed.

"It's The Guard, you've brought them back!"

Big Red dropped a heavy hand on his shoulder and squeezed gently.

"Yes, I did. I thought you would probably need them. Besides, Goose was most insistent about it. He kept at me all during breakfast."

Goose pivoted in front of them, took two steps forward and swung his sword up in salute. The band launched into *The Gallant Seventh*. The two rows filed past, uniforms gleaming red and blue. They stopped, stomped their feet, and pivoted in unison, and snapped to attention.

Tinker whispered to Big Red, "Don't you think you should have used a British melody, they're Grenadier Guards, after all?"

"**HA!**" Big Red gave Goose a snappy salute.

"They work for you and they are not exactly British nor are they exactly Grenadier Guards."

"There not?"

"No, more like Variation On A Theme, Op. #1 by B. Red. They wear berets, their jackets are more like a tunic than a jacket, and other small details."

"Ummmmm, I see."

"I am sure that you do."

Tinker stared at them. "Seems to be a lot more than the last time."

Big Red smiled, a wide happy smile.

"Thought you would probably need a bit more help than last time. So I doubled their number. There are now twenty-four. But they are the same sturdy lads, same hearts of oak."

Goose flashed his blade through the air and shouted, **"TO THE DEATH, SIRE. HIP, HIP, HOORAY!"**

The Guard bellowed, **"HIP, HIP, HOORAY!"**

Goose swivelled on his heels and marched off. The Guard pivoted on their heels, and to the thump of *Sabre and Spurs,* they marched after him and disappeared around the corner of the house. The band faded away, taking the music with it. The platform lowered itself to the ground and faded into nothingness.

"AHHHHHH," sighed Big Red. "Sousa was always my favorite. Shall we sit down?"

Tinker took his chair and turned it slightly so he could watch Big Red.

"That was some display. Thanks for The Guard. But that must mean this trip is worse than the last."

Big Red's face was grim, all pretense at jollity gone.

"Fraid so, John, fraid so. You are going to need all the help you can get. So remember, take it from anywhere you can get it, in what ever form it may appear."

"Sounds bad."

"It is."

"So what it is, this time? Monsters, demons, Dram?"

Big Red folded his hands over his stomach and exhaled heavily. "Worse, worser, worse-est."

"What?" Tinker was leaning forward, hands on knees.

Big Red leaned forward and patted one of Tinker's hands.

"Bear with me on this, John, the explanation is strange. But it is true. Coffee?" A small table materialized next to them bearing a coffee pot and two cups.

"Sure."

Big Red poured, handed one cup to Tinker, took one, sipped, and sat back. "Ahhhhhh." Then he cast one eye at Tinker and paused before beginning.

"Let me start this way. Dram, who you also know as The Evil One, stole The Egg of Time. He means to keep the universes of times and places from regenerating. He wishes chaos to reign forever. Your job, if you chose to take it, is to find The Egg of Time and take it to the end of the universe, that place where it will soon become a great collapsed stuff, and see to it that the whole thing gets restarted again."

"And that's all?" Tinker stared at him, frowning darkly.

"Just restart the universe?" Tinker laughed. "Not bad for an impossible mission."

"Sure," answered Big Red. He nodded.

Confusion wandered over Tinker's face.

Big Red twisted his lips from side to side as he watched.

"Not too clear, huh? O.K., look out there, I will illustrate the story as I go along."

Tinker looked out into the open air where a soft fog bank was forming.

"First, let me tell you about the Phoenix, John."

The fog cleared and Tinker saw a strange bird. It was similar to a pheasant, but had a long tail like a peacock. The body was plum-colored, the tail a brilliant blue with intermingled feathers of rosy hue. The shoulders shaded from deep purple into golden flashes along the neck. It strutted before them, tail on full display.

"The Phoenix," intoned Big Red.

"The King of the feathered race. A symbol of peace and prosperity. Among the Chinese it was counted as being the second of the four supernatural beasts, the others being the dragon, the unicorn, and the tortoise. The bird was also sacred to the Egyptian god Ra, the Sun God. When that bird felt that its life was drawing to a close, it build a nest, laid an egg, and then set fire to itself and the nest. From the funeral pyre a new phoenix would arise, the heat hatching the egg. And the process would repeat itself."

Tinker could feel the heat from the flames leaping high into the air. As they died away, the egg crackled and a new bird emerged, stretched its wings and flew away.

"That is the first part," explained Big Red. "Now behold!"

Tinker looked into swirling blackness and raging sea.

"That is Chaos, The Beginning and the End of the Universes."

A mound of brown earth pushed above the swirling waters. Something flashed down. It was the Phoenix. It settled itself on the mound, and laid an egg.

"That is The Egg of Time," whispered Big Red.

The Phoenix flared into flames, the process repeated, but this time the two halves of the egg shell shoved aside the swirling waters causing the universes to form. As the universes expanded, their material swirling and eddying throughout space, chaos was shoved to the furthest outer edges. And there it stayed, waiting.

"There you see it, John, the endless war between Order and Chaos. It will never end, but merely ebb and flow in an endless cycle. Remember my message: evil never dies. The hatching of The Egg of Time is the astronomical Big-Bang, the beginning of the universes. Of course, your scientists would never accept that explanation, but then, their explanations are as fantastic as any, right?"

Tinker nodded his head. "Very interesting stuff. But?"

"But, what?"

"But, so what?"

Big Red leaped to his feet. "**BUT SO WHAT?**" He dropped back into his chair as his words came echoing back, bouncing from distant hills.

"You saw The Egg of Time. Dram took it and hid it somewhere. If it doesn't hatch, then chaos will not be pushed aside and everything will end, forever." He clapped Tinker on the shoulder, almost twisting him around.

"So that is your job, if you chose to take it. Find The Egg of Time, take it to the end of the universes, and see to it that it hatches. Simplicity itself. That was another of the messages: Dangers foreseen are the sooner prevented. So there you are."

Big Red leaned back and beamed at him. "And I am not self-destructing at the end of the message."

"Right," laughed Tinker.

"And here I am. And you know what?"

"No, John, I do not know, what?"

"And here I stay!"

"OH, no, you don't."

"Ha, ha," stated Tinker as firmly as he could.

"O.K., what do you want?" Big Red stared into his eyes.

"Some guarantees," stated Tinker.

Big Red frowned. In the distance Tinker heard the faint rumble of thunder.

"What sort of guarantees did you have in mind?"

Tinker smiled at him. It was time to bargain.

"For starters, I do not want to lose Chicken or Smoke again. We cannot be ripped apart again. I don't think that we would survive if it happened."

"Ummmmmmm," mumbled Big Red, stroking his chin, eyes crinkling, a merchant eyeing goods being offered.

"Well, I suppose I could manage something along those lines. For starters."

"And that goes for the rest of them as well."

"WHAT!" Big Red crashed to his feet and began to pace, and grow. He was twenty feet tall when he spun to face Tinker. His voice boomed forth,"**CAN'T BE DONE, NOT THE ENTIRE GROUP. THAT IS TOO MUCH INTERFERENCE!**"

Lightening flashed in dark clouds, his voice shook leaves from the trees. Suddenly he shrank back to normal size.

"Sorry, John, sorry. But I can't interject that much. The Princess Chicken and Smoke I can manage, but the rest will just have to take their chances. I can't do much more than that, not unless Dram does. Everything has to remain balanced, you see, that is the problem, everything must be balanced." He joggled empty palms up and down, a weighing gesture.

"But," he clapped his hands together.

"Smoke and Chicken, through the portal, every time. And when you return home, they will be with you, as you wish, as you wish."

"With me, with me!"

"Of course, with you. Just as you wish them to be." He smiled gently.

"All back in Grandeville, just like you. Alive."

The magical one leaned back and watched Tinker's face carefully, the faintest of smiles tugging gently at one corner of his mouth. "Not as before. Is that all?"

"You've already produced The Guard." Big Red nodded.

"Used up some of the balance right there, doubling them. Limits, always limits. That is what Dram doesn't realize. There are always limits."

"How about supplies?" The laughter was hardy.

"No problemo, J.T. Sure, all the supplies you can use. Just give me a list and it will be so."

Tinker slouched in his chair. "Fine, I will get it to you as soon as I can draw it up."

"That it?"

"Nope!"

Big Red's eyebrows shot straight up. "Now what?"

"How about Mountain and Sorrowful?"

Big Red snapped his fingers. "Oh, them. They will be here tomorrow. Now, are we done?"

Tinker shrugged his shoulder.

"For the time being," he suggested. "I think that we are. But, I will let you know, um, if anything should come to me, later."

"Ummmm, yes, you do that." One large hand reached toward Tinker, palm up.

"Show me what you have collected so far."

"Collected?"

"You know, little trinkets from here and there, from this elseplace or that."

"Well, not much." Tinker unsnapped his jacket pocket and rummaged in the deep side pocket.

"We got this from the Snojin just before we arrived here. That was the only elseplace we visited." He handed the white sphere to Big Red.

"Oh, very nice. A Heatdrain. What else?"

Tinker leaned forward to retrieve the small sphere. "That's it."A small object flashed golden as it swung forward on the fine chain around his neck.

"What is that?" Big Red pointed.

Tinker fingered the charm.

"Oh, this, just something Master Chen insisted that I wear. It keeps Chicken and him happy."

Big Red thrust his hand out. "Let me see it."

"I promised them both that I wouldn't remove it."

"Our secret, John."

Tinker reached up and lifted the chain from around his neck."Don't tell the Princess." He handed it to Big Red.

Big Red took a careful and dramatic look around the patio. "Not a peep from me, the ladies get unmanageable, at times." He held the charm close to his face and peered at it intently.

"Well bless my soul," he mumbled. "It is The

Golden Dragon of the House of Chen."

"You recognize it?"

"Of course I recognize her. Just like I recognized the Heatdrain. You forget, I am magic. There is nothing in all the many universes of times and places that I could not recognize, know or understand. Of course, I do tend to forget quite a bit. But show me a thing and I will remember. Wear it well." He handed chain and amulet back to Tinker who slipped it back over his head, dropping it inside his shirt.

"My, you have some rare treasures." Big Red smiled.

"What do I do with them?"

"That I can not say, just think this. I, and you, and them, will play our parts as our parts need to be played. At least, that is the great hope."

Big Red stood and stretched and stared at their surroundings.

Tinker glanced around. It was getting on toward dusk.

"I am hungry," announced Big Red. "We have missed lunch. Shall we join the others? Back in the house? They are waiting for us." He strode toward the house. Tinker followed.

It was dark.

It was evening.

The stars twinkled about them.

Walking down the hall, headed for the dining room, he bumped into Chicken, who had stepped from somewhere.

"**OOOF.**" He saw tears glistening in her eyes as she grabbed him.

"Thank you, My Lord.]ohnLove." She buried her face against his chest.

Startled, confused, and more than a little surprised, he stood and held her gently, wondering, now what?

"What's going on, Princess? Something happen?"

"Smoke do tell Us," she answered, tilting her face and straightening up, still holding him in a tight embrace.

"What did she tell you?"

"She do say a'Us thee do make most fierceful magic one agree that henceforth nary would we three be severed, one from t'other."

Smoke?

True, MindMate. I heard and told her that the dzent we are would survive and remain whole. Unlike the last time.

How did you know?

I peeked.

I see.

What see thee, Sweet Prince?

Happy face, happy minds.

"Let's to dinner go!" Chicken tugged him into motion.

They headed down the hall and into the dining room. Chicken walked at his side, tightly clenching one of his hands in one of her's.

Tinker sat at the table, sandwiched between them.

Smoke purred loudly all through the meal.

When all assembled had finished, Big Red waved a hand for quiet, and said loudly, "Most Noble Ladies and Gentlemen, fierce warriors and stalwart soldiers, a toast." He held a glass high. It was filled with a deep, rich burgundy wine.

Goose, sitting in the midst of The Guard thrust his glass high, sloshing all within reach.

"To John Tinker."

Goose and The Guard leaped to their feet.

"Hip, Hip, Hooray. **HIP, HIP, HOORAY!**"

Big Red stared down the long table and cleared his throat loudly.

"I have a cautionary word for one and all. It was my third message to John. The one cruel fact about heros is that they are made of flesh and blood. May all of you make it your business to see to it that his is neither rent nor spilled."

Toucan stood, glass held high.

"As mine very own Noble Brother, the glorious but rowdy Goose wouldst so speak, I do drink to that."

He took a great swallow and banged his cup down hard.

"Pon my solemn oath, Highness, we do most strongly promise for to keep thee sound of life and limb."

He bowed stiffly at Tinker.

Goose waved his cup, once again sloshing wine hither and yon. "To the death, Sire!"

The Guard jostled each other and Goose and shouted, "To the death, Sire. **TO . . . THE . . . DEATH!**"

They all collapsed backward into their chairs, The Guard bursting into some raucous song having to do with beautiful young maidens and The Guard.

Big Red spoke through the noise, "May this evening's entertainment begin."

Tinker laughed and bent toward Chicken, speaking into her ear. She shook her head, she couldn't hear him through the din.

I have to leave the party, Princess, and make a list of supplies we need so Big Red can furnish them. He will see to it that we are very well supplied this time. Catch you when I am done.

Indeed, my love.

Tinker headed for the living room and settled by a small table that he could use for a desk.

Smoke drifted after him and sprawled across the rug past his feet.

It does seem that your folk have some interesting customs.

Tinker nodded his head and mumbled, "Suppose so." He was already concentrating on making his shopping list. After a while Smoke slipped un-noticed from the room, seeking the warmth and quiet of outside night air.

He worked on, adding, subtracting, crossing out, adding in, hardly noticing the din that washed in violent crescendos down the hall. Finally he stood, stretched, and headed for their bedroom. It sounded to him as if the party was still in full swing. As he rounded the last corner of the corridor leading to their chamber, a lithe figure leaped from the shadows and looped her arms around his neck.

"Gats-zha, ma'Lorb! Now thee do be most really and truly begottin'."

She planted a kiss on one side of his nose.

"Oooooops, mished! Ah well, take better aim, nextch shot."

"Princess!"

"Righto, me bucko, tis Us, thy Verra Own Queen."

She leaned back, disengaged her arms and winked lewdly at him.

"Wouldst thee care to inspect fair merchandize? Wouldst thee a'escorting Us to most pleasing of BED chambers do?" She grabbed one of his arms and leaned suddenly to one side pulling them crashing into the wall.

"Steady on, matey!" she ordered.

"Maybe I better take both your arms?"

She laughed as she straighten up and lightly nibbled on his shoulder.

"Thee might take what er portions thee might wish, Our booooony Prince John." She rolled her eyes at him.

"Our Verra Own pretty blue-eyed a'King." And began to fumble with the buttons on her shirt with her free hand.

Tinker hauled her toward their room.

"Throw one arm around my shoulder," he told her as they wove their way down the hall.

Perhaps I'd better get you to our bedroom." He banged open a door. "Here we go."

She rolled sideways and glanced at him.

"Med Loooor'dah, hast the great red wizard us betaken out to sea? This vessel do itself rock with most unseemly a'gait."

"Nope. We are still on solid, dry land. I think that you might have had just a wee bit too much to drink."

She yanked her arm away, straightened into rigid stance and gave him a poke in the stomach with an elbow that took his breath away.

"Right thou art, Our Own sweet loverly. We do be One-Over-The-Eight. We do be, most right and regally in-ebri-ated-ted. A dram of this, a tot of that."

She beamed brightly and spun in a complete circle, falling back against his chest, her arms swinging back to hold him.

"Drunk as a lord, show to bespeaken. In fact, We do be fou, as dower Scots do say." She yanked his hands up and clenched them against her chest.

"Drunk as a tinker, as a fish, as a goat, as an emperor, as a Goose, who most certainly tis, as a piper, as a beggar, as a horse-fly, as a wheel-barrow, as David's sow. TIGHT! As a tick." She laughed, deep in her throat.

"Our Primce?"

"What?"

"Thy verra own hands do clench Us in most erotic manner." She pushed his hands up and down.

"Princess, stop that!"

Yanking forward and out of his arms, she spun and bounced casually from one wall, cupped her hands around her mouth, and bellowed at the ceiling. "**ALL HANDS ON DECK, ALL HANDS ON DECK!**" Turning back to him, she grabbed one of his hands and, leaning forward, towed him into their bedroom.

"Most safe harbor at last. Whish."

Letting go, she turned and sat on the foot end of

the bed and squinted up at him.

"Me'lurb, didst We thee tell that thy true bed woman of honour do drink all, as some wouldst say. In fact, We do it give most right noble attempt, We do, didst/">." She toppled backward.

"Fair Prince, wouldst thee care for to de'vest Our Own self of vestments restraining?"

She laughed softly as he yanked off her boots and unfastened her belt, slipping the sword free and leaning it in a corner. She wiggled further onto the bed. As he yanked her shirt loose she grabbed him and yanked him down on top of her.

"OOOOOOF, Randy Knave, thee do ponch most heavily pon Our bod. Knowest thee not that We do win tonight most mightly, ummmmmm?"

He tried to sit up, she wouldn't let go.

"No, Princess, I didn't know that. What did you win?"

"Thine own self."

"Me?"

"Indeed. T'was a wager, some small flutter." She wiggled her fingers against his ear to illustrate the point.

"T'was Our Own Brother Goose do be at fault. He do Us bet, he do, that We couldst not this far get what with heavy seas and all. Of coursh, We did bespeak Ourself his utterance do be mosht falsh, and hast We not proven just such a fact? And do We not knock down three, count'em, Our lordloverly lusty own, three of The Guard as well."

Tinker wrenched himself free, sitting back on her out thrust legs and stared down at her.

"Three of The Guard? What were you guys doing in there? All of you?"

She gave him a slow knowing smile.

"Tish, tush, m'lorp. Only used stave, you know, a mere cosh of smallish size. Ba'Red do himself produce them." Winking slyly, she stated solemnly, "He was be'fozzled." Then she gurgled.

"Received nary a bruise. Thee may ever so carefully search the underpinnings if thee do so wish."

She unsnapped her belt and tugged unsuccessfully at her trousers.

"Bashen them all a fait hee well, We do. Corsh they do'unt have their sea-legs under them, not t'all, nit t'all." She eyes flew wide.

"Quickly, Johntinkerlove, kiss Us quick. We be a'falling."

He bent down and did.

She was sound asleep.

He walked around to the side of the bed, grabbed her under the arms and dragged her up the bed, rolled her sideways, yanked the covers back, and rolled her in and under.

Kissing her forehead and brushing the hair from her face, he smiled and thought to himself what a morning she was going to have.

Then he undressed and slipped into the other side of the bed.

Farewell Again

Paradise.

The sun oozed its way gently up over the far horizon as if afraid to suddenly disturb last night's roisterers.

Tinker slowly woke, then stretched and lay still, drifting quietly awake. A bright shaft of sunshine poked through the window. His eyes popped open, he yawned. It had been a long night for him, much longer for the rest he suspected. One of his arms reached sideways and gently brushed against the lump next to him in the bed. Chicken was still fast asleep.

He sat up and smiled, remembering their trip down the corridor. He reached over and lightly lifted the edge of the covers. She was still dressed in last night's garb. He frowned and tried to remember the dream he had been having. It had something to do with Smoke and Chicken. And soft plush fur. All he remembered was sensation.

He slipped noiselessly from the bed, gathered up his clothes and tip-toed into the hall. There, he dressed and still in his bare feet, slipped down the hall, boots in hand. He figured she would not want a lot of loud noise this morning. He headed down for breakfast after yanking on his boots. As he entered the dining hall, a low murmur of conversation stopped.

A small, child-like figure jumped from its place

and ran around the table, and with a light spring landed on a nearby chair and peered up into his face.

"A fine morn, John Tinker, now what have you been up to?"

"SORROWFUL!"

Tinker grabbed the small man and twirled him around and around, and then set him on the edge of the table.

"It is good to see you. I see you are ready to travel."

Sorrowful made a dainty pirouette on the table top.

"As you can see, I am dressed and armed for what may be." He looked down at the floor. "But I chose to wear my clothes in their entirety."

He was dressed in the same flat black clothing as Tinker. At his belt hung his weaponkin, the dagger called Cutthroat. Down the left hand sleeve, from shoulder to cuff, ran a bright red strip.

Tinker pulled out a chair, sat down and began to do up his boots.

"What's the racing strip for?" He pointed.

Sorrowful sucked in a deep breath, drew himself up to his full three feet height, then dropped to sit on the edge of the table, legs swinging.

"That is the Badge of a MASTER Teller of Tales. I am The Right Honorable MASTER Sorrowful Mistidings, Teller of Tales, large and small, noted so throughout the Six Lands, which is A Tale In Its Own Right." He slipped lightly to the floor and walked around to his chair, waving regally at Tinker.

"Have something to eat, John Tinker. Join with

us." He pointed at a great hulk of a shadow at the far end of the table.

"Before this great thing eats all and then some."

"Join us?" Tinker looked puzzled, and then frowned at the far end of the table.

A gigantic form rose up and up, head seeming to brush the rafters.

"Well, BY DUMPF, you are able to see a small nit-nat like this talking mouse, but you overlook me." The deep rumbling bass voice shook a loose pain of glass somewhere in the hall.

"ROCKS AND STONES, but your eyesight must be failing."

"MOUNTAIN," gasped Tinker. "That truly you?"

"Who else do you know that is that big?" said Big Red, now standing at Tinker's side.

"Didn't I say that they would arrive. Here, let me throw a little light on the subject." The far end of the room glowed with soft golden light.

Tinker stood and walked over to peer upward.

"Have you gotten bigger?"

Mountain patted his stomach and sat down.

"Maybe just a little. After all, it has been a long time since we were last together."

"A long time?"

"Seat yourself and have some breakfast, John," suggested Big Red. Food appeared in front of Tinker's chair. And more in front of Mountain.

Big Red walked around and took his chair as Tinker sat down and began to eat.

"It has been a long time for Mountain. He is now

in the middle of his life cycle. When first you met he was just approaching his adult stature. Four of his years have passed. It has also been a long time for Sorrowful."

Tinker began to eat the breakfast that appeared in front of him, sausage, hash browns, eggs, over easy, toast, jelly, and coffee.

When Sorrowful noticed that Tinker was finished, he rapped the side of his cup with his fork and smiled at him.

"Now that the day has started properly, perhaps you will tell us what you have been doing since last we were together. But first I will tell you how we came to be here." He stood as was proper for a Teller of Tales.

"SO! In a time and at a time, I was at home, having just returned from a small trip, when the portal appeared by my door calling me. I bade goodbye to wife and children and relatives, dressed appropriately, and stepped through to Paradise. Mountain had been on some sort of wander when the portal plucked him from the side of a cliff, dropped him at home for a change of clothes, rather nice of it I would say, and here he is. Do you know," he bounced up and down on the balls of his feet, "that a new tale comparable to the last one would earn for me the Green Banner of Grand Master when I return. Ummm, if I return. NEVER. When I return. And that will make me the first GRAND MASTER in several generations."

Tinker smiled at the two of them. It felt good to be once again in the presence of this inquisitive teller of tales and the enormous, ever grumbling hulk from that time and place the residents called Stumpf, a terrible curse in their language. So Tinker related everything and Sorrowful recorded it all in his capacious memory. He left out the year of anguish, however, figuring that wasn't germane to anything but his personal business.

Sorrowful smiled when Tinker finished. He enjoyed a good tale well told.

Mountain grumbled softly, softly for him, loud for everyone else.

"Well, BY DUMPF, I, for one, am overjoyed to have missed a land of ice and snow. This land is cool enough. RUMPF, it is no wonder that the Gett went into hibernation. John Tinker, where is that stony creature? Or did you leave it somewhere to hold a door open?"

Small, sharp pinchers pinched him on the calf.

"YOWP! BY DUMPF, something bit me!"

The Gett scurried up a table leg and onto the table top and stopped in front of Mountain. Four crystalline eyes peered at him.

"Greetings, Strange Creature, I am Quartzeye, son of Quartzeye, son of Quartzeye, son of Quartzeye, son of Quartzeye with whom you did once upon a time journey. We bear a message from the Gett'tda."

Mountain looked at the rock-like being, a smile of some sort on his face.

"Tell me your message, down slope relative of my old companion from the land of The Gett."

The Gett slipped closer, multiple feet making slight scratching noises on the table top.

"Greetings, Strange Creature. The sand-trells are crying. May your way be clear."

It settled with a sharp bang to the table top and watched him.

Mountain glowered at the stone creature and

reached out to rap it sharply on the top with one knuckle.

"That is the message? That is it, BY DUMPF! My message is that The sand-trells are crying. May my way be clear. By all the ROCKS AND STONES, SAND AND PEBBLES, that is a RAR-RUMPFING, dust mote of a message!"

The Gett raised itself up and popped two long arms from slots, reached under its edge and extracted some small object.

"That is the message. We bring you a gift, Strange Creature, from the Sand-Trells."

It scooted forward and thrust at Mountain a crystal vial incased in fine woven silver mesh, the whole suspended from a equally finely woven silver loop.

"Wear it around your neck, Strange Creature, always."

Mountain reached out and lifted his gift up to his eyes and stared at the vial.

"MUMPF, what is this gift you give?"

Inside the vial he could see purple sand that seemed to swirl and eddy to its own inner rhythm.

"HUMPF, a strange gift. What am I to do with this, Quartzeye descendent?"

"The Gett'tda say, they do say, you are to keep it until it is required. Only you will know when this is to be. The Sand- Trells are crying, they miss you, their great friend and more. The Land of The Gett is cured of the evil which once befell it, thanks to you. Now all is well." The Gett backed up.

"Our function is over. May your way be clear, Strange Creature."

It turned and began to walk up into the air at a very steep incline and dwindle in size, it final words echoing down at them. "May your way be clear." It was gone.

Tinker looked at Big Red.

"Did you do that?"

Big Red shook his head.

"Not I. Those Gett have their own strange qualities, now that they may once again use them, thanks to Mountain. Interesting gift you have there, Mountain?"

"BY DUMPF, it is." Mountain slipped the chain over his head and dropped the vial inside his shirt.

"WUMPFING warm gift. Must be the sand inside. Now that was a properly comfortable place, that Land of The Gett." His head swivelled.

"John Tinker, where are the rest of The Company, or is it to be just the three of us, this time?"

Tinker laughed and shook his head.

"Oh no, there's more. But I think they might all be rather slow this morning, it seems our host put on quite a party last night."

Big Red smiled sheepishly at him.

"Speak for thyself, My Lord."

Chicken strode briskly into the hall, waved jauntily at Sorrowful and Mountain, planted a heavy kiss on Tinker, sat down and stared pointedly at Big Red, and demanded in a very stem voice, "Where do be Our break fast? We do be most ravenous this fair mom."

The food appeared, she started eating. Tinker stared at her, mouth dropping open. She gave him a sly wink.

"Thy mouth do hang some open, My Lord. From what source do spring thy great surprise so?"

Tinker stammered, "It. . . it is just, urn, well, it is just that you, ah, urn seem . . ."

She smiled all innocence at him and purred, "Yes?"

He reached over and rubbed her shoulder apologetically.

"Well, after last night I felt sure that one and all would be so hung over that the mere thought of food would turn them green."

"Ahem."

Big Red cleared his throat by way of interjection.

"That was my doing. I felt it was my duty, as host and all, to see to it that everyone didn't have any painful after effects from last evening's little celebration. Of course, they will probably sleep a lot today. But it will be just pure fatigue." He stood.

"Come, let us walk outside and finish our business, John."

Tinker stood and followed him outside. Stepping onto the patio, they met Goose, Toucan and The Guard straggling along, headed for the house.

"Good morn, Highness."

"Morning, Toucan."

"Bright sunny day it do be, Sire. How do fare Our Noble Sister this morn?"

"Right as rain, Goose. You'll see."

The Guard saluted Tinker as they passed.

"Everyone looks fine," said Tinker. "Not at all what I expected."

"Like I said, John," murmured Big Red, leading

Tinker over to a large mound of backpacks, bulging with supplies. He pointed at them.

"There you are, as ordered, just as your list specified. Everything is ready to go. Do you wish to inspect them?" Tinker shook his head.

"Nope, I am sure they are fine."

Big Red clapped him a solid, hearty bang on the back.

"Well, if you think of anything else, just let me know. It is the least I can do."

Tinker looked at him. "There is one thing."

"Yes?" Big Red looked suspicious, very, very suspicious.

"You did agree about keeping Chicken, Smoke, and me together, right?"

"Yes. At the end of the quest you will be together."

"Guaranteed?"

"Yes, yes, yes! All three of you, together, just as you wish, John, just as you wish." He smiled broadly. Then frowned and waggled one finger at him.

"But remember, I can't make any other deals. Smoke has explained to me about your joining, so I understand why you make such a request. So, no matter what Dram tries, or does, when you finish and return home, you three will be together, just as you wish, John, just as you wish. Ah, there is one small thing you probably ought to know."

"What's that?"

"They both love you deeply."

"We all feel that. That is why I didn't want to come on this quest of your's. I didn't think we, I, could stand to be separated again. But, here we are. So, what else will you tell me?"

Big Red gestured at two chairs that had just appeared.

"Let's sit."

They did.

Big Red looked at Tinker and asked, "Well, what else?"

"Ummmm, any little old piece of information that we might be able to use. Forewarned is forearmed, you know."

"There is little else that I can tell you. You will have your total company including the twin robots and Tai."

Tinker scanned their surroundings.

"I don't see them."

"They are off in another direction, but they will be here."

Tinker's eyes unfocused as he stared into the distance and wondered what more he could ask for. Then he looked at Big Red.

"AH, we are still traveling by portal?"

"Oh yes," he intoned in rolling tones. "It is the only way to travel." He chuckled.

"Then fix it!" Tinker jabbed a finger at Big Red. "It seems to malfunction, every now and then."

"Only the times when you were all separated. And that was Dram's doing, and undoing. So what do you have to worry about. Whether you want to accept this or not, where you go, where ever it takes you, there is always a reason. It is just that the reason is not always clear, that is all."

Tinker leaned back and frowned at him.

"Humpf. Any way to know where we are going before we get there?"

"Nope."

"Back to being the ping-pong balls of the universes, right?" Big Red smiled.

"In a manner of speaking, I suppose. By the way, that thing seems to have taken on a life of its own with some sense of direction toward our goal. Follow it, you have no choice. Nothing is aimless in maintaining the balance between Chaos and Order. You know the zen of action/no-action, use it." He stood.

"Come, let's walk a little. After the party people have finished their naps, it will be time to go."

For some distance they walked in silence, then Big Red broke it.

"I care for you very much, John, but I worry about the universes even more. Dram must not succeed. You are better at coping that you realize. Accept help from any quarter that offers it, in whatever shape or form. Stay alert, be careful, and maybe you will survive. Ahhhhh, there are no guarantees, you know, none that I can make. You might all die."

On that cheerful note, they walked deep into the grassy plain.

In the open courtyard, Toucan and Goose labored to pack as much of the additional gear and supplies as they could on the back of Tai the stegosaurus. She stood munching contentedly on a heap of grass.

The Guard adjusted and readjusted their own

packs until everything hung just right. Then they stacked them in two neat rows and wandered off to sleep.

Toucan yanked heavily at the final strap, pulling Chicken sideways.

"There, Sister Queen, that should hold thee fine."

"Indeed Brother, it do pear so. We do think Us to follow Great Guard's lead. T'was most long a night."

Toucan yawned and stretched.

"Oh t'was that. Me'thinks yon couch in quiet hall do me beckon. Thee?"

"Upstairs."

They walked back into the house and headed for their chosen sites.

And all too soon, their naps were over.

As Tinker and Big Red wandered up to the patio, they could see Goose and The Guard rechecking everything for the last time. Chicken stood to one side watching them.

Nearby stood Tai, patiently chewing on something. Behind the guard stood Two-Byte, the electronic siamese twins, softly crackling to each other.

Toucan strode from the house.

"Good rest, Brother?" asked Chicken.

"Indeed, pears we do be most ready."

Dancing-All-The-Day and Silly came from around one corner of the house as Smoke padded silently from around the other.

Tinker walked up to Goose.

"Ready to go?"

"Indeed, Sire."

"Well, everyone looks rested and fit. Guess it is

time to leave."

"Sire?"

"What?"

"This do be marching sequence. Thee three, Mine Own Self, Count Sorrowful, The Guard, Mountain, Two-Byte, Tai, then Brother Toucan who will check that all supplies do pass through."

Toucan made a slight bow and took his place at the end of the line.

Big Red walked over to Tinker, his wife walking at his side.

"John," he said, "it has been good having you with us for this short time. One of these visits we will have to make longer, just for the fun of it."

He stepped over to Chicken who had taken her place next to Tinker, bent forward and kissed her on the forehead, and whispered, "Take good care of him, daughter."

Chicken smiled gently. "Detect We some small tear, Mighty Wizard?"

Big Red laughed, pointed at the sky. Instantly it was dark, multitudes of stars twinkled brightly.

"Good night, good night," declaimed Big Red crushing her in a great bear hug. "Parting is such sweet sorrow."

Day flashed over night. He stepped back and nodded to them.

"Goodbye, goodbye."

As Big Red walked away, Chicken whispered after him, "Say naught good-bye but au revoir."

Grabbing Tinker's left hand, she tugged him toward the portal. It stood there flames curling up and around all sides, the fire snakes watching them.

"My Lord, shall we go?"

"Right, let's get this show on the road."

The portal glowed, the fire snakes roiled and hissed and flashed their tongues at them.

"JOHN TINKER, ONE MOMENT!"

Silly ran up and grabbed Tinker's free hand.

Off to one side the military brass band appeared and began to thump out *Solid Men To The Front*.

Silly pumped Tinker's hand vigorously while his left hand deftly slipped a slim ebony rod tipped in silver into one of Tinker's pockets.

"Here, a small gift. I waited until the last possible moment, didn't want my pater to see. It is one of his wands."

Silly stepped back, turned and quickly walked away, saying over his shoulder, "Perhaps we may visit again some time."

Tinker turned toward the portal.

"I think we had best hurry, Princess. Ready? Smoke?"

She trotted up to them.

I am here.

Tinker waved at Big Red who waved back. They stepped through. The rest of The Company followed.

Toucan carefully walked around the area and stopped by Big Red. He bowed to the magician.

"Nothing do seem for to be left behind. Fare thee well."

He strolled to the portal, took one last look, turned and disappeared.

Big Red took his wife's arm.

"Shall we have some small snack?"

"Will they be all right where they are going?"

He frowned.

"I really can't say, given what they must face. Who can tell? Ummmmm?"

"Yes, husband?"

"What do you think your son gave to John?"

She gave him a sharp poke in the ribs and told him to promise not to ask.

He promised.

Three Trees Town.

Sluba mage Ransapal was relaxing in a side room over a pleasant beverage and pondering nothing at all when the nice feeling of the moment was ruined. He hastily cast multi-layer protection and eyed the nearby open window. There was a slim chance that he could leap out that way and survive.

The tall figure in the deep forest green almost black robe had strode over and now stared down at him with unblinking eyes from inside her hood.

"This one is Lady Fairdeath. May this one sit at your table?"

His eyes jumped from empty table to empty table. He wondered how he could say no to one of them. No one with a sane mind ever did.

Laying the short gold staff on his table top, she sat.

"Silence is assumed agreement. What is that stuff?" She pointed at his mug.

"Quril's Best," he rasped. "Brewed here." And frantically waved a hand at a cowering server who was peering cautiously, ever so cautiously, around the edge of the door, and called, "Another for The Lady!"

"Most kind." She sat still as still until her drink arrived. Then she took a sip and laid a gold coin on the table top.

He looked but couldn't see a face inside the deep hood just the eyes watching him. How that could be he had no idea.

"Is there something?" he every so gently asked.

"It is said," replied the soft whisper, "that this Ransapal has studied the Dark Under and is most learned in ancient witch history."

He nodded, vigorously, and stated, "Most true." And began to worry. A lot. In some places it was told that the *The Divineal of Thantala* were a breed of witch that had split into a darkness all their own. It was a research area he had chose not to follow. It had not seemed to him to be a safe area of endeavor although he had been, and was, quite curious about that group and their history.

"This one would wish that the most learned Ransapal would teach this one all he knows of the long ago split that brought the new witch clans and the sorcerer clans into existence."

He blinked. And stared at her.

"For this," continued the soft whisper, "much gold coin will be paid and The Divineal would owe debt to the most knowledgeable Ransapal." She took another sip from her mug.

He drained his mug and gasped. And cleared his throat. "It will take some time to do that."

"This one has time. Shall we start?"

"Such matters are not to be told in such public places."

"We will go to your lodgings."

She stood and picked up the short gold staff. And waited.

He leaped to his feet and hurried from the room and the inn and then to the edge of town to his dwelling. And wondered how he was going to survive this. It was going to take a long time to cover all that she was wanting to know. The Divineal were not noted for their patience.

She walked along by his side not making a sound.

Unfortunately, While There Are Few Great Friends, There Is No Little Enemy

A Place Unnamed.

Tinker walked down the path, turned through the sharp bend, and bumped smack into the rotund figure blocking the way. "OOOOOP!" Startled, Tinker jumped back and looked him over.

He was shorter than Tinker, but wider, dressed in dark clothing. His attire looked distinctly tarnished. He had a broad face, merry dimples, rosy cheeks and nose. The blue eyes twinkled at Tinker, carefully inspecting this stranger in his land.

The man smiled around a short pipe tightly clenched in his teeth. The smoke drifted up, circling his head like a wreath. His noticeable round belly pressed against a wide, leather belt. He nodded at Tinker and winked knowingly.

"Welcome to my land, John Tinker." His voice was low, sonorous.

"Macabre's the name. And terror's the game."

"What?" Tinker wasn't sure that he had heard clearly what this guy had just said.

"These little imps are my helpers." Macabre ignored Tinker's question and waved grandly at his surroundings.

"Come Darter, come Caper, come Springer, and Shrew. Run Sun Stream, run Eros, run Thunder and Lightning, too."

Eight small, buzzing creatures darted from the underbrush and gathered in a jostling throng around his legs. They were small folk dressed entirely in black. On their feet they wore boots with pointed toes. They stared at Tinker with blank-faced malevolence. Sharp-pointed teeth barely protruded below their upper lips. Yellow wolf eyes watched him.

Tinker took an involuntary step backward.

Macabre dropped his hands on the shoulders of the two standing closest to him.

"Well fellows, this is John Tinker. And those are his friends."

Chicken walked around the corner, the rest of The Company behind her. All stopped and stared.

Macabre made shooing motions with his hands.

"Now buzz away, buzz away all. These people and I must talk in the hall."

The creatures melted into the underbrush with soft whirring sounds.

The hairs on the back of Tinker's arms raised. It was the sound of threat, of sudden and vicious death, waiting eagerly to be delivered.

With a lively and quick motion, Macabre turned, motioning Tinker and all to follow, and started down the path. They did. Right behind the rotund figure as he rolled from side to side. His legs, apparently stiff, never stumbled over anything on the path. Down twisted paths and through thick underbrush, under tall trees, blocking out the light from above.

It was a world of grey-green shapes, grey-green forms, and grey-green shadows. As they followed Macabre, they could hear the faint buzzing trailing along on both sides of the path. Macabre paid no attention as he trundled along. It was apparent that something, long ago, had injured his legs. Badly.

Chicken nervously fingered the hilt of her sword.

"This do be most dark and drear a'place, My Lord."

Tinker tucked her arm under his.

"Don't look so worried, Princess, look at the bright side. It may not be as sinister as it appears."

Her expression told him she didn't believe that for a moment.

"Did you notice. He called me by name. As soon as he saw me. Now, what do you think about that?"

She clenched his arm tighter and whispered in his ear, "We do Ourself believe Us t'would do be best do thee carry most fierce weaponkin in thy hand."

"Why is that, Princess?"

"Because, My Lord Johnny, for of all elseplaces where do we slay Dram's most foul minions, they also do know thy name. But nary a'one do we aid."

"Ummmmmmmmm." He reached up over his left shoulder.

Stay your hand, MindMate.

He quickly dropped his hand.

Why?

Those creatures of his are nervous about us. And I feel

that this person means you no harm.

"You heard, Princess?"

"Oh, aye." She still fingered her sword hilt nervously.

The vegetation waved and swayed as they passed, making soft rustling sounds.

"Tis most fell a'place," she grumbled.

"How so?"

"Ugly vegetation do itself move unaided by fair breeze. Tis foul witchery, indeed." She pushed closer to his side.

Tinker glanced back down the line. The rest were strung out in a long column, each walking as near to the center of the path as possible.

They had all noticed the same phenomenon. Ahead, the greyness was lightening.

They walked into a wide spot on the trail.

Macabre stopped and turned, and nodded at them.

"If you will just wait here, I will go ahead and tell the guards that I have guests." He spun and disappeared around another bend in the path.

Smoke.

Yes?

See anything?

His dwelling is not far and is watched by two strange beings, his guards. All around us are his other creatures. Then nothing but vegetation.

Tinker looked around the clearing.

Goose had placed The Guard around the periphery.

Two-Byte stood and crackled to themselves.

Tai sniffed at one of the moving shrubs, reached out, and delicately took a mouthful, snipping it off with surgical precision.

The bush seemed to recoil in horror. All around them they could hear slight rustling as the growth stirred. Now everything appeared to leaning away from the clearing.

Tinker hastily called out, "Two-Byte, see if you can keep Tai from eating anything else." Under his breath he mumbled, "At least until we can figure out what is going on here."

The two robots, crackling blue flames, slowly pushed the massive lizard back to the very center of the clearing. She stretched out her long neck and made a last snap at a slower moving limb. The plant thrashed. Out of reach.

Macabre suddenly stepped into the opening.

"Come ahead, please, the guards have been forewarned." He turned and walked off. They following.

Chicken clenched Tinker's arm tightly again and murmured low, "Passing strange growth do be in this place. Where do Tai a piece be'bitten, it do look as if wounded stem do constrict and thus seal itself from leaking precious fluid."

Tinker started to answer, but stopped and stared ahead of them. They had reached Macabre's dwelling.

A flat, blank, vertical wall slowly curved away and disappeared into the dense plant growth. Far overhead, swelling up from behind the wall, they could see the slope of a gigantic metallic gray dome. It appeared to Tinker to look much like one of those gigantic enclosed football stadiums. More or less the same size.

Macabre stepped onto a small platform, pressed on the wall with right palm and waited until, with a quiet hissing, an opening appeared. Turning his head, he said, "One moment," and stepped inside.

In a few moments he returned with two creatures the size of large St. Bernard dogs. They glittered bright white brilliant shafts of light that danced over everything, except Macabre.

Tinker squinted into the light display and thought that he could vaguely see what they were. They appeared to be mostly claws and fangs. As Macabre and the two things walked out, Tinker could hear the clatter of sharp toenails on the metal floor.

Macabre stepped to one side and waved them through the opening, announcing, "You may come in."

Tinker indicated the beings standing next to Macabre, and asked, "What are those things?"

Macabre laughed, a deep, belly laugh, devoid of humor.

"Ho, ho, ho, ho, ho, ho. These are The Sparkling Tigers. They are quite rare and will not hurt you. I told them you could enter." He gestured again.

"NOW, enter! Everyone, including that strange purple creature. The opening is large enough. Everyone. In!"

As he passed Macabre, Tinker was given directions. "Straight ahead to the main cabin. It is large enough for all. I will close up behind you."

Tinker walked down the wide, very wide and very tall, corridor, Chicken at his side, Smoke on their heels.

"My Lord," gasped Chicken. "All things herein do appear of metal for to be made."

"Yes, Princess, I've noticed."

And he had. It reminded him of being aboard an ocean liner. The door in front of them hissed open, the lights inside popped on.

"Well, this must be the main cabin. Watch your step."

They walked into a great, round room with a high, domed ceiling. In the exact center stood a console of some sort. Tinker walked over to take a look. It was shaped like a doughnut with a chair in the central opening. All around were dials, knobs and switches.

"I trust you haven't touched anything, John Tinker?"

Macabre entered the room flanked by The Sparkling Tigers.

Tinker spun and faced him.

"Oh no, looks much too complicated."

Macabre gestured at a row of seats that lined one part of the curving wall.

"Seat yourselves and make yourselves comfortable. The beasts will have to make do with the open floor."

He settled into a large, heavily padded chair, leaned back and thrust his legs straight out. The Sparkling Tigers prowled aimlessly around the newcomers. As one passed Tinker, he could hear heavy sniffing. One of them circled around and around Smoke before finally walking off to join the other sitting next to Macabre's outstretched legs.

"NOW! What may I do for you?"

Macabre twined his fingers together over his stomach and looked expectantly at Tinker.

Tinker looked back. This was a surprise. Meet a perfect stranger who knows your name and what does he do, he asks you what he can do for you? He started to respond in his usual direct manner.

"Ummmmmm, ahhhhh, wellll, it is, ah, a bit of a surprise, um, to find out that you know us. Er, and that you wish to help us. Eh, we don't know you at all, not not all, you see . . . "

Chicken leaned against him and whispered in his ear, "Well bespoke, My Lord."

Macabre furrowed his brow and stared at Tinker.

"WELL! This. . . is. . . most. . . strange. You do not know me, about me? Really?"

Tinker nodded.

"Then why are you here?"

Tinker shrugged his shoulder, they were on familiar ground now.

"Beats me. I suppose that must seem strange, but, we really do not know you, or where we are. We are here. Just . . . here."

Macabre was frowning even heavier and beginning to finger a black thing hanging from his belt.

"Why," continued Tinker, "we are here is just a part of the mystery. You see, we, ah, never know exactly where we are going for sure, that is, we do know where we are going, it is just that we do not know how we are going to get there, soooooo . . . "

Macabre burst into the middle of this convoluted explanation. "Then why land your ship here? And come down the only path to my dwelling?"

Tinker tried to inhibit it, but he couldn't. He started laughing.

"Well, our, ah, ship just dumps us here and there. And then it comes back and picks us up. In between we are, sort of, on our own, so to speak."

Macabre straightened up and stared at them.

"What you say sounds very crazy to me." His face suddenly went very blank.

"I think you had better try to explain, once more." The black weapon slipped from its holster, to be held on his stomach.

"OOP!" said Tinker. "Ah, it is a rather long story. I will let our story teller tell you. Sorrowful, tell him."

The small man bounced to his feet and walked to the center of attention. As he passed Tinker, Tinker spoke to him in a very, very low voice, "Better make it good."

Sorrowful turned his head. And winked. Then he faced Macabre and made a deep bow. A difficult audience did not bother him.

He took a deep breath.

"SO! In a time and at a time . . ." And then he was inside the story, telling of their first quest. And the horrible ending. Then without missing a beat, he told of everything up to this moment. He made a short bow and walked back to his seat.

Macabre was slumped deep into his seat, deep in thought. He looked up, his eyes flicking from one to the other. Finally, apparently making up his mind, he lurched upright, holstered the weapon, and rubbed his hands together.

"An amazing story. A remarkable tale." He looked around the room.

"I have never heard anything like that before. And I have never met any thing or being like you describe yourselves before. But, I see it is true. Now I understand who you are and how you came here. But I do not understand the why of it, not at all. And I do not see how I may be of any aid to you." Then he chuckled, making Tinker's skin crawl.

Tinker heard the hiss of Chicken's intake breath.

Macabre smiled, of a sort, at them, eyes scanning from face to face.

"Well, maybe I do at that. We will talk about it later. Would you like to go to your cabins, you have been walking most of a day. The robots and the purple creature may stay here. They are perfectly safe."

Tinker waggled hand at him.

"Ummm, one question?"

"Yessss, what would that be?"

"How did you know my name?"

"HO! Ho, ho, ho, ho, ho. I was called on the communicator, told you would be here. So, naturally, I took a little stroll just to meet-and-greet, maybe take some little project or other where I might utilize my, eh, rather specialized skill services. That is why I was puzzled by your behavior. You were not behaving like a usual customer, ah, client."

Tinker frowned at him.

"O.K., but who called you?"

"I do not know. I just found the message waiting for me when I came in. It was stored. I was taking my daily stroll. Have to keep fit. As you can see, I have a bit of a weight problem. HO! Ho, ho, ho, ho."

"May I ask another question?"

"Blast away." Macabre shot Tinker a quick smile, of a sort. "Ah, ask."

"What do you do? What are your, ah, rather specialized services and skills?"

Macabre stood and stared at him.

"That I have already told you. Terror. Terror's the game." He gestured sharply.

"COME!" he ordered.

"This way, into my gallery. Let me show you my souvenirs." He shrugged. "Of a sort."

One wall of the room slid open. Inside soft lights came on.

Macabre gestured impatiently.

"Come on, come on!"

Tinker, Chicken and Toucan followed him. The rest stayed outside.

It was an art gallery, tastefully illuminated and furnished. Art work hung on most of the walls. Here and there were displayed pieces of statuary. Macabre pointed at one painting.

"Here. We will start here and walk around the room. Everything is arranged in chronological order. It is a full record. I am the artist, by the way." He stopped in front of the first painting, pointing to it.

"This one was my first commission."

It was the portrait of an individual seen close up. His eyes were staring, mouth open, neck cords straining in fright. Fear radiated from the drawing. It was a charcoal sketch.

Macabre murmured softly, "A very good

likeness. That is King Kartark. He ruled Iron Arm, the homeland of my ancestors. He was responsible for the deaths of my parents and my clan and is the reason why I do what I do. I am almost the last of the Santos lineage.
This job had a nice retribution to it, him and his being my first commission."

Tinker managed to speak through dry mouth, "What, what happened to him?"

Macabre chuckled, "HO! Ho, ho, ho, ho. He died. His was a military society that preyed upon others. Those that live by the sword oft get themselves eliminated by one. Horribly. I saw to that." He pointed at the sketch.

"That is the moment when Kartark realized who I was and what was in store for him and his."

Macabre stepped to the next drawing and pointed at it.

"Now this one I did in soft pastels. I really think they capture the soft shading that smoke and haze produce."

The drawing was made from a high perspective as if the artist was hanging in the air. It was the ruins of a vast city. They could see that it had once been a beautiful place.

"This was the Green City of Tray. This job bought me my ship."

Macabre walked to the next and nodded.

"Now this is the Planet of Wurt."

It was grey shattered landscape.

Slowly he led them through the gallery that commemorated destruction in all its shapes and forms.

Twisted, blacken worlds, beings screaming in horror and fear.

By the time they left the room, Tinker felt his knees trying to quiver and the urge to mayhem bubbling up. And a deep underlying fear of this seemingly jolly person with the hollow laugh. And twinkling, merry appearing, cold, dead eyes.

As they stepped out, Tinker reached up for his weaponkin.

Stay your hand, MindMate.

Something, some slight change in air pressure, perhaps, caused Macabre to swing around.

Tinker rubbed his left shoulder and walked past him.

Chicken looked decidedly uneasy.

Toucan's face was a carefully held blank. He watched Tinker, waiting instructions.

Tinker leaned against the wall, totally wrung out by the gallery tour. Why were they here? Why with such a person as this?

Macabre looked at him.

"As you can see, IT IS a rather specialized skill."

Tinker managed to rasp out an answer, "Yes, I could see that, all right. It certainly is that."

"Hear, hear," softly murmured Toucan.

Macabre walked to one of the many doors. It hissed open.

"This way, please. I will show you to your cabins. We may talk after dinner. Your belongings will be safe where ever you leave them." He waited beside the door.

Silently they filtered past and down the corridor.

Macabre opened various doors and got them

settled in their quarters. With a sly smile he offered Tinker and Chicken a large, plushly furnished cabin.

Smoke slipped in and lay on the thick rug.

Macabre turned and stepped back into the hall.

"When you are ready to eat, just come back the way you came. The dining cabin will be open. You can't miss it." The door closed behind him.

Chicken grabbed Tinker and held him tight. "What manner of creature do we now face ?"

He rubbed her back.

"I don't know, Princess. But I think we had better be very careful. He seems to be a rather nasty sort." He lightly stroked her hair and then suggested, "Let's freshen up a bit and go eat dinner. Maybe then, we will get some idea of why the portal dumped us here."

She stepped away and went into the adjoining room. When she came out, he took his turn.

Finally Tinker stepped out, ran his hands through his hair, and said, "There, let's go. The sooner we can leave this place, the better."

He stepped toward the door. It hissed open.

In the corridor they looked right and left. Far to the left they could see light streaming from an open door.

Slipping her arm inside his, Chicken headed them that way.

Smoke followed, her tail slowly waving from side to side.

The dining cabin was a large space, filled with tables, all set, waiting.

Macabre sat at one, his back to the wall, flanked by The Sparkling Tigers. He waved at them with his fork, gesturing for them to join him at his table.

"Eat. No waiting, no formality. The rest of your crew can eat when ever they get here. It is serve yourself, noble guests."

He pointed at a long shelf covered with steaming vessels and jugs of something to drink. They followed their host down the line as he lifted lids, naming items, and resettled themselves at his table.

Tinker heaped one platter with the stuff Smoke wished and set it on the floor and tried to push his chair back. It was bolted to the floor. He glanced down. Everything was bolted to the floor.

Macabre had paid not the slightest attention to him, but began to eat.

"I do hope you find my cuisine palatable. I don't have many visitors and hardy ever a guest. It does seem most folk are far too nervous to stick around. I like you, John Tinker. And I like your crew. Well controlled, well mannered. That is rare, very rare. You may be nervous but you do not show it, very much. Good! And, of course, you have chosen to stay." He waved his fork in the air.

"Although, from that tale I was told, you do not have much choice. HO! Ho, ho, ho, ho. But still, I admire a professional bunch when I meet them. Hardly ever see that. And you have kept your curiosity under control as well. HO! Ho, ho, ho, ho, ho."

With his laughter and twinkling eyes, it was hard for Tinker to match the man to what they had seen in the gallery. The two aspects appeared poles apart. Jekyll and Hyde?

At the end of their meal, with Macabre leaning

back in his seat, Tinker decided this was the time, as good as any, to try and find out more about this strange person.

He cleared his throat, "Ahh, ahem, Macabre?"

Macabre looked at him. "Yes?"

Start with something safe, John Tinker, he thought. "Where did you get The Sparkling Tigers? We haven't seen anything like them in our travels."

Macabre clapped his hands together, rubbing them lightly, and smiled at them.

"They are something, are they not? Where did I get them, ummmm? Now, it is my time to tell a tale." He past Tinker's shoulder and waved, beckoning.

"Sorrowful, Teller of Tales, if you would come here, I will add to your storehouse of stories."

Sorrowful wiped his lips and hurried over to their table. He sat across from Macabre and nodded.

"You may start, I am ready to hear."

"HO! Ho, ho, ho, ho, ho. Good, you are ready and so am I. Here we go."

He hung in space, not too far above the surface, and viewed the result of his visit to the Kingdom of Plfanmt. Over the land drifted smoke and ashes. Red splotches flickered and glowed through the haze. He nodded at the sight. It had been rather messy, but it had ended well. Plfanmt had gone phfoot. It was a small joke, but he smiled, a smile of no mirth, and turned to the viewscreen, hands still clasped behind his back. The Vipers stood and watched.

"So, fellows, where do you think we should go from here? How does home sound?"

Their buzzing rose to a higher pitch.

"I thought so. Everyone is ready for home." He clapped his hands together and rubbed them lightly.

"That is what we will do, then. But, I think we will take the scenic tour, at least for part of the way."

He walked into the console and adjusted various of the knobs and dials, pushing this button and that.

"There, all done. Now we can sit and relax. And enjoy the ride." He looked at the eight small creatures,

"Know what I did?" Their expressions didn't change, they never did.

"I told the ship to fly in a straight line, at least in as straight a line as you may when traveling through the universes. But whenever we meet something, to carom off it. We are going to ricochet our way home. I allowed for eight bounces, then we head straight back. No other side trips."

He stepped from the console and rubbed his hands together, lightly, watching the stars flow past in the viewscreen.

"Who knows, we might find something interesting." He glanced at his companions. "Or even something different to eat."

Their buzzing started to warble.

"HO! Ho, ho, ho, ho, ho, ho. I thought you would like that. Well, everyone to their chairs and we shall see what we shall see, eh?"

They all settled down to wait.

Macabre thumbed through a catalog of the things he had taken from Plfanmt. He had portions being installed, integrated into the ship. The ship's automated repair systems were patching, merging, blending in all the new parts.

The trip was uneventful. They sailed along, rebounding from place to place. The seventh tangent took them deep into a vast empty quarter. Days passed.

Macabre became so bored that he prowled the ship, tinkering, adjusting, this and that. Finally he began to seriously think about changing the ship's instructions. Suddenly the warning gong began to clang.

Macabre trundled up the ladder, closed the hatch and hurried to the main cabin and stared at the viewscreen. There was something ahead and to the side.

It appeared to be a small dying sun with a single satellite. It did not look promising. But when you are this bored, anything is better than nothing.

He told the ship to run the standard search pattern. He might be lucky. Dying civilizations often left behind vast quantities of cultural materials. There might be some artifacts lying about, some useful, some even valuable.

The ship lazily circled, closer and closer. At the end of the pattern, the needle flickered slightly. Metal, some metal deposit.

He decided to see what it was. Probably some geological feature of no import.

Then he laughed, "HO! Ho, ho, ho, ho, ho, ho."

He certainly wasn't the first to come this way. From a stationary position he peered down at it.

It was a gigantic ship, many times the size of his. It had struck the barren planet, scraping a long, shallow groove across the rocky face, shedding pieces of itself all along the gouge mark it had left. The bulk of it lay draped and broken over a sharp ridge.

As he checked sensors and sent the ship lower, a small patch of red formed on the screen. There was something alive down there. It was deep inside the bowels of the wreckage.

"Suit up Vipers," he called, clapping his hands together, rubbing them lightly.

"We are going down for a visit. Full precautions, you little horrors, but wait for my signal before you do anything violent. There is something alive down there. Who knows, it might even be friendly."

They cut their way through the outside hull of the wreck and resealed it. They had heard the hiss of escaping gases blowing outward.

Macabre's suit analyzed the atmosphere and pinged to notify him that it was breathable. He unscrewed his helmet and handed it to one of the Vipers.

"Here, hold this. What luck, this thing's system is still making atmosphere." He sniffed loudly. "And it is not too bad."

They prowled up one corridor and down the next, peeking into rooms, wending their way deeper and deeper into this mystery.

They found nothing of interest. Strange skeletons told them that this disaster had happened a long time ago. Finally, they entered the heart of the vessel. Row upon row of containers faced them. Many were cracked open.

Peering through the transparent walls, they saw unusual and grotesque skeletons.

Macabre puzzled over this as they walked along

one of the catwalks that laced through this space. Then it dawned. He clapped his hands together with a soft *whomp* and rubbed them lightly. The gloves made a soft rasping sound. The Vipers turned, stared and waited.

"Do you realize what this ship was? It was a collection of the unusual. Who ever they were, they must have been collecting for years and years. Judging from the numbers of cages, they must have visited hundreds of places."

They dropped to the bottom of the cargo hold and entered a dark tunnel. Macabre's suit sensors and The Vipers' agitation told him that there was something ahead of them, and that it was alive.

He screwed his helmet back in place, touched up full suit defense, and pulled the face plate down. The twin beams from the helmet pierced the darkness, casting warped, strange shadows.

There was more skeletal material scattered all along the corridor. There was much more here than elsewhere. They stepped into a junction.

"Which way? Right? Or left?"

The Vipers indicated right.

His suit agreed.

Sidling that way, his back to the wall, he slipped silently down the corridor.

Far ahead, he could see bright shafts of light, dancing and twinkling. Something small was illuminating the far space.

He slipped toward it, waving the Vipers behind.

"Wait for my signal!"

Closer, it appeared to be a ball of light. Macabre stepped out to take a better look.

It broke into two, the pieces hurtling toward them. One struck his chest, the other flashed past into the midst of The Vipers.

The impact drove him backward to thump heavily against a bulkhead. He whirled and hammered at the thing still sticking to his chest. As he spun he saw The Vipers as a roiling, angrily buzzing mob, rolling and thrashing, grappling with whatever it was.

The bright shafts of light made it hard to see what it was that was clinging to him. His visor had self-darkened. It did not seem to help.

He could feel a number of limbs as he tried to grab it. Finally he had two limbs firmly clenched in either hand, but the others still clawed at him. Arching his back, he thrust his arms outward. With a ripping, metallic screech, the thing came loose from his chest plate. It twisted and turned in his grasp. It was wiry and strong, but not very big. It ripped at his armored hand and arms. With a touch of his chin he snapped on the visor lights and squinted through the lancing shards of light.

The thing appeared to be all claws and fangs. From a startling white surface, shafts of light flashed in all directions.

Slowly, carefully he gathered all the limbs, one after the other, into one hand. It weighed very little, it was about the size of his head. Thrusting it as far from him as possible, he turned to see what was happening with The Vipers.

They had untangled themselves and held their captive. It was a struggling, flashing ball of light, grasped firmly by four of The Vipers. Trapped by the eight steely hands, it still struggled and snapped. It appeared to be the same size as the one he held.

"We had better put these things into one of the intact cages. Then I will try to figure out what they are. I will tie the ship's brain into this junk heap and hope its memory still functions. Perhaps we may learn something, useful."

But all he was able to learn from the shattered computers was that these things were called Sparkling Tigers. The rest of the records were scrambled. It indicated that they were rare, the first two in captivity.

"And that is how I found them. After that, I fed them and they became amazingly tame. Must have some larger social structure than two. They are quite intelligent. When we returned to my ship and I inspected my suit, I received quite a shock. The little bugger had clawed deep into the armor plating. I had to replace the entire front panel. It appears that there is little that they can not penetrate. Or eat." He nodded at them, one on either side of his legs.

"Since then they have grown quite a bit." Macabre checked his audience.

"Have you ever seen anything like them? I am most interested to know where they came from. No?" He shrugged his shoulders.

"Oh well, someday, somewhere, I will find out. I have searched every record on every place that I have visited, not a trace of them." He stood and stretched.

"I think that it is time for me to sleep, I have had a long day. You may do as you wish. Feel free to wander about. Tomorrow we will talk business. Good sleep."

A door hissed open and waited until he had walked through, The Sparkling Tigers at his heels. Their claws clattered sharply on the metal floor. The door closed.

Tinker nudged Chicken gently.

"Shall we retire, Princess? It has been a long day. And, somehow, I think a good night's sleep will help us cope with Macabre in the morning." He swivelled his chair around and stood.

The rest of The Company rose and headed for the door. Toucan touched his arm.

"Highness, what business have we with the likes of that?"

Tinker shrugged.

"Beat's me. Just have to wait and see."

Mountain thumped a table top with one heavy hand.

"BY DUMPF, those things of his are worse than any rock demon the old ones talk of. And their master is a gorge of horror. ROCKS AND STONES, we would be better away from here."

He lumbered to his feet and clumped over and ducked out the door and down to his cabin.

Goose and The Guard eased out the door, spreading up and down the corridor, waiting for Tinker and Chicken to proceed.

Tinker smiled to himself at their caution, but he felt that they were all perfectly safe in Macabre's company. At least, right now.

He took Chicken's arm and headed for their cabin, said good night to Sorrowful and Toucan at theirs, thanked Goose and went into their chambers.

Smoke followed and flopped on the rug.

As they slipped under the covers, Chicken nestled against him.

"Do hold Us, My Lord, for We do feel most cold."

"Ummmm, feel pretty warm to me."

"T'was not what We do mean."

"I know."

Soon their breathing slowed and they drifted into sleep.

After checking that Tinker and Chicken were well asleep, Smoke stood and stared at the door. It hissed open. Casting her hunting sensenet to its maximum, feeling hindered, closed in, by the metal walls, she drifted into the corridor and silently slipped away.

Lock Heraur. An Isolated Solitary Place.

They crashed into the Central Green of the town called Pikel Fermda, tumbling and rolling, trailing streamers of green and grey smoke.

Turintor struggled to her feet, angrily waving away the smoke and repaired her robes, the grape and green design of the Potri witch Clan. Lurching over, she dragged her black clad companion to her feet, pulled one of her arms up and around her neck and headed toward a building on the far side. It looked like an inn ought to look. They required a place to stay and to heal.

Her companion mumbled something.

"Yesssss," hissed Turintor. "We are finally out of that place. But we are strangely blocked off. Most uneasy a feeling to be so."

The pair staggered across the green grass and across the red brick road and in through the wide front door. It had been a good guess. The inscription on the front of the low counter's face told them that they had entered *The Fair Inn*.

The night clerk gasped and stared at them. Vagrants were not allowed in this establishment. He started to protest. A heavy leather sack thumped onto the counter top.

It clinked with the sound of gold coins.

"Lodgings?" he managed to ask.

Turintor nodded.

"With bathing facilities attached. Send two large meals. What ever is good."

He nodded and wrote something on a slip and handed her a token.

She pointed at the sack.

"Take enough for two hands of evenings. I will require assistance to get my friend to our rooms. Now!"

The clerk beckoned over a porter, woken by the entrance of the pair, issued instructions, and hurried to the kitchen to rouse up the night cook.

A Trip. An Adventure.

A Place Unnamed.

A soft chime announced that it was morning. Tinker slowly slipped into wakefulness.

During the night while he had been sleeping some part of him had been thinking, thinking about what it was that he was doing this time. The last time he had been out in the elseplaces he had been snatched from his home and thrust into an unwanted world, a series of worlds, to interfere in the plans of Dram, often called The Evil One. That time it had all been some strange twisted journey which he now thought had been planned, in some devious way, by Big Red, Dram's opposite.

So what was he doing this time? He sat up, gently shoving Chicken's arm over. She was sprawled on her back, a pillow covering her eyes and forehead. He laughed silently to himself. The same thing, that's what. Only this time it was different. This time he had come willingly. It was after all exactly as Chen had suggested. He had a strange obligation to that Red Magician to help him in another twisted plot to foil Dram, if possible. And, he added to himself, after that past hard year of training and study, a duty to do so. At the moment he wasn't sure what that obligation, or duty, really meant. But, for the moment, he would live with that.

Smoke rose, stretched and yawned widely. Her great canines glistened in the soft room light. With a sharp *clack* she snapped her jaws shut.

New day, MindMate. All are rested. Tai is eating something brought in by The Vipers. Two-Byte has been conversing with Macabre's devices.

And what have you been doing, Smoke?

She sat and stared at him, golden orange eyes glowing quietly.

I have been investigating this dwelling, during the night, when all were sleeping. Much of this place is his ship.

She didn't tell him that she had listening to his mental mussing and selftalk. As the days passed she would, ever so carefully, follow those memory traces of his deeper and deeper and deeper and ever so carefully nudge them into his awareness. His reason for being as he was had certainly been a more complicated process than he seemed to realize. As the hub of a band of telepathic carnivores whose minds were constantly intertwined she thought that this was an aspect of him that was very interesting and more than a little strange. Especially for a consort. She would set one of her minds to work on this small problem. It would take a long time.

Tinker gestured at the cabin.

"This is a ship? All this structure?"

Smoke's ears twitched.

Much of it is.

Fingers ran up and down his rib cage. "Fair morn, LordLove." The pillow was now crammed under her head, she stretched and yawned. "Fair morn, Dark

Sister."

Princess, all conversations to be kept private, speak this way.

Yes, My Lord. She pinched him just above the hip.

"What are you doing?"

"Mere checking of thy reflexes."

"They don't need checking." He half turned and slid his hand under the covers.

"What do thee be about?"

"Checking your reflexes."

"Passing strange a'manner."

"Oh?"

"Indeed, thee do nantle some full handful most familiarly." She grinned and lifted the edge of the cover.

"Think these small lumps do require some such fair massage?"

"Guess your reflexes are all right."

"Unleash Us so We might move."

Kittens.

"What?"

"Sister?"

This is Macabre's ship.

I'd say, if it is, that it isn't going anywhere. Looks pretty well anchored to the ground.

Smoke walked over, and flopped her forelegs onto the bed, her ears cocked forward. The bed sagged. Her tail floated around and gently tickled Chicken's nose.

"Whish," hissed Chicken.

What we saw outside is the support structure. The ship may leave anytime Macabre wishes it. The outer structure is a gigantic cradle.

Is he getting ready to leave?

He is hard to read. Ask Two-Byte.

Chicken threw the covers away, sat up and began to dress. Then she spun and kissed the tip of his nose, turned back and yanked on her boots.

"YECK!" shorted Tinker. "Get that thing away."

He batted at the end of Smoke's tail as it darted away. She had begun to tickle the end of his nose. He grimaced.

"What is there about my nose that attracts you two this morning?"

"Thy hooter?"

"I suppose."

Chicken smiled, all innocence at him.

"Tis most like a'climbing great mountain, My Lord."

"Like climbing a mountain?"

Because it is there, added Smoke.

"Ha. Ha," grumbled Tinker, bending over and tying his boots. Then straightening up, he whirled around and grabbed Chicken, yanking her against his chest. When she looked up, he gave her a kiss on the tip of her nose.

"Shall we go get some breakfast? See what business we have with Macabre?"

She wiggled in his arms.

"We might do thus, if thee do wish it to be so?"

"Right," he said, letting her go. She took one of his hands in one of her's and stepped toward the door.

It hissed open.

She popped into the hall, giving him a sharp tug.

He had to step quickly to keep from tripping

over the door jamb.

"Watch it!"

She grabbed him and gave him a hard kiss, right on the chosen target.

"UMMMMM?"

She jumped back and laughed.

"Most like a'climbing most fair a'mountain, Me'LordLove."

He threw an arm around her waist, pulled her against his side, and patted a sleek flank.

"We are certainly feeling frisky this morning, aren't we?"

She blew into his ear.

"My Lord, We do naught but sleep deep some full night. Thus well rested We do be."

His arm wandered up her rib cage as he nuzzled the side of her neck.

"Ummmmm, yes."

He lurched. "OOOOOOOF!"

Smoke had given him a heavy butt with the top of her head, just to start them down the passageway for breakfast and Macabre.

"O.K., O.K.," grumbled Tinker. "Pushy female."

They ambled toward the far doorway, Smoke's head floating just above their touching shoulders, humming softly, deep in her throat.

When they entered the dining room, they could see that Macabre was in the last stages of finishing his meal. The Sparkling Tigers stood on either side of his chair. He grinned at them and waved happily.

"Good dawning to you. You slept well, I hope."

Macabre shoved himself to his feet and made a

courtly bow toward Chicken.

"Please join me. It is good to have company, ahhh, that is, different company. I have company but my companions have rather limited outlooks. It is good to have cultured guests."

Tinker and Chicken sat across the table from him, Smoke stood by Tinker's free side.

Macabre dropped into his seat.

"Yeeeeessssss, most pleasant to have visitors. Especially ones with such interesting backgrounds. And capabilities. Ah, ha, here is your food."

Two of The Vipers shot up to the table, deposited a number of platters, and whipped away.

As they ate, Macabre kept up a stream of inconsequential talk. The weather, the vegetation, and on, and on. As soon as they had finished eating, a Viper snapped up, grabbed the dirty dishes, and vanished. Macabre clapped his hands together, rubbing them lightly.

"NOW, it is time to get down to business."

At the mention of business, Toucan left the table where he had been sitting and joined them. The rest of The Company had been filtering in while Tinker and Chicken and Smoke had been eating.

Macabre cast a puzzled look at Tinker. Tinker nodded at Toucan.

"My consigliere."

As Sorrowful took a place next to Chicken, Tinker said, "My recorder."

He raised Chicken's hand to his lips.

"My Lady."

"Ah, I see." Macabre smiled, sort of.

"To business, then."

Tinker smiled back. A smile equally devoid of warmth.

"Sure, to business, then."

Macabre leaned forward and stretched his massive forearms out on the table top.

"From what I was told yesterday by your, um, Recorder, it would seem that I am to give you aid of some kind. Hence, we have a bit of business to transact, we do. For aid given I must be returned something. After all, I have expenses, like any other business. Staff to feed, equipment to maintain, standard overhead costs, you know, all those normal sorts of things."

He clasped his hands together and watched Tinker's face.

"What can you offer in exchange for services rendered?"

Tinker stared back.

"Beats me. What may we offer, that is if we chose to utilize your services?"

Macabre leaned back.

"IF? If you wish to utilize my services? You have no choice, young fellow, none at all. That portal thing put you here. And here there is nothing else. Just me and mine. Ergo, you will utilize my services, like it or not. And were you not told, and here I quote, most accurately mind you, 'Accept help from what ever quarter, in what ever shape or form it may be offered.' End quote. So, you see, you have no choice." He laughed, "HO! Ho, ho, ho, ho, ho, ho." And nodded at Tinker.

"I am offering my aid, or assistance, or what ever

you might wish to call it. All we are doing is agreeing upon the price."

Macabre shrugged his shoulders and leaned back, dragging his arms back until only the hands and wrists were still on the table top.

Tinker looked at Toucan and then at Sorrowful, the unspoken question on his face.

Sorrowful wrinkled his brow.

"He quoted most correctly."

Toucan winced.

"He do be most correct, Highness, we have naught but acceptance."

Macabre grimaced.

"Come, come. You need not spare my feelings, John Tinker. Few folk understand my chosen profession. I do not require your approval. Just accept the aid offered. But, you might not like the price."

Tinker sighed.

"O.K., what is the price?"

Macabre's face became all blank and unreadable, his hands dropped and began to fidget with various devices hung on his belt. The Sparkling Tigers shifted restlessly, feeling the building tension in their master.

"The price is . . . your great, purple creature."

"WHAT?"

"**SIRE**," shouted Goose, dodging between the tables to stand behind Tinker, his hand on his sword hilt.

The Guard began to scatter throughout the room.

Macabre watched every move made by everyone.

Tinker could see his muscles set.

Light beams blasted around the room as The Sparkling Tigers, claws scratching loudly, readied themselves to attack.

Tinker voice's ripped through the gathering storm, **"SETTLE DOWN, SETTLE DOWN! EVERYONE! EVERYTHING!"**

He grabbed Chicken's arm and said, in a quieter tone, "That means you too." And looked over, "Goose, go sit someplace."

"As you do command, Sire."

Goose sat at the next table, The Guard sat down where they had been standing, all eyes fastened upon Macabre.

Macabre loosened up, a little.

"Why Tai?" asked Tinker.

Macabre placed his hands on the table top.

"Why, John Tinker Lord? Because I have never seen anything like that before. And it would make an interesting addition to my, as you will admit, rather strange companions. And, I would take very good care of it."

"Her."

"Her?"

"Yes."

"Oh. Her."

Tinker leaned back.

"What do we get in return? Other than some vague promise of aid?"

"You get these."

Macabre fished around in a loose side pocket and then handed to Tinker a stack of small, domino shaped objects. They were gray in color and made of some kind of metal.

"What are these things?"

Macabre waggled one between his fingers.

"These things will tell me where you are, or rather, they will tell shipbrain where you are, and it will tell me. If the device is turned on it will mean that you need help. And when, and if you do, why there I will be. Ready, willing, and able. To deliver our finest professional services. HO! Ho, ho, ho, ho, ho, ho, ho."

He clapped his hands together, and rubbed them lightly.

"And those services will be quite a surprise to who ever or what ever has decided to give you trouble."

He pointed at a design incised in the surface.

"See here, my initial, M. And just below it, see there, this little circle. All you do is push it, hold for the count of three, and that is that. Simplicity itself. Now, how many of these do you need?"

Tinker looked at Toucan.

Finally, after a long pause, Toucan spoke. "One."

Macabre's eyebrows shot up. "ONE?"

Toucan held up his hand. And spoke to Tinker.

"Highness, we do need but one. For thyself. The rest do share thy danger. But thou are the key and the pivot around which all do revolve. Thus, thee must have the device magical for tis thy well-being do most need be insured, not our's."

Toucan reached out and took one of the gray things and set it in front of Tinker, pushing the rest back toward Macabre.

"And, Highness, it must remain on thy person at

all times."

Tinker picked it up and dropped it in his pocket.

"There, now what?"

Macabre ducked his head. It was a somewhat sheepish gesture.

"There is one more small thing. I require your assistance on the next globe over. If your, ah, company would all return to their cabins, I will explain what I need in the main cabin, to you alone."

Tinker rose, turned and looked around the room.

"O.K., everybody back to their rooms. Smoke, you stay with Chicken."

Yes, MindMate, we will watch.

The room emptied. Macabre rose to his feet and beckoned to Tinker.

"This way."

A door hissed open. Tinker followed him.

In the main cabin they found Tai munching contentedly on heaps of greens being piled up by The Vipers.

Two-Byte was whirling around the main console.

Macabre gestured at the robots.

"A very interesting pair, but why are they called by a single name?"

"Actually, explained Tinker, "they have two names: Red Byte and Blue Byte."

Macabre nodded.

"The reason they are called Two-Byte is that they are siamese twins. That transparent blue band stretching between them is a connection of some sort."

Tinker waved at them.

"Hi fellas, what's up?"

They whirled to face him.

"We have communicated with Gyreship. Its capabilities far exceed ours. We have learned much, there is still more to learn."

The robots spun around and went back to what ever it was they were doing.

Macabre stared at them.

"Gyreship? I have never called the ship that. Perhaps the ship is getting away from me."

"How's that?" asked Tinker.

Macabre patted the console gently.

"I keep adding things to it. Every world has added some piece here or there to the ship, always advancing its capabilities. There are nooks and crannies, rooms and holds filled with apparatus from dozens of cultures, all wired together, all interconnected. All part of ship's brain."

He beamed.

"Long ago the ship became self-repairing. So all I do now is bring new things to it, new capabilities."

Macabre leaned closer and whispered into Tinker's ear.

"I no longer have any idea what the full range of its abilities are anymore, I have lost track. And besides, there are too many permutations. I think it might be becoming sapient."

He pulled back and said loudly, "Anyhow, this is the hub of the ship, or I suppose we should now say, Gyreship."

Macabre swung open a panel, stepped inside and sat down. With one foot he spun around.

"This is the point where Gyreship and I interact."

His fingers danced over a keyboard.

"Well, there we go."

Tinker could feel a faint vibration start in the floor. He leaned on the console and asked, "What's up?"

Macabre almost bounced as he laughed, "HO! Ho, ho, ho, ho, ho, ho. We are, John Tinker, we are. Look."

He pointed at a portion of the far wall which had became a giant view screen.

They were looking straight down. Far below, and receding fast, Tinker could see the thick circular outline of Macabre's dwelling. The interior was concave. The vast bulk of the structure was gone.

Macabre poked Tinker on the shoulder with one fingertip.

"We are on our way."

The curvature of the planet came into view. Then the view spun and refocused.

"That is our destination."

A bright speck of light pierced the blackness of space.

Cross-hairs drifted across the screen and centered on the dot and shifted until both were dead-center on the screen.

"We won't be gone long. It is just a small matter, just something that I have been putting off for far too long."

Macabre stood and exited the console.

"Come, let us go get a warm drink."

He headed for a door which hissed open at his approach.

They sat at one of the tables in the dining cabin.

Macabre set his cup down with a heavy sigh.

"Don't look so glum. Your service, I hope, will be passive at best. All I want you to do is watch my back for me, that is all. Just you, and your weaponkin, of course."

He rapped the table with one knuckle.

"Everyone is perfectly safe back there. All your cabins are in the outer ring. Except Your Lady and the black creature. They are elsewhere in, ummm, Gyreship. All cabins were sealed as soon as we lifted away. Nothing lives on my world that can scale those walls. Even if something did, nothing can penetrate. Everything is made of the same stuff as the ship, er, Gyreship, and it is impervious to almost everything."

Suddenly he stared past Tinker's shoulder.

"We are almost there, let's go."

He jumped to his feet and hurried away, doors hissing open as he hurtled forward.

At one point they passed Two-Byte standing against a wall. They had opened a panel in one of the walls and were fiddling with some kind of mechanical device, half in, half out of the opening.

"What's going on, Fellows?" asked Tinker.

Blue-Byte buzzed at Red-Byte as it shoved something deeper.

"Minor modifications, upgraded design."

Red-Byte withdrew everything, Blue-Byte fastened the panel. The wall resealed itself.

Macabre called at Tinker, "We are almost down, we better find a seat. Sometimes we bump a little."

Tinker followed him and grabbed the first seat he saw. Suddenly the vibration under his feet stopped. No bump.

Macabre stood and smiled at him.

"That was certainly smooth. We are down. Follow me, please."

He opened a large panel and tugged out a large harness and squirmed into it.

"UMMMMMMphf, seem to have gained a little weight. Have to watch that." He wiggled.

"There, all settled in place. Ready to go?"

The harness was festooned with strange pieces of apparatus.

Tinker nodded.

"Sure, let's go."

As they walked down a long corridor, the ship gave a sudden shift, then a lurch.

Tinker threw a hand against the wall to steady himself. Macabre grabbed the other arm.

"Steady. Gyreship is just adjusting its stance. Nothing else."

At the end of the corridor, The Sparkling Tigers waited. Macabre touched something on the wall and the outer doors hissed open, the ramp extended down to the ground.

The Vipers shot from a side passage and disappeared down the ramp and into the dense plant growth, buzzing menacingly.

Macabre looked at Tinker.

"They are just making sure that we do not have any unpleasant surprises waiting for us."

He stepped outside onto the small platform. Tinker followed and took a quick look.

This world appeared to be much like the one that

they had just left, but it was more open, not quite so closed in feeling.

Macabre pointed toward one side.

"That is the way we have to go. You stay about twenty paces behind me, weapon in hand, please. I will have one of The Tigers stay with you. The other will accompany me."

He leaned over and said something guttural, growling, mumbling to them, and walked down the ramp, one of them by his side. The other stayed next to Tinker, waiting for him to proceed.

Tinker waited until Macabre was the set distance ahead, then he started down and into this new world, sword in hand. With his new companion, who carefully did not hit him with shafts of light.

It was only a short walk to their destination, a large, sprawling structure. Macabre waved Tinker forward as he peered upward at the dark structural mass.

"Ummm, it has gotten larger since last I visited."

He walked forward and yanked at the front door handle. Nothing.

He turned back to Tinker.

"The place is sealed up. He must have seen us arrive. Ho-hum, this will only take a moment or two."

Pacing a measured distance, he unhooked one of the devices from his harness, turned to face the door, setting the contraption on the ground, pointing the knobbly end at the door. After a few moments of wiggling one of the small dials, Macabre straightened up.

Suddenly the ground exploded in front of him.

Pieces of the device flew in all directions. They whizzed past Tinker, who was shielded by Macabre's bulk. Fragments bounced off Macabre's suit. Macabre shoved Tinker violently backward.

"Watch it, someone up there is shooting at us."

Tinker leaped into dark shadow next to a cluster of trees, his clothes blending into the gloom. He looked up. It had seemed to him that the shot had angled downward. There was one open window almost at tree top height. Someone was moving in the dim interior.

Macabre was looking at the same place.

"**YOU THERE!**" he shouted. "**STOP THAT**!"

He made a quick gesture with his hand. A small black form shot from the undergrowth and began to slip straight up the face of the wall, far to one side. It was one of The Vipers. Soon, it clung just above the window, hanging face down. It was totally silent. All The Vipers were silent.

Macabre mumbled to Tinker, sotto voce, "Do not give any sign that you know that it is there."

He stepped into a shaft of sunlight and waved one arm, a flapping motion.

"**YOU THERE! OPEN THE DOOR!**"

The figure stepped forward and looked down at them, leaning on the railing.

"Leave this place, Macabre. Leave this place. Now!"

"**NOT UNTIL I HAVE MY TALK! OPEN THAT DOOR. NOW!**"

The figure leaned further, pointing some kind of weapon at them.

"You must leave. The Master does not wish you

to be here. Begone. Or die!"

Macabre grumbled, "Happens this way all the time."

He snapped his fingers.

The Viper dropped, wrapping itself over the figure's head and shoulders. The impact toppled them over the balcony. As they tumbled, a gout of blood sprayed everywhere. Another Viper scrambled up the wall and slipped through the open window.

From the bloody wreckage on the ground, the first Viper stood, licked its lips, and crawled back up the wall. It left a bloody track behind it.

"HO! Ho, ho, ho, ho, ho, ho."

Macabre clapped his hands together, rubbing them lightly.

"That should keep them occupied for a while."

He looked over his shoulder at Tinker who was still staring at the remains of whoever that had been. Macabre banged him on the shoulder to get his attention.

"Now. Let us go fix that door."

He walked over and bent down to where the device that had been shot was lying, picked it up and gave it a good shaking. Setting it on the ground, he took replacement parts from a small pouch and rapidly rebuilt the damaged sections.

Standing up, he said, "Shield your eyes, John Tinker, it is bright."

The device gave a soft hum, the door was illuminated by a blinding flash.

"All right, let us go in And I can have my talk."

Tinker opened his eyes. A large section of the

door was missing. The edges of the holes were rounded over. Small tendrils of smoke drifted from the sides of the hole.

"Step through carefully," cautioned Macabre, "and watch it. It is hot."

Macabre gingerly eased his bulk through the opening. Once inside, he plucked some other small device from his belt. It looked to Tinker like a tuning fork.

"This way, we have to visit The Master. Pretty fancy name he is going by these days."

Macabre rolled down the corridor, swaying from side to side, holding the device in front of himself.

"Guess I should have attended to this matter some time ago."

Tinker followed. Twisting and turning through the maze of intersecting hallways, they reached an ornate set of doors.

Macabre paused and looked at Tinker, then shrugged his shoulders.

Macabre smiled.

"This is where you really pay me, John Tinker. This is the fee for my services. Watch my back, keep that monstrous thing in your hand, and keep a steady eye cocked for action. If we are not fast enough, we will both probably die. Ready?"

Tinker nodded. His weaponkin hummed softly as he pulled it up and over his left shoulder.

Macabre gave him a wink and the doors a heavy kick, trotting inside as they swung open. The doors banged back against the walls. The Tigers leaped after him. Tinker slipped in and crouched low, the sword dancing level to the floor. He could hear the sharp clatter of claws as The Sparkling Tigers changed direction, leaving deep gouges in the stone floor.

Macabre's weapon cracked.

ONCE!

TWICE!

Tinker slowly straightened up.

Each Tiger was straddling a struggling figure, arms and legs thrashing. From the Tigers came dry, crackling sounds as the bodies were sucked underneath and disappeared. The Tigers moved sideways, then forward, leaving behind a faint stain and a few nondescript fragments.

A tall figure stood facing them.

"Call those things back if you value them."

Black pits for eyes glared at them. In one hand he held a red-glowing rod.

Macabre said something, The Sparkling Tigers stopped their forward motion.

From the hall behind came a loud, high-pitched buzzing. The Vipers whipped through the doorway, dripping gore as they scattered throughout the open space.

Tinker felt his stomach leap for his throat. He gulped hard, focusing on the man in front of them.

Who screeched at them, "Sooooooooooooooo, you have come again. And you think to rid this place of ME! I, Philius Santos, am greater than you, I am more powerful."

He stalked forward.

"I serve Chaos. NOTHING may now stand against me."

His voice fell to a low hiss, "Not even you, Macabre."

Macabre shrugged his shoulders.

"Be that as it may. I have come to say . . . farewell."

His hand flicked, the weapon flashed. The bolt of fire glanced off Philius, who smiled at him.

"You see, old man, nothing may harm me. It is I who say farewell."

Philius slowly raised the ruby staff, the end pulsating brightly. A scarlet beam flashed out and through Macabre's upper left shoulder. The shock dropped him to his knees, gasping. "Now, John. NOW!"

Tinker snapped the great blade up and over with both hands, heaving it pass the top of Macabre's head, and dropped to his knees as a flash of red snapped past his ear.

The weaponkin struck Philius in the sternum, plunged through his chest, and drove him back-pedaling into the wall. The blade popped free and clattered to the floor.

Macabre lurched to his feet and staggered forward to watch the tall figure crumble and slide down to the floor. Macabre knelt in front of him and wiped hair from eyes rapidly beginning to glaze over.

With a last breath the dying man managed to whisper, "So, you won after all . . . pater."

Macabre gently eased him to the floor, straightened his limbs and placed both limp arms at his sides, and chanted softly:

> "Farewell, farewell, Santo Philius;
> Warrior bold, cast from a mighty line.
> Now the mighty be vanquished, The Mightier arise.
> Farewell, farewell.
> SANTOS forever."

Then he stood, turned and walked slowly from the room. Tinker picked up his weaponkin, wiped it clean on a curtain, and followed.

As they walked down the hall, Macabre reached into a side pocket and began to scatter a handful of small metallic objects in all directions, calling, "Everybody out, everybody outside! In a few moments this place will no longer exist!" He pointed at the shattered door.

"Quickly, John, I will be there shortly."

He turned and walked back toward the room they had just left.

Tinker stepped through the door and headed back along the path.

The Sparkling Tigers waited

The Vipers, buzzing like angry hornets from a disturbed nest, boiled from the entrance and disappeared into the brush.

Tinker waited, then Macabre stepped from the door. Behind him, Tinker could see flashing lights.

Macabre gestured and began to trot.

"Hurry, we do not want to be too close."

Tinker turned and ran.

The shock wave threw him forward, dirt and debris swirled around him, along with tree limbs, leaves and parts of the brush. He stumbled, kept his feet, and ran. Underfoot, the ground heaved and shook.

Banging up the ramp, he saw bloody streaks where The Vipers had passed.

On the small platform, Tinker turned and waited.

Macabre trotted up the ramp, The Sparkling Tigers by his sides. He stopped, patted dust from his clothes with one hand, before passing inside. The other arm hung loose. Blood was dripping from his slack fingers. He lurched to one side.

"Better give me a hand. Not to worry, the Medical Section will soon take care of this."

Following Macabre's directions, Tinker soon had him in the indicated room. Within minutes Macabre was almost entirely covered by a confusing nest of apparatus, only his face remaining visible.

"I have told Gyreship to take us home. I will be released by the time we land."

His eyelids flickered and closed. Tinker left the room and wandered back to the central cabin where he slumped into a chair.

And fell asleep.

A gentle hand shook his shoulder. His eyes popped open. Worried blue eyes peered into his.

"My Lord, do thee be well?"

"OH? Hi, Princess, we must be back."

"Oh aye, My Lord."

She dropped to her knees, crossing her arms on his legs and looked deeply into his face. He could feel her mind tracing out the memory of his trip.

NOOOOOOO. Stop her, Smoke.

His anguished cry echoed through their collective mind and soul.

She jumped back as he surged to his feet, wild-eyed, frightening.

"My Lord," she gasped, stark disbelief distorting her face.

"Thee would lock us out? We do be but ONE!"

Tinker pulled her into his arms and held her tight, mumbling into her air, "Princess, Princess, there are some things that are better not shared."

She pushed at his chest to stare at him, blinking back the tears.

"But We would share thy pain."

Smoke. Just a quick glimpse, that is all.

Smoke did it.

Chicken gasped, the color drained from her face.

Behind them a high-pitched buzzing erupted as The Vipers shot into the room. Still gore entangled they waited for Macabre to walk through the doorway.

Tinker stared at the creatures, his stomach taking another surge. One of them turned its head toward him, a human finger still dangling from the corner of its mouth. It slowly sucked it down.

Chicken thrust herself away from Tinker, spinning around, her wild scream of rage punctuated by the slither of steel as she whipped her sword free.

"**BLACK LIZARD! SLIME AND DUNG! MIDNIGHT HORROR!** Show your fell self. Come forth, carrion ghoul, We do earnestly command it."

She glared around the room, searching the many doors for signs of motion.

"WAIT!" Tinker stepped toward her as he heard a voice respond.

"You wished to speak with me?"

Macabre stepped into the cabin.

"YESSSSSSS!" hissed Chicken as she lunged, sword flashing. It stabbed through one of Macabre's eyes, and sprang back. For good measure she drove it through his chest, piercing his heart.

"Die, foulest creature, fell shade."

She yanked her weapon free as he crumpled at her feet.

Goose and Toucan hurtled into the room, swords flashing. They had heard her scream and recognized the battle lust driving their sister. Goose ran toward Tinker's side.

Toucan stopped and looked at the fallen form of Macabre

Goose quickly scanned Tinker for injuries.

"Sire, what do be a'foot? We do hear Our Sister's rage and do expect the very hounds of hell for to be a'coursin' through this place, yet we but do find nothin' here?"

Tinker spoke, a very flat, toneless response.

"It is hard to explain, but it appears that the bargain we struck has just been terminated."

"HO! Ho, ho, ho, ho, ho. An apt choice of words, John Tinker Lord."

Macabre stepped from another door flanked by The Sparkling Tigers.

Chicken took a step toward him, disbelief written on her face.

"Hold your hand, fire-breathing Princess." Macabre held out one hand, palm facing her. "Stow your blade, allow me to explain."

Chicken whirled around and stared at the fallen form. It was slowly fading away. She spun back toward Macabre.

He waggled one hand at her.

"It was only a projection, nothing else. It saves wear and tear on this old body which has just been repaired and which is scar covered enough from the honest toils in the fields I plow for you to add anything else. Please, sheath your weapons and join me in something to eat."

He turned and stepped from the room as the door hissed open. His voice floated back toward them.

"I am always famished after coming out of the Medical Section."

Chicken looked at Tinker, who nodded. She slipped her sword into its scabbard.

He walked over, slipped an arm around her waist, and said softly, "Come on, PrincessLove, I think that he might not be as vile as we first thought him to be." He tugged her gently.

Together they followed Macabre.

As Goose traded glances with Toucan, Smoke slipped between them and followed her mates. All trailed after Macabre to the dining hall.

Chicken and Tinker joined Macabre at his table as he sent The Sparkling Tigers from the room.

"There," he said. "I am now alone and

unguarded. Princess, if you wish to murder me, you may."

He reached over and lay one hand gently over one of her's.

"Feel that, it is me. Warm, fully capable of bleeding or dying." He peered into her face. "Well?"

Chicken jerked her head from side to side.

"Good, good. Ahhhh, you will like this."

One of The Vipers, now spotlessly clean, carried in a tray loaded with large mugs from which steam slowly curled and eddied, pleasant aromas drifted from the concoction.

Macabre grabbed one and took a sip.

"Ahhhh, that puts the old body to right again."

He plunked the mug down and looked into each face.

"Now, I will explain. I am an exterminator. It is a very grizzly business, as your Lord Tinker saw. And not without its hazards. I would not be here now to explain if he had not acted as swiftly as he did."

Toucan leaned forward.

"What do you exterminate?"

Macabre pointed toward the art gallery.

"As you saw. People. Places. Things. Sometimes just a small group, an evil just starting to grow, like my son. Sometimes a city, sometimes an entire world. Once a planetary system. It is a hard business, but as my race used to say: 'If you are afraid of the scars, stay away from the battles.' Of course, in my youth, long, long ago, I did not realize that also meant the scars of the mind and the soul."

He sighed and shrugged.

"Ah, the shallowness of youth. Ho-hum, collected another scar this time, did we not?"

He stared at Tinker who stared at the wall past Macabre's shoulder.

"Yes," said Tinker softly. "One more scar."

Macabre grabbed his mug and drank deeply. Then he looked around the table.

"It works this way. Someone comes and says that this or that, such and such, is doing thus and so. If this place, in actuality, has become so estranged from civilized society as to become leprous, then I eliminate it. For a price. I have excellent training for recognizing such a condition when it exists."

He paused, eyes passing from face to face.

"My race, my world, my friends and neighbors had become such a thing."

Macabre's shoulders slumped.

"So, I destroyed them, every last man, woman, and child until nothing remained. Except my son whom I saved, thinking that I had saved him from such an, ah, existence."

He waved one hand loosely in the air.

"A short time ago, I corrected my error, I, Nicolos Santos, once called 'Nick' by my friends, friends who now blow as ashes in the wind, a wind they no longer can feel, I did that."

He paused and straightened up in his chair and shuddered to his feet.

"I am tired, so very tired. You have free reign of my home, do what you will. I will see you, perhaps, at the start of the next period."

He trudged slowly from the room. The others

stood and silently headed for their quarters.

In their cabin, Tinker dropped onto the couch and set the weaponkin on the floor underneath it.

Chicken unfastened her belt, letting it and sword bang on the floor and then crawled into his lap so he could hold her.

He could feel her silent tears soaking through his shirt.

Smoke sat and watched them until both fell asleep.

Morning.

Chicken, Tinker, Smoke, and Sorrowful sat finishing their breakfast.

The rest of The Company crowded around the other tables.

Sorrowful nodded his head as Tinker ended the tale of his most recent adventure.

Macabre rolled through the door.

"HO! Ho, ho, ho, ho, ho."

Grabbing a food dish from a Viper, he sat at their table.

The Sparkling Tigers sat behind him, flanking him so they could see everyone else.

"Ahhhh, John Tinker Lord and Ladies, a fine morning. The cool, clear air of dawn is always the best part of any day. Sleep well?"

He radiated health and well-being.

Tinker smiled at him and observed, "You seem to have recuperated."

"HO! Ho, ho, ho, ho, ho, ho."

Macabre nodded his agreement and smiled.

"Nothing like a good night's rest to recharge and restore the soul!"

A Viper shoved another food dish in front of him and buzzed away.

"FOOD! Just what the Medical Section ordered."

After awhile, Macabre daintily dabbed at his lips with his napkin and sat back, sighing happily, or so it seemed. He peered at Tinker over the top of his cup as he sipped and winked at him.

Setting it down, he said, "A little unfinished business and you will be on your way, I suspect."

Toucan joined them and frowned at Macabre.

"What unfinished business, everything was over and done with yesterday?"

Macabre took another sip and banged down his cup. Heads snapped in their direction at the loud *crack*.

"Not quite, not quite. There is the matter of YOUR Lady, The Most Noble, and Vicious, Princess Chicken, attacking and DESTROYING one of my projections. What about that?"

"WHAT? Surely you are not going to charge us for that?"

Tinker half-rose in his seat.

Toucan placed a restraining hand on his elbow.

"Highness, praps we ought hear all to be said? First?"

Tinker plopped down.

"O.K. What else, Macabre?"

Macabre threw his arms wide, a slight wiggle to the outer edges of his mouth.

"NOTHING, absolutely nothing. It was a small

joke, a petite witticism, a jest, nothing more. You can't injure a projection, that is the purpose for them, you see. And a good thing, too."

He jabbed a finger at Chicken.

"That beautiful exterior hides a Sparkling Tiger if ever I did see one. And that is a compliment, fair maid."

Then he winked at Tinker.

"But you be forewarned."

"So, we are done, then? Our business is completed?"

Macabre shook his head vehemently.

"NO! It is not! You may keep your strange, purple beast. I think I tried to extract too high a price."

"But . . . ," said Tinker.

"No buts, my mind is made up!"

"You are sure?"

"Absolutely!"

"Sorry," said Tinker shaking his head. "No dice?"

"What? Dice?"

"She is your's, that was our deal."

Tinker sat back and folded his arms on his chest.

"True?"

"True."

Macabre pushed himself to his feet.

"HO! Ho, ho, ho, ho, ho, ho, ho, ho. I AM in your debt, doubly now. Remember, John Tinker Lord, one touch on the calling device and I WILL BE THERE!"

Hunching his shoulders, Macabre lowered his voice.

"Nothing, and I do mean nothing, can, or will

keep me from making that engagement."

His voice dropped another notch, filling the room with menace as he spoke.

"Nothing in this world, or the next, will stop me. I . . . will . . . be . . . there."

His shoulders dropped to normal, the room seemed to warm back to normal.

"But come, introduce me to my new possession. What does she eat, etc., etc?"

He bustled from the dining hall headed for the main cabin where Tai was kept.

Goose began removing bundles and packs from Tai's back handing them to The Guard who began to redistribute the load among themselves.

Tinker told Macabre everything he knew about the care and feeding of the stegosaurus. It wasn't much. But it seemed to satisfy Macabre.

He dropped to the floor and carefully crawled under her belly and crept out from under the far side.

"It is true, there is writing on her gut. HO! Ho, ho, ho, ho, ho, ho, ho, ho."

He strode around, stepped over her long tail, and grabbed Tinker in a bone-crushing embrace, patting his back. Then he shoved him to arm's length and peered into his eyes.

"It has been a pleasure meeting you and the rest of your company, John Tinker Lord. And there are few beings to whom I may say that. I feel you are finished here, with your visit. Your strange craft will pick you up?"

Tinker smiled at him.

"I suppose so, but I don't really know. That is

one of the more frustrating aspects of traveling the way we do."

The Sparkling Tigers suddenly began shooting shards of brilliance throughout the room and jostled up to protect Macabre.

Tinker jerked back and away, reaching up over his left shoulder. Then he relaxed.

The portal stood in one of the uncluttered spaces. Its surface crackled, the heat waves distorting the view on the other side. The fire snakes roiled and hissed around the edges.

Tinker pointed.

"There it is, our faithful carriage. It is time for us to go."

He spun and called to Goose, "READY?"

"Righto, Sire."

Turning back to Macabre, Tinker said, "Time for us to leave."

He reached for Chicken's hand, beckoned for Smoke with his free hand, and headed for the Portal.

Two-Byte crackled up and barred their way.

"We are not going."

"What?"

"We are not going, we have joined with Gyreship."

They rolled aside, crackling and humming.

Tinker looked back at Macabre.

"It looks like you've just gained another two crew members, if you wish them."

Macabre walked over and grabbed both Chicken and Tinker in a farewell embrace.

"They are welcome. Remember, may you never

need my aid. Tread carefully."

Chicken leaned forward and kissed him on the forehead, and replied, "Tread most carefully yourself."

Macabre stepped back, brushed a sleeve across his face, turned and headed for the door, waving a silent farewell as he exited.

"Time to go, Princess."

Tinker gripped her hand firmly, waited for Smoke, and then the two of them stepped through.

Smoke bounded after them, hard on their heels.

The rest followed, Toucan waiting till the last. He turned slowly around checking the cabin for materials overlooked and saw Macabre re-enter the room to stand watching.

Toucan gave him a stiff, formal bow, rotated smartly on his heel, and disappeared through the heat haze.

The Portal blinked away.

Macabre settled into a large chair and wondered whether they would ever require his aid. He hoped not.

Did Ever A Dragon Be so Fair?

Lair Of The Dragon.

As Tinker and Chicken stepped from the portal, a flash of color exploded against his chest yanking him head first, away from her. Instantly he released Chicken's hand, stumbling, seeking balance.

Chicken screamed. "**MY LORD!**"

He pitched over the edge of the large hill they had stepped onto and went sliding, tumbling, rolling, downward, down through thick green, the deep grass cushioning most of his careening impacts. In a jumbled twisted sprawl, he finally thudded to a halt, lying at an awkward angle, staring up at the sky. It was a nice clear blue.

Tinker noticed that. He noted that it was a nice clear blue sky with a decoration of cotton ball clouds dotted artistically here and there.

That damn portal, he thought to himself, had opened at the top of a hill, right on the edge, and now here I am, lying at the bottom. Gingerly he began to feel his arms, then ribs, searching for the pain of broken bones. Sliding his right hand down, he fondled his leg. His fingers told him it was there. His leg didn't say a thing. His leg couldn't feel his fingers digging into the soft flesh of the thigh. Broken back, he thought. Now what?

The leg jerked itself from his grasp, something wiggled against and under his back.

"What?"

A musical voice spoke to him, right next to his ear. "Aiiye, Master, stop tickling so. That horrible fall wasss my fault. Please forgive this humble one, frail girl that she isss, for doing such a thing. Aiiye, what will Grandfather Chen say? In my abysmal clumsinessss, I have brought untold shame upon the House of Chen! For thisss I will surely be beaten."

"WHAT?"

Tinker hastily rolled to one side and sat up, thoughts of broken back forgotten. He now realized that he had been lying sprawled on top of someone. He scurried backwards to see who it was.

That person was now kneeling, facing him, bent over, nearly flat, hands and arms stretched upon the ground, forehead touching, hands pressing into the thick grass.

"Who are you?"

No movement.

"All right, that's enough of that! Sit up, sit up."

"Yesss, Master," replied a voice, muffled by the grass.

She sat up and back upon her legs, placing both hands demurely in her lap. She was Chinese, dressed in silken trousers over which she wore a silk jacket covered with multicolored embroidery. She stared into his face, then hastily cast her eyes away, looking downward.

"How may thisss unworthy one serve you, Powerful Lord? Great shame hasss befallen my lowly estate in causing such a worthy person asss yourself to fall such a great distance in such an undignified manner. A hundred thousand pardonsss, Great One."

She bowed forward, striking her forehead against the ground three times, then did it again. And again.

"O.K., O.K., STOP THAT! Who are you, anyway? And how did you get here? And what do you want? And how come I am down here, with you?"

She sat up, then leaned toward him, bowing her head submissively.

"Please forgive thisss worthlesss one for disagreeing with your righteousss self, but I wasss with you, Noble Lord, Master of All Time and Place, since you first started thisss journey."

"You were?"

Tinker stared at her, disbelieving.

She bobbed her head.

"It isss true."

"Where were you?"

"Hanging meekly around your neck, asss Chen Adam Liu, that most wise Head of The House of Chen, directed me to do."

"Humbug."

Tinker reached up and felt. The necklace and amulet were missing. He squinted, then frowned at her.

"You?"

She bobbed her head again, looked up, and smiled shyly at him.

"It isss so, I am the one given to you by Grandfather Chen in hisss wisdom. But now I have caused great, greviousss injury to your person and to your dignity. How may I gain such small forgivenessss asss you might bestow on such a clumsy girl child for her unforgivable behavior?"

"Well," he said. "You could help me stand up and tell me your name."

She uncoiled in one fluid motion, grabbed him by both forearms and lifted him straight up, setting him lightly on his feet, quickly dropping her hands and stepping away.

"Are you injured, Noble One?"

Tinker patted his cloths, banging away pieces of grass.

"Nope. I guess this grass cushioned my fall."

She smiled slyly.

"The hill and I. May I reply to the latter part of your statement?"

"Sure"

She bowed.

"I am called, formally, Chen Gum Lung."

"**MY LORD, WHERE BE THEE?"**

"DOWN HERE, PRINCESS, AT THE BOTTOM OF THE HILL! And you claim that you are the amulet?"

She straightened to her full five foot stature, tucked her hands inside her sleeves, and replied, "It isss so. I have been with The House of Chen since the beginning of time. In all yearsss, the Head of The House decidesss who isss to be the keeper. Grandfather Chen decided. Thusss it isss so. I am your'sss, to command, to do whatever you will wish with my humble self."

She bowed her head and waited, perfectly

motionless.

Tinker noticed that her final s-sounds tended to be a slight hiss, then dismissed this small item of information as trivial.

"Ummmmm, yes, all right, ah, sure. Just stay with us and we will see what ever."

He turned away and peered up the steep slope. Then he turned around and looked at her, carefully this time. She was really very pretty, certainly didn't look strong enough to pick him up so easily and set him on his feet.

"What does your name mean, in English?"

She lifted her head, jade green eyes stared deep into his.

"The Golden Dragon of The House of Chen."

"**HALLLOOOOOO, MY LORD, BE THEE WELL?**"

Tinker hadn't noticed the color of her eyes before, or the light golden color of her skin either. He spun at the call and searched the hill side. The Company was clambering down, Chicken in the lead, her lithe figure clothed in yellow as the sun reflected from her garments. A great black shadow close by her side.

"Aiiye, Great One, a Golden Princess asss well."

He waved at them.

"Hi gang, good to see you."

Chicken bounded up to him and lightly touched his cheek.

"And We thee, Our Verra Own Prince."

"Righto, Sire."

Goose jolted to a halt and gasped, "BY GEORGE,

SIRE, BY GEORGE!"

He was staring past Tinker.

"Oh," said Tinker. "This is Chen Gum Lung."

He gestured toward her. She wasn't there. She was standing three paces away, off to his right side, her face a mask of blank composure, arms crossed in front of her chest, hands tucked inside her sleeves.

"What are you doing over there? Come over here, let me introduce you to the rest of this bunch." Tinker waved at Chen.

"Come on."

Without speaking, she walked over, and with formal dignity, bowed to each of them.

Tinker sighed, "Oh well."

Then he cleared his throat and began, "Ahem, Miss Chen, this is Princess Chicken, the Princes Toucan and Goose. Goose is the one with the big grin."

Chen was eyeing Smoke with deep suspicion. He pointed at the rest.

"Those are The Guard." Then he asked her, "What were you doing standing over there?"

She bowed to him.

"Master Lord, asss the assigned guardian of your august person, it isss not proper for me to take a position that would shadow your magnificence. My proper place isss three paces to the back and to the right."

"MY Lord," gasped Chicken, staring at him, horrified.

"WHAT? What's the matter, Princess?"

"The amulet that Master Chen did bestow pon thee, tis gone. Thee did wear same as we did but step into flaming portal." She spun, waving her arms. "Quickly, quickly, fan out and search thick grass. It must be found. Our Lord do be not safe till it do be returned."

The Guard scattered.

"HOLD IT! Everybody stop, right there. Just hold it up for a minute."

Everyone looked at Tinker.

"I have not lost the amulet, it has just changed, ahhh, a little." He pointed at Chen. "This is the amulet, The Golden Dragon of The House of Chen, in person, so to speak."

Chen bowed to all the others, and stepped back and to his right.

Chicken stepped forward, opened the neck of his shirt, then looked up.

"Tis true, My Lord?"

"Sure is, Princess."

Goose beamed. "BY GEORGE, SIRE, BY GEORGE! Tis quite a gift, if I do say so."

Chicken glared at her brother. He ducked his head.

"Yes, it is," said Tinker quickly, then he looked around the area where they were standing.

"Well, looks like we are all here. So, which way do we go? Any suggestions?"

He looked over at their newest member.

"You may join in, if you wish."

Goose continued to stare at the dragon girl and her emerald eyes.

"Amazin', truly amazin', such a green color they do be."

He walked over and looked down into her face.

"Really and truly you do be fierce dragon? Amulet?"

She nodded her head.

Tinker cleared his throat, loudly, "Ahem, shall we put our minds on which way to go?"

Goose jumped back, ran up to them, snapping to attention.

"Righto, Sire, righto!"

Mountain thumped to a halt, Sorrowful perched on his shoulder.

"BY DOUBLE-DUMPF, it is about time. A pleasant climate at last." He set Sorrowful on the ground.

Tinker wiped some beads of sweat from his face.

"Well, a little warmer than Paradise, I'd say."

"ROCKS AND STONES, John Tinker," Mountain's face twitched. It was his version of a smile.

"It is just right, reminds me of home."

"Well then, which way do we go?"

"HUMPF-DUMPF!" he grumbled. "Do not ask me. In the midst of grass covered hills with no road or trail, who can say? But I, for one, am happy to be outside where I can see the sky."

He shrugged his shoulder and sat with a heavy thump. "UMPF!" And looked at Sorrowful, who just grinned at him.

Chen was eyeing these new persons with some suspicion.

Tinker hastily made the introductions. "Mountain, Sorrowful, Chen."

Goose turned from his low conversation with

Toucan.

"What say, Sire, that I do pop to the top of yon grassy hill and see what there be for to see."

"Good idea, Goose."

As Tinker settled into the grass, Goose and six of The Guard trotted up the next hill.

Chicken sat and leaned against Tinker's side.

Chen suddenly leaped to his other side, hissing loudly as a long black tail floated over his outside shoulder, curled around and tickled the tip of his nose.

Tinker shoved it away and glared around Chicken at Smoke, and grumbled at Chen, "That is Smoke. She is with us and, ummmm, she is mine, just like the Golden Princess."

Chen nodded and stepped away.

"She do be most pretty, My Lord Grumble," murmured Chicken, as she gave him a gentle nudge with her elbow.

"Well, I suppose, she is, if you favor large, fur-covered, feline looking carnivores with enormous canines, a really long tail and a weird sense of humor."

The sharp elbow dug into his ribs.

"OOOF!"

"We do be not Ourself a'speaking of Our Dark Self, but of thy fair dragon with the silk soft skin of golden hue."

Tinker rubbed his ribs.

"Well, now that you mention it, I guess she is, ah, she has."

The tip of the tail lazily tickled him in the ear. He batted it away.

"What is it with you two, anyway?"

Chicken smiled, all innocence at him. He winced.

"Mere most lady-like curiosity, My Lord," she murmured sweetly.

Tinker glared at her, then leaned forward and shot an equally fierce glare at Smoke.

"Lady-like curiosity, huh? Why don't I believe that, do you suppose? And let me tell you two something else, in case you don't know it all ready. You two are more than enough for anyone to handle."

His eyes flickered toward Chen.

"I am not interested in any more, if you get what I mean? You are too much as it is."

Chicken rose in a smooth, undulating motion, and gave him an exaggerated wink. She leaned over, batting her eyelashes at him, smiling, a picture of little girl innocence.

"Handle, My Lord? Praps t'was some fondle thee did mean?"

Tinker stood, looking stem and strict. At least that is what he thought he looked like.

"COPE!" he snarled. "It is all one mortal man can do to COPE with a bloodthirsty warrior woman and an equally bloodthirsty carnivorous telepathic black lump of fur."

Then he jumped between then, swinging one arm around Chicken's waist, yanking her against his side as he threw the other arm over Smoke's neck.

Smoke leaned heavily and shoved them into a squirming heap.

"HEY!"

"Smoke, this fella do pear a'me for to be most recovered from stay with Macabre."

Princess, he is.

What's that? What are you two talking about?

Nothing, My Lord.

Nothing, MindMate.

"You would lock me out? We are but One," he grumbled at them.

"What your ladies wish for to bespeak themselves pon tis nary thy business," stated Chicken, firmly. Most royally.

"Oh, is that so?" he laughed, and grabbed her.

She laughed.

Smoke purred.

Fully recovered, Princess.

Indeed.

Chicken and Tinker sprawled side by side, heads propped comfortably upon Smoke, who was stretched out enjoying the coolness of the grass.

"She do be most attractive, My Lord?"

"Not going to give it up, are you?"

"Mere observation, Sweet Prince."

"How about I rip her clothes off so you can take a good look?" he mumbled.

"MY LORD! That do be most unseemly a'thought. One do not treat thy concubines thus. She do be thy gift."

"She is a dragon amulet, not my concubine."

Goose trotted up and looked at them. "What ho, Sire?"

Tinker shoved Chicken off his chest, batted away Smoke's tail, and struggled to his feet.

"What did you see, Goose?"

Goose shot at quick glance at his sister and giggled. "Bloody all, Sire." Quickly composing his face, he reported smartly, "Nothin' there, Sire. Hills, hills, and more hills. Same as far as mine eyes do see. We be awash in sea of green. Pon circlin' around about we do see nary discernable a'pattern nor sign of road nor trail. SIRE!"

He snapped to attention, hoping his first remark would be overlooked.

Tinker wandered away, stopped, took his pack from one of The Guard, and began to rummage in it.

"There it is."

He stood up and turned slowly around and around, singing, somewhat off key,

"East, west, north, south.

Close your eyes, and open your mouth."

"What say, Sire?"

"Just a children's rhyme that came to mind. Which direction would you like to go? Anyone?"

Silence.

All waited for someone else to speak.

Mountain thrust himself up.

"BY DUMPF, let us go that way."

He shot one great arm out and pointed. It was a very dramatic gesture.

Tinker checked his compass. "West, it is."

He beckoned to Sorrowful, and said, "Come here and I will show you how this thing works. Then you and Goose can take the lead. O.K., Goose?"

"Indeed, Sire."

He spun away shouting, arms waving, **"SERGEANT, SERGEANT!"**

"SAH!"

"You know the drill, front, rear, and sides. Do get cracking, shall we?"

"SAH!"

The Guard scattered under the bellowing of The Sergeant.

Goose trotted back to Tinker.

Sorrowful was nodding his head as Tinker finished his explanation.

"Simplicity itself, John Tinker. Of course, in The Six Lands we have no need for such devices."

He gestured at the surrounding hills.

"We do not have this confusion." Looking at Goose, he stated, "I am quite ready Prince Goose, if you are?"

"All do be in order, Sire, Duke Sorrowful."

Goose stepped back and waited.

Sorrowful turned to Tinker and whispered, "I thought that I was a, ahm, Count, the last time."

Tinker bent over and whispered back, "It seems you have been promoted."

He straightened up.

"O.K., lets get this show on the road."

Sorrowful headed for the lead group with Goose.

Goose said something to him and turned back, and stopped near Tinker, looking very nervous.

"Yes?" asked Tinker, wondering.

Goose was nervous. It was strange for him to look this way.

"What?" repeated Tinker.

"Ahhhh, Sire, do think thee t'would be right, and proper, do thy Lady Chen come some way with us?

With thy permission, Sire?"

"Us?"

"Duke Sorrowful, The Guard, and meself."

Tinker stifled a smile and turned. She was waiting, three paces back and to the right, arms tucked in her sleeves.

"Ahhhhh, Chen, would you like to accompany the advance guard? Oh, and by the way, what form of address would you prefer we use?"

She bowed to him and spoke in a most subdued tone of voice, "Great One, you may call me Chen. I am hardly a Lady."

She straightened up and spoke much firmer and louder. "However, my place is here. Near you."

Tinker beckoned to her. She walked up to him.

"You go with Goose and Sorrowful. But if anything happens, you hurry back to me."

She bowed. "Asss you command so shall it be."

She turned and walked swiftly toward where Sorrowful stood waiting for Goose.

"Go, Goose," said Tinker.

Goose had to trot to catch up with his group.

The Company started off, wending its way around the bases of the hills.

Mountain elected to walk at the back, with the Rear Guard.

Tinker reached for Chicken's arm.

"Well, here we go again, again. So far we haven't seen any sign of Dram or his monstrosities. But I think we had better be on our guard. This kind of good fortune can't last forever."

Chicken slipped her arm through his, and said,

"Thee do be most likely correct in that." Her free hand fingered the hilt of her sword.

Toucan nodded to himself.

Smoke cast her sensenet to its limits.

We are alone.

"Good," said Tinker. "At least it is a nice day for a walk."

The day wore on.

Muscles slowly adjusted to walking again and the loads they were carrying.

Lunch came and went.

Then dinner.

Then along came twilight.

John Tinker?

Sorrowful?

Goose wishes to camp on the top of this next hill.

O.K., lead the way.

The Company reassembled itself on the top of the chosen hill. Packs were cast down, sleeping bags shaken out and positioned. Goose selected the first section of The Guard and had The Sergeant place them around the hilltop. Satisfied with their placement, he returned to the center of the camp.

"Sire, all do be ready. Should any thin' approach, we forewarned will be."

"Good."

Tinker flapped his bag again and laid it over the edge where he could lie on the slope and look out at their surroundings, out at the far horizon. The hills seemed to stretch forever. The sky dimmed and darkened.

Chicken threw her bag next to his, pushed and shoved it around, then lay down on it and pressed against his side. Finally she nudged him with her elbow.

"Oh."

He swung an arm around and pulled her close as she rolled onto her side.

"Lots of stars up there, Princess."

"Ummmm, My Lord."

She plucked at his shirt and slipped one hand inside.

He was already falling asleep.

A hand was violently shaking his shoulder.

"Highness, Highness!"

"Umpf? Huh? What?"

"Highness, do wake up."

"Morning already?"

Tinker opened his eyes. It was pitch dark, all he could see were the stars overhead.

"It is still night."

Toucan gave him a gentle shake.

"Look at yonder horizon, there pon thy right."

Tinker sat up and looked.

"What is it?"

A reddish, pulsating glow filled one spot on the edge between dark hills and dark sky.

"I know me not, Highness. It do start some time ago. The Guard do wake me. It do seem most important."

"Quite right. Smoke?"

Too far.

"I wonder what it is?"

A soft musical voice spoke to him, "Dragonfire. It isss dragonfire, Great One."

She was kneeling by his side.

Tinker hadn't heard her silent approach.

"Dragonfire?"

"Yesss."

"There is a dragon out there doing that?"

"Yesss."

"Friend or foe?"

"From this distance I cannot say. If you wish I shall go and see. It would take but little time."

"Ahhhhh, NO, it can wait. You had best stay here."

He lay back, and mumbled, "We might as well get back to sleep. It seems to be staying way over there."

Toucan and Chen left as he lay back and rolled onto his side.

Chicken kissed the tip of his nose and pulled him close as he adjusted the blanket.

The Company settled back down.

A solitary figure walked to the edge of the hilltop and stood facing the glow. Her eyes flickered green flame. A low hissing sound issued from her lips.

They had been traveling for three days now. Still wending their way through the hills. Still walking through deep grass. Still wondering what the dragon on the far horizon was doing. And why they were here.

Tinker spoke to no-one in particular, "You know, I think I am really going to be glad when we leave these hills. I am ready for a change in scenery."

"Indeed, Highness, I do agree. Quite."

Toucan bobbed his head and waggled one hand, observing, "It do pear most seamless sea of swelling green."

"Most poetically bespoken, Brother. Not so, My Lord?"

"Ummmmmmm, yes. An interesting image."

Tinker looked over at Toucan and said, "All right, spill it."

"What would thee have me pour pon lush ground, Highness?"

Tinker sighed.

Chicken suppressed her smile.

Toucan waited.

"Ahhhhh. Well. Lets just say that you have been frowning about something all morning, so what are you frowning about?"

"Ahhhh. I do be mere casting me'mind back pon last quest and it do seem a'me that then we do be a'progress toward something, but now not."

"How so"" asked Tinker and Chicken in unison.

Toucan smiled at them and began to explain.

"In the past travel, each time in some new spot, there do be some foul demonic minion of Dram a'waitin'. So far, none at all. Even Macabre, a personage worthy, in a sense, of Dram's level of destructive tendencies, do seem to be allied not with that one."

Tinker shrugged his shoulders, and said, "Something to think about, all right."

Toucan continued, "There do be more."

"More?"

Toucan nodded gravely.

"Indeed, Highness, indeed."

"What? More?"

Toucan frowned. "It do pear a'me, it do, that we do be much less well armed than time past. Yet Guiding Wizard do Us tell of far worse things to be a'coming."

Chicken burst into the middle of Toucan's dissertation, "Brother, think thee we do be less well prepared? Do we be not twenty times more provisioned? Do thee forget a'sleeping pon most hard rock and having naught for empty bellies? Hast not The Royal Magician," Tinker smiled to himself at her labeling of Big Red, "doubled The Guard?"

"Aye, Sister, most true. But where do be our magical weapons? What have we a'gathered to sweet bosoms thus far?"

Tinker opened his mouth, Chicken cut him off.

"We do have pale globe of Snojin. We do have Master Chen amulet."

He nodded at her, and shrugged, and replied, "Most true, My Lady Queen." It was a very slow, very deliberately response. "Our Lord do carry fine orb in pocket. Amulet do be enow most delicate and young woman." He held up his hand. "THAT! TWO! That do be most thin sum and substance of thaumaturgic armory. Passing small, me'thinks."

"Ahem," said Tinker, pushing his way back into the argument. "That is not quite all. We have this."

He fished the wand from his pocket.

"My Lord, tis naught but small stick."

"Not so, Princess." He flourished it before them.

"This, my love," he waved it at her.

"This, Toucan," he waved it at him.

"This is one of Big Red's very own magic wands. Taken fair and square by Silly from his father's desk and handed to me just as we departed Paradise. Silly thought it might come in handy."

"One of The Wizard's magical devices, Highness?"

"Yep," replied Tinker, tucking it back into his pocket. "It ought to be very powerfu1."

"Indeed." Toucan nodded.

Chicken tugged at his arm and smiled.

"Sweet Prince, do some small legerdemain, some slight trivial for to pass time."

Tinker laughed softly at her expression, and cleared his throat, "Ahem. Well, there is one small problem with that."

"Indeed?"

Ummmm, yes. We were on our way, and Silly didn't want his father to see what he was doing, and so . . . "

"And so?" asked Chicken.

Toucan waited.

Tinker ducked his head, and mumbled, "And sooooo . . . he didn't have time to tell me how to work it."

With that, all conversation dropped back into the pit of silence it had been dragged from.

Another day wandered to a close.

And another started, to be greeted by Mountain, as he had greeted each one and every one since they had arrived.

"BY DUMPF, another beautiful, balmy day."

They had altered the direction they had been heading since they had seen the dragon-fire on the far horizon. For days they had steered in that direction. But nothing shone out there. The glow had been a solitary event.

On the evening of the ninth day, as he fluffed up his sleeping bag, Tinker called Toucan over and pointed at the horizon, and asked, "What do you see?"

Toucan squinted, then smiled. "Mountains, Highness. I guess me t'will do be yet two, three days err we leave these hills behind."

Tinker waved his arm. "Goose, come over for a minute, would you?"

Goose bounded over to them. "Righto, Sire. What do be a'foot?"

Toucan pointed at the spot.

Goose looked, leaped into the air, clicking his heels three times, and landed, smiling broadly.

"BY GEORGE, they do be mountains. Three days iffen we do but amble, two if we do be a'hurryin'. Might we not hurry, Sire?"

"Lets amble. No sense getting tired before we get there."

Goose looked disappointed.

"However," suggested Tinker, "you could send an advance party to study the countryside before we get there."

"Jolly good, Sire, most jolly good. By your leave."

He quickly bowed, spun and ran, shouting, **"SERGEANT, TO ME, TO ME!"**

"SAH!"

They met down the slope.

Tinker watched as Goose threw his arm around the Sergeant's shoulder and pointed the direction they would be going. The conversation became more and more animated. Finally The Sergeant turned and hurried down to the picket line of The Guard. Goose ran back up the hill and bowed deeply and ornately.

"Pon me word, Sire, I do mean me nay disrespect a'runnin' off."

Tinker laughed and smiled at him.

"Hardly something to worry about. I am as excited as you are to get out of here. What's up?" He pointed down the hill.

Goose watched Tinker's face carefully as he spoke.

"I do me think for to go ahead with small Duke and guidin' machine." Before Tinker could say something, Goose hastily interjected, "He can keep thee most well informed, Sire. Sire?"

"Ummmmmmmm." *Smoke?*

She padded over and sat and looked from Goose to him.

Too far. I could go partway and overlap, each being at the opposite edge of the sensenet. I have seen nothing, yet.

A small, dark figure bounded up the slope and over to them. "I am ready to go."

Sorrowful smiled, his backpack on his back, and frowned slightly.

"This has not been much of a tale to tell. My sons

will be disappointed."

Tinker looked at him, and asked, "Sons?"

"Yes, three."

Sorrowful shook his head sadly, and said, "But they are not interested in telling tales. They must take after their mother." Then he smiled and added, "But my Grandson, Tears, seems to be. But it will be a few years yet before it becomes apparent."

Tinker nodded. "Yes, I guess I remember you saying something about a wife."

Sorrowful laughed and smiled broadly. "It all happened after I returned. I was walking and telling The Tale and that is how we met, my wife and I."

"How old are your sons?"

Sorrowful stared into space and wiggled his fingers.

"Twenty, the oldest is twenty."

Tinker stared at him. "Twenty, it was twenty years between this time and the last?"

Sorrowful shook his head. "A bit longer than that. We did not have children right away. It has been, urn, twenty-four years. I had always assumed that was my one and only Great Adventure."

Tinker took a closer, more careful look at his small companion. Now that he knew what to look for, he could see the subtle changes. He dropped his hand on one of Sorrowful's shoulders.

"It had only been a single year for me, just one year."

Chicken slipped her arm around his waist, feeling his pain at remembering that year.

"Well, no matter," said Sorrowful with a slight

shrug, "it just makes The Tale more telling." Then he gave Tinker a wide smile. "I am ready, shall we go?" He looked at Goose.

"Sire?" Goose looked at Tinker.

"Go ahead. Smoke will see to it that we are always in contact."

As everyone headed off to settle a last few details, Goose called to Sorrowful, "Tell The Sergeant to make ready."

Then he looked at Tinker, face carefully held blank.

"Sire?"

Tinker tried to look as serious as Goose did.

"Yes?"

"Think thee Lady Chen might fare a'us?"

Tinker rubbed his chin thoughtfully, prolonging his response time. Goose almost fidgeted. Almost.

"Sure, Goose," said Tinker. Then he called, "CHEN!"

"Illustriousss Master," said a small, musical voice from his other side. No-one had seen or heard her approach.

"OOP!" Tinker jerked slightly, then frowned at her. "Goose wants you to go with them. Do you want to go?"

"Asss you wish."

"Then I wish you to do that. O.K.?"

She bowed and murmured, "Yesssss, Wise Master, it will be so." She straightened up and looked at Goose. In the gathering dusk, Tinker couldn't see the flush rising on his cheeks. Chen didn't mention the fact that dragons could see as plainly in the dark as during the day. She smiled, a small smile, and followed Goose.

Blurratha. Hidden. In Plain Sight.

"We saw the unusual in the Anaza viewing pool."

Fairlan stroked the fur on her beast's back.

"It was that one and those strange companions that aided on the assault on the Evil One. I observed this."

The four, small, slim beings, each the Head of their Cluster, stood in a loose group, their beasts at their sides, holding a Formal Cham.

This type of discussion was a rarity, and only convened for the most important of decisions. The Wood With kept to themselves and were so successful that only one group of *Others* even knew of their existence. Those others were the Anaza Sorcerers, who were almost as reclusive as the Wood With.

Clearlar scratched his beast behind one ear and nodded. "So this unusual one is to be respected?"

Faerlar sucked in a sharp breath. His beast growled. He hissed at it to quiet it down.

"Respected?" He looked at Fairlan.

She shook her head. "Not suggested!"

Ringlan nodded. Her beast grumbled. She tugged gently on one long ear, just to quiet it, and asked, "Does Fairlan suggest that we have an interest in this creature?"

Fairlan patted her beast on the side of the neck.

"I feel some sense of that. The Anaza watch it and discuss a future involvement told by their ancient verses."

Clearlar frowned at her. "Know these of our watch?"

Fairlan shrugged slightly. "A little." She smiled at him.

"Our presence does leave some small olfactory trace. Somehow the Anaza have learned to recognize this. No other beings have this understanding. The Anaza are guarded and wish us to not know of their interest."

Clearlar ruffled the fur on his beast's head and nodded slowly.

"Send Flerlan to see this unusual one. Now and then. She is the most talented at slipping through."

Fairlan nodded and the group dispersed, each carrying the decision to their Cluster so all would know.

Pleasant Trip, Fair Surprise

Lair Of The Dragon.

Twilight kissed the edge of day as Smoke drifted past the outer ring of The Guard and down the slope. She would get close enough to the advance party soon enough. It was a pleasant morning for a run. Behind her she heard and felt Toucan rousing up those still sleeping.

Tinker mumbled in the tangle of his sleeping bag, oozing his way toward waking consciousness. Chicken rose, for once before he did, slipping quickly from her bag, the low hum of excitement in the encampment pulling her into action. The lethargy of the long past days was being shaken off.

"Brother, what say thee bout all this?" she asked.

Toucan gave her a quizzical look, one eyebrow arching sagely.

"Tis naught but change. In but three days we shall quit these hills. Beyond, unknown. Further still, mountains. And a creature. Unknown. Two days hence, we do begin to know."

Chicken stretched, yawned and rubbed one hip.

"These pads do be most marvelous. Yet, some small stone do bite me still." She grinned at Toucan as she grabbed some breakfast.

"Me'thinks, Dear Brother Wise, that thee do best keep fine watch pon wall-eyed Goose lest most fair

Dragon do roast him well."

Toucan frowned at her, casting a quick glance at Tinker who was squirming but not quite awake, and said softly, ever so softly, "Think thee so?"

Chicken gave him a heavy comradely thump on the shoulder, rocking him to one side, and grinned.

"Oh aye, Brother, We most do. Our Own thoughts do say fair Dragon would play goose to that gander but do be most uncertain bout propriety, her being Our Lord's Verra own guardian amulet and all. Whish, speak no more."

She twirled on her heels, took two long strides, and shoved, not too gently at the figure just sitting up with the tip of one boot.

"Rise and shine, Me'Lord, fair sun do shoot cross fair blue sky. The Company do be most eager for to proceed yet thy Verra own slothful dalliance pon most hard ground do even now confound the plan."

"Ump? Huh?" He grabbed her ankle, twisted and pulled. She tumbled more or less into his lap.

"What is all this Elizabethan gibberish, this morning?"

He swatted at one of her hands, and yelped, "Hey, stop that!"

Now fully awake, he lurched to his feet, dumping her onto the heap of sleeping bags. Leaning over, he glared at her, and snarled, kinna, "Now what is going on? Huh?"

Glancing up at him through her eyebrows, she answered in her most demure manner, "Nary a'thing, My Lord. Tis naught but most high spirits pon most fine a'morn."

His mouth wrinkled at one corner as he watched her face. There was something else. He could see it in her eyes. He could feel it in her mind, but he didn't push. So he shrugged.

"I am not going anywhere until I have some breakfast. If that would be all right with you."

She leaped up, kissed the tip of his nose. "Most certain Own true loverly. Brother Toucan do fix most fine repast. Whilst thee do eat, t'will pack, most carefully, this thy pack."

She knelt down and began to gather everything together, giving Tinker a heavy shove with one shoulder, removing his foot from the sleeping bag.

As soon as he had finished breakfast, and stood up, she lightly swung the heavy pack onto his shoulders, fussing over him as he adjusted its fit.

Toucan cleared away the remains of the meal, Chicken grabbing this and that as he did. She was still feeling quite hungry.

Then they followed Toucan down the hill. He strode in front, leading the way.

Tinker wondered, really wondered, as he slyly watched Chicken, who seemed to be bouncing with each step, what was going on. This time.

So he tired a tentative probe, "Princess, you seem to be in high spirits this morning?"

She beamed at him, and replied "Tis most true, Our love."

"Ahhhhh, any special reason?"

She gave him an innocent look, and replied gently, "Oh, nay. Tis but most fine morn we do feel."

"Hummmmmmm." He didn't believe it, not for

a moment. There were aspects of his ladies he knew he would never fathom.

"Just the way they are put together," he mumbled to himself.

"Sweet Prince?"

"Nothing," he mumbled.

The rest of the day was just another day, just like all the previous ones. Finally toward the start of dusk he heard from Sorrowful, using the Golden Eye jewel set in the hilt of his weaponkin.

John Tinker, we have arrived.

What do you see, Sorrowful?

Desolation. A vast area of cinders and slag, porous rubble and ash. Not a living thing out there. We will camp on a nearby hilltop and wait your arrival.

"Well, Princess, no news is good news. I suppose."

"Indeed."

Tinker turned to Toucan and told him, "Just heard from Sorrowful. It seems we are facing some sort of volcanic wasteland ahead. We will have to make sure that all the water containers are filled to the lip at every opportunity. We will catch up with them tomorrow."

Toucan jogged back to relay the news to the rest of The Guard and to Mountain.

Mountain shrugged his shoulders, it didn't seem to be much of a problem to him. What's a little desolation? Just like home. That was a comforting thought.

Late the next day, suddenly, rounding a hill, they exited into a long valley sided with dwindling hills. Off to the right they could see small figures standing on the top of one of the last hills. When they reached the top of this hill, they could look out toward the distant mountain ranges.

Between the mountains and the hill where they stood was an open, grey space. A faint breeze out there stirred wisps of ash into faint plumes making drifting smudges in the air. Everywhere there were crags and spires, glistening black points on a dull background. Here and there, reddish blotches, splashes of something.

Tinker though they could be looking at the moon's surface if it came in these colors.

Mountain thought that this didn't look as bad as one of the Empty Wastes on Stumpf.

Goose and Sorrowful came trotting over.

"Greetings, Sire."

"Almost eventime, John Tinker."

Tinker addressed them jointly. "What do you think?" He pointed at the scene before them.

Sorrowful answered. "John Tinker, it appears that we have left sterile green for barren grey."

"Certainly looks that way. Where's the camp?"

"This way, Sire." Goose led them around to the other side.

By the time they had settled in, twilight had fluttered into night.

Goose gestured broadly, and explained, "Nice spot. Good view. Easily defended. Has own water just yonder. Fair spring do spout cool water."

Tinker allowed himself to be led upon an inspection. It was a good spot to camp.

A dark shadow slipped up over the edge in front

of him.

Good evening, MindMate.

"Hi, Smoke."

Chicken walked over and ruffled the fur behind her ears.

Tinker turned toward Goose, "Any problems on the way here?"

"Nay, Sire." Goose shook his head. "Nary a'problem durin' fair trip."

"But?" asked Tinker.

The words came all in a rush, "The Lady Chen do herself disappear durin' last even. Sire."

Tinker stared at him. "What? How could she disappear?"

Goose bit at his lip. "I know me not, Sire. One moment, she do be here, then she do not. Dark evenin' t'was quiet and peaceful. One great cloud do itself appear, then disappear, driftin' out and away." He pointed. "Yonder, over emptiness vast." He waved toward the shattered plain.

"A cloud?"

Indeed, Sire." He nodded. "T'was most large a cloud t'were. Barely a'skimmin' top of The Guard as it do pass."

"Strange. Smoke, did you see anything?"

No. She disappeared from my sight.

"Well," he sighed. "It is too late to do anything about that now. Is there anything to eat, we haven't eaten since lunch time?"

"Meals await thy party, Sire. The Duke do set some of The Guard to preparations when first all were seen a'comin' in."

"Good. Well, let's eat. Tomorrow we can figure out what we need to do, if anything." He nudged Chicken as they walked along.

"Pick a spot, Princess."

She pulled him to one side.

"Here, My Lord."

"Just right." He dropped his pack, rolling and stretching his shoulders, and smiled at her. "Care to join me at dinner, Fair Maid."

She linked her arm through his, and wondered, "Thee do pear most light-hearted pon The Lady Chen's disappearance, Our Prince."

"I figure a dragon ought to be pretty good at taking care of itself, ah, herself, don't you ?"

"Really think thee she do be actual dragon monster. She do pear most delicate and fine of form and feature. A most luscious oriental morsel, this thy concubine."

Tinker laughed softly and bumped her with one shoulder, and said, "That delicate little lady, when we first met, picked me up and set me upon my feet with the same ease that Mountain picks up Sorrowful. Say, that smells good."

He sniffed heavily at the cooking smells. Then he glared at Chicken and growled, "And she is not my concubine."

The Guard tending the cooking pots smiled at the compliment to their cooking, saluted, handed them two plates, and left, deciding a royal debate was not for them.

Tinker and Chicken were shortly joined by the rest of their party who scattered around, sitting on the grass.

When all had finished they headed for their chosen sleeping places, Chicken and Tinker pushing and shoving their sleeping bags around until they could stretch out on the slope and stare at the view. Slipping one arm around, he felt her slowly drift to sleep.

Tinker watched the strange star pattern and wondered where in the universes they might be. Then he saw it, some large shape blotting out the stars, drifting silently overhead, coming from out there. He jolted upright, snapping Chicken wide awake.

"Did you see that?"

"What, My Lord." She rolled sideways and snatched for her weapon. Her sword slithered free.

"I thought I saw something go by, up there." He pointed.

"What, pray tell?"

"I don't know, just a large something, blotting out the stars."

She shoved her sword into its scabbard, set it to one side, and wiggled into a comfortable spot, tugging at his arm.

He lay back, rolled over and kissed her.

"Ummmmmm, JohnLove," she murmured.

"Ummmmmm," he agreed.

She began to unbutton his shirt.

At the first edge of dawn, Toucan woke, and circled the encampment. One of The Guard waved at him from the perimeter, signaling all was well. Toucan stopped and stared. Chen was preparing breakfast. He hurried over to her.

"Lady Chen?"

She stood and bowed. "Illustriousss Counselor Toucan."

"Ahhhh . . . here, do allow me." She didn't move.

"Please, it isss not proper work for one such asss you. Please, please allow thisss humble servant to finish her work."

Toucan stopped and smiled. "Ah, well, yes. Do proceed then." He walked away to rouse the rest of the camp.

Chen turned back to her chosen task. With two long fingers, she picked up a glowing coal, blew it carefully into flames, and then carefully poked it under one of the pots. From all around she could hear the waking sounds of the camp. She selected another coal and repeated the process until all the pots were heating.

Suddenly she looked up. Two great, orange-gold eyes were staring at her from a face covered with dark fur. The long canines glistened brightly in the first rays of the rising sun.

Chen stood and bowed. "Noble Lady Smoke."

Smoke's long, rabbit like ears, stood straight up, twitching here and there as she listened to the morning noises.

Tinker strolled up, and smiled at them.

"Morning ladies. Good to have you back, Chen."

Chen whirled around, fell to her knees, palms flat on the grass and crouched before him, forehead pressing into the thick green.

"Aaaaiyeeee, Mighty Master and Lord of All, if I have offended you, beat me."

"Stop that, Chen! You are going to have to stop

saying that. Up, up!"

She flowed to her feet.

"Right," said Tinker, "much better." He walked around her and peeked into one of the pots, and sniffed. "Looks, and smells, good."

Behind him the rest of The Company began to form a line. He glanced back.

"Guess it is time to eat."

Tinker heaped his dish and walked off, gesturing for Chen and Toucan to follow as soon as they had served themselves.

Tinker found a place to sit, on the edge of a large earth slump, his feet dangling over the side. Chen sat nearby. Toucan handed Tinker a cup.

"Thanks. So, what did you see out there?"

"All of that isss a dragon'sss playground, Great One. Beyond, in a small valley, at the furthest end, isss a cave of tangled complexity. Thisss isss the place where the dragon dwells. It isss the ruler of thisss land. And it guardsss the treasure that you seek, The Egg of Time. To get it away we shall have to kill that worm."

Tinker stared at her, startled by the vehemence of her tone, not by her words.

"Couldn't you just talk to it? I mean, as one dragon to another?"

She hissed at him, and shook her head, "Thiss iss a Western Dragon."

"Ah, O.K., a western dragon. Um, so what? I mean, why is that so bad?"

Chen bent at the waist, her forehead pressed into the grass. "Forgive thisss humble girl, Lord, for her terrible mannersss."

"Chen, will you stop doing that! Please? Tell us about this dragon, this, eh, western dragon."

She sat up, shame-faced, and spoke in a very soft voice, "A Western dragon isss a vile creature with stinking breath and poisonous fangsss. This one is big and old. The entryway isss stained by the fire and smoke of itsss fell breath, the dark interior isss littered with the bonesss of itsss victimsss. It will not give up itsss hoarded wealth easily."

Tinker looked out at the desolation they would have to cross. "And we have to kill it?"

"Yesss, Great One, there isss no other way to separate these greedy reptilesss from their long guarded treasuresss."

Tinker looked at her, and asked, "Chen?"

"Yesss?"

"How do we do that?"

She slowly shook her head as she replied, "The firey onesss are hard to kill. Perhapsss," she looked across the camp, her eyes fastening upon the figure of Goose standing among The Guard as they ate, "The Rightousss General of the Imperial Guard will find a way."

She bowed her head and stated, "He isss most wise in the waysss of the warrior."

Tinker smiled. "Perhaps."

"Honorable Master, may this poor female speak with the Warrior In White about these mattersss?"

"Sure." He nodded. "Ah, please feel free to do whatever you might feel is best, urn, without asking, all right?"

Chen bobbled her head and stood, halting as he

continued, "And tell Goose to start preparations for leaving, we might as well head out into that mess." She smiled, bowed, and walked away. Toward Goose.

Tinker ate the last bit on his plate and rose to his feet.

"Ready, Toucan? It looks like a long, hot, dusty day or two lies before us. And then all we have to do is kill a western dragon." He snapped his fingers. "No problemo."

Toucan stared at him.

"Just a joke," said Tinker. "Let's go."

The Company moved, merged and broke into parts as Goose assigned each section its proper place in the planned movement across the waste lands. Soon the lead contingent of Guard moved off, Goose, Sorrowful, and Chen in their midst. They hadn't taken twenty steps when they were halted by a loud bellow.

"**HALT! By DOUBLE-DUMPF, stop I say!**"

Mountain came stomping from the rear spot he had been assigned, and grumbled at them, "ROCKS AND STONES, halt, I say, HALT!"

He stopped and glared down at Tinker. It was a very dramatic glare as he stated firmly, "John Tinker, on my time and place, from which I have been so rudely taken, again, once again forced to help you small folk out of your many problems, such as they are, we have places such as those. And I have crossed these places, many, many times. I think it would be wise if I went first, to find the proper way across. On STUMPF such places are hard places to cross. Few leave who enter. Only the most experienced can find their way."

He gave a great thump to his chest with one fist,

and said, "And this boulder is one of the very most experienced there is."

Sorrowful had walked over during this tirade. He gave a mighty kick to the side of Mountain's boot, just to draw his attention.

Mountain peered down, and exclaimed, "The talking flea has joined us."

His voice dropped to his normal tone as he asked, "Do you not think I am correct, Sorrowful?"

Sorrowful looked up and around at them and smiled.

"John Tinker, this mountain of sound is probably correct, this time. From all I have been told of our respective times and places, this place is most like the stony homeland of this bellowing stomach."

"You need a guide. I am that guide." Mountain gave his chest another thump.

"O.K., lead the way," said Tinker. He looked down at Sorrowful and suggested, "He probably knows what he is doing."

"Probably knows what he is doing," grumbled the large man. "ROCKS AND STONES, SAND AND GRAVEL, I should just let you all get lost in there. Just to prove the point." He paused, then continued, in a slightly less loud tone of voice, "But I will not. For the good of the quest." Then he bent at the waist until his head was level with Tinker's.

"Beside, I was getting tired of drifting along at the back of the line." He swivelled, still bent, and looked at Chicken who had just joined them, and rumbled, "Give this piece of stone a good-luck kiss, Princess. This land we must pass through is more wicked that it appears."

Chicken stood on her toes, stretched, and kissed his cheek.

Mountain straightened up, almost smiled, and strode off, announcing loudly, "**ROLL ON!** As my twice grandfather would say, **ROLL ON!** The sooner in, the sooner out."

The lead party followed him and soon disappeared into the wastes. At measured intervals, the rest followed.

As they struggled along, it rapidly became apparent that Mountain did know what he was doing. The trail he marked was erratic but always skirted the worse places and always kept them heading in the right direction.

Evening found them perched on the edge of a deep chasm that bisected their path.

Peering over the edge they saw shear walls glistening in the faint light. Looking out, the dimly seen opposite walls rose from shadowed bases. On the bottom, tangled with mist, nothing moved.

Goose hurried up to Tinker's side. "Sire, it do appear that here we must camp. Mountain do feel pon fair morn's light he will himself find some passage down. T'will be dry campin' as all water do far below lie."

Tinker nodded.

"O.K., lets make camp, eat, and sleep. Tomorrow will be a day of hard work."

"Righto, Sire!" Goose saluted and hurried off to set up the camp as he felt best. Soon it would be too dark to do anything orderly.

Camp stoves flared as the simple meal was prepared.

The Company settled down right after dinner, wondering what they would find below. And soon fell asleep.

Goose snapped awake. It was dark, nearly pitch dark. Something heavy was pressing down upon his chest. He couldn't inhale. In the faint light cast by a tiny moon he could vaguely see something reptilian crouched there. Its legs had pinned his arms to his sides and trapped his thighs firmly. He could barely kick his legs. He tried to shout.

Nothing happened. His vocal cords were numb.

The things eye's glowed orange as it opened its jaws wide, the rows of teeth flickering pin-pricks of moonlight. Slowly it reached for his face, its tongue flickering in and out, judging the distance.

The creature snapped into the air. It writhed in agony, tail flaying wildly.

Something cracked. The head tumbled to the ground, the body was flung into the canyon.

Goose rolled onto his side, rasping deep burning breaths into his lungs, chest heaving. He desperately scrabbled sideways as something clamped onto his forearm and lifted him up.

"Are you injured, White Warrior?"

Chen stood next to him, easily holding him upright by one arm, eye checking him for damage.

"Please sit and allow me to inspect your neck and shouldersss, Noble Prince."

She released his arm, he thumped to a sitting

position. Leaning forward, she gently prodded here and there, inspecting, seeking signs of damage. She sat in front of him and looked into his face.

"Beautiful eyes," murmured Goose, finding that his vocal cords now worked, staring deep into the green glow.

"Dragon eyesss, Beautiful Prince."

Her hands softly caressed his throat. They were warm and dry. Her breath lightly touched his cheek.

Goose reached out and clasped her hands in his. "My Lady Che . . . "

She blinked.

He was in the darkness of night. Pulling her hands free, she stood and lifted him to his feet.

Gently he pulled her close, looking down into her face. The green glow returned, greatly subdued.

"What do that thing be? And what do slay it?"

She allowed herself to be enfolded in his arms.

"Great Warrior, that thing wasss a Durag, a carrion-feeder, a creature of the worm we will soon slay. I killed it."

Goose dropped his hands, jumped back. "You?"

She laughed, the soft tinkling of bells. "Yesss, Great Warrior."

A swirling cloud surrounded her, billowing outward in all directions, not touching him. Then an immense, five-fingered, taloned foot reached out and gently tweaked the end of his nose with two talons and stated, "I am The Golden Dragon of the House of Chen."

The talons floated over his face, tickling his throat.

The cloud swirled and she was back, leaning heavily against him, breathing gently against his chest.

"Fair Lady. . . "

"Beautiful Prince. . ."

Taking one of his hands in one of hers, she led him to the edge of the cliff.

The Guard on duty only saw a cloud drift over their positions and disappear down the canyon.

Surprise, Surprise

Lair Of The Dragon.

Dawn and daylight sprang into being quickly on the high rock where the camp had settled. For once Tinker was up before Toucan. He strode around checking the encampment. Toucan beckoned and pointed. Goose lay sprawled on his back, still deeply asleep, Chen was sitting by his side. The sparkling white of his clothes had dark rusty-brown stains splashed across it. Not far away lay the head of something ugly. A puddle of gore, rusty-brown, had oozed from the mangled stump of a neck and dried on the bare stone.

Tinker walked over and asked in a soft voice, "Chen, is Goose all right?"

She stood, a faint smile on her face.

"Yesss, Great Master Of Usss All, your Tender Warrior merely sleepsss the sleep of the pleasantly exhausted." Then she told Tinker about the Durag attack and that Goose had escaped unharmed. She neglected to mention what had happened later.

Tinker smiled. "Guess he can sleep a little longer. While breakfast is being prepared I will have everyone come and take a look at that thing. Chen, would you stay and tell them whatever you know about these things?"

"It shall be asss you wish." She sat down, lightly

placing one hand on Goose's forearm.

"For having been up all night, you don't look all that tired, Chen."

She smiled, her eyes twinkling. "Dragonsss have no need of sleep."

"Oh."

Tinker walked away, found the right lump, and lightly nudged it with the tip of one boot.

"Time to get up, Princess."

Mountain stomped by searching for a way down. By the time all had finished eating, packing, and were standing, waiting, ready to go, Mountain returned.

"BY DOUBLE DUMPF," he announced, "there is one small crevice we can use."

He called The Company around and quickly explained how they were to proceed, and cautioned them firmly, "And BY DUMPF, save the sight-seeing until you reach the bottom. We do not want any plummeting bodies striking me on the head and shoulders. John Tinker, are you ready?"

"Right. Let's go."

Mountain stomped away, and started down the selected crack.

It was late in the day by the time the last of them stepped out onto a well beaten path on the canyon floor. Down here everything was different. The light was dim, filtered through a haze they hadn't noticed from above.

The grass was lush and green. Somewhere, towards the middle, hidden by thick, entangled, head-high growth, they could hear the pleasant sound of running water, splashing over rocks.

Tinker looked around and saw a group of The

Guard clustered around something.

Sorrowful waved for him to come and see. It was the body of a lizard-shaped thing, the long neck missing the head. It was already in an advanced state of decay.

"OOOOOOF!" Tinker wrinkled his nose. "Let's get away from here, that is awful."

Everyone moved far enough away so as to minimize the smell.

Sorrowful pointed back at it.

"There is one good thing about those beasts, John Tinker."

"What?"

"Short legs, they can not run very fast."

"Ummmm. Maybe they only come out at night."

"That would be bothersome. With that soft dark skin color they would be hard to see."

"The Guard will have to watch extra carefully. Where's Mountain?"

Sorrowful pointed at the only path, just where it entered the thick growth. "He went in there to see about the water, whether we can cross it, something like that."

"So where is he, there is nothing down there growing taller than he is."

Tinker stood, ready to call Goose and The Guard, when he saw Mountain rise above the surrounding vegetation and begin to walk toward them. As he trudged out into the open space they could see water running from his cloths.

"Do not, BY DUMPF, speak a HUMPFING word, not one! I was taking a drink at the edge of a deep pool and slipped on some DOUBLE DUMPFING, SAND SUMPFING, moss covered stone!"

He shook himself like a gigantic dog, scattering water over everyone close enough to be hit. His stomach made a loud sloshing noise. He patted it happily.

"As long as I was in there I drank my fill. Shall we proceed? This path leads to a clear spot which we can easily cross, fill all our water containers, and drink all we might wish."

The Company followed Mountain, single file. As they walked into the growth, Tinker started to hum to himself.

From behind him, Chicken asked, "What merry tune do be that, Me'Lord?"

"Would you like a little rendition, Princess?"

"Indeed."

He began to sing, "Hi Ho, Hi Ho, it's off to work we go, with a . . . "

Tinker sang all of the song that he could remember. "Like it?"

"Tis most merry a tune, but nay appropriate, me'thinks."

"Seemed appropriate to me."

Chicken laughed softly. "My Own True LordLove, it do seem a'Us thy humor do be some bent ."

"Humpf."

"And thee do be a'catching most foul habits from yonder great hulk, Mountain."

"Yes, dear," he said sweetly.

A small boot tip caught him squarely on the hip pocket.

"OUCH!"

Soon The Company reached the stream, crossed to the spot selected by Mountain, and stood milling around while the numerous water bottles were refilled. That deed done, Mountain hurried away, pushing to reach the far side of the gorge before the light grew too faint for them to see where they were walking.

None-the-less, they were stumbling over small unseen objects by the time they began to set up their camp.

The Guard scouted around, found sufficient dry material and started the cooking fires.

It was this flickering light that guided in the last of the hikers. Sorrowful took charge of the dinner preparations and soon announced that the food was ready to eat.

"Goose!"

"Sire?"

"We had better space The Guard quite close and keep that fire going all night. We don't want another Durag to visit."

"Most certainly not." Goose hurried away to set the picket line

After a quickly consumed meal, The Company settled down for the night.

Goose began to make a last tour of his watching troops, speaking to each man. A small figure slipped silently up to his side.

"May thiss humble one join you, Great Prince?" In the darkness her fingers twined with his. Her's were longer.

"Why, yes, Lady Chen, thee most certainly may."

Slowly they walked the rest of the circuit.

"Would it slight your honor if I called you Goose, Mighty Prince? In private?"

"T'would give me great pleasure, My Lady."

Finally they stopped and stared into the darkness of the narrow canyon.

"And what may I call you, Lady Chen?"

"My name iss The Golden Dragon of the House of Chen, rather lengthly and cumbersome. Sometimess, Grandfather Chen calls me Huo Hua which meanss Fire Blossom."

"A pretty name. May I give you one also?"

"Yesssssss . . . Goose, please do."

He turned and stared down into those wonderfully bottomless fire-like, verdant glowing eyes.

"Ember," he murmured to their flickering pulse, thinking of Fire Blossom.

"It iss a good name. Red iss the color of joy."

"Tis truly how I do feel."

They stood, aware of each other and their closeness.

The Guard on duty neither heard nor saw the great cloud that drifted silently high overhead, settling far down the canyon in a small meadow. It was a clearing Chen had seen as she had stared down into that long gorge from high above.

When the first rays of dawn filtered into the bottom, The Guard on duty were startled to see Chen and Goose walking up a small trail toward them. They were coming from somewhere down slope. Goose and Chen were laughing and smiling over some private joke.

Mountain roused the camp, almost beating Toucan to the chore, hustled everyone through their breakfast, and charged along the path they had been following and started them climbing up a narrow crack in the rock face. It was the way out, it was the way up.

Mountain went first, followed by some of The Guard. These, he positioned at strategic places to help the climbers on their way.

Hours later, hot, dusty, with muscles screaming fatigue, Tinker hauled himself up and over the lip at the top. Two great hands lifted him to his feet.

"BY DUMP," he announced, "was not that a wonderful climb. Nothing like scrabbling over rock to maintain fighting trim."

Mountain pointed at the first climbers who were now sprawling where ever they found a comfortable place.

"HUMPF, might as well find an ash pile and rest. It will be a long time before the tail of this group wags itself to rest."

Tinker staggered over to Goose and Sorrowful and flopped down. "Well gang, how goes it?"

Sorrowful lifted himself up on his elbows, grimacing and said, "One of these crawls down and crawls up is enough for a lifetime. In The Six Lands we do not have country such as this. I feel as tired as you look."

Goose, flat on his back, stared up at the sky, and stated, "All too true, Sire, all too true. I do be fair clapped out.'

Tinker sat and watched the rest as they, one by one, eased themselves up onto the flat ground.

"Make camp here, Goose. We all need a rest. We will start tomorrow."

"Righto, Sire."

Goose slowly levered himself upright and lurched away, calling, "**SERGEANT, SERGEANT!**"

"SAH!"

"On the double, man!"

"SAH!"

After receiving his orders, The Sargeant snapped around and began bellowing orders. The Guard scattered and rapidly began to set up the camp. By late afternoon the entire Company had reassembled itself and sat or lay and relaxed.

The region they were now facing was flat and stretched to a far horizon. A scatter of ash mounds dotted the surface.

Tinker stood and scanned the dismal scene. A path started at the edge of the crack they had just climbed and disappeared into the flatness. Smaller trails wandered along the cliff edge. He smiled at Chicken as she joined him.

"Care for a little stroll, Princess? A little sight seeing? It should be safe enough."

"Surprisingly, My Lord, We do believe that We can still walk."

She curled her arm through one of his. Smoke brushed past them and padded down a trail in front of them paralleling the cliff face. They followed.

"A stark land, Dusty Love."

"But it has its own beauty." His arm snaked around her waist.

She gave him a quick peck on the cheek, and

suggested, "As does Mine Own Brother Goose."

Tinker laughed softly. "So he does, so he does."

Chicken pointed at the far horizon.

"When do we reach far sere peaks, LordLove?"

"Mountain thinks we can get there in two or three days. We had better, we can't carry much more water than that."

They stopped and stared across the gorge at the far side. It was already turning into night at the bottom. Chicken stepped in front of him and leaned back. His arms coiled around and held her gently.

"Sweet Love?"

"Ummm?"

"Thy hands do be some fair gritty."

"Ooop!"

"Mayhap t'will be fine pool yonder."

She turned and wrapped her arms around him.

"You look pretty gritty, yourself," he said.

She had a grey smudge running from the ridge of her nose across her left cheek. Her clothes were gray patched and stained.

"Guess we better start back."

"She slipped from his arms, and nodded. "Indeed, My Lord."

As they walked, Chicken flapped the edges of her open shirt.

"Tis ever much cooler but most unseemly for to so stroll into camp."

She grinned at him and slowly buttoned it.

Smoke butted her gently in the small of the back.

Approaching the camp, they could smell cooking food and hear soft laughter as The Company relaxed.

After dinner, Sorrowful told them a rollicking tale that had them all wiping tears of laughter from dirty cheeks, leaving clean streaks in the dust grime. And then, little by little, the camp quieted down as each found a comfortable space and drifted into sleep.

"Me'lord?"

"Umm?"

She tugged him onto his side and murmured, "Do give Us a kiss, dirt'n all."

Across the camp, Chen stared into the black of night and watched the faint flickering. That monster was stirring restlessly. She hissed softly and moved closer to Goose.

The next three rock filled days passed as the small party trudged on. On the plain the temperature rose, the heat radiated from all sides. The bottoms of their feet ached. Endless time, filled with stumbling, cursing forever. Each camp was dry and dusty. Each pathway wander along deep inside great cracks splitting the plain, bottoms roped with onetime molten rock.

Good news boomed at them, finally.

"**PRAISE THE BOULDERS, BY DUMPF!**"

Mountain had just returned from his afternoon's reconnaisance as they were making camp and announced to one and all, "We are almost out of this ash pit. By mid-day next, we meet foothills, greenery, and water."

He dropped with a thump to a sitting position on the ground, creating a large dust cloud near Tinker.

"Lady Chen will have to guide us from there."

Mountain jerked his thumb up and over one shoulder, indicating where there was.

"That mountain range is an evil, jagged pile," he rumbled. "It will be hard climbing, hard passage, a monstrous place for a monstrous thing."

Tinker slowly nodded and looked around at his crew. Only The Guard and Lady Chen didn't wear deep lines of fatigue etched in their faces. Even Smoke seemed to be sagging. They were a real mess.

Food was eaten, not because of hunger but because all knew they must, appetites were non-existent.

Tinker slipped one arm under Chicken's head as she sprawled next to him.

"Holding up, Princess?"

"Poorly, My Lord. Tis a most ugly a'land, this."

He brushed her hair from her forehead. It was matted and tangled, and laughed softly.

"You are a real mess."

"Sweet Prince, thee be some peasant muck foulsome thyself."

Goose tried not to laugh.

Toucan frowned at her.

But . . .

the next day. . .

Mountain's prediction came true.

By late afternoon, The Company was thrashing in deep, cool pools of water. Everything that needed washing was washed together: bodies, clothing, gear.

Chicken, Chen and Smoke found their own, secluded spot.

The warm air quickly dried everything and everyone.

In the dying rays of the day, Goose flashed brilliant white again. Tinker leaped to his feet and spun as he caught the golden glow coming around a great boulder. Chicken smiled at him.

Dinner was quickly made and quickly eaten. All fell into deep sleep as the comfort of the thick grass eased cramped muscles, stiff from sleeping on hard surfaces. The mats had helped, but not enough.

Chen slipped silently past the outer Guard and headed deep into the mountains.

Toucan's eyes popped open at the first traces of dawnlight. Someone was already awake and murmuring.

He sat up and saw Chen and Mountain deep in soft conversation.

Over breakfast, Mountain explained what faced them, arms gesturing wildly and dramatically.

"BY DUMPF, the monster is so fat and heavy that it has worn a smooth path not too far from here. It leads directly to its cave. We have a long and steep hike to make. But an easy one."

Goose stood up.

"Sire, t'would do be best do we send some small advance party ahead by even intervals. Thus, if fierce dragon do us attack, thee do acquire most ample a'warnin'. Sorrowful, Mountain and I will lead. Lady Chen wilt stay with thee."

He shot her a quick glance.

"Thus between us, we shall be most small and widely spaced groups." He saluted sharply

"Your leave, Sire."

"As you wish, Goose," answered Tinker. "And Goose. . . ?"

"Sire?"

"Be careful, Mighty Warrior."

Goose giggled, and stated, "Pon my very word, most careful, indeed."

He spun away, calling, "**SERGEANT!**"

"SAH!"

"Let us be away."

"SAH!"

The lead party trailed over to and up the path, disappearing around a distance cragstone.

A faint, echoing cry came down the slope, "Tallyho, Sire . . . tallyho . . . tally . . . ho . . ."

They waited the allotted time, ate a hasty meal and prepared themselves.

Toucan sent little groups of The Guard ahead.

Finally at their turn, Tinker started up the trail, Chicken on one side, Chen on the other.

Smoke bounded ahead of them.

Then, at intervals, Toucan send the remainder of The Guard, giving final orders to the last ones as he left the camp.

He waited the allotted time, and strolled up the smooth stone passageway. As they passed around the stone outcropping, a Durag came sniffing out from under an overhang and waddled after them.

By the time that the sun crested noon, the three Guard who were the rear party entered a narrow defile and quickly hid themselves among the cracks and crevices. And waited silently.

The Durag waddled past, loudly sniffing. It hesitated. And started to back up.

A Guard leaped out, sword whipping down. The thing's head bounced to one side as the body thrashed and twitched down the sloping path, trailing gore. One of The Guard charged upward to notify Toucan while the others walked behind, watching for more unwanted visitors.

Toucan rubbed his chin. "Ummmm, praps t'will be best if we three do join with you three and wait to see whether more foul beasties do be adogging our steps."

He sat on a low boulder and waited for the two to join them. And when they did, he stood, and gestured, "Now chaps, do let us dispose ourselves amongst rocks and boulders and wait ever so patiently. And praps see whether our tail hast tail."

They disappeared. And waited.

And waited.

And waited.

Finally they heard it. Soft snuffling coming up the path. A Durag shuffled into view, its nose just above the dust on the path.

A Guard leaped out and hacked off its head.

Toucan leaped out, grabbed the head and heaved it into a deep crevice. One of The Guard chucked the body after the head.

They slipped back into their hiding spots. Small carrion eaters flitted down into the crevice, seeking a meal.

Soon, the silence was broken by the snorting of another Durag coming up the trail.

Its parts were added to the crevice.

The day wore on. One by one, more Durag joined the first.

As day began to fade into twilight, Toucan motioned them all back onto the trail.

"Lads, there do be something most wrong. Tis all too easy. We do spend day a'making carrion and now we do be most greatly separated from our fellows. Me'thinks t'was all some sly ruse to split one from t'other. Quickly, we have naught but hard run err we rejoin safely most far advanced Company."

Toucan trotted up the trail, two of The Guard ahead of him, three behind. It was a long grade, winding ever upward.

As they ran, Toucan stared at the dust, at the footprints of those who had proceeded them. All he saw was boot prints. The only tracks those of Smoke.

Dusk enveloped them . . .

Toucan's legs ached, their leaden weight dragging scuff marks in the dust. His breath rasped into heaving lungs. Slowly, slowly, his trot became a jog, became a stroll, became a stumbling walk.

High overhead, he heard it. The crackling roar of a great mass starting down, taking everything with it.

"**RUN, LADS, RUN!** Tis all for themselves, else none shall live to tell of this treachery. **RUN!**"

He lurched forward and gasped as loud as he could at one of The Guard, "**RUN, MAN, RUN!** Our Lord must be warned."

The Guard nodded and spurted ahead.

Toucan's foot slipped on a small stone, he stumbled, and knew he wouldn't make it. Dust swirled past his face, small pebbles rained down around him. The roar pained his ears.

Two of The Guard grabbed him under the arm-pits and raced forward, dragging him along, his feet barely touching the ground. Behind them came the others, glancing right and left, searching for the enemy.

The roar of avalanche drove all thought from his mind as the avalanche crashed down, the pressure wave driving them forward, knees buckling. Dust whirled in waves, rocks poured down. The ground shuddered and heaved under the pounding. And silence soft as the powder dust that covered the path settled across the scene.

Smoke sensed someone coming as they waited for the last of their party to join them.

Long moments later, The Guardsman thudded to a halt and stood at rigid attention in front of Tinker.

"What is it?"

"HIGHNESS!" The Guard spoke evenly and unhurriedly, "Prince Toucan do wish you for to know that rear party do be lured into ambush most foul."

He carefully related all the details of the event from the first Durag on. Then he pointed down the path.

"The last sound do I hear t'was sound most like mountain face collapsing pon one and all." He waited for instructions.

"OH, My Lord!" gasped Chicken.

"Let's go."

Tinker started forward, flicking on a flashlight, thanking himself for thinking of bring that. He walked as fast as he could.

It was a long walk back down the path into the narrow defile. Here, still drifting clouds of dust coated them in fine grit. The path was littered with broken shards of rock.

The shattered stone became deeper and deeper and then the main fall blocked their way.

They stood and stared up at the mass towering overhead. Chicken and Tinker flicked their flashlights over the jumble, searching for signs of their missing companions.

Tinker turned to The Guard who had brought the message. "Trooper, do you have any idea where in this mess they might be?"

"Nay, Highness."

He is here.

Tinker swung around, the beam of light darting over the great black shape of Smoke sitting up the path where the rubble was less complex.

Here.

Tinker shrugged off his pack. "We will have to dig them out."

A small hand lightly touched his arm, as she said, "Great Master, if this humble girl might offer some small suggestion?"

"Sure, what?"

"If all would move uphill to safety out of the way, I can move these pebblesss faster than you."

Chen reached down and casually tossed a boulder away.

"Whoa, wait until we are clear." Tinker danced back, swinging his pack wildly.

Everyone scattered.

Chen rapidly cleared the space before them, boulders and rocks flying down the slope. In the flickering beams of the flashlights they saw the blue and red of The Guard uniforms, torn and tattered. As Chen removed the last of the pinning rock, they struggled to sit up.

A pained voice mumbled at them, "Highness, do be that thee?"

Chen lifted The Guard free and gently picked up Toucan, setting him on his feet in a clear spot.

He grinned crookedly at her. "Tis good to see thee, Lady, Highness. T'was day spend most unwisely, I do me fear."

"You all right?"

Toucan nodded and searched the small group around him. "Only four Guard?"

One of The Guard nodded.

He sighed. "Then we have lost two. Even solid oak could withstand that not."

Tinker stared at the wall blocking the path. "We better move out of here, there could be more rock falls."

The group hurried up the path, seeking the open canyon above. As they hurried along, a small hand plucked at Tinker's sleeve.

"Master?"

"Yes?"

"Solid oak?"

"Guess no-one told you about them, The Guard. They are made of solid oak. A surprise, huh?"

"Uh, yesss. Are the rest also made of wood?"

"Nope, flesh and blood, very human. It is a good thing those two Guard covered Toucan or he would be as dead as dead can be."

They hurried in silence until Chen touched his sleeve and indicated that they had reached the wide place in the canyon where the camp could be made.

Everyone dropped their gear and flopped down without bothering to eat.

Chen and The Guard kept watch.

Morning light arrived much too soon.

Wearily, they all prepared themselves for a new day.

The advance party was soon far ahead. The rest headed out at the predetermined intervals.

It was a day spent plodding higher and higher into the reaches of dark mass mountain fastness. Time dragged leaden feet

It was two long days.

John Tinker.

What, Sorrowful?

We have arrived at the mouth of a long, blackened valley, reeking of sulphur. We are now withdrawing a small distance to await your arrival.

"Toucan, we are almost there. Sorrowful just told me that they are at the mouth of the dragon's valley. If we hurry we ought to get there before it gets too dark."

Tinker hiked his backpack into a more comfortable spot and lengthened his stride.

It was dark by the time they smelled dinner

smells drifting down slope. Goose waggled a flashlight at them, guiding them to the camp.

"What ho, Sire? Come, come, dinner awaits weary travelers. Tis some days since we do part. What ails thee, Brother? And were do be those laggards? Two of The Guard do their feet drag."

Goose stared carefully at Toucan, his flashlight running up and down the weary and dirt stained figure, and frowned.

"Praps t'would do be best do thee tell me what hast occurred these past days."

Over dinner, Toucan did.

Heavy feet thumped from the darkness.

"Well, BY DUMPF, there you finally are, John Tinker. And here we are." Mountain sat near the food, eyeing the pots and rumbled, "This is as evil a place as ever I did see."

Sorrowful stepped doser, carefully listening to everything told, steadily adding to the tale he was building in his mind, the tale of this adventure.

As they scattered to spread their sleeping gear, Tinker called, "Goose. Two days. We will camp and rest for two days."

"Righto, Sire, two days t'will be! I do send two scouts into yonder valley just for to see what might do be seen. This do be last greenery afore passin' into that sere land."

Tinker found the place where Chicken had spread their things and flopped heavily down.

"Boy, oh boy, do I need a rest."

She tugged his boots off and nodded agreement.

"Goose do himself state some smallish but deep

pool do be most nearby. Wouldst thee care for to bathe thyself, Me'Lord?"

"Sure, it will be good to feel clean again."

Reaching over, twining her fingers in his, she pulled him to his feet and led him to the spot.

At the edge, they shed their clothes and slipped into the warm water.

"We do Us bring cloth for a'scrubbing."

She began to rub his chest gently, slowing working her way around to his back, and reached over his shoulder and handed him the cloth.

"Favor for sweet favor, Our Verra Own Prince."

"Right," he snatched the offering, "gimme that thing."

He turned and began to scrub her back and side.

She twitched. "Thee do Us tickle." She spun and wrapped her arms around his neck, and sighed, "Oh my, oh My Lord."

He quickly tossed the wash cloth onto the grass.

"We can wash later."

High above, unseen, unnoticed, a great shape floated silently, drifting up the valley.

Chen looked down and decided that they would be sleeping late.

Blurratha. Hidden. In Plain Sight.

Flerlan The Observer stood with her beast in the dense shadows of The Great Tree close to Fairlan and spoke ever so quietly to her.

"From all that I have seen of the unusual one and his strange companions I feel that we, we all, have a strong interest in this one."

Fairlan jerked and stared, hard, at her. "This is a most serious thing to suggest! Explain!"

Flerlan ducked her head, and hissed, "Best most calm. I saw strange occurrence, now and then, that speaks to this suggestion."

She stood silent and gathered in her courage to proceed. Touching her beast lightly, she carefully watched Fairlan.

"I have tracked the unusual one in the other's lands, called elseplaces by most. That one is overtangled and event intertouched by the force of the one that thwarts the other."

Fairlan gasped and touched the Great Tree for strength, and nodded continue.

"I saw the females of mortality, a few. I believe something in and of the unusual one is attracting them."

Fairlan dropped to the ground and leaned her back against the trunk of the Great Tree, feeling the gnarled bark pressing through the material of her jacket, all rough edge against her, and gasped, "Those?"

"It was seen."

Flerlan knelt close to her side and whispered, ever so softly, "It was seen."

Madness Says I Love You So

Lair Of The Dragon.

Morning arrived, bright and clear. Toucan carefully kept everyone away from the sleeping pair. Goose and Chen spend a long time talking quietly, The Guard huddled around them, listening intently, all listening to what the evening scouts had to say and to what Chen had seen. Then the group dissolved as one by one The Guard filtered into the valley, passing through the narrow mouth of the desolated valley. Toucan and Sorrowful straightened up the camp while Mountain left to climb in the rocks, to peer over the high ridgeline down into the valley they would soon be traveling through.

The sun was high above the horizon when Tinker's eyes popped open. Something had him around the waist and was nibbling on his chest. He flung the sleeping bag wide, one arm grabbing wildly for his weaponkin.

Chicken pressed herself tightly against his body.

"Hist, My Lord, We do be Ourself most unclothed."

He yanked the cover back.

"You startled me."

"T'was but some verra small wake thee moment."

"I thought a Durag had me."

"Did ever so foul a'beast feel so soft?"

He rolled onto his side and peered under the cover.

"I couldn't say. I never had one in bed with me before."

She slipped up, blue eyes staring into his, and purred, "Would we but do be in more private a'quarters, this Durag would fix thee most right and proper, My Prince."

"Perhaps we ought to scout around, see if there isn't some place like that here abouts. Where's my clothes."

"Just there, by thy boots. Wouldst fetch Our own?"

He sat up, yanking on his trousers, and grumbled, "Sure. Here." He shoved them under the covers.

"Want me to make a screen while you get dressed?"

"Nay need." She sat up and thrust her arms rapidly into her shirt. "Fair morning Brother, Lady Chen."

Tinker's head snapped around. Goose and Chen were almost upon them.

"Fair Morn, Sire, Sister Queen."

"Morning, Goose, Chen."

"Fair Morn to thee both," Chicken stood, stuffing her shirt into her trousers.

"Breakfast do await," announced Goose, catching Chicken's eyes as she scanned the encampment.

"What's up, Goose?" asked Tinker.

"A'scoutin' drear valley, as thee do direct. Lady

Chen do say great worm we do seek hast most foul a'lair at far end of yonder black valley, up great and final hillside, far up enclosin' flank of most great a'mountain which do make most tight a'box of this place so dire."

Goose pointed at a narrow crack that meandered into and along the valley floor, and explained, "In cracks and crevices will The Guard soon find some most subtle a'path wherein we might creep most unseen."

"Mighty White Warrior, the vile thing knowsss of our presence but it sleepsss the sleep of evil complaisance. With itsss great size and foul helpersss, the Durag, it feelsss no need to fear. Sun Tzu said, 'He who exercisesss no forethought but makes light of hisss opponents isss sure to be captured by them.' However, I urge that we take the greatest of caution. It isss an old and mighty beast and we must plan carefully so that it attacksss when and where we wish."

She bowed to Goose and Tinker.

"Of course, Most Noble Sirsss, your humble servant, pitiful girl that she isss, merely offersss these worthlesss commentsss asss idle woman'sss chatter."

She bowed again, turned and walked away with Chicken. They were headed toward Toucan who was supervising breakfast preparations.

Goose frowned at her back. "Sire, she do have most strange ways. Be'times."

"Not strange, Goose, just different. She is a product of her culture as you are of your's." Tinker clapped him on one shoulder, and waved, "Let's go eat. We will stay here a few days and rest up. And wait for The Guard to report back. I leave the dragon assault in charge of you and Chen."

They walked over and joined the others for breakfast.

Then all wandered around the area, resting and relaxing, as much as they could, knowing what they would soon be facing.

Late in the afternoon, heads bobbling just above the water in the pool, with Smoke sprawling along the edge, carefully staying clear of the water, Chicken and Tinker relaxed.

Lunch was long past.

"My Lord, such pain to be separated so." His eyes popped open. Tears were glistening in her eyes as she looked into his.

"Don't think about it, Princess, it is over, it is in the past."

"But it do linger deep within thee. Dark Sister felt less as her clan, The Velvetmist, do surround her and keep such agony away. But thee do be but most alone."

A muscle in his cheek twitched. "Stop, stop, stop! I do not want to remember that." He forced a smile.

"Won't happen again, Big Red promised." He leaned forward and kissed her tears away.

She murmured softly, eyes glittering, "We will Ourself slit him open do he that promise fail, My Own Sweet Love."

He laughed and reached for her.

"Tis nay a'jest,"s he grumbled, frowning darkly.

"I know that."

His hands drifted down her rib cage and

wrapped around her waist, pulling her close.

It was two days later when four of The Guard returned, dirty, dusty, but bearing good news. They had found a passageway through the valley.

In the twilight of the next day The Company began to file silently into the narrow crevice and head out into the blackened valley. The Guardsmen guided the rest in a twisting turning passage up the broken and splintered valley floor. It was slow going, and warm. The black rock retained the heat from the previous day. In the confined spaces they were traveling, no breeze penetrated. The temperature soared. Overhead an unfelt breeze brushed fine grit down upon them.

Other than The Guard and Chen, Mountain was the only one who appeared unaffected by it all. His only complaint, grumbled softly, now and then, was that he would have preferred wider passageways, BY DUMPF!

Finally, ever so carefully, as the sun slipped behind a far ridge, they quietly eased themselves up and out, and luxuriated in the cool air beginning to flow downslope to the valley floor. They were led to a small depression where they were met by the rest of The Guard who had remained here, waiting for The Company's arrival. They were standing off to one side of the dragon's lair, the cave entrance looming large, a blackened shaft piercing deep into the mountain rock.

Tinker looked at his companions. They were all covered in grey. He smiled, they looked like human moles.

Chen slipped to his side and whispered softly in

his ear, "Stay here, Great Master, I will see what thisss maggot iss doing." She ran on silent feet to the cave entrance and darted inside.

"Sire!" hissed Goose.

"Shhhhhhhh." Tinker waved his hand to silence any other outbursts and sat down, waving them all to follow suit. They did. Goose watched the cave entrance, brows furrowed, hand fingering his sword hilt.

Behind them, the sky turned golden, then faded into deep, dark blue. Then black.

Few stars decorated the night sky. As they waited a soft glow eased from the home of the sun. The larger moon rose with silent, pale majesty, full and bright, illuminating the valley floor. They became stark shadows on midnight ground.

The ground vibrated. A low rumble, small stones rattled from above. Sudden, dense cloud curls erupted from the upper lip of the cave mouth.

Goose leaped to his feet, sword hissing free, as a slight figure slipped into the moonlight and darted over to rejoin them.

"Chen!" Tinker stared at her, checking for injuries.

"It iss so, Master."

"What happened."

"The worm merely turned in itss sleep. It seemed to be having a bad dream. I think that it feels usss, but it hasss not yet become alarmed. We must be ready to act at first light."

"Chen, it is your party, tell us what to do."She bowed three times.

"It will be asss you command."

She walked from person to person and whispered to each what they were to do. The Company settled to the rock and tried to get some rest.

Chen, Chicken, and Smoke disappeared into the darkness.

No one had to be roused at first light.

Tinker stood and stretched, stiff and aching. He waved Goose over.

"Sire?" whispered Goose.

"I don't see Chen, Chicken, or Smoke."

"The Lady Chen do say all must do be in place err first rays of sun do pierce this most foul abode. Look just there."

Goose pointed to the rock face high above the cave entrance.

"Is that who I think it is?"

"Indeed, Sire, tis Lady Chen."

She stood on a small ledge of rock, saw them looking in her direction, and waved, then pointed toward the valley floor.

They turned and looked. Someone down there stood in the gloom and mist, facing the cave. The sun began its slow rise into a new day and shot the first bright beams onto the valley floor, dissipating the swirling mists. The beams wandered yellow spotlights and stroked the standing figure who flashed a brilliant golden answer.

"It's Chicken," gasped Tinker. "Somehow, they washed her clothes."

He started down the slope. "I hope whatever

they are planning works. The dragon won't be able to miss seeing her."

Goose laid a restraining hand on his arm, holding him back. "Tis the plan, Sire. Lady Chen did tell that Western Dragons do have most overwhelming fondness for most fair, young maidens. And Mine Sister do be that, mongst other things."

Tinker frowned, and grumbled, "Goose, I don't like this. I don't like her being the bait."

"Hist, Sire," cautioned Goose, "something comes."

They could feel the deep rumbling beneath their feet. Puffs of smoke surged from the care. The Company scattered, ducking behind great splinters of rock and stone. Goose and Tinker shared one huge monolith.

Flames arched from the cave. They could clearly hear the rattle of sharp claws on hard rock. The creature looked out at its kingdom. The scale covered head floated from side to side on the end of a long sinuous neck, forked tongue tasting the air, seeking prey.

The fat, bloated body eased into the open air, bulging sides scraping the cavern walls, dragging behind it the long muscular tail.

Once clear of the entrance, the creature lifted it head and scanned its surroundings from high overhead, bulging, flame-tinged eyes carefully checked everything. It sniffed at the rock slopes. Chen was gone.

"**HARRO, UP THERE!**"

It was Chicken calling, jumping up and down, waving her arms, a flashing, agitated golden lure.

Hissing steam, the creature eased forward. Sunlight glistened from the slimy, green hide. Its tail waggled, brushing the few stones from the path beside it. It roared, bellowing smoke and fire. The dragon's eyes glittered hungrily as its gaze fastened upon Chicken.

Goose and Tinker choked on the sulphurous fumes enveloping them, tears streaming from their eyes. The monster brushed past their hiding place. They felt the stone column shift, and resettle. In the clearing air they drew in deep, rasping breaths, and wiped their eyes with grimy sleeves.

"**YOU,! UGLY THING!**" shouted Chicken, as the dragon hesitated, hearing foreign sounds.

"**DOWN HERE, MOST THING STUPID!**"

The head arched forward, salvia dripping from gaping jaws. It shuffled down the slope.

Tinker reached back, yanking his weaponkin down, and started to rise.

Goose grabbed his shoulder, and whispered, "Sire, we must wait, we must wait."

Suddenly the light began to dim. Overhead a gigantic cloud was billowing and growing. It capped the valley and cut the brilliant sunlight to soft twilight. A huge form moved within. The cloud dropped, enveloping all in cloaking mist. Something bellowed in rage and anger. And howled in agony. Flame and smoke boiled over their heads. Heavy thrashing shook the ground. Lightening crashed, thunder roared. Something was hissing loudly. Rock and debris crashed down the mountain slopes. The rock spire wobbled.

Goose and Tinker leaped away as it toppled over.

In the clearing mist, they could see two great

struggling forms.

Tinker stared.

Goose gasped.

The green monster writhed and struggled in the clenches of another.

This monster had its long, snake-like body thrown into an S-shape as it gripped the smaller at the shoulders and haunches with gleaming, eagle claws. Its jaws were snapped tightly behind its victim's head, pinching the neck so tight that only a slight trickle of smoke and flames burbled free.

Tinker rose from his crouch to take a better look at the struggling pair, wondering where this other thing had come from, and how they were going to escape.

The larger unsnapped its jaws from the smaller's neck and spoke to him with a voice that sounded like tinkling bells.

"Stay back, Great Master, thisss humble servant hasss yet to fully subdue thisss ugly worm and take it far from here." The great, green eyes blinked at him.

With a sudden roar, the Western Dragon twisted its head around and shoot a gout of flame and smoke down the valley floor, enveloping the yellow figure who stood watching the battle.

"**PRINCEESSS** . . ." Tinker hurtled forward, his blade singing through the air.

"**AAAAAAAAAAAAAAAAH . . .** "

Before either of the monsters could react, he had spun in a full circle and brought his weaponkin down in a whistling, overhead stroke. The dark blade clanged loudly as it struck sparks from the rock floor and rebounded. The Western Dragon's head tumbled free, jaws snapping, tongue flicking in and out. The neck flailed back and forth, showering gore in a ruddy arch, drenching Tinker.

The other dragon released its prey and lurched upward, great wings pumping.

Below, in a mad fury, Tinker spun, leaping and hacking, slashing at the thrashing carcass.

Goose leaped forward, then hurtled himself backward as the great sword flashed past his face.

"**SIRE, SIRE! STOP! TIS DEAD, TIS DEAD!**"

The mad assault seemed to increase. Pieces of the beast showered to all sides to be kicked and stomped under Tinker's boots into a pulp. Finally, when no slight shiver animated the dead thing, Tinker stopped, his breath whistling through his throat. He swayed back and forth, sword held out from his side, eyes wide, glazed, staring around him.

Goose started forward. A firm hand grabbed his shoulder and yanked him back.

"STOP! Brother, leave him be. Tis the killing madness pon him now. He do now be most berserk. We must wait, at some safe distance. Quickly, we must withdraw."

"But Brother . . . "

"We must! He do be most safe, tis ourselves who do be in greatest danger. Come, up to cave entrance let us go. There we may watch, safely."

Toucan tugged Goose away.

They joined the rest at the cave entrance. The Company stood, watching.

Tinker was motionless, apparently unmoving, unseeing.

A small winged creature floated by to inspect the carnage. The weaponkin flicked. Pieces tumbled in all directions.

Toucan spoke softly. "We must leave him be."

Sorrowful grabbed Toucan by the sleeve. "Prince, what is wrong? What is he doing?"

Toucan explained.

Mountain bent over to listen.

"DOUBLE DUMPFING DUMPF! That breaks the rock. If he has gone off the cliff, this quest is doomed. And us with it. And the treasure we have found in that filth-pit behind us."

"What manner of treasure?"

Mountain reached around and heaved a large sack from the pack on his back. He gently placed it on the ground and carefully began to unfold the cloth swaddling, exposing a gleaming white surface. He stepped back and pointed dramatically, and announced, "There, BY DUMPF, there it is!"

Goose peered at the thing. "Passin' strange treasure, I do me'self say."

"MUMPF!" snarled Mountain. "That is the ever LUMPFING, BE-DUMPFING, QUEST QUMPFING, Egg Of Time!"

Sorrowful almost danced on his toes.

"So you see, Goose, and Toucan, that is the Egg of Time. And we found it." He stood straight, and tall.

"Mountain and I, we did it. We found it. Now we can put it back where it belongs and the quest is done, almost over before it has begun." His eyes darted from face to face.

"Is not that correct?" Then he bent forward and

flicked some small speck of dirt from the flat white surface of the egg.

Toucan slowly shook his head.

"Duke, ever do I wish it t'were so, yet it do pear yet not to be. Our King do stand below, fair raging out of mind. And we must stand above, patiently a'waiting till he do become himself. As he is nought but the very key to the quest, I do be most sorely a'feared till that happy moment do occur, we must wait and wait again."

Mountain kicked a boulder down the slope.

"By TRIPLE-RAGGING-RUMPF, Prince, are you suggesting that we just sit quietly here and die. Here, in this rock rotten worm hole."

Toucan cast a wary glance up at the glowering face and suggested, "Well, I do suppose in interim we might take ourselves to far side of stark mountains and have a glance."

A soft voice spoke to them as she stepped from behind a jagged outcrop, "There is little beyond here but more of the same. This is almost an empty world, now inhabited only by those things which that death monster utilized for food."

"Lady Chen," gasped Goose.

She smiled at him. "White Warrior."

Toucan turned toward her. "You return."

She nodded at him.

"Yes, I have . . . There wasss no purpose for me to stay near that hacked and battered corpse. Even for me, the Mad Master might be dangerousss." She crumpled to the ground and wrapped her arms around Goose's legs, her head bowed.

"It isss my fate to die by your handss for it wass

my fault that The Master isss so."

Goose bent over and gently lifted her to her feet and shook his head.

"Nay Lady, speak not so. A useless death wilt cure not that which has him befallen."

Her eyes fastened upon his as she stated firmly, "Great General, it iss not proper to live with such a great shame. If you will not relieve me of my dishonor, I shall have to exile myself." She turned and began to walk away.

Sorrowful trotted up to her and grabbed her arm.

"Wait, Lady Chen, for one moment, wait. Please?" He pointed down into the valley.

"Out there, someone, or something, is coming this way. And over there is another. What do you see?"

Chen turned to looked at the specks as he pointed. Suddenly she reached down and lifted him up, her eyes boring into his.

Sorrowful twisted slightly in her grasp, and smiled wanly, "Lady?"

"I am in your debt, Master Teller of Talesss."

She set him down and walked over to stand next to Goose. He slipped his arm through her's as she pointed.

"Those specksss are Smoke and the Lady Chicken picking their way toward usss through the rubble."

Goose stared. "By George, she do be right."

He twirled Chen around and planted a kiss on her startled expression as he wrapped her in a bone-jarring embrace. Then he released her and started down the slope.

Chen yanked him to a standstill with one hand.

"WAIT! The only living thingsss that may approach him are those two for they are each a portion of himself and of hisss mind and being. And it isss hisss mind and being that requiresss healing. Leave them be."

She pointed with her free hand.

"See, even now he isss turning toward them."

Standing in the midst of the gore that he had created, Tinker turned slowly toward the approaching enemies, his sword flicking gently back and forth, waiting.

My Lord, leave it be, tis nay real.

Princess?

Soft tendrils twined through his mind and he was back on Paradise, basking in warm sunshine, a gentle breeze caressing his hair, Smoke and Chicken on either side.

Smoke?

We are both here, MindMate.

Tinker began to shuffle downslope, arms by his sides, the sword tip dragging through the rocky debris.

Chicken ran toward him as Smoke loped in from the opposite side.

They met in a heavy thump that the watching group high up the hill could hear.

Chicken wrapped her arms around him as they crashed heavily to the hard ground.

Smoke draped herself across them both. The sword clattered to one side.

He looked into blue eyes and murmured, "I saw you die, enveloped in smoke and flame. Then there was nothing, nothing left . . . nothing . . . nothing at all. Gone, gone . . . gone . . . "

Their minds slipped together, Chicken and Smoke working together, pushing the madness of loss deeper and deeper, feeling his tenseness flow away, peace slowly returning.

Sensing his return, Chicken wriggled into a more comfortable position and brushed her lips gently across his.

"Nay, My Lord, My Sweet Prince, t'was not so. As thou may see, and feel."

Smoke poked the tip of her tail into one of his ears.

Tickle, tickle.

He tried to reach for it but Chicken had her arms wrapped tightly around his chest, pinning his arms to his sides.

"T'was but some small idea that we do borrow from most fell creature, Macabre."

"Macabre?"

Yes, MindMate.

Tinker struggled and finally managed to sit up, Chicken sprawling across his lap, arms now around his neck. Smoke leaned heavily against them.

"Macabre?" he repeated.

Chicken smiled.

"Oh aye, Love, just so. Smoke do project Our Own image for foul worm to see. When he do spout smoke and fire, We do be far, far below, far down yon rocky valley, beyond most foul breathy reach. We were, and are, quite fine."

Smoke? Sister?

He is all right as well, now. But we shall have to watch him.

Watch him?

Yes. I think he is much too excitable for this kind of life.

Smoke stood and slowly padded up the hill.

Tinker surged to his feet, Chicken rolled to one side.

"Too excitable? You over grown tabby cat."

He charged up the slope and grabbed for the end of her tail, intending to tie a knot in it. The tip twitched away at the last possible moment.

He snarled at her, "Damn it, stand still."

Am I supposed to stand still while you perform such an indignity?

Chicken hurtled past him and slapped him.

"And there for thy verra own backside, Me'Lord."

Tinker yelped and jumped sideways.

"**OUCH!** Hey, that hurt." He spun angrily around and glowered at them.

Teach you to mess with your fair ladies, MindMate.

Smoke stood immobile while he walked up to her. Throwing one arm over her shoulders, he reached up and ruffled the fur along her neck.

"I surrender, you've got me outnumbered."

He walked away and picked up his sword, and started up the slope toward the watching group. They stirred uneasily as he approached.

Toucan spoke first, carefully, cautiously, "Be thee well, Highness?"

"Sure, Toucan, feel fine."

Tinker looked from face to face and asked, "So, what's up?"

The madness is trapped deep within, Princess. It will fade. But we must be careful until it becomes merely an unpleasant memory.

Indeed, Dark Sister. He is now most himself.

Mostly. But also some of us.

"Ahhhhh, Sire, if thee mindst not? Ummmmm ." Goose was looking quite uncomfortable.

"What?"

Goose pointed at him and frowned a wee bit, his nose wrinkling.

"Sire, thou art fair ruddy mess and do stink most highly."

Tinker looked down at his clothes, for the first time aware that he was drenched in congealed dragon blood. It was a surprise. And a shock. His mind danced wildly.

Smoke's mind snapped out and grabbed him. And the madness was pushed deeper.

Sorrowful lightly touched Tinker's arm and suggested, gently, "John Tinker, inside the dragon's cave there is a deep warm-water pool. You, and your clothes, might be best served if you took a long soak. We, the rest of us, can search through that lair and see what things of a useful nature might be found."

Tinker smiled at him. "Good idea, lead me to it!"

Sorrowful stepped smartly away with Tinker hard on his heels. Chicken jumped to Tinker's side.

It was only a short distance before they stood staring down at the steaming water, warm mists curling up to condense sweat drops on the ceiling which tinkled down to the floor.

"We do think Us, Me'Lord," said Chicken, "to join thee in fair tub. It do seem, it do, that thou hast bemucked Our Verra Own attire as well."

Tinker looked at her clothes, heavily stained and smeared with dragon blood.

"Certainly are," he agreed, shoved her into the pool and jumped.

Much later, some after long later, they wrung their clothes out and draped them over the nearby hot rock. Tinker bobbled in the water, his expression solemn.

"Princess, I thought that I had lost you again. And Smoke. And something just took over. Something terrible, murderous."

"T'was thy fearsome blade. And mental shock. So Smoke did say."

"It was real. The flames. Then nothing . . . nothing."

"Do leave it be, Love, do leave it be."

"I should have known, I could have been told."

"Nay so, My Prince, for most foul a'monster do be telepathic some. It do take most of Smoke's energy just to keep it a bay, blocking, shoving. She do have no strength for other matters. Thus, it do think We do be most real. And, thus, thou wert given opportunity to close with and slay great stinking beast."

"I suppose so."

He reached for her, lightly ticking her ribs, and grumbled, "Wonder what will happen next."

"Next? Do thee say next, My Lord?"

"Ah, sure, that is what I said. Why?"

She bobbled in front of him, her eyes glittering happily.

"For next tis naught but most grateful, fair maiden giving sweet reward a'her most Noble and Handsome Knight that do rescue her from most foul and terrible beast. Do thee take most deep a'breath."

"What?"

"We would not wish thee for a'drowning be."

She grabbed him and sank.

"PRINCESS!"

He barely had time to fill his lungs.

They sat, relaxing against the warm walls at the mouth of the cave, watching the sun set. Chicken's clothes glowed soft golden in the fading light. The color cast light color on his face.

His arm was draped over her shoulders.

Goose pointed. "Now do we have great Egg Of Time, what do be next, Sire?"

Tinker watched Mountain carefully wrapping the egg after he had been shown it.

"Next?"

Chicken nudged him in the ribs and gave him a lecherous wink.

"Ahhhhhh . . . next? Oh, right. We camp here and wait and see. Nothing else to do."

"Righto, Sire, camp and wait."

Goose spun around and strode off bellowing at The Guard, "All right, chaps, straighten up, do let Us get this encampment in order. Chop, chop. **SERGEANT!**"

"Yes, SAH!"

"Let Us see some little action, shall we? We do be all most hungry and tired. And most ruddy sun do be almost set. Get crackin'. **ON THE DOUBLE!**"

"SAH!"

The Guard, reacting to the bellowing commands of The Sergeant, quickly set up the camp, and started dinner bubbling in a number of pots and pans.

As soon as dinner was over, Tinker sprawled on his sleeping bag and mat and promptly fell asleep. Chicken gently pulled the top of his bag over, snuggled against his side, and joined him. Smoke flopped down on his other side, a deep thrumming sound coming from her neck and chest.

As the rest settled down, Goose wandered along the rock face and disappeared, Chen at his side.

All slept soundly.

Except for The Guard on duty.

And Goose and Chen.

Toucan's eyes popped open as the first rays of morning light shot past the far ridge. He stood, stretched and casually scanned the sleeping camp. Then his eyes popped wide in surprise. He ran to where Tinker slept and began to violently shake him awake.

"Highness, Highness . . . "

"Ummpf. Huh? Toucan?"

"The portal, Highness, tis here, now."

Toucan pointed. It stood next to the cave

entrance. The fire snakes coiled and hissed, their breath steaming in the cool air of morning.

Tinker threw his sleeping bag aside and sat up, shaking Chicken by the shoulder.

"Princess, let's go, our carriage awaits. Rouse the others, Toucan, we better get a move on."

Toucan ran through the encampment and within moments had organized the bedlam.

"What Ho, Brother?"

Goose and Chen strode into their midst smiling happily at one and all. He asked, "Do be there yet another worm?"

The Sergeant ran up and began reporting on the state of their preparations for moving out. Goose's head snapped around to stare at the portal, and gasped, "By George, device be most early a'riser."

Then his eyes danced around the turmoil, noting that The Guard had everything almost ready for travel.

Tinker joined them.

Smoke was nudging the still attempting to sleep Chicken with her head.

Goose saluted him. "Sire, it do pear all do be near readiness."

He saw Mountain swing his pack in place and heard Sorrowful cautioning him to be careful with The Egg.

Tinker smiled at Chicken as she walked up to them, handing him his pack and sleeping bag, stretching and yawning.

"Looks like we are ready to go." He stuffed his bag into its sack, fastened it to his pack, and swung the pack up and into place.

"Princess, your arm." He tucked it firmly against his side. "We can take a nap on the other side."

Smoke waited for them by the portal.

The Company formed itself into marching order as Chicken and Tinker walked over to join Smoke.

Then they stepped through.

The rest of The Company followed.

Leaving behind. . .

Silence . . .

The portal faded into nothingness.

Total and absolute quiet reigned in the desolate wasteland.

Forever.

To What Purpose Is This Waste?

A Strange Place This Is.

Tinker stepped from the portal, his right hand tightly clenching Chicken's left wrist, and promptly lost his footing.

They slid, stumbling, half-running down an immense pile of something, as Tinker yelled, "Watch it, Princess! We've come to a bad spot. **AGAIIIIIIIN!**"

They hit the bottom and staggered to a halt. Turning around, they looked up the slope, and ducked as a shower of stuff banged and clattered around them as the others emerged to stumble, wallow down toward them.

Up above, Tinker and Chicken saw the portal wink out.

"Oh, no," gasped Tinker, feeling the sudden loss ripping through his mind. One third of him was gone!

My Lord, she do be gone!"

"**AHHHHHHHHH!**"

It was Tinker screaming as he spun around searching desperately for Smoke. Chicken leaped in front of him, her arm swinging in a wide arc to smash against his face.

"**OUCH!**"

She hit him again.

"**OUCH!** Stop that! **STOP! OUCH!**"

"My Lord?"

"I am all right. Now. Thanks, I needed that."

"Indeed." She nodded.

"It was a sort of a joke, Princess."

"T'were no joke. Thy mind do be a'jittering most madly."

"Probably bruised my cheek," he grumbled, rubbing it.

"Well, I am all right now." He gently touched the side of her face. "As long as you are here." It was a useful lie. A piece of himself was missing.

"Sire?" It was a tentative question. Goose had seen his sister walloping Tinker.

"I am fine. We are fine. Momentary lapse."

Tinker stared at them, then scanned the slope of trash in front of himself.

"Just you three?"

Toucan spun around and scanned their surroundings, and nodded.

"It do pear so, Highness. We do abandoned be, it do appear."

"Damn portal," hissed Tinker.

"Do calm thyself, Our Sweet Prince. Tis most like some very subtle need that do bring we four here."

"Whoopie," snarled Tinker.

"Passin' strange name for most rubble a'filled landscape."

"I doubt that is it's name, Goose. But it does look like we are standing smack dab in the middle of someone's dump."

"Dump?" asked Toucan.

Tinker nodded and pointed at the heaps

stretching to either side of where they stood.

"Yep, looks like garbage to me. But it doesn't have the usual smell. You sure no-one else came through?"

"Indeed, Highness." Toucan nodded. "I do follow Brother Goose who do follow thyself and our Noble Queen Sister. Smoke and rest do trail behind mine own self. It seems that fey portal do itself fade err they do step forth. Where do they be?"

"Beats me." Tinker shrugged his shoulders. "They are not close, I can't feel Smoke." He looked at Chicken who saw the pain welling in his eyes.

She swung. He blocked the blow and jumped back. "Easy does it, Princess."

"Our minds must hold fast together, My Love. Else that which we, Dark Sister and Ourself, do push deep, will surface again be."

"Let's work on the mental rather than the physical, O.K.?"

Chicken stepped close and kissed his cheek.

"With some exceptions," mumbled Tinker.

Goose and Toucan had stepped back and were now eyeing the two of them with very suspicious eyes.

Tinker nodded at them. "It's O.K., you two, it really is."

"Highness?"

"Yes "

"Where might we be?"

"Beat's me. We are just here, down in the dump, for some reason. Which I suppose we will eventually figure out. This quest is even more irrational than the last time."

He turned, slipped an arm around Chicken's waist and stated firmly, "And we are staying home never again to wander. Ah, when we get home, that is. Understand?"

"Indeed, My Lord and Master," replied Chicken in her most demur voice.

"And you better believe it!" He smiled, and asked, "Or do you like to stroll through someone's garbage?"

"Nay, tis most strange a'place this."

They looked around. They were all standing knee-deep in crumbled metal containers of some kind. In every direction, as far as their eyes could see, there were gigantic mounds of the stuff. All the slopes tended in the same direction. They appeared to be at the base of a mountain range of refuse. The debris slopes curved away from them to either side. They were standing on the bottom of what appeared to be a box canyon.

Suddenly Toucan pointed up slope.

"Look, yonder, rising above these stuffs! Tis a wall."

Barely discernable in the soft mists, that they now also noticed swirling overhead, was the wall. It was a dull metallic gray blending into the dull metallic gray, mist coated sky. The wall followed, or set, the curvature of the trash mounds.

As they stared upward, a door popped open, hissed, and poured forth a torrent of material. A new slope rapidly formed nearby. The door snapped shut.

"Highness?"

"Yes?"

"Me'thinks t'would be best do we remove

ourselves some distance from here else we do becomen buried alive deep in discharge next."

Far to their right, they heard another door pop open and heard the roar of another discharge.

"Most active a'place, this do be," stated Toucan.

"Most true, Brother," agreed Goose. He pointed.

"Just there do seem to be surface firm and path a'leadin' away. Let us slither yonder and begone. Sire?"

"Lead on, MacGoose."

"MacGoose, Sire?"

"Nothing. Let's go."

They clattered through the debris after Goose and soon found themselves walking on hard, bare ground at the edge of the trash slopes.

It was a well-worn, hard-packed path that appeared to skirt along the edge of the garbage slope.

Goose stopped to rummage in the debris and looked up.

"Sire, look you here. All be naught but containers. Each shaped and sized like all others. Passin' strange, what?"

"Certainly is."

He nudged Chicken.

"Which way shall we go, left or right?"

"Left, My Lord."

"Left it is. Goose, scout ahead, if you will. Toucan, watch our backs. Princess, stay on my left side. Maybe we can find a way into this city."

"City, My Love?"

"Sure. That wall up there must be the edge of a city of some size. The portal set us down in the place where they put their garbage."

Behind them they heard a hiss and loud clatter.

Tinker waved them forward.

"Let's hurry, shall we?"

They did.

The path followed the edge of the junk heaps, intersected by many other paths coming and going from places unseen. They hurried on and finally stopped in the middle of a slight depression.

It was an intersection of some size. A dozen paths converged here, lines radiated in all directions.

"Hold up troops, this looks like an interesting spot. It looks like a main traffic node of some kind. Let's sit for a moment and think about it. We are far enough away from the trash to be safe. Let's check our packs and supplies."

Tinker shrugged his off and set it on the ground and began rummaging around in it.

"Well, Toucan, what do you think?"

"Highness, it do seem we do be adequately furnished. Goose and I have tent parts. Our Sister and thyself have cooking apparatus. We all have food stuffs. And we are all well armed. But I will sorely miss The Guard."

"And the Dukes Sorrowful and great Mountain, Brother."

"And Lady Chen," added Goose, looking most forlorn.

"What about this intersection? Any ideas?"

Tinker pushed them back to the immediate problem not wanting to think about missing Smoke.

Goose knelt and ran one hand over the smooth surface and pointed out, "Do seem some most heavy tred do pack and polish soil neatly. Fair caution tis desired as we do travel err we happen suddenly pon what manner of thing do trample this ground hard so."

He stood and dusted his hand on his trouser leg. "Very dry."

"Pick a direction again, Princess." Chicken nodded and point.

"Let us away as we were about."

"Good as any."

They walked along the chosen path watching everything that they could see.

The path swung wide and wandered between small clumps of shrubs that managed to grow on the dry, mostly barren soil. Few things managed to grow on the tightly compacted path. The soil was brown, the growing things were green.

Overhead, they caught tiny glimpses of blue-green sky through the mist cover. It was a silent place, the only noise being that of more and more trash being disgorged.

No birds sang, no insects buzzed, only the hiss and clatter of waste disposal.

"Highness, how do this trash laden a'place not overwhelm itself?"

Goose hissed and held up his hand. They halted and watched carefully.

"What is it?" whispered Tinker.

"I do hear some thin', just ahead, near yon tall clumpery. It do sound most like mumblin' to me."

"Mumbling?"

"Oh, aye, Sire, mumblin'. And a'crunchin'. Do listen most closely as we ourselves steal most cautiously forward."

Goose pointed at the small stand of tall shrubs.

"But no further than small tangled growth."

"Right."

They started forward, carefully placing their feet, hands ready to pull weapons free.

Goose shot one hand straight up.

"Listen," he hissed.

They stood immobile and strained to hear. It was a faint sound, a steady, rhythmic, metallic sound. It was drawing closer, and growing louder. At times it almost made sense.

"Toucan," said Tinker. "Your ears are the sharpest, what is it saying?"

Toucan stood, eyes closed, all concentration focused upon hearing.

"Tin-tin, Highness, it do bespeak itself thusly, tin-tin."

"What?"

"Tin-tin."

"Sire," suggested Goose, "let us hide just there and wait some small time for to see if creature wilt come this way. If so, then we might see what manner of thing do speak so."

He pointed at one of the clumps of taller vegetation.

"Good idea," agreed Tinker, "let's do it."

They did, deep inside the shrubbery, they hid. They sat on the ground and peered out through the limbs and leaves.

And waited.

And waited.

And waited.

The sounds receded into the distance.

Finally Tinker shoved his way clear and stood.

"Come on. Let's follow it, see what's going on."

They headed in the direction of the strange noise, their path now swinging straight for the edge of one of the trash mountains.

Stepping around some shrubs they found a deep swath cut into the garbage, the area littered with bits and pieces of crumpled and cut containers, the fresh edges glistening in the light.

"What ever it was, it went that-a-way."

Tinker pointed and swung his arm around and pointed in the opposite direction.

"Let us go this-a-way."

They hurried back the way they had come, past the disturbed section. Suddenly the trash in front of them began to bulge outward.

"Sire!" gasped Goose. "What do be this?"

"BACK UP, GOOSE, BACK UP!"

The bulge burst open, great quantities of junk surging across the path in front of them, blocking their way.

A large silver head poked out and twisted around. It had a high forehead, a long snout, glittering red eyes. It stared at them. And with another surge of debris, it stepped out.

"Bigger than an elephant," observed Tinker.

The neck lowered the head. Massive teeth mashed and gobbled trash, the jaws working slowly, steadily. It chewed, nosily, paying them no attention.

"This thing sounds like a garbage disposal," said Tinker.

"What do be that, My Lord?"

"A device some folks have in their kitchen sinks to dispose of garbage."

"This creature be one of them?" asked Toucan.

"Mighty great sink, Sire," suggested Goose.

"Let's get out of here."

Tinker hurried back the way they had come.

The creature turned and watched them depart.

"Tin-tin," it said.

Goose laughed softly and said, "Now we do know what manner of creature does speak so."

"Certainly we do. OH, OH!"

"**MY LORD!**"

Chicken's sword whistled from its scabbard.

"Trapped," snapped Tinker.

Another of the things had burst from the trash in front of them. It now stood on the path blocking their way, red eyes staring in their direction. It moved forward.

"Tin tin."

Behind them they heard an answering reply, "Tin tin."

Tinker spun around. The other one was coming their way. The two voices repeated the single phrase, echo and re-echo.

"Tin tin."

"Tin-tin."

"Tin-tin."

"Tin-tin."

Tinker inched toward the closer of the two, his great weaponkin held in both hands.

He jumped forward and swung a heavy side-stroke.

CLANK!

The sword bounced back, vibrations wrenching his shoulder.

"Metal, it is made of heavy metal."

There was a thin, bright scar on one of the thing's legs where the sword had struck it.

"Tin-tin."

"Tin-tin."

"Tin-tin."

"Tin-tin."

"Sire, I will greatly distract these metal things whilst thee three do flee."

"Too late. There's another coming from over there"

"**TIN-TIN!**" it bellowed at the two on the path.

"**YOU! DOWN THERE! STRANGERS,**" boomed at loud voice down at them. "**UP THE LADDER, QUICKLY!**"

They stared upward.

Some sort of craft hovered over them, a flexible ladder rapidly descending toward them from an opening in its bottom. The bottom rung thumped against the ground.

Tinker shoved Chicken toward it. "GO!"

She leaped at it and clambered up.

Tinker, Goose and Toucan followed.

As they worked their way toward the craft it lifted rapidly, yanking them beyond the reach of the creatures below. The three things met with a heavy dull *THUNK!*

"Tin-tin."

"Tin-tin."

"Tin-tin."

The ladder rolled itself onto a drum and pulled them in through the opening which closed beneath them.

One by one they clambered down and looked around at the large empty space where they now stood.

A door opened and someone walked through, and announced, "If you were not strangers, I would have left you to the Tin-tin. Only crazies wander out there. And The Collectors. But you are neither crazies nor Collectors. So, let me welcome you to the planet Rinn, the city Rinn."

He gestured imperially at them.

"Come. Forward go and sit. In my quarters we will discuss your presence here."

Tinker held up one hand.

"One moment, please."

"Yes?"

"What is the name of this place?"

"THIS IS the planet Rinn, the city Rinn."

Tinker smiled at him.

"That is what I thought you said."

Then he started to giggle, finally bursting out into loud laughter, crashing sideways into the wall.

Chicken jumped to his side, grabbing one of his arms.

"My Lord, do be most strange relapse from foul dragon world?"

Tinker gasped for breath and started another fit of giggling, and managed to gasp a reply, "Oh no. No, no. It is just that this must be a Big Red joke. A really bad one."

She stared at him as Goose and Toucan edged closer.

"Look, this is the planet Rinn, the city Rinn." He sucked in a deep breath fighting to restrain his grin, and added, "And if it is, then those things down there are called. . ."

He lost it in a fit of laughter, finally managing to burst out, "Rin Tin Tin."

This time he slipped slowly down to the floor.

Chicken dropped to her knees next to him, fearful for what seemed to be affecting him.

"MY LOVE, what be so laughable bout most strange metal beastes below?"

He swallowed hard and nodded.

"Right, you do not know, do you."

He shoved himself to his feet and threw an arm around her waist as she stood. He smiled and managed to regain control.

"Ahhhh, I will tell you later. Ummmmmm, all right?"

"Indeed, My Lord." She glanced at Toucan, who gave the slightest of shrugs.

Tinker managed to make his face mostly blank and turned toward their rescuer.

"Sorry about that, momentary relapse."

Chicken quickly threw her arm around his waist.

"I am John Tinker and this is the Princess Chicken and the Princes Goose and Toucan."

The small man peered at them as if they were some kind of new and strange bug under his lens.

"Jon'tinker, I am Collector Ran'k."

He gestured them forward to a small cabin and arranged them in a row of seats along the wall. Then he settled into what appeared to be the pilot's chair. Ran'k glanced over his shoulder as he headed the vessel toward the city wall.

"You are lucky to be alive. The Tin-tin wouldn't have noticed whether they were taking you in or not. They are very efficient but somewhat non-discriminating. The only thing that is supposed to be out there are empty containers. Nothing else."

"Other than strange Tin-tin," added Chicken.

"They are not alive, they are machines."

"Machines?"

"Mechanical dogs," mumbled Tinker, starting to smile, laughter on its way back to the surface.

"Whish, My Lord."

"Machines," restated Ran'k. "They start the recycling process."

Tinker giggled, and mumbled, "Yo, Rinnie."

"They crush and reprocess and eject clean ingots which are used to make new containers," continued Ran'k, more or less patiently.

"Most clever that," stated Goose, watching Tinker who was once again struggling not to laugh.

Toucan looked worried.

"Most necessary," explained Ran'k turning back to face the outer window.

"Hold tight please," he said over his shoulder. "Please remain seated until the vehicle has come to a full stop and the pilot has turned off the seat belt light."

This sentence was said in a hurry and a jumble, words tumbling on and after each other.

The craft slipped through a wall opening.

Tinker stood and stepped forward to peer over Ran'k's head.

The city seemed to stretch to forever. Corridors and tunnels interconnected in endless patterns. Other craft passed them as they twisted and turned and drifted silently along. Finally they settled into a small chamber whose door slipped closed behind them.

"This is Bin'One," said Ran'k. "I hope you have enjoyed your flight with us. Please wait until the craft has come to a complete stop before attempting to embark."

This is a weird place, Princess.

How so, My Lord.

Tell you about that later, also.

Tinker looked around the chamber as they stepped down.

"Where do we go now, Collector Ran'k?"

"To my office, Jon'tinker. We have to fill out the required forms."

"Forms?"

"AD 252-59ZBS2X; Tin Accident Report; Alien Encounter Report, short form; Safe Flight Form; Vehicle Usage and Travel Document; Expendables, Consumables, and Combustion sheet; Docking Fee Schedule Trip Tick."

He held up a small clip-board that he had just

slipped from a large pouch on the front of his right trouser leg.

"Just initial, here, and here, and there and there. . . . and there. That signifies that you had a pleasant trip and would fly this way again on your next planned vacation. Thank . . .you."

Ran'k folded the paper into even thirds and pushed it into a small slot next to a door. The wall grunted, a sign began to blink on and off.

EXIT

EXIT

EXIT

EXIT.

The door opened.

"Follow me."

Ran'k bustled away from the craft, led them into a hall and down a staircase. They entered a large corridor where a shouting crowd began showering them with confetti.

Tinker whispered in Chicken's ear, "Now I am sure, this place is a figment of Big Red's imagination."

Goose looked at him and asked, "True, Sire?"

Chicken yanked on Tinker's arm, and murmured, "Shhhh, My Lord."

"I will try."

Collector Ran'k led them through the crowd and into a long, vacant corridor, brushing the streamers and confetti from his cloths. Small slots opened at the base of the walls and sucked the debris away.

"At least we will not have to do the Debris Form," mumbled Ran'k.

He gestured. "Come."

Three intersections later they turned and entered a reception area.

"Good moment, Collector Ran'k," said the receptionist.

"Any messages?"

"None. Conductor Bun't stepped in and suggested that you come to his office when you have time."

"Conductor Bun't," he gasped, eyes wide, mouth dropping open.

"Most sure."

"Yes, yes . . . Tell him I have returned and will be along shortly."

The receptionist turned and picked up a small instrument. She began talking.

Ran'k waved an arm in their direction, and ordered firmly, "You four, come with me."

He walked rapidly past the front desk and into the office. Dropping behind the large desk, he gestured for them to sit.

"There. Now we have much work to do. And I will have to go see Conductor Bun't as well. More forms, no doubt."

He sighed heavily. It was the practiced sigh of a civil servant who had more than his share of the burden to carry. Reaching down, he opened a desk drawer and removed a stack of forms. They came in all colors, a rainbow of information needs. He beamed at the four of them with a rigid attempt at a pleasant smile.

"Shall we get started?"

Thumbing through the collection he selected the mauve one, and beamed at them.

"Alien Encounter Form, " he stated. He glanced up at them and nodded. "Rather obvious that is what you are. Strange costumes, funny language. Names, please."

Several long hours later, Tinker watched Ran'k with unbelieving eyes as he stuffed yet another form into the already stuffed and bulging folder.

The desk beeped.

"Yes."

"Collector, it is time for your appointment with Conductor Bun't."

"OH. My," he sighed. "How the time flies. Bring our guests some refreshment."

Ran'k smiled a crooked apology at them.

"Must go! Don't wander off, you might get lost, even get injured. We still have a bit to complete."

He stood and hurtled through a side door as the receptionist came through the front one carrying a large tray with four mugs.

"Kay?" She handed each a mug and left.

Goose took a tentative sip.

"Most like that which we do drink a'home."

Tinker took a sip and nodded, and asked, "Well, gang, what do you think of this place?"

Toucan indicated the bulging folder.

"Highness, I do me most astonished be. It do seem for to be most endless forms, sheets and papers.

This be most pettifogging a'folk."

"Oh, aye, My Lord," agreed Chicken. "This Ran'k do have manners like foul sokeman although me'thinks he do be some manner of villein born. Warrant reaction to superior's beckon."

Tinker smiled and shrugged.

"Whatever. This is a strange place all right. Much of what we have seen seems to be ritualistic, spoken for form rather than content."

"Highness, what do propose thee?"

"Beats me. About all we can do is wait and see."

They did.

They sat.

And sat, and sat, and sat, and sat, and sat.

Toucan and Goose dozed.

Tinker was lost deep in thought.

Chicken wandered aimlessly about the room. Finally she opened one of the doors and peeked outside, attracting Tinker's attention.

Princess?

We do Us have great uneasiness, My Lord. This abode do be passing strange with deep underlying threat.

Threat?

Indeed. Thee may wish to say woman's intuition. But We say do so tis a'warrior's. Tis time for to loose ourselves from constraining space.

Cabin fever.

What manner of illness do be that?

Comes from being in one small space too long.

Nay, JohnLove, We have no fever from cabin. Let Us away from small room and smaller person.

She shut the door and spun to her brothers

banging their shoulders.

"Someone do come."

Their eyes popped open, they straighten themselves in their chairs.

Chicken leaped across the room and took her seat, her left hand settling around the top of the scabbard.

"Someone?"

"Indeed, My Lord."

"Awfully sharp hearing."

"Tis that."

The side door opened and Collector Ran'k plunged back into the room, his arms full.

He dropped the thick sheaf of paper on his desk and then fell with a heavy thud into his chair.

"Trash and Trash," he snarled. "Bun't has swallowed a zpft and regurgitated a Tin-tin. Your pardon for my word choice but I get so upset when this happens."

His hand slammed down on top of this new pile of paper.

"Special forms. In hexaplic. Do you know what this means?"

"Lots of paper," suggested Tinker, not sure what that peculiar term was.

"The Conductor designed special forms, just for the occasion. These."

He thumped the pile again. It sagged to one side, sending portions sliding toward the edge of the desk.

Ran'k captured his errant charges before they could make their escape and sighed.

"Let's get started."He peered at the form he held.

"Alien Vehicle Registration Form." He looked at Tinker and asked, "Make. Model. Year of manufacture."

Tinker grinned. "Bit of a problem there."

Ran'k's eyes flew wide as he visualized another form.

"Well, Yes, ummm, you see, it is this way. . . "

"My Lord," said Chicken. "Make do be Portal, model do be Firesnake."

"OH, right," agreed Tinker, "that is it! Portal and Firesnake."

Tinker flashed a quick smile at Ran'k who flashed an equally empty one back.

"Portal? Firesnake?"He filled in the appropriate blocks and mumbled, "Quaint names you aliens use. Year?"

"Yes, ah, yes, year? What year is it here? Asked Tinker.

"20 Bong 41, of course."

"What would it be after the planet Rinn, the city Rinn makes one complete revolution around your sun?"

"Sun? Ahhhh, the Fireglobe. Then it will then be 20 Pip 41."

"Ummm. When will either 20 or 41 increment one point?"

"Why after a complete appropriate cycle, of course. Why do you ask?"

"Tell me the complete cycle and I will tell you the year of our vehicle."

Collector Ran'k bobbed his head. "I see, I see. You are translating your cycle date into ours. How useful, how very clever. The cycle is as follows: Zee, Nin, Pop, Whe, Bong, Pip, Umm, and Dit."

"I see. Our vehicle then is, ehhhhhh, 20 Zee 41."

"That old? Carrying capacity?" Ran'k made two checks and scribbled something.

20 Zee 41, My Lord?

"Twenty-four passengers."

"That large. It must be a sizable craft. We will have to issue you a Carrier's License as well." Ran'k sighed.

"Now, what is next?"

The remainder of the day was spent filling out forms.

And more forms.

Etc., etc.

Goose and Toucan lapsed back into apparent lethargy.

Chicken moved from place to place.

Finally, with a dramatic and grandiose gesture, Ran'k signed the last form and announced in ringing tones, "DONE!"

Two sets of eyes popped open. Chicken walked over and stood behind Tinker.

Goose cleared his throat. "Praps, Sire, we might find ourselves fine food and fair lodgings?"

Tinker grinned. "Good idea. Collector Ran'k, how do we go about doing that?"

"What Jon'tinker?"

"Getting something to eat and a place to sleep."

"Ah, yes. That. I don't suppose you have any of the Best with you?"

"Best?"

"Exactly what I thought." Ran'k fell back in his chair and stated with a deep frown, "Indigent."

"Not exactly," said Tinker.

"You do not have any of the Best, do you?"

"Nope."

"Indigent!"

Ran'k eased open a desk drawer and slipped out one more form and pushed it toward Tinker and stated firmly, "Fill this out and take it to The Cashier. One of the many Social Services provided by the Planet Rinn, the City Rinn."

Tinker, shrugged, spun the form around, and read it. It was titled, in bold, black letters, ***The Penurious Alien Fund***.

Collector Ran'k tapped it with the tip of one finger and ordered, "Just sign your name here and put in the green block, ummmm, there are four of you, soooooo, let's just say 4,000 should do. Put 4,000 right there." Tinker did as he was told.

Ran'k snatched the form back, snapped off his copy and stuffed it into the folder, which ripped just a little more along one seam, and handed the other copies back to Tinker.

"Take this to my secretary. She will show you the way."

He stood and ushered them to the door of his office, stating loudly, "Take these four to The Cashier."

The secretary stood and guided them out and down the hall. After some zig-zagging through numerous intersections she pointed to a small window set in a wall. A sign over it stated plainly, in red letters, ***CASHIER.***

"Give them the form." She spun on her heels and rapidly walked away.

Tinker stepped in front of the window. He couldn't see in. It was mirrored, one-way glass. He slipped the form through a narrow slot in the window.

After a short wait, a narrow shelf slipped out from the wall. It had another form lying upon it.

"Initial the purple block," said someone. Tinker did. A door popped open and a large stack of brightly colored currency was shoved out.

Tinker grabbed the stack, the door snapped shut. The shelf, with form, slipped back inside the wall.

Tinker rapped sharply upon the glass and asked, "Can you tell us how to find food and lodging?"

"Follow this corridor to Z-80, turn onto Q-28, watch for the sign. You can't miss it."

The sign over the window changed and began to flash.

CLOSED . . . CLOSED . . . CLOSED . . .

"Goose?"

"Sire?"

"Lead on. We're off to see the city."

They walked through a bee-hive of a city. Corridors branched in every direction.

A set intervals they passed vertical shafts. People stepped into or out of these. Some sort of elevator, thought Tinker. Arrows frequently pointed to this or that. Goose rapidly figured out the naming conventions of corridors, halls, and shafts. The people they passed, ignored them.

"Highness," said Toucan. "They do seem most dower a'folk."

"Sire." Goose pointed. "Me'thinks one turn and

we do be there."

They made the turn.

"By George, that must be fair inn." Goose pointed.

The corridor was very wide. The far wall had a glowing orange sign with a flashing blue border.

LODGINGS

To one side, a gold star flashed on and off under a series of golden curves.

Tinker laughed and swung his arm around Chicken. "Shall we, Princess?"

"Any port in a storm, me'love."

They walked over and pushed through the door. The room looked like most any hotel lobby Tinker had ever been inside. Behind the counter a small man looked up and adjusted some forms into a neater stack as they approached.

"Welcome to *The Lodgings,* part of the *Cushion Chain* of fine food and finer accommodations."

He beamed at them and asked, "How may I help?"

He ripped an ornately embossed form from the top of a pad and spun it around, pushing it gently toward them. He nudged a writing instrument against one edge of the form.

Tinker started to fill in the various boxes on the form. Finally with a flourish he signed it and looked at the clerk. "Are all your forms this complex?"

The clerk smiled and shook his head.

"Nope-a-loo. This one is quite simple. The Hotel and Lodging Directorate protested quite loudly to keep it as simple as it is. The previous one was driving away business."

His head bobbed up and down as he gushed, "Yep, yep, yep, that is what was happening, just driving away business." He waved pudgy hands back and forth. "Four pages and a Currency Declaration. Much too much. Yep, yep, yep."

He stopped moving, smiled, and peered at Tinker. Then quickly scanned the form, and frowned.

"How many rooms? How long will you be with us?"

Tinker shrugged his shoulder. "Well . . . "

The clerk clapped his hands together and announced, "We have a special, just for this period, yep, yep, yep. Just for Aliens, if you will pardon the expression. Although that is what you are, after all. WE HAVE a New, Improved, Ever-So-Extra Special! Stay five nights, the sixth night is free, yep, yep, yep. PLUS, if you take the Deluxe, Two-Bedroom, *Special Accommodations For Aliens' Suite,* we throw in the Ultra-Deluxe, Wider-Than-Wide, *Wonder-Screen, Vision-Master.* PLUS, all meals are free. For you, for all four of you."

His voice dropped to a confidential whisper, "And you may order from the Hotel Menu. Room Service for a minor fee." He straightened back up and stated grandly, *"The Gold Star Packet."* He smiled broadly. And waited.

"How much?" asked Tinker.

"Cash up front? Ten percent discount."

Tinker nodded. "Figure it that way."

The clerk bounced in his chair as he worked out the calculations and began filling another form with figure after figure. Finished, he looked up and stated, "Total cost of The Package, after discount, comes to, exactly, Six Long. All righty?"

"Ummmmmmm . . . "

The clerk pursed his lips, his eyes darting to the right and to the left and whispered softly, "If you promise not to blab it around, I will make it five, Five Long." He waggled his shoulder and sighed, "Best that I can do." He smiled at his pun.

"We will take it."

"GOOD! Goody, good, good. You are the first one in this period to whom I have made such a sale. I have just won a *Free, ALL Expenses Trip, for TWO, to The Furthest Reaches*. Yep, yep, yep. For this, I will send a container of our own, my compliments, to your rooms."

Tinker interrupted, "But . . . "

The clerks happy expression fell. "But?" he murmured.

"It's this way . . . "

The clerk sighed. "Yes?"

"AH, we don't know what five long are."

"No problem."

"There isn't?"

"Nope, nope, nopey."

"Good."

The clerk began to sing, in a dry, squeaky voice, "Da-da-dum. Long are Purple, short are Green, and Brown are everything else in between. Doooooooo Dah!"

"Purple are long?"

"Yep, yep, yep, yeppy."

Tinker thumbed through the thick wad of currency and placed five purple bills on the counter. Then he put another five next to the first five.

"For yourself. For being such a wonderful, good host."

The clerk waved a hand. The bills disappeared.

"You are most generous."

He handed Tinker a small, cone shaped object that glowed blue light.

"Push it in the door."

His head began to bob up and down as he announced in rolling tones, "On behalf of The Management and Staff of the *Golden Larches,* a wholly owned and operated subsidiary designed with YOU in mind, may I wish you and your's a Pleasant Stay."

He pointed at the wall. "Follow the Golden Stars. They lead to The *Gold Star Suite*. That way."

Rows of gold stars began to flash on and off.

Tinker and the group turned and followed them, down the hall, into an elevator, and somewhere high above, into a small alcove. A single door flashed a gold star at them.

Tinker walked up to it and shoved the cone into the only hole he could find.

The door slid open, the cone popped free.

The room they walked into was spacious. It was large, it was hard, it was sterile.

Metallic walls, metallic furniture.

As they stood and stared at their accommodations, Chicken stepped into one of the adjoining rooms, came back and purred softly into one of Tinker's ears, "Fair bed do appear most large and comfortable, My Own Sweet Prince."

Tinker smiled at her and rolled his eyes at the room. "Toucan, see if that room is the kitchen."

He turned slowly around and asked, "How about we go outside and see if we can find a restaurant."

He threw his arms wide and spun slowly around and announced grandly, "Welcome to the planet Rinn, the city Rinn. And all that it holds."

He dropped into a chair, a double-wide chair and grunted, "UMMMPF, not too uncomfortable, just ugly."

Chicken walked around and sat next to him, pushing him aside. Throwing an arm around him, she lightly tickled his ribs. "Sweet Prince, what be there here that do strangely thy mood affect? Thee hast been most ferlie since we do come a'here."

He looked into bright blue eyes. "Strange? Ferlie? Me?"

"Quite right, Sire," agreed Goose smiling broadly, sprawling in a thing resembling a couch. "Passin' strange."

Tinker looked over at Toucan, who nodded his head. "Most unanimous opinion, Highness. Strangely bothered, I do say."

Tinker slipped an arm around Chicken and drew her close and explained, "Right. I don't like this place, not at all. It is too hard, too cold, too bureaucratic. And something else which I can't quite figure out. There is something wrong here, somewhere. I do not trust these people."

Toucan wandered into another room of their

suite. Then he called, "Highness."

"What?"

"I do think that I do find me that which thee do wish found."

Tinker stood and walked over to see. "Yep, looks like it. Shall we order something to eat?"

It arrived after a short wait.

The Gold Star Special turned out to be a surprise.

As they sat back from the meal and relaxed, Tinker sighed, and stated, "Not too bad, I had my doubts, but it wasn't too bad. Guess we don't have to go restaurant hunting just yet."

Goose smiled and stated, "Not Master Chen level, yet it do be most pleasant."

"When we take a stroll we still better keep a weather eye cocked."

"How so, Sire?"

"The portal dumped us here, did it not?"

"Oh, Aye."

"And separated us from the rest of The Company?"

"Most true."

"And even after Big Red's promise, Smoke is elsewhere?"

"Oh, aye."

"And, in the past, where ever the portal put us, there was something nasty and evil?"

"Indeed."

"And there was always something that we needed?"

"Quite."

"So, have you seen anything lurking about that

looks or feels nasty and evil, or that we need?"

"Nay, Sire."

"That is why we ought to be careful."

"How so, Sire? Most other places t'were neither nasty nor evil."

"I don't know. There is just something about this place that bothers me, that's all. This is a single planet, a single city, all carefully ordered and carefully papered over. But somewhere, right here in River City, there is trouble. And that's spelled with a capital 'T'."

"River City, Sire?"

"Ahhhhh, Rinn."

"Oh."

Tinker dropped back into his seat, he had been stalking back and forth, and asked, "Sooooo, what do you want to do?"

Chicken brushed her lips against his ear and blew a soft breath at him.

He smiled. "Other than that, lusty wench."

Goose giggled.

Toucan waited.

Tinker waved a hand toward the front door. "Shall we take a stroll? See if we can spot anything, anything at all?"

So they did.

They prowled the corridors.

The city Rinn apparently stretched out beyond them forever, layer upon layer. They finally reached the uppermost level. It was marked *HB*.

The interesting thing that they noted was how few people they actually saw walking the corridors. They gave up and went back to *The Gold Star Suite*.

Inside they found a large jug of the complimentary beverage which they poured into waiting cups and sipped. They were sitting in what they had decided was the kitchen.

"Well, group?"

Toucan and Chicken both shook their heads.

"Nothin' Sire. In all places this warren do pear most the same. Be there some thing here we do need, tis most well and cunnin' a'hidden." Goose shrugged.

"Seems so. Tomorrow is another day, let's hit the sack."

"A game, Sire?" Goose beamed at him.

"A saying."

"Oh."

"It means, that it is time for bed." He stood. "Good night. Rouse us early, Toucan."

"As thee wish, Highness." He bowed his head.

Tinker and Chicken left the two sitting at the table talking quietly.

As she closed the door behind them, Chicken swung Tinker around, tucked one shoulder into his stomach and thrust him backward across the floor and into the large bed.

"OOOOOOF!"

She leaped upon him, legs straddling his waist, and began to unfasten his clothes.

Now let us see what evil does lurk in the minds of men. Heh, heh, heh.

Tinker dropped his hands and stared up at her.

"Where did you hear that?"

Grinning as evilly as she could, she rolled sideways and grabbed him.

Master Chen do play a'Us magical sound story.

He gasped. *Foul play, Princess.*

Seems most pleasing fair to Us. Stop that!

He pulled her over.

Thy most humble of servants, My Lord. She nestled in his arms.

Much later, they slept.

The Gold Star sensors recorded all.

Busy hands made notations on forms and charts. Copies were sorted and filed and routed to the appropriate offices. Data was checked and tabulated. The reports began to filter upward through layer after layer of Rinn bureaucracy.

Lock Heraur. Pikel Fermda.

The pair sat on the small balcony three stories above the street and sipped at their beverages. They had just finished the morning meal.

Their clothes were clean and neat again. And they were mostly healed.

Turintor yawned and stretched. And glanced at her silent companion. She hadn't said a word since their escape and their arrival in this elseplace. That witch appeared alert enough but strangely closed into herself.

Turintor sighed. "We have been here for three hands of days and are mostly healed and rested."

It was stating the obvious but at the moment she didn't know what else to do.

She stared darkly at the table top and watched a small spot burn into the wood and said, "I can not feel my clan. Either they are all dead or I am still badly damaged. How are you?"

Her companion nodded. Then she reached out and ran one fingertip over the burned hole and lifted her hand. The tabletop was smooth and unblemished. She shook her head.

Turintor set her cup down, stood and leaned on the railing and peered down at the street, at the people wandering up and down and said, "There is another town not too many walks from here. Let us go there. We have seen all there is to see in this one." She turned and added, "Maybe we will find a friendly clan there that might aid us."

Her companion stood and headed for the door.

Turintor strode after her. It was the most activity that she had seen from that black clad witch. She nodded to herself. Maybe that silent one might even speak one of these nights.

Will These Adventures Never Cease?

Some Place. Some Time.

Smoke dropped lightly to the ground, took a quick look around, and spun, and made a twisting leap toward the portal.

The rest were stepping through. She tumbled Sorrowful head over heels and crashed into Mountain.

"BY DUMPF, Smoke, this is no time to become playful. The Guard are behind me."

Mountain stomped straight ahead, waving his arms in warning. With a quick movement he scooped up Sorrowful and hastily stepped to one side.

"Wouldn't do to have that group tromp you into mud, little teller of tales."

Twenty-two Guardsmen marched out.

Smoke danced around and around trying to find an opening, trying to find a way back into the portal.

Sorrowful squirmed in Mountain's clutches, and gasped, "Where is John Tinker? And the rest? I do not see them?"

Mountain craned his neck around. "Neither do I. Now what, BY DUMPF?"

Sorrowful yelled, "**BACK, BACK! BACK THROUGH THE PORTAL!**"

Mountain turned, took one step and halted and grumbled, "Too late."

The portal faded away.

Smoke's leap took her through the empty air where it had been.

Mountain gently set Sorrowful down and rumbled, "Well, Talking Flea, it appears that we are on our own again. This DUMPFING quest is beginning to take on all the bad characteristics of the last one. And that, BY ALL THE SAND AND GRAVEL, is not good!"

He spun slowly around and waved one arm. "I see neither John Tinker nor Goose nor Toucan nor the Princess nor the Lady Chen. That whole outcrop is missing, BY GUMPF."

Sorrowful stared at Smoke.

She had crashed into a heap. Tumbled over. Twitching. Her minds struggled for control as the Hub Center screamed in agony.

ALONE.

ALONE.

Monsters.

Demons.

Nightmare fright.

All around her these things appeared. Swirling, flashing into existence. And disappearing again.

The Guard charged up and surrounded her, their great blades drawn, ready to attack whatever it was.

"BY DUMP!" Mountain yanked his cudgel free and stood watching. Anything that burst through The Guards ranks would have to face him.

"Oh dear, oh dear, oh dear."

Sorrowful peered between two of The Guard, his

weaponkin held ready.

Then there was only Smoke lurching upright, sitting, front legs wide spread, head hanging low, looking up through her eyebrows at him, tail thrashing angrily.

Sorrowful slipped inside and cautiously approached her, his thumb rubbing the Golden Eye, the jewel set in the hilt of his dagger. "Smoke?"

I am all right. Now. It was separation shock. But I have it under control.

"It really and truly does seems that we are on our own, as Mountain has implied. This reminds me of a most appropriately named tale, *The Group That Lost Its Head.*" He sucked in a deep breath.

So!"

The deep base voice cut into his tale, interrupting, "BY DUMPF. I think that we should first decide what we should do, take some course of action."

Mountain watched Smoke as she stood, wobbling upright.

"Am I not right?" Mountain's finger caressed the golden jewel set in the end of his cudgel.

Yes. Good of you to remember the power of The Golden Eye. Sorrowful has joined us.

Mountain?

Smoke? Can you hear me?

Yes.

Yes, BY DUMPF!

Then what should we do? Smoke?

The portal has done this before, has it not?

Yes. You and I went to the Land of the Gryerd, Mountain to the Land of the Gett, and John Tinker was off by himself. Well, not exactly by himself, he was with all the others.

And now, BIDDLY-BUMPF?

Now we decide which way to go.

And which way would that be?

Why I think we should follow the advice told in that old tale.

"It was called *The Man That Followed His Nose.* There is a small roadway, just there." Sorrowful pointed.

One of The Guard was already investigating it.

Smoke?

That way.

"Mountain?"

"BY DUMPF, downhill is better than up. It appears that there might be food down there. That way it is."

Sorrowful smiled at them and said, "Smoke can run ahead and we can set eleven of The Guard in front and eleven behind. Sergeant, you heard?"

"Yes, SAH, Lord Sorrowful."

"Smoke, are you all right?"

Yes. Sudden loss of your selves can drive one mad.

She rolled her eyes at Sorrowful, who leaped back and away.

But I am the Center of The Center. Have no fear. We are in control.

Deep inside, carefully controlled, it still whispered, still said . . . *Alone.*

The Sergeant took ten of his comrades with him. They headed down the roadway in single file. The rest waited for Mountain and Sorrowful to proceed.

Smoke trotted past the lead contingent and disappeared into the shadows of the vegetation growing thickly right up to the edge of the stone they walked upon.

Sorrowful looked around, taking in their new surroundings.

"A pleasant place to visit," he observed, and added, "It seems to be mid-afternoon here."

Mountain nodded. "BY DUMPF, you are right if these shadows tell correctly. But it is a bit on the cool side. It seems that most of the places we visit are cooler than Stumpf."

"You will warm up as we walk."

"True. So . . . ?"

"So?"

"So, tell me one of your everlasting, endless supply tales, Master Teller of Tales."

"Since you asked so politely, I will."

"HUMPF!"

"I thought you would never ask."

"DOUBLE-DUMPF!"

Sorrowful laughed softly, pleased that everything appeared to be back to norma1.

"Yes. Let us see, which one? How about that appropriate tale, I believe I mentioned it just a moment ago. The tale titled *The Group That Lost Its Head.* It should do nicely. Ready?"

"BY DUMPF, yammering mouse, I am."

Sorrowful took a deep breath, and began.

"SO! In a time and at a time, there was a group that wandered far and wide throughout The Six Lands. Some even said that they had journeyed beyond. But, of course, no-one believed that. Now The Leader of this odd collection of travelers was called May'Hap Be'Hap." He paused, for just a moment, just for effect.

"Some people suggested that it would have been better if he had been named Hapless Pap for it seemed that he would usually have bad luck. Now, most of the time, no-one would call him by this name to his face as he was the type of person who tended to get overly excited."

Sorrowful glanced meaningfully at his gigantic companion, who seemed to pay no attention to that meaningful glance.

"But, as it happened, one day the group entered a town of a rather ill-mannered folk, a town known far and wide as Callowville. As the group was strolling down the main street, searching for the local tavern or inn, a bystander shouted to a friend on the other side of the street, 'Look there, there is Hapless Pap.' And within minutes everyone in sight was chanting, Hapless Pap, Hapless Pap." Sorrowful smiled slyly.

"Of course, as things tended to occur in these cases, May'Hap Be'Hap got rather agitated at this. He started running back and forth hitting people. Wellllll, before you knew it, a regular riot broke out. When the dust settled, the group could not find a bit or piece of May'Hap Be'Hap. But they were standing in front of the local combination tavern-inn, so they went in to find food and lodgings." Sorrowful paused and quickly glanced up at his companion who was strolling along staring far ahead.

"Inside, they tried to order rooms and a meal all at the same time. The inn-keeper managed to quiet them down with much arm waving and into the silence asked, 'Which one of you is the spokesman for this mob?' And one of them answered, 'We don't have any, he disappeared.' With this the inn-keeper roared with laughter and shouted at them, 'What, do you mean to tell me that this group lost it's head?' And . . . "

"Stop right there, BY DUMPF!"

Sorrowful looked up and asked, "Why, what is the matter?"

"You are just making this up as you go along. This is a tale with no point."

"A less than sharp rump?"

"RUMPF BY DUMPF! Your tale is cut from words of no meat."

"A sausage of talk?"

"**DOUBLE-DUMPF AND ROCK DUST!**"

Mountain's voice boomed out over the open slope, startling a flock of some things from the nearby foliage. They appeared to have glowing red eyes.

Mountain glanced at them, shrugged one shoulder, and walked on. He reached over and touched The Golden Eye.

Smoke.

Yes.

A group of things just flew from some brush near us. Do you see them, or anything else?

Yes. This region is teeming with life forms. Tasty, too.

Tasty?

Urp.

Ah. Anything else? Anything we should worry about?

No.

Well, BY DUMPF, is there anything, anyplace ahead, where we might rest and get a bite to eat, also?

I haven't been resting.

BY BIBBLY-BUMPF, I know that, I just meant.

I see what you meant . . . See what I meant?

Mountain could suddenly see a round, rather fat thing hopping through the underbrush. It wobbled as it hopped. He knew he was watching with Smoke's eyes. The image was superimposed over what he was seeing as he walked along. It was a novel experience.

The round creature was covered in gray scales and appeared to have an excessive number of teeth in a long pointed snout. Its eyes glowed a faint yellow.

A large paw snapped into his sight and knocked the creature into a nearby, heavy stemmed plant of some kind. Then he could taste it in his mouth. It was rather pleasant to the palate. And somewhat crunchy.

See?

Yes, very tasty.

There are no other sapient creatures other than ourselves within the sensenet. Just these edibles and other shapes and forms.

MUMPF! Evening is coming to greet us. We shall need a place to camp.

Yes.

She guided them to a large clearing. Smoke sat in the center. Waiting.

Sorrowful charged past Mountain and flung himself at her neck. His arms couldn't reach around. Then he dropped to his feet and clasped The Golden Eye set in the hilt of his dagger.

Here we are again, Smoke, off by ourselves.

Not exactly by ourselves.

He smiled happily and nodded.

"True. But we are separated from John Tinker and the others."

He could see the muscles suddenly rippling under her fur.

"OH! Apologies, apologies."

It is all right. We will be rejoined.

Mountain stomped up and rumbled at them, "BY DUMPF, you two may reminisce after we have set up camp and eaten dinner." He cast a crafty look at Smoke.

"You won't happen to have, somewhere about this place, one or two of those tasty creatures, would you?"

Smoke stood and stepped daintily to one side.

Next to her lay two of the creatures she had shown Mountain

Mountain roared, "SERGEANT, MAKE A FIRE, WE HAVE FOOD THAT REQUIRES ROASTING!"

"Yes, SAH, Lord Mountain."

The Sergeant hurried away, shouting orders in all directions.

"Lord Mountain?" grumbled the large man.

A voice spoke to his leg, "Indeed. It seems that we have been promoted to the status of Lords in the absence of John Tinker."

"Smoke is also a Lord?"

Sorrowful laughed. "I do believe that they address her as Lady."

He waved his arms in a grand, wide gesture.

"This is a beautiful land we have been dropped into."

Un-noticed during their conversation, Smoke had come and gone several times, dropping six more of the fat creatures in a pile near the small cooking fire started by The Guard.

"ROCKS AND STONES!" bellowed Mountain, finally taking notice of her activities.

"We will need more wood than that for this feast."

He charged into the nearby tall vegetation. Crashing noises echoed from the thicket as he gathered firewood. He stomped back into the clearing, a large tree-like plant slung over one shoulder. Dumping it to the ground, he began to break it into smaller pieces and heave them into the small fire. He gave his hands a quick dusting as he kicked the final piece into place.

"There! If The Guard will just roast these little morsels we can eat." He sat down with a heavy thump.

"HUMPF!"

The Guard did. And they all did.

At the end of the meal, Mountain peered around, decided that there wasn't anything left to eat, decided that, perhaps, this was enough anyway, and leaned back upon his elbows.

"So, BY DUMPF, Sorrowful, what do we do next?"

"I really do not know."

"HUMPF! On that last quest, it seemed that the natives were always pointing the way. This time, BY DOUBLE-DUMPF, it seems to me, it does, that we are just banging from rock to boulder. Does it not seem that way to you?"

"It does. This has been a strange adventure. So

far."

"Then, BY ALL THE SAND AND GRAVEL, I propose we follow my twice Grandfather's advice and favorite piece of wisdom."

"And what is that?"

"Roll on, Great Stone, roll on."

"Smoke?" asked Sorrowful.

As far as I can sense, nothing but vegetation and small life forms.

Mountain thumped the ground with one hand, raising a cloud of dust and rumbled at them, "That CRACKS THE ROCK, BY DUMPF. We will just have to roll on until we thump into something, then back off, and take a good look. No sense worrying about a slip that might be a slip."

He sat up and began to rummage in his pack, pulling things out to make his bed and announced grandly, "And that is that!" He rolled over and fell asleep.

Sorrowful stretched out and looked up at the night sky. It was dark with just a light scattering of stars. So where are we now, he wondered to himself.

We will probably never know. Sleep deep. Nothing may approach without my knowing of it.

They all drifted off to sleep. Except for members of The Guard, who rotated shifts, watching the perimeter of the camp throughout the night. They felt better doing it.

And Here's . . .

The City Rinn, The Planet Rinn.

Voices screamed.

Music thumped out a heavy military beat.

A loud, happy voice shouted, "And heeeeeere's ZON'NIE!"

The audience went wild, leaping up and down in their seats, screaming, laughing, beating the back of the seats in front of them.

A small, dapper man strode onto the stage, stopped, backed up, and smiled shyly.

Vast laughter, an in-group joke.

Then he stood on the lip of the stage and beamed at them. "Are you ready to play?" he asked.

"YES."

He smiled out at them. "Really?"

"YES! YES! YES!" they chanted."

"Are you ready to bet?"

"YES! YES! YES!, the bellowed.

It was a measured, steady chant.

"YES! YES! YES!"

"You bet your . . . ?"

"LIFE!" they screamed.

He turned, walked to a large desk and sat behind it, and swivelled back and forth, and smiled at them.

Heavy applause.

Thunderous applause.

"What are you watching?"

Tinker walked from the bedroom, yawning and stretching.

Goose sat in one of the chairs facing a great image that covered most of the wall.

"Know not, Sire. I do just be a'sittin' here, touchin' end of chair arm when suddenly do appear this."

"Look's like a game show to me," said Tinker bending over to peer at the end of the chair's arm.

"Game show?"

"I will explain when we get back home."

He couldn't find the volume control so he walked into the kitchen and shut the door. As he puttered around, the noise filtered through the door. Just as he was finishing setting the table, the door slammed open.

Goose burst through. "Sire, come quickly." He turned and ran back into the main room.

Tinker dropped the cutlery and dashed after him.

The image on the screen was of some vast arena. The camera was high up. From its vantage point they could see row upon row of spectators dwindling down to tiny specks.

It seemed to be a great, round space. The round, open field looked immense, several football fields across.

In the exact center stood a tiny white dot. The camera panned down and down and down until they could see that it was a man, a very terrified man.

"Looks like he is in a domed stadium to me," observed Tinker. "A gigantic one."

"Sire, that person do be the very one answerin' strange questions."

"Questions?"

"Aye. The smilin' one do be named Zon'nie who do ask this one numbers of questions, half-jest type, and he did reply, gainin' vast quantities of stuff. The crowd did scream and shout, urging him on and on. Then he did fail, the mob did moan, and there he be."

"He must have missed the question."

The camera drifted around the arena, panning across the sea of excited faces until it stopped, focused upon a single door set into one wall. The audience slowly sank into silence.

From somewhere high overhead, a single, crystal clear trumpet note sounded. It echoed through the dome.

The spectators cheered as the door slowly slid open.

They were looking into a dark chamber.

The audience sucked in their collective breath.

Something moved, light glistened off it.

It charged into the light.

Goose leaped to his feet, staring. "What manner of beast do be that?"

"Beat's me. But it certainly looks lethal."

The thing was rectangular with a spindly leg on each corner. Light flashed from a number of thorny appendages protruding from the front. It hurtled forward.

The camera panned back and back and up. They watched as the thing charged towards the standing figure. The camera zoomed in for a close shot.

The terrified man jumped back and sideways.

Spikes flashed in the bright light as the thing whipped past. A small shred of cloth fluttered from one spike.

Tinker stared at the picture. "It's a bull fight. Of some sort."

"Barbarian Spaniards, Sire?"

"Of a sort. But this seems rather one-sided. That is a mechanical bull and he is no matador."

The bull-machine turned, sand flying from beneath metal hooves.

Before the victim could properly react, it tossed him high into the air.

Again and again.

"Turn that thing off," snarled Tinker.

"How, Sire, how?"

Tinker jumped forward, one boot heel snapping into the air. The arm rest crumbled in upon itself. Sparks flashed the screen went blank.

"My Lord, what do be that?"

Chicken stood in the bedroom door, eyes staring at the empty wall.

"That, Princess, is the horror of this place." Tinker walked over and gathered her in his arms.

"It seems that the planet Rinn, the city Rinn has some sort of game to entertain its citizens. What we saw is what happens to the losers."

She stared into his face.

"Thou wert most correct, My Lord. There do be great evil here."

Toucan stepped into the room looking puzzled by what he could see.

"Highness?"

"Yes?"

"Has something happened?"

Goose leaped to one side, left hand clenching his sword hilt and stated firmly, "Rah'ther, Brother, rah'ther."

Tinker waved them toward the kitchen.

"We can discuss this over breakfast. I was just getting it ready when all that started."

Breakfast was mostly a silent affair.

Finally Tinker set down his cup and sighed. "O.K., what do we do now?" He looked around the small table.

Blank faces, shrugged shoulders.

Finally Toucan spoke up, "Highness, do be there anything we might do? Tis a most vast a'place and we be but four."

"About that." Tinker jerked a thumb toward the living room. "Nothing." He looked from face to face.

"But we can go out there and try to find what ever it is that we were dropped here to find. And get out of town. The sooner the better."

He stood and headed for the bedroom.

Toucan tossed down the last of his drink.

Goose reached out and stuffed the last of the meal into his mouth, daintily patting his lips with a napkin. Cheeks bulging, eyes twinkling, he headed for the front door.

Chicken rose and waited until all three had passed into the living room. Then she reached into a pocket and drew out a small, gray domino shaped object given to her by Tinker for safe keeping. She turned it over and over in her fingers, lost in thought.

Tinker called from the living room, “Princess, ready to go?”

Her head snapped up, a very grim expression on her face. She pressed the small, engraved circle on the object, held it firmly, counted to herself, and then slipped it back into her pocket. Then she stepped briskly into the living room.

“Stand not blocking the way, Fair Gentlemen, let us away and find what we may.”

She gave Tinker a bump with one hip as she passed and threw open the door.

The morning passed in aimless wandering. Level to level, corridor to corridor.

Unmarked doors, blank-faced people. Everything looked like everything.

Tinker mumbled that this place was the quest in microcosm. They didn’t know where they were going; they didn’t know what they would find; they didn’t know what to do with it, if they found it.

Toucan suggested that this was what they had agreed to do.

Tinker growled.

Chicken took his hand.

Finally, they settled in some small eatery, stomachs grumbling. The place was small and cramped. They hurried through lunch. And waited. Goose had placed another order.

As he crunched the last morsel, he spoke to them in a low whisper, “Yon fella, just there, near outside door, do be most nervous . . . “

"What about him," asked Tinker.

"I do believe me that he do be a'followin' us about. Me'thinks I do see him here, there and everywhere, behind us always."

"We have a tail?"

"Oh, good image, Sire."

"I borrowed it."

"Well, tis most apt, none the less."

"Right. Shall we go and see if he follows?"

They trailed out of the eatery and wandered the corridors, deeper and deeper into the maze that was the city Rinn, the planet Rinn.

The nervous man followed them.

For the rest of the day.

At what they felt was the dinner hour, Goose announced in ringing tones that it was time to eat.

At the next intersection Goose turned left. Toucan turned right.

Tinker and Chicken walked straight ahead.

Their follower stopped, hesitated and then walked after Tinker and Chicken.

Goose and Toucan swiftly stepped out, slipped an arm under each of his, and walked laughing and smiling toward Tinker and Chicken who were waiting.

The man's feet barely touched the floor.

"O.K. guy, what is this all about," demanded Tinker.

The man, more nervous than ever, struggled to be free.

Goose and Toucan set him down, but stood close against him.

"My name is not Gu'y, it is Trim't."

"Well, Trim't," snarled Tinker. "What is going

on? Why are you following us?"

"I must!"

"Why?"

"I lost in The Game and this is what I must do. I must follow you and report all that I see. Or . . . "

"Or what?"

Trim't's face broke into sweat, tears began to run down his cheeks. He licked at his lips with quick jabs of his tongue.

"Or," he whispered harshly, "I will have to face the torhorrus."

His body twitched as he looked nervously about the corridor. There was no one in sight.

"You must let me go. Please?"

His feet danced nervously.

"I don't wish to die, not that way."

"That way? You mean with that thing in the arena?"

They could barely hear his whispered reply, "Yes."

"Let him go," said Tinker.

Goose and Toucan stepped away."

Tinker nodded. "O.K., Trim't, follow us all you wish."

He turned and started walking away, down the corridor.

Chicken slipped her arm under his.

Goose and Toucan walked several paces behind them.

Trim't followed at a circumspect distance.

Goose found them another place to eat. This one had a flashing sign that claimed that good food was inside.

As they settled at their chosen table, they saw Trim't slip into the place and take a table near the door, nervously scanning the room.

Once their orders were taken and they were alone, Goose leaned forward and spoke softly, "It do pear a'me, it do, that this sprawling Rinn do be Rome incarnate."

"Rome, Brother?" asked Chicken.

"Indeed, Queen-Sister. Bread and circuses. Roman at most decadent stage."

"Where is their empire?" asked Tinker. "This planet and city are one."

Goose shrugged his shoulders.

Toucan spoke up. "Highness, me'thinks thy feeling of early day t'was most apt."

"How so?"

"Well, Highness, if this warren be strange incarnation of Rome, from that fact alone there rises great caution. Mighty Romans did have one set of rules for citizens, another, less fair, for barbarians."

Tinker frowned. "And we were labeled as aliens. Let's finish and get back to the Gold Star Suite. Tomorrow we will change quarters. We better not stay in one place too long. We better keep moving."

They rushed through their meal and headed directly back to their rooms. Behind them trailed Trim't.

Around the kitchen table they made their plans, drank another complimentary beverage, and went to bed.

And quickly fell into a deep, bottomless sleep.

Tinker woke with a metallic taste in his mouth and a throbbing headache. Someone sat down next to him on his bed. Slowly turning his head, he squinted up at this person.

It was a stranger smiling a wonderfully insipid, meaningless smile full of gleaming white teeth.

Tinker worked at clearing his throat. Finally he managed to croak, "Who are you?"

The teeth flashed. "I am Zon'nie, the 128th. Perhaps you have seen me on the wall?"

"Just once."

Zon'nie, the 128th beamed, glitterflash. "A wonderful show, don't you think. It has been top-rated all these many years."

"Horrid."

Zon'nie, the 128th beamed and cleared his throat. "That is probably because you are aliens. Aliens are, if you don't mind my saying it, so uncultured, so unappreciative of the civilized life, here in the planet RINN, the city RINN!"

"Certainly seems that way, doesn't it?"

Flashing radiant dentures, Zon'nie, the 128th rose to his feet and said, "No matter, you will do wonders for our rating, it is that time of the cycle. Aliens are always so entertaining. And, whether you will appreciate it or not, you will be A STAR! For a short while, at least. Fickle fame, it comes and goes. For some."

Tinker lurched toward him, gaining his feet and falling sideways. His fingers clenched at the wall for support.

Zon'nie, the 128th quickly steadied him.

"Careful, careful, we wouldn't want to damage one of the featured performers, now would we? It does take some time for that stuff to wear off."

As the multiple images settled down and ran back together, Tinker squinted at him and asked, "What stuff? What star? What are you talking about? Where am I?" He sagged down to sit on the bed.

Zon'nie, the 128th smiled at him, flash, flash.

"Reading from back to front: a holding pen; a series of four Special Segments, titled *Aliens In The Pit,* with special music and narration. Each of you four will be the stars, each with your own segment; and, we put a certain chemical in your complimentary beverage so we could bring you here without a struggle, and without damaging the goods. You have slept for a few periods. We wanted the merchandise to be in prime condition for THE BIG SHOW!"

Turning away, he rapped briskly on the door. It slid open, burly guards peered inside.

Zon'nie, the 128th, stepped outside, then leaned back in, around the door jamb. "Jon'tinker, called Lor'dtinker by your companions, DO put on a GOOD SHOW, will you? Ta, ta?"

He waved one limp hand and disappeared. The door snapped shut.

Tinker sat, head in hands and pondered this new development and thought, so, we are to be a piece of that ghastly show. He looked at the corner and smiled. At least they left my weaponkin. Either it was too primitive for them to recognize or else they don't really care. But, how was he going to escape from this place and find the others.

PRINCESS?

OUCH! Less fierce, My Lord.

Princess?

My Lord?

You heard?

That Zon'nie creature do visit Us earlier. Thee do be some slower to recover.

Where are Goose and Toucan?

I know not.

Still armed?

Indeed.

Well, don't stick anyone or they will take it away. Save it for the arena.

He heard a soft hissing. The door opened, a guard stepped into the entrance holding a small jug which he shoved at Tinker's face.

"Drink this, it will fix you."

Later, LadyLove.

Tinker drank the stuff. It worked. Suddenly he felt ready to go.

LoveJohn, do be most careful, careful.

Another guard carried in a large tray of food and set it on the floor. They backed out. The door closed.

Tinker was left with his meal and silence.

Time passed slowly. He ate meals and exercised. But never with his weaponkin. He figured they were being watched all the time. As the hours, or the days, passed, he and Chicken talked about different ways to disable the torhorrus, the mechanical monster of the arena, and what to do after that.

Then the door slid open and Zon'nie, the 128th appeared, teeth flashing.

"Finally, everything is set. They were going to fit you up in new costumes but I prevailed. What you are wearing is quaint enough. Saves on the over-head costs also. One more meal and it is SHOW-TIME. Just walk down the corridor toward the light and sound. It will be The Arena! The Crowd! A door will open and you will stride out into what we call *The Pit.* And one more thing."

"What?"

"Do try to last as long as possible."

The door slid open and Zon'nie, the 128th walked away. The door slid shut. Within moments the door slid open again. The guard shoved in the familiar tray.

"Last meal, short-term star. Eat hardy."

Tinker ate the meal and progressed through a complicated set of maneuvers, bringing his body to readiness. He stood, his center calm, the great black sword nestling on his back, humming its soft song of blood-lust and destruction. They were ready.

A soft voice announced from the ceiling, "Five minutes, everyone to their places. Five minutes."

The door slipped open.

"Lights coming up. Cameras pan down."

Tinker stepped out. The corridor was empty, his end blocked. Far to his left he could see light and an opening. As he ambled toward it, he could hear the crowd noise growing louder and louder.

Stepping out onto the hard packed sand, he looked around.

It was that vast open space, the one that they had

seen on the screen in their room. He judged it to be at least four football stadiums in size, maybe larger, maybe much larger, tier after tier of seats rising into the dim reaches overhead.

Cupping his hands around his eyes he could make out the faint details of the roofing span.

The crowd murmured, wondering what he was going to do. Behind him, he heard the door slide shut. This was the place that they had seen on the wall of their suite.

He headed straight for the center point, scuffling his feet, testing the surface. It was firm with just enough texture to allow for sudden and hard changes of direction without slipping. All this information he relayed to Chicken. Reaching the center, he turned and waved gaily to the crowd.

They cheered wildly. They laughed delightedly. It was going to be a good show, just as advertized. They told each other how lucky they had been to get tickets.

A light flashed, the audience became silent. A crystal clear trumpet note sounded and died away. In the far wall a door opened. The thing hurtled out, skidded to a halt, sending sand flying.

The crowd roared.

It turned this way and that, seeking him. Finding its victim, it charged. On a straight unswerving line.

Tinker stood and watched it approach, the four legs flailing sand in the air. It left a series of ruts behind. At the last moment he pivoted on his left leg.

The thing zipped past, light flashing from the bristling front spikes.

"Olay," mumbled Tinker to himself.

The crowd roared its approval.

By the third pass they were jumping up and down in the seats.

As the monster ripped past, it bobbled toward him.

He danced back. "OOP! Almost got me. Time to end this show."

He waited while the torhorrus spun end for end and began its charge. He could hear the servomotors whining to an even higher pitch.

Tinker slowly reached up over his left shoulder and gripped his sword hilt. The tingle ran down his arm.

As the thing roared down upon him he rotated toward it, spinning completely around. The weaponkin sang through the air. The sword cut started low and curved sharply upward. Sparks flew into the air with bits and pieces of horns.

The crowd leaped and danced.

Metallic shards of sensors cascaded down around him.

The monster charged wildly. In the wrong direction, smashing into a wall. It bounced and stood, smoke trickling from a broad crack down one side. One leg kicked aimlessly.

Down the wall a door opened and something crawled into the arena, grabbed the collapsing mechanical beast and dragged it away.

Tinker bowed to the audience. Debris rained down in torrents.

The crowd stood on their seats, shouting themselves hoarse. Over the turmoil, Tinker barely heard the trumpet note ring out.

The door snapped open. Out charged another of the things. It hurtled toward Tinker. He swung.

The thing veered away.

"Oh, oh, this one knows what happened to the other one."

The torhorrus stood waiting. Coming to some sort of a decision, it hurtled toward him, jerking its front rapidly from left to right.

Tinker stood and waited. Then he leaped to his left, sliding to his knees and swiveling around. The black sword sang murder as it swept level to the ground.

Ripping past where his chest would have been, the monster sailed by. The blade slashed through the thin legs, severing them at the knee joint.

The thing plowed a deep furrow into the hard packed sand.

Tinker jumped to his feet, ran forward and bashed sensors and antenna in all directions.

The watchers in the stands were in a frenzy, screaming, crying, tearing their clothes, tossing pieces down to the sands below. Over the bedlam, Tinker couldn't hear the trumpet sound but he saw the door slide open again.

Two of the things charged into the open space and stopped, watching, seeking him.

Tinker turned and ran for the opposite end. They watched him as he took his position and shot forward, charging down each side, racing blurs, gaining greater and greater speed.

Tinker knew he would have time for one cut, but

never two. He wiggled his feet, setting himself, the great sword held to one side. It would be a dangerous maneuver but maybe it would be successful.

From high overhead came a loud *POP!* Debris rained down. Two bright flashes, semi-molten scrap bounced from the sands. Something had shot the torhorrus pair.

He stared upward. The ceiling had a large hole in it. It sagged and bent downward as something heavy settled up there. Then the roof dissolved.

Tinker ran and huddled against the wall seeking some minimal protection from the falling thing.

The lower edge of the great spheroid hung above the sand. It curved downward, bulging into the vast open space. Three legs extended and steadied it. Everything was a flat, black color. The bulk of the thing pressed up through the gaping roof.

"Now what?"

Tinker stood and readied himself. This was something unplanned for, something different that what they had expected.

All around the great stadium the crowds fell silent. They stared at the thing and whispered to each other.

The thing sat, ticking quietly to itself. With a snake-like hiss a door opened. A ramp extended and stretched down to the ground.

Something moved inside. Then a large, rotund figure dressed in glistening dark garments of some hard looking material strolled regally down the ramp, casually firing two ugly looking weapons into the crowded stands, blasting holes through the tightly packed tiers of spectators. He stopped and smiled happily up at the crowds. It started a panic.

Tinker ran to the base of the ramp and stared upward. "Macabre?"

"You called?"

"How did you . . . ?"

"Tut, tut, my boy, not now, I have business to attend to."

He snapped two quick shots into the crowds shoving toward the exits. Then he spun around and called into the interior of his ship, "Vipers out, everybody out!"

The buzz of maddened hornets answered him as eight small, black figures flashed down the ramps and scurried up into the now open corridors above.

Tinker saw the flash of eyes glittering angrily as they ran past, teeth chattering.

They scaled up the wall as if running on flat ground. He heard screams of terror intermingled with that terrifying buzzing. The sound faded deep into the interior of the planet Rinn, the city Rinn.

Macabre casually shot two spectators who were peering down at them. He turned his attention back to the ground.

"John Tinker, if you would kindly lead me to the responsible agent or agents who put you in here, we will settle their hash or hashes. HO! Ho, ho, ho, ho."

It was a jolly laugh totally devoid of humor but of one who enjoyed his work immensely.

"Oh, I almost forgot, I brought a friend. Come out."

An electronic crackling noise sounded from the

interior and Two-Byte glided down the ramp and stopped in front of Tinker.

"Greetings, John Tinker. We will speak with city brain and locate your missing companions. They are still well?"

"Chicken is, I don't know about Goose and Toucan."

Two-Byte glided off and began to investigate various openings in the walls of the nearest corridor.

Macabre thumped Tinker heartily on the shoulder, jolting him to one side and stated, "Not to worry, we will soon open up this can of garbage."

He stretched and groaned, "Ahhhhhhhh, it does my old bones good to have a little exercise again." He smiled happily.

"This paper shuffling mound has long been overdue for a little stirring around. Come on, let's go, I want to talk with the head man. HO! Ho, ho, ho, ho, ho. It will be delightful."

Without looking up he fired ten times into the overhead. Nine lights fixtures blew away.

"Not too bad, nine out of ten."

Tinker followed him into corridor A-I.

It was the corridor that had led Tinker into the arena.

Macabre strolled along firing left and right. There was a subtle rhythm to the destruction as each door fell outward, crashing on their faces just as Macabre and Tinker walked past. As the ninth door banged to the floor, a voice called out.

"By George, that wert some trick."

A head poked out and peered up and down the

hall. Then the smiling Goose leaped out into the dust and debris.

"Most humble greetings, Sire. And you, Macabre. Tis good bein' free of that hole. Whither go we now?"

"To find Chicken and Toucan," answered Tinker.

"Let us do be fast a'foot." Goose pointed into the dust and noise.

Macabre was far down the corridor, doors steadily crashing behind him, littering the space between them.

A yellow blur snapped into the corridor from one of the openings behind Macabre.

"**HOLD DEMON! STAND AND DIE!**"

Chicken hurtled herself at him, blade flashing.

Tinker bellowed through the dim dust blurred air, "STOP!"

She skidded to a halt and spun around. "My Lord?"

"And Goose," he said.

Chicken whirled to look at her almost victim.

Macabre smiled at her and asked, "You called, fair Princess?"

"Matter of fact, We do indeed do the deed."

She fished something from her pocket and pitched it at him.

Macabre caught it, carefully inspected its surface, and returned his gaze to her.

"Why so you did, so you did. And a good thing too, I got here just in time." He smiled.

"We do see that. Now We do stand deep in your debt."

She smiled at him and made a courtly bow,

sweeping her blade to one side.

Macabre's face flushed. "Here, here, no need for that. Business is business. John and I struck a bargain. So there is no need to speak of owing debts. Come, there are many doors to open, much work to do."

He pitched the device back to her and nodded. Then he spun around and trundled ponderously off, weapons flashing destruction all around. Turning into a cross-corridor he waved jauntily and called back over a shoulder as he turned, "See you later, I have some private business to attend to."

A figure stepped cautiously from the last open cell and looked around.

"Toucan."

"Brother."

"Highness, we do be free?"

Tinker smiled.

"Yep, we are all back together again, although I had my doubts back there. We had better hurry. Macabre is moving fast, that way."

They ran down the corridor, around a corner, and stopped. Macabre was nowhere in sight. His passage was obvious. As far as they could see there was smoke and wreckage.

From somewhere they could hear people screaming. They ran toward the sound.

And out into one of the large, main corridors. The floor was covered with broken walls, parts of the ceiling and bodies. At the next intersection, a great cloud of smoke suddenly puffed out.

Tinker ran toward it. "He must be down there."

As they ran around a corner a section of wall fell

outward, the panel crumbling softly in the middle. Smoke billowed out.

Macabre stepped from the swirling folds, light shooting in all directions around him. Two glittering things stood behind him. They were as tall as his shoulders. He turned and started away.

"Macabre," called Tinker. "Hold up."

Macabre spun around. "Why John, what are you doing here?"

Tinker took a deep breath. "Just trying to catch up with you."

Macabre tilted his head to one side, listening, and asked, "The Sparkling Tigers want to know where your dark companion is?"

"We don't know. The portal dumped just the four of us here."

"UMMMMM."

"Ummmm, it is. What are you doing?"

Macabre clapped his hands and laughed, "HO! Ho, ho, ho, ho, ho, ho. I am doing my job, John, doing my job. Fire and smoke. Death and destruction. TERROR!"

He smiled and started to turn away. And stopped. He looked down the corridor. "Two-Byte is coming."

The electronic siamese-twins came from the undestroyed portion. They stopped and crackled excitedly at them.

"Greeting, John Tinker, Macabre. We must disable the mainmind, the master computer of this place. Just back this way is a terminal box. Hurry!"

Crackling and buzzing they headed down the

hall and into a small alcove. By the time the rest had joined them they were hooked in. Bright blue energy surged over and between them. Tinker could smell the pungent odor of burning insulation. He started forward.

"Stop them, Macabre, they're burning up. They are going into overload."

Macabre's arm held Tinker back.

Fumes began to seep from small cracks in the twins plating. Electric arcs danced from walls and ceiling.

Through the crackling, they heard the twins' voices, "John Tinker must have The Heart. We are with Gyreship. Gyreship will guide Macabre."

A brilliant flame banged across the twins and scorched the wall. Soft silence, acrid fumes drifting lazily from splintered shells as their casings began to sag from the intensity of internal meltdown.

Chicken clenched Tinker's arm tightly.

"Ohhhhhhh, My Lord, they do die."

Macabre gently touched her sleeve and spoke softly, "Not so, Princess. They are now part of Gyreship who is even now giving me coordinates of where we must go." He touched his right ear and pointed.

"This way, this way. The mainmind is disabled, the Heart Of Time untouched. John, you must have it for your quest. Run, run, run."

Macabre hurtled forward, the Sparkling Tigers trotting on either side.

Tinker and the rest ran after them.

It took a not too long just a little while, for the panting, sweating group to reach their destination.

It was a towering room, the ceiling far, far above.

The walls were blackened with streaks and splattered with globs of exploded circuitry.

In the center of the room, sitting on a tall pedestal, sat a crystalline box.

Macabre pointed at it. "All your's, John. Take it!"

Tinker crossed the sagging floor gingerly. It seemed to be dropping lower as he walked. He touched the box. It felt cool to his touch. He held it easily in one hand as he walked back to his companions.

"This is The Heart Of Time?"

Macabre nodded. "That is what gyreship said." He waved them back into the corridor.

"We must hurry from this place. The main power source is overheating. Now that mainmind is destroyed, it will continue to do so until everything is consumed, city and planet. Everything."

He pointed back at the floor. It was sinking downward. They could see it begin to flow.

Macabre led then away, strolling nonchalantly along. "Well, that is that." He smacked his gloved hands together and smiled.

"You know, this place really needed to die. It has been preying upon this sector of the universe much too long. The planet Rinn, the city Rinn has consumed dozens of other worlds and depopulated great portions of others." Macabre laughed.

"It is a kind of retribution. Now it is consuming itself. If mainmind hadn't started such a mess, there might have been some survivors. But not now. We must leave or we will soon be in the same oven."

He jerked and jolted to a halt. The smile dropped from his face and pure rage poured forth as he snarled,

"I WILL KILL THEM, EACH AND EVERYONE! Slowly, cruelly, painfully. They will feel an agony like they have never imagined. Before this place eats them."

His voice dropped to a still lower register, "I will give them something to die with." He smiled.

Chicken gasped and reached for her sword.

"STARK RAVING TERROR!" growled snarled Macabre.

Macabre muttered something to the Sparkling Tigers who flashed brighter and brighter shafts of light.

Tinker leaped backward, his weaponkin swinging down and in front of him as he crouched.

Chicken, Goose and Toucan jumped away, turning to face in all directions.

Tinker shouted at the raging figure before him, "MACABRE, WHAT'S WRONG WITH YOU?"

Macabre growled at him, his face twisted in fury, "They have holed Gyreship. This nest of paper-shufflers have somehow holed my ship. We are doomed. Gyreship can't make repairs fast enough for us to get away from this soon to be molten ball. Although ship will try." The terrible smile returned. "But I will get them first."

Tinker straightened up and dropped his blade.

"Wait a minute, will you. It isn't that bad."

"Don't speak nonsense, John. I have millions and millions of them to take care of and very little time to do it in." Macabre started to turn away.

The great sword snapped up in front of his face.

He stopped.

"WAIT, I said."

Macabre turned just his head, death leaking from

his eyes. A soft smile rippled across his face. "Don't try to stop me, John."

Tinker smiled at him. "Wouldn't you rather escape from this place? Friend."

"There is no escape."

The Sparkling Tigers leaned forward, barely restrained by Macabre's outstretched arms.

"I think there is. So, if you can restrain yourself for just a few minutes, I will be right back. That was the main control room wasn't it? With the main power source under the floor?"

Macabre nodded.

"You three stay with him."

Tinker spun and ran down the corridor, back toward the towering room with the sagging floor.

Chicken started after him. Toucan grabbed her arm.

"We are to here stay."

Macabre watched the figure disappear into the fumes and smoke. He began to fiddle with various pieces of lethal looking apparatus hanging from his utility belt.

"It does appear that John is running back to the mainmind chamber," he grumbled.

Tinker poked his head through the door and looked down. The floor was mostly gone, the edges hanging in slow dripping shards. Far below he could see a deep, red glow.

The rising heat stung his face.

Stepping back, he unfastened his pocket and lifted out a small, white sphere. He pitched it into the shaft. And stood and waited. And hoped. Then he peeked back inside. The red glow had faded a little. He spun and ran back.

Macabre saw him coming. "There he is."

Tinker thudded to a halt, drawing in deep breathes.

Macabre stared at him through lowered eyebrows. "Well, John?"

"WE are safe, that is well enough! The fire is going out. You should have all the time you need to repair gyre ship and leave this place."

Macabre seemed to unfold. "How did you do that?"

"I pitched the heat sink into it."

Macabre reached out and grabbed Tinker by both shoulders. "It seems, once again, that I am in your debt."

He winked at Chicken. "And your's has now been paid."

He handed her a heavy ring which he had just twisted from one finger. "Take this, a mere bagatelle."

He held one finger against his nose and looked at Tinker. "But it may come in handy, son."

He stepped past Tinker and mumbled in passing, "It appears that it is time for you to leave this trash heap to my tender mercies." He pointed past them.

They turned around.

The portal stood in the corridor, shimmering, heat waves distorting its surface. The fire snakes writhed and twisted, hissing at them, snapping at the Sparkling Tigers who had stepped close to investigate.

Tinker turned back toward Macabre, and said, "Must be time, all right. Well . . . "

"Well me no wells, John. Till we meet again, tred carefully."

Macabre managed a very stately bow. He smiled at Chicken, it really was a warm smile, as he straightened up.

"Fair Warrior Princess, take care, tred carefully." He turned and waved casually back over his shoulder as he started off. "Farewell, farewell."

Macabre disappeared into the clouds of dust and smoke billowing from holes and craters. His weapons jumped into either hand. Firing left and right, they heard him laughing in the gloom, "HO! Ho, ho, ho, ho, ho, ho."

Tinker turned to face the portal as a great cloud of dust, smoke and burned particles drifted toward them. Something crashed out there in the dust and gloom.

"Let's get out of here."

"Lead on, Sire."

"As you wish, Highness."

Chicken slipped her arm through his. "Indeed, My Lord."

They stepped into the portal. Goose and Toucan followed.

The portal winked out.

A massive section of the ceiling collapsed into the corridor, blocking the passageway .

Far in the distance a voice could be heard, in the midst of explosions and the din of falling structure, a voice could be heard laughing . . .

"HO! Ho, ho, ho, ho, ho, ho . . . "

A Strange Thing It Is, Indeed

Some Place. Some Time.

It was morning and they were on the trail again.

Sorrowful was quiet, walking along the path, paying little attention to his surroundings. Smoke had bounded ahead to see what she could find. Behind her came the front half of The Guard. The rest trailed along after Mountain and Sorrowful.

The day warmed up rapidly. This event cheered Mountain no end.

"BY DUMPF, this world is showing signs of having a passable climate after all."

"Ummmmmm, yes, Mountain, passable climate."

"No tales for such a pleasant day?"

"Ummmmmmm, no, Mountain, no tales."

"BE-DUMPF, what is your problem?"

"Ummmmmmm, no, Mountain, no problem."

Mountain spun and glowered down at his small companion and grumbled, "BY ALL THE ROCKS AND PEBBLES!"

He grabbed Sorrowful under the armpits and swung him up to eye-level, holding him out at arm's length.

"There most certainly is, my Talking Mouse." Mountain shook the small man gently. "Now speak. What is this strange thing that makes you so quiet this first of day? This is an un-natural event for you to be so silent. Speak, BY DUMPF!"

Sorrowful gave him a wan smile.

"If you would set me down. Gently. I will tell you."

Mountain did.

Sorrowful carefully shook his clothes back into place, patted some small spot clean, and started walking along the path.

Mountain ambled at his side, casting a wary glance down at his tiny companion.

"If you promise to contain yourself, I will tell you."

"MUMPF! Get on with it."

"I had a night thought."

"A what?"

"I had a night thought."

Mountain stared wide-eyed at Sorrowful. "You had a night thought."

Sorrowful nodded, "Yes."

"Might this one ask a question? That is, if you do not feel that I might be interjecting myself too DUMPFING much?"

"Ask."

"This, ah, night thought thing you had. What is it?"

"A night thought."

"BY DUMPF, THAT IS THE DIM-DUMPFING POINT! You are telling the name not the what!"

Mountain's voice echoed from a distance hill.

"What kind of thing is this TRUMPF-HUMPFING, DOUBLE-DUMPFING, RE-RUMPFING so-called night thought?" He had tried to keep his voice down but had failed.

Sorrowful looked up at the glowering face and stated firmly, "A night thought is a night thought. Do you not know what a night thought is?"

"A foreign word, thing."

"You do not have night thoughts?"

Mountain sucked in a great breath and grumbled, "I do believe that I have just mentioned the very plain fact that this thing is foreign to me, did I not?" Mountain stared around them, searching the landscape.

"But, BY ALL THE MINERALS AND GEMS, if I see one skulking around after us, I will pound it into dusty-dust. You just point it out to me and I will fix that BE-BUMPFING thing the next time it comes around."

Mountain's hand gently stroked the handle of his great cudgel.

"A kind offer, but it would be difficult for you to handle."

"HUMPF! We will just see about that."

Mountain took something edible from his pocket and began to munch loudly.

"Mountain?"

"Yes?" He stopped chewing. "You want something to eat?"

"Remember when Smoke showed you that animal, the one like those we ate?"

"Yes."

Mountain's stomach rumbled remembrance.

"If you had been sleeping and if she was not responsible and if you then woke up and remembered what you had seen when you had been sleeping, then you would have had a night thought."

"That is a night thought?"

"Pretty much."

"HUMPF! I almost had one on the world of the Gett. But it was not."

They walked on.

For some time.

In silence.

"So?"

"So, what?"

"SO, BY DUMPF, what was this night thought thing of your's like?"

"Oh, that."

"Yes, BY DIDDLING-DUMPF, THAT!"

"Let us sit for awhile and I will tell you about it."

"Right!"

With a heavy and loud thump Mountain dropped into a sitting position, tucking his legs underneath. Small dust puffs eddied around him.

Sorrowful selected a small and convenient boulder. It was a good size for sitting. For him.

"SO! First you have to realize that my folk tend not to have night thoughts. Some of our wiser ones have suggested that this is because our tale telling proclivities have substituted for them. Hence, when we sleep there is no need for them. It seems, it does, that night thoughts only come to certain of us, at certain times. And when they do, they tend to be prophetic rather than recreational. Now. . . "

"Now, BY DUMPF, get to the point."

"I asked you not to interrupt."

"HUMPF!"

Sorrowful watched Mountain resettle himself, more or less, and regained his narrative string.

"Well, then, to get to the point. And a frightful breach of manners and poor taste and lack of proper upbringing it is too, most suitable for barbarians, of which we do not have any in my world, by the way, which is why I have to borrow the term, of other poorly educated beings, of which I have met more than my share, I assure you, on these quests of John Tinker's . . ."

"BY ALL THAT FALLS, I swear that your jaw is hinged back and front. "

"SO!"

"SO, indeed, BY DUMPF! So, indeed."

Mountain's eyes were flashing from place to place, his expression suggesting that he was ready to begin tearing trees up by their roots.

Sorrowful was staring into space, focusing inward, seemingly unaware of the great mass of agitation sitting nearby. He restarted his tale.

"The night thought seemed to be here, on this world, in this world. Strange creatures, who walked on two legs, gave us a rod of crystal. They passed it through a box of similar material. They called the rod The Key Of Time. It will take us to the end of time. But there is a thing here which will keep us from attaining this gift. It is great and powerful. And neither dagger nor great cudgel will have an effect upon it. This path we walk will lead us straight to it. And a great wasteland. All I could see was this great waste land. It stretched on and on. Desolation. On and on and on and on and on and on and . . . "

"STOP!"

"And on and on and on and on and . . . "

"STOP! BY ALL THE ROCKS AND STONES, STOP!"

A gigantic hand slammed flat on the ground next to Sorrowful. The jolt lifted him from his perch.

" . . . what? . . . "

"Stop telling of this night thought thing of your's. It is not good to hear."

Mountain stood and stretched.

"Come, it is exercise that you need, not dreary remembrance. If some unkind being awaits us, there is little we can do about that but face it, if, and when, we do."

He held one finger up in front of Sorrowful's face, bending deeply at the waist to do so.

"But, until then, we enjoy the few pleasures of life we have: hiking, eating, and sleeping." Mountain gestured roughly.

"Come, we have but one way to go. And with but one choice there is no need for tedious debate." He waved one arm in a broad and grand sweep, taking in everything in their surroundings, and urged, "Come. As we walk you may thump my ear numb with one of your everlasting tales."

Sorrowful stood and nodded. "You are correct, we have no choice. We will hike. But out there lies. . ."

"STOP! BY DUMPF, another word of that and you might become squashed bug blotch. Tell me a tale!"

Mountain stomped down the pathway.

Sorrowful trotted to catch up with him and asked, "All right, all right. Which one would you prefer?"

"One that I have not already heard."

"Ummmm, fine, I have one of those. This tale is most befitting the occasion considering our present circumstances, I do believe."

"Good."

"It is called *The Tale of the Pf'rindle-Df'indle And The Endless Road.*"

Sorrowful took a deep breath.

"So! In a time and at a time, there was a Pf'rindle-Df'indle who decided to leave home and see the world. So he set out upon his journey. But first he had to say good-bye. To his brother and to his brother and to his brother and to his sister and to his sister and to his sister and to his sister and to his mother and to his mother and to his mother and to his mother and to his father and to his father and to his father and to . . ."

"WAIT ONE DUMPFING PAUSE!"

"What is it . . . now?"

Mountain squinted down at Sorrowful and frowned. "BY DUMPF, it is this. Explain this creature's mother, mother, mother, mother, father, father, father."

Sorrowful smiled shyly. "The Pf'rindle-Df'indle have a rather interesting procreational system."

"It would seem so."

Sorrowful glanced up and sideways at his companion and said, "I suppose I shall have to explain it, in order to get on with the tale?"

Mountain nodded. "YES, BY DUMPF, I think you ought to do that." He almost smiled. "How else am I to understand the subtleties of this tale?"

Sorrowful smiled. "It is fortunate that we do not

have any ladies with us. For if we had, I would not be able to explain."

"HUMPF!"

"I assume that means you are ready to listen. The process among the Pf'rindle-Df'indle goes this way. When a female Pf'indle-Df'indle feels a certain urge, she starts to . . . "

Far ahead of them, Smoke padded silently through the brush. Suddenly her ears shot straight up, twisting slightly from side to side. In the dim distance she had perceived something new at the edge of her sensenet. She started to lope in and around brush clumps toward it. Part of her minds focused upon these things. Part was listening to Sorrowful's explanation of the strange thing of his tale to Mountain. She found it somewhat amusing. Part was casting back through all her accumulation of clan memories, generations deep, for guidance. But, before she could fully focus upon these strange creatures, they scattered and disappeared. Smoke stopped and sat down, puzzled by this strange behavior.

She looked around. There were many other living things all around, scattered throughout the vegetation. They were running over or burrowing through the ground. They paid no attention to her nor was she paying much attention to them. At the moment neither was a threat to the other.

Whatever had happened, should not have. She was The Hub. Among the Velvetmist, her clan, she was the most powerful mindlink. She pulled the sensenet in and focused all her energies and mind levels on the search for an answer to this puzzle. Then slowly she expanded the sensenet outwards, slowly, ever so slowly, probing every living thing, plant or animal. Foot by careful foot the unseen energies flowed outward.

She had it.

With all the stealth of the great carnivore that she was, she slowly turned her head and stared up into a tall tree. A leather-winged flyer sat on a high limb, brown-glowing eyes watching her. It was a passive watcher. The far away beings were using it to observe and monitor her movements. Something out there felt her touch them. She had been careless. It would not happen again.

Smoke's mind flowed into the other and then released it. The watcher leaped from its perch and floated high into the air on a thermal. There was nothing to see in the clearing below. The black creature had disappeared.

The Breem puzzled over this. But others would see it and report the location.

Smoke sat in the clearing and watched the leather-winged flyer soar higher and higher. Nothing on this world could see her now. She padded through the brush.

" . . . and so you see, that is how they do it." Sorrowful looked up to see how his companion was reacting to the long, complicated explanation.

Mountain nodded slowly. "BY DUMPF, that is truly remarkable. You tiny folk certainly have active imaginations."

"Among other attributes."

"HUMPF!"

They strolled down the path as Mountain

pondered all that Sorrowful had told him. He thought about what his twice-father would say if he had heard this tale.

"Heh, heh."

"What?"

"UMPF, nothing, just a stray thought. Heh, heh."

Sorrowful smiled up at him and stated, "It seems to me, that for you, you are in the midst of unbridled merriment."

Mountain looked down at him. "BY DUMPF, you are correct in that. Heh, heh."

Sorrowful smiled to himself.

A leather-winged flyer perched in a nearby tree. Its brown eyes clouded over as it watched them walk past.

The Breem puzzled over what they saw, these things with the dead eyes. They apparently came in assorted sizes and shapes. What ever these things were, they were brave. They were walking down Endfate Holdtrack into the Emptyspace. None had ever returned from there. These creatures appeared unconcerned. Perhaps it was because they were unaware.

The Breem thought about this. And discussed it, many times, carefully.

The day flowed on.

"Mountain?"

"Yes?"

"Let us make camp early."

"BY DUMPF, why not. **SERGEANT!**"

The blast of sound focused twenty pairs of glowing eyes on them from the surrounding vegetation before their owners fled for their lives. The Guard came at a run.

"Lords"

Sorrowful said, "Sergeant, we wish to make camp early."

"As you wish, Lord Sorrowful. Just ahead there lies a small clearing. We can put up there."

"That sounds fine. See to it, will you Sergeant?"

"At once."

The Sergeant spun on his heels and trotted off shouting orders. By the time Sorrowful and Mountain arrived, The Guard had the camp set up and had started cooking the evening meal. It was ready to eat by the time the rear Guard arrived.

Mountain and Sorrowful sat eating their meal in the center of the clearing. The Guard had insisted that they occupy that spot.

"BY DUMPF, this meal is not as fine as that we had last."

Mountain was eating hefty portions, none the less. "Where has Smoke run to? She could have brought in a few more of those fat, tasty things."

"Ask her."

"What?"

"Use your Golden Eye and ask her."

"DIM-DUMPFING DUMB! I forgot."

Mountain wiped his hands on his pant legs and hefted his cudgel around, slamming one palm down over the jewel in the end.

Smoke?

Yes?

Where are you?

Far ahead.

Far ahead?

Yes. By next evening I will contact The Breem. They have been watching us. Then I will guide you here. There is nothing around for you to worry about. Sleep comfortably.

But not well.

Catch your own food.

HUMPF!

Smoke's image faded away. The Breem had seen her. Then she disappeared from their sight again.

The Breem puzzled over this. Never before had anything behaved this way. The Breem thought about this. And discussed it, over and over.

Evening seemed to come upon the camp slowly.

Sorrowful told Mountain and The Guard various tales until it was too dark to see faces. Then all settled down for the night.

Far ahead, Smoke drifted silently toward her quarry. She ate some of the fat creatures that Mountain had so enjoyed.

One by one they disappeared.

The Breem saw this and puzzled over it. The pattern was clear. Some thing was coming their way. But they could not see it. Never had anything behaved this way before.

Not even the creature that lived in Emptyspace. This must be something new. The strange in Emptyspace must feel it also. It stirred sluggishly. The nearby watchers felt the vibration in the earth.

The Breem thought about this. And discussed it, over and over.

Smoke drifted closer and closer.

The Magic of The Tongue Is The Most Dangerous of All Spells

Clear Bandler.

The Magician shuffled onto the stage from the right wing. The house lights dimmed as a single spotlight picked him out of the gloom and followed his wandering path toward the front of the stage. The bright light made the strangely patterned cloth of his rather tattered robe appear to twist and curl with a life of its own. If anyone had been close enough to see, they would have noticed that the bottom edge of the robe was badly frayed. Small pieces of lining hung from his sleeves.

The Magician lurched forward carrying two suitcases, each tucked high under either arm. His loud mumbling carried to the last row.

"Oh dear, oh dear, late again. Have to do something about the transportation system." He stared into the bright light, squinting his eyes, searching and finding the audience.

"AH, there you are."

Standing, looking outward, he managed to tangle his feet, one over the other, and started toppling sideways. Hopping and bobbling from foot to foot, he finally regained his balance. The spotlight jerked around the stage and finally caught up with him.

Trapped in the brilliant circle he sighed, and set down the suitcases.

"Well. Here we are. Ah . . . YES. Urm . . . Here we are."

He stared for a long moment, blinked his eyes, and smiled, a shy smile, and announced, "LADIES AND GENTLEMEN, LET THE SHOW BEGIN . . . "

Nothing happened.

Long, deadly silence.

Cautiously he peered around the stage and whispered loudly, "Em? Where are The Heralds?"

Then his face flushed bright red. "Oh dear, forgot to unpack them."

He smiled weakly out across the stage front at his audience.

"Hold on a minute, won't you? This will only take a moment or two."

With a few quick tugs and pulls, he unfolded the suitcases. Two tables popped into existence, gleaming with reflected light. He yanked a heavy brown robe from one suitcase, flapped it loosely, shaking out the dust, waved one hand at the small cloud, and walked over and dropped the robe at one side of the stage. Then he repeated his actions with the other suitcase and dropped that robe on the other side of the stage. The spotlight managed to follow him as he wandered back and forth and finally returned to stage-center.

"Now, where were we? Oh . . . yes. Ahem, ahem. LADIES AND GENTLEMEN, LET THE SHOW BEGIN!"

He waved a wand grandly and jabbed it at either side of the stage. The brown robes billowed, filled and rose to stand looking out, their hoods filled with . . . nothing.

One spoke to the audience with a deep bass voice, "ATTENTION! ATTENTION! THIS IS THE MAGICIAN. LET THE SHOW BEGIN!"

From the other side, the notes of a trumpet blared forth.

TAAAAA!

TAAAAAAAAAAA!

The crystal clear notes caused ringing in the ears of the people sitting in the rear-most rows of seats, up into the fourth and last balcony. A drum beat shook the building. Dust trickled down from the high ceiling.

"Oh my," sighed the figure staring at his phantom helpers.

"Much too loud. Really much too loud!"

He waggled his wand at them. "ENOUGH!"

The robes collapsed into jumbled heaps as he mumbled mostly to himself, "The show must go on, and all that sort of thing."

With a dramatic gesture, he picked up an object and twirled it on one finger.

"As you can see, Ladies and Gentlemen, this cylinder is empty and light as a feather."

He peered out at the audience through one end. "Peek."

Setting it on one of the tables, he covered the cylinder with a yellow cloth and waved his wand over it and told the audience, "Now for a few magic words. Ummmm, let's see, what were they?"

His face went blank as he stared into space. Then his eyes popped wide.

"AH! Riggle-de-piggle-de-de. HOOP and BAM!"

He jerked the cloth away and slid one arm into the tube.

"And what do we find in here." Jerking his arm out, he cried loudly, "OUCH!"

He began to jab at something deep inside the cylinder, the wand making rattling and banging noises as he leaned over, his arm thrust down into the cylinder up to the shoulder.

Straightening up, he leaned over and peered inside. "Out, out, out. You get out of there!"

Three black creatures flew out and began to circle over the audience before they disappeared up into the rafters over the stage floor. The audience gasped. One vaguely resembled a bat, the other two something else. Better not seen too closely.

The Magician gestured angrily and wildly over his head.

"YOU! Come down here."

The bat-like thing fluttered down and perched on the end of his wand, held out in front of him. It looked more or less like a bat. With a human head. With a quick snatch of his free hand he grabbed it by the legs and stuffed it head first into the short cylinder on the table.

"Back in you go. We can't have mythological creatures trying to seep across the cracks of time and universe."

He got rid of the other two in like fashion.

"THERE!"

He threw the wand over his shoulder. It disappeared. Dusting his hands with a quick motion, he smiled at the audience and reached into the cylinder again. And began to throw great quantities of flowers and ribbons and handkerchiefs of many colors into the audience. Then he stopped and took a quick bow. The audience cheered and clapped.

"Now," he stated loudly, "For my next trick, I need a volunteer from the audience."

He stood, waiting, patiently. Someone would come. They always did, if a little slowly. A strange noise caused him to whirl around and look toward the back of the stage.

"What's this?"

Four feet above the stage floor something strange had appeared. Flames licked over its surface. The fire-snakes roiled and hissed at him.

"WHAT IS THIS? I didn't order this thing!"

He shook his head and murmured to himself, "Now who could be volunteering is such a fashion? Where is that wand, never find one when you need one. Ahhhh, there it is."

The magician reached into the air and snatched it forth just as the first figure tumbled out and landed heavily on the stage floor. Another followed. They seemed to be coming from the strange device.

"WATCH IT, CHICKEN! OOOOOOOOOF!"

"Most sorry, My Lord, t'was most far drop. Roll quickly aside."

Something dressed in black followed by one in white landed next to them.

The Magician looked into the stage wings and yelled, "RING DOWN THE CURTAINS!"

He jerked back toward the audience as the

curtains began to roll closed.

"Ladies and gentlemen, that is the show for tonight. Your tickets will be refunded until the next performance. It appears that, ah, things beyond our control have interfered with tonight's performance."

He bowed and bowed and waved. "Good night, good night."

The curtains closed with a heavy thump. The magician whirled around and glared at these intruders.

"Who are you?"

One of them stepped forward.

"Me? I am John Tinker." He waved one arm. "These are my, ah, helpers. Who are you?"

The Magician stared at them.

"ME? You mean to tell me that you volunteered and you do not know who I am. I am the $1.98 Magician." He made a sweeping bow. "At your service."

All the stage lights flared into brilliance. He smiled and asked, "So, John Tinker, where is the rest of your company?"

Tinker frowned at him. "Good question. Who knows. How did you know that?"

Toucan, Goose and Chicken began to spread sideways, hands drifting toward sword hilts.

The Magician smiled at Tinker. "Big Red told me that you would be appearing soon. But I hardly expected you to do it this way." He waggled his hands aimlessly and shrugged. "But that is neither here or there or anywhere else." He started for one side of the stage.

"Come, we can discuss all this over dinner. I

know a nice place. It is just around the corner."

He strode rapidly toward the side door. His two suitcases, magically packed, jostled each other as they floated after him.

Tinker glanced at his companions.

Toucan raised one eyebrow.

Goose giggled.

Chicken took Tinker's arm in her's.

They followed the Magician outside. Behind them the stage lights dimmed.

They were standing on a broad wooden sidewalk running down one side of a dirt street. All the buildings they could see were made of large diameter logs. It was twilight on the frontier. No one else was on the street.

$1.98 gestured at their surroundings and explained, "A rather primitive town. But it has a theater."

Tinker nodded. "Seems that way. Where's the inhabitants?"

"This is a back way. Follow me please."

The magician waggled one hand loosely.

They walked down the sidewalk until they came to a smaller, more narrow passage way.

$1.98 turned in and led them a few paces forward, then stopped and pointed at a red line on one of the wooden slats.

"See that, the red stripe?"

"Yep."

"As soon as you step over it, turn right, like this."

$1.98 stepped forward, pivoted on one foot and stepped. And disappeared. The suitcases bobbled right after him. And disappeared. One after the other.

Behind him, Tinker heard Goose hiss, "Most amazin', Sire."

"Certainly is."

A disembodied voice spoke to them, "Come along, come along. It is perfectly safe."

Tinker slipped his arm under Chicken's and tugged her forward. They stepped, turned, and disappeared.

Toucan looked at Goose.

Goose bowed him forward. Then followed.

They all were standing in an alley of what sounded like a large and bustling city. Just past the alley mouth where they were standing they could see traffic and people passing by.

$1.98 smiled at them. "I said it was just around the corner."

Tinker smiled back. "Some corner."

Yes . . . well . . . I travel muchly. It saves a lot of time and wear and tear."

$1.98 pointed.

"The restaurant is just around that corner. Actually is that corner, this time."

They followed him and the jostling suitcases out onto the main street of the city, turned the corner and entered the first door available. Into a small restaurant.

The suitcases slipped onto the shelf below the coat rack. $1.98 led everyone to a small table, just big enough for them, located in a quiet corner.

After they had all seated themselves, he nodded his head and explained. "This place is named *Mudas*. I used to work here. That is how I know the name and taste. I met Big Red here."

A pot-bellied, red-faced man popped from the kitchen door, beaming at them as he shuffled over to their table.

"$1.98, good to see you again. Need a job? Ha, ha, ha, small joke, small joke."

$1.98 waved one hand at his guests. "Lord John Tinker, Princess Chicken, Prince Toucan and Prince Goose. This is Brizbittle, otherwise known as Muda, after whom, of course, this place is named."

Muda beamed at them and threw both arms wide and gushed, "Lords and Lady, welcome to my place, my very humble place." He winked at them. "But the food is the best anywhere. Of course."

"Of course," agreed $1.98.

Muda smiled at the magician. "It seems you have moved up a notch in the world to be in such royal company."

"More like sideways," suggested Tinker.

Muda frowned. "Pardon, Lord?"

$1.98 smiled at the owner. "Nothing, Muda, nothing. We will have the speciality of the house, of course. And a container of bu-juice."

"OF COURSE! Right away, right away."

Muda bustled back to the kitchen and returned almost immediately with a large, very heavy serving tray laden with steaming dishes and several crystal containers filled with a murky, pale orange liquid.

$1.98 jumped to his feet and began to serve his guests.

Goose beamed as the food was silently slipped in front of them. "By George, Sire, it do smell jolly good."

He carefully tasted one of the food stuffs and

smiled happily. "Jolly good tastin' too."

Muda returned to the kitchen and $1.98 sat down.

"It is all in the sauces, Prince, all in the sauces. I should know, that used to be my job, helping the sauce chef prepare the various ones, one for each different dish."

"You do cook?" asked Toucan.

"Yes, Prince Toucan, I did. But that was before I met Big Red."

"Maybe you could tell us about that?" mumbled Tinker around a mouthful.

"Certainly, John Tinker."

$1.98 held out one of the crystal containers.

"Here, try some of this. It is made from a local berry, the bu berry, and is renown for the subtle flavors."

He poured a generous measure into Tinker's glass and then topped up his own. And looked around the table.

He began to tell his tale as they ate.

"Well, let's see, how to start? Ummmmm. It was a number of years ago and I was a hard working helper in the kitchen. And quite happy in my work. Then, one day, this new customer came in. Every week or so, he would come in for a meal. Always the same meal, always the same dish."

$1.98 smiled at them and continued, "This went on for quite a long time. Finally, after one particular meal, he called for me. So I came out, from the kitchen you see, and walked over to his table. I was ready to be complimented for my sauce work, you see. It had been one of my better efforts. He introduced himself."

"Duzriddle, my name is Big Red. I think that it is time for you to begin to learn your true calling."

"But Sir," I stated. "I have a good job."

"Yes, yes, of course, you do." Big Red smiled warmly. "But it is not your true calling. SIT!"

"I sat, quite confused and asked him, what do you mean, Sir?"

Big Red beamed and smiled and then frowned. He did it in that order.

"First, stop this Sir stuff. My name is Big Red. And that is what you will call me. Second, it is time to start your training. I will be your teacher." He looked toward the kitchen.

"Muda won't mind. It will bring fame, perhaps even fortune to this place."

Big Red started doing little things on the table top. "You see, I am a magician. And I can tell that you have the potential to be one also. You will be my student."

I leaped to my feet, surprised. After all, to be a magician is to have a special gift, a special thing. And what he was telling me was that I was to become a special person. But I felt he was wrong, that it wasn't meant for me. After all, I already had a good job. Eventually I would become a sauce chef. It was enough.

So, I told Big Red that. And sat down.

He laughed. "You do not understand. You will study with me, as my student, a kind of under-study. It will take a number of years. But then, it will only be a minor change."

He reached over and tapped me on the chest

with one finger tip.

"I am the greatest magician that is, or will ever be. And you are to be my student. After all, you are already the saucier's apprentice."

He laughed so hard that the rest of the customers started staring at us.

He disappeared.

The next day he came back and started my training. Always at the same meal time.

It took years.

When I was done, he gave me my name and said, "For all this you will aid me if I should need it. I will tell you when. And when, and if, you must use all your powers and then some."

He stood on the last day and patted me on my shoulder.

"Believe me, when that time comes, you will need all the skills that you have developed."

He disappeared again, this time for good. For one moment, it seemed as if some other creature stood there. It said cock-a-doddle-do. Or something like that.

$1.98 gestured around the table.

"Now, here you are. Just one day after Big Red told me to expect you. But I thought there were more of you."

Tinker shrugged one shoulder and said, "It seems that is how things are." He nodded toward the magician. "What are you supposed to do, to help us, that is?"

$1.98 shook his head. "Big Red didn't say. Just provide all help possible. I assumed that you would know what kind of help that was to be." He looked around the table.

Everyone shook their heads.

$1.98 held up the container of bu-juice.

Goose pushed his cup forward. "Jolly good idea."

$1.98 refilled all the cups.

"Welllll, I suppose you could all stay at my place. It is not far, it is . . . "

"Just around the corner," interjected Chicken.

$1.98 looked startled.

The rest laughed.

Chicken touched the magician lightly on his shoulder. "It do seem most appropriate, not so?"

$1.98 nodded. "Yes, I suppose." He stood. "Shall we go?" And headed for the door.

Muda met them there.

The suitcases jostled next to his legs.

"Always a pleasure, $1.98. Return soon. Bring your friends."

Muda pushed open the door and waved them through.

They walked out.

Followed by the suitcases.

As they headed down the street, Tinker whispered to $1.98, "How did you pay for all that?"

$1.98 laughed. "I didn't pay. I am a magician."

He led them into a different small, side street and pointed.

"There. Just past that pole. It is just a hop, skip, and a jump."

Tinker smiled. "Really?"

$1.98 looked puzzled.

"Just so. Turn right, take one hop, one skip. And jump."

He turned past the pole, hopped and took a small skip. And disappeared.

The suitcases pushed past Tinker and company. And disappeared.

Tinker looked at Chicken. "Well Princess, shall we?"

She reached out and took his hand. "Like two innocent children, My Lord."

Tinker gave her an exaggerated wink and leer, and using his W.C. Field imitation, stated slyly, "Not too innocent, My Dear."

He turned her in the correct direction.

"Ready. Hop."

Toucan watched them disappear and followed.

Goose watched the process, smiled broadly and followed his brother, flapping his arms wildly, giggling happily.

"HOP! SKIP!"

Tinker and Chicken landed lightly on their feet and stepped to one side to inspect their new surroundings.

Toucan landed sedately and looked around.

Goose thudded down, arms windmilling, up and down. "JUMP!" He circled around them. "Hop. Skip. Jump."

Giggling and beaming, he came to a halt in front of them. "Oh, I say, Sire, this place do have most novel manner of gettin' about. Where do be mage?"

"Over here, Lords and Lady."

$1.98 was leaning against a wall, eyeing his

guests carefully.

Tinker strolled over and peered out a large window. "Sunshine."

$1.98 stepped to his side.

"We have come some distance around the ball. I assume that you are probably tired from your journey." He waved one arm. "I made adjustments."

He turned and started to walk away.

"Just follow me and I will take you to your accommodations."

An opening appeared in one wall. He led them through and down a short hall which began to widen as they approached the end making a short wall with two doors set side by side. The doors swung open as they approached.

$1.98 gestured and left them to choose.

Tinker looked at the two Princes. "Which one?"

"Either, Highness."

"Quite right, Sire."

Tinker pointed to the left door. "Your room. See you in the morning."

Tinker and Chicken stepped into their room.

The door swung shut behind them. It was a large room with a large window. Most of the floor appeared to be knee deep in thick quilts. They dropped their gear by one wall.

Chicken stepped out onto the softness, spun on one heel and toppled backward. And thumped and disappeared.

A muffled voice spoke to him, "Most soft and pleasant, Me'Lord. Wouldst care to join this thy Verra Own Queen?"

Tinker stepped to the spot where he figured she had disappeared and bent over and poked with one finger.

"I would, if I could tell where you are."

An arm reached out and grabbed him, yanking him forward. "GOTCHA!"

He disappeared into the coverings.

"PRINCESS . . . ?"

"Yes, My Lord?"

"Ummmmmm. Never mind. Gotcha."

"Oh, my yes, thee certainly has Us in thy clutches."

"Ummm, hummm."

"OH!"

Outside, the light faded.

Night had enveloped day.

Lock Heraur. Pikel Antar.

It had taken four fingers of a hand to walk the nights from Pikel Fermda to this much larger town, a near city in size.

As they strolled along one of the large wide street searching for good lodgings, Turintor nodded to herself. The long walk had been beneficial. Two nights past, finally, her dark companion had finally spoken. Two words.

"Witch debt," she had said as she had finished the meal, leaning back on the comfortable pillows mounded up in soft overgrown heaps.

Turintor had taken care of the food and anything else that they had required.

"No debt," snapped Turintor. "I would still be

trapped if you had not done that."

Her companion nodded.

And so here they were, wandering along one of the large wide streets seeking lodgings.

Folk very carefully did not jostle them. It was not a good thing to do, jostle wandering witches. Even if these witches appeared to be calm and very relaxed, or at least as calm and relaxed as witches ever appeared to be.

The pair strolled into the *Triggle Inn,* acquired a three-room suite situated on the fourth floor, outside corner, with a wrap-around balcony.

Turintor stood and peered down at the busy intersection and idly watched the local folk going about their business. Suddenly she jerked and hissed and spun around. Her companion stood, calmly watching, holding a thin black wand in one hand. It was her first magical manifestation since their escape.

Turintor twitched and watched as the thin black wand was shoved up her companion's left sleeve, who explained, "I just felt a touch of strange witch." She spun and pointed. "Out there."

Rocks and Stones

Some Place. Some Time.

"Wake up, wake up."

It was Sorrowful, singing merrily, as he poked at a vast heap with the toe of one boot as he announced, "It is a bright and sunny morning. Adventure beckons us onward into the dawn."

The great heap creaked into an upright position and mumbled deep inside its chest.

"BY DUMPF! I would prefer a more subdued wakening."

Mountain made a slow sweep with one arm. "BEGONE, nattering nitterly."

"Nattering nitterly. A fine choice of words to greet one who has seen fit to fix you a fine, one might even say, a wonderful, morning meal."

Mountain's eyes popped wide. "Morning meal? Did you say morning meal?"

He stood, sweeping covers to one side, tumbling the small man under the jumble. Mountain bent over, pushed here and there, and lifted Sorrowful with one hand, unbent, eyes sweeping the clearing, searching for the promised food.

"Mighty Master of Tale Telling," he rumbled. "This is a generous act. BY ALL THE ROCKS AND STONES, you tiny folk might be civilized after all."

Mountain stomped off in the direction nose and

stomach directed him.

"But, BY DOUBLE DUMPF, it certainly has taken a long enough time for you to demonstrate that fact."

Thudding down to the ground next to The Guard, he carefully set Sorrowful on his feet and held out one hand for a platter. One of The Guard handed him a dish and set food upon it.

"BY DUMPF! BY DUMPF, indeed. You have cooked more of those fat little tasty things."

Mountain patted Sorrowful gently on the shoulder. It buckled Sorrowful's knees.

"A true mark of civilization, Sorrowful, a true mark. May we start?"

"Of course, of course."

Smoke padded along, far distant from their camp, amused by Mountain's reaction. She had herded a number of the small creatures into a clearing and held them there until The Guard could catch them for the meal. Then she had roused Sorrowful and told him what she had done. Now she had turned her attention back to her task and put the full focus of her minds on the task ahead.

"BY DUMPF!"

Mountain burped softly to himself, dabbed at his mouth with his sleeve and beamed at Sorrowful.

"So it was Smoke's idea. Even a greater surprise."

He took a deep swallow from his cup and eyed the empty cooking vessels.

"MUMPF, she deserves great thanks for this."

"You may do that this evening. She said we would catch up with her by then."

Sorrowful jumped to his feet and nudged Mountain just above the straining belt and asked, "Will you be able to hurry with that great lump?"

"GREAT LUMP?"

Mountain shot to his feet and bent over to stare into Sorrowful's face.

"Such a small repast has never slowed me down. And it certainly will not do that here, today."

He waved one arm. "Where ever we are." Straightening up, Mountain gestured dramatically. "COME! Let us pack our belongings and start."

He stomped heavily over to his pack and began to stuff everything into to it, mumbling to himself, "BY PUMPF-DUMPF! Something knee-tall to a rock fall wondering whether I will be able to hurry. HUMPF, HUMPF, and DOUBLE-DUMPF!"

While all this was going on, Sorrowful spoke to The Sergeant who then finished preparing the camp to move out. By the time Mountain had completed his packing the front half of The Guard were well down the trail. Sorrowful waited for Mountain, smiling happily at him.

"WELL WUMPF, what are all the teeth for?"

"I smile in enjoyment at your radiant personality."

"HUMPF!"

"HUMPF, indeed."

Sorrowful started down the trail, Mountain at his side.

"This reminds me of *The Tale of The Great Stone Tr'indle.*"

"Well, BE BUMPF, go on, be-numb my ears

again. But don't swear so much."

Sorrowful laughed and took a deep breath.

"SO! In a time and at a time, there lived a Tr'indle. Now this Tr'indle was . . . OH. By the way, Smoke has found intelligent life in the place. They call themselves The Breem."

"Breem?"

"Yes. We should meet them this evening."

"And Smoke?"

"Yes, yes. And Smoke. She said that these Breem have some of the same skills that she has. And that they have been watching us all along."

"Then, BY DUMPF, why do these Breem not show themselves?"

"Smoke said that they are puzzled by us and by her. They are trying to make up their minds as to what to do."

"Minds?"

"Yes, yes. They are some sort of collective entity."

"Oh. SO . . . ?"

"SO . . . what?"

"SO, BY DIFFIBLE-DUMPF, on with it."

"It?"

Mountain flapped one arm in exasperation.

"HUMP! DUMPF! AND TRUMPF! I do not think that your mind has recovered yet. THE GREAT STONE TR'INDLE!"

"Oh, yes."

"OH YES, INDEED!"

Sorrowful took another deep breath and started again.

"SO! In a time and at a time, there lived a Tr'indle. Now this Tr'indle was . . . "

They passed down the trail and around the curve.

Out of sight of the leather-winged watcher perched nearby. But another saw them. Further, much further, down the trail, another took over. And watched them. At all times, careful eyes kept them in sight.

Just beyond the furthest of far ridges, Smoke waited for them. She stood in deep shadow and observed The Breem. She could have been standing out in the bright sunshine but it was cooler here in the shade.

The Breem sat in a cluster across the trail. They were waiting for the strange things to approach. They had made a decision.

Smoke watched them and pondered their small size. They were short, squat creatures, smaller than Sorrowful. With large splayed feet. Their agile, many-fingered hands were never still. They fondled small objects they carried. They touched each other. It was a wiggling, squirming cluster.

She now understood that it was their close proximity to each other that gave them their far reaching mental capabilities.

The Breem sat and discussed the approach of the strange creatures. The disappeared one had never reappeared. This was a puzzle. They discussed this. And the strangeness of these things. They came in many sizes and shapes. This was also a puzzle. They discussed this. Even their texture varied. The Breem discussed all these matters. And puzzled over them. At the end of the track, EndFate HoldTrack, they sat, blocking the way. Waiting for these strange ones.

Behind them, the thing in the Emptyspace stirred. It seemed to be becoming more aware of these approaching strange things. If it came from the crystal wastes the Breem would have to flee.

Smoke sat and watched them.

Long after it had become dark, Mountain, Sorrowful and The Guard approached the Breem and stopped. All they could see was a jumble, an ever shifting cluster of purple spots, the eyes of The Breem, watching them.

A tentative voice spoke. "Smoke?"

Sorrowful?

"These spots are The Breem?"

Yes.

"What do they want? Or perhaps it would be better to ask, what do they have that we were brought here to get? Or perhaps it would be better to rephrase it this way, what relationship is there . . . "

"BY DUMPF, STOP! Smoke, tell us what ever it is that you have discovered. When you have finished, this bottomless pit of unanswered questions, rephrased and restated, can start up again. HUMPF, HUMPF, HUMPF!"

A heavy thump in the dark signaled to all that Mountain had sat down.

"Well, it does seem that Mountain has some small point. Ah, so, if you would proceed, my dear."

Each of them placed the tip of a finger on the jewels set in the end of their weapon.

Yes. Sorrowful? Mountain?

"Yes."

"UMPF!"

These are The Breem, their world Bril. They are similar but different than the Velvetmist. We remain individuals within the sensenet. They are a single composite organism of one mind which spends most of its time discussing things. It took me a long time to contact them because of this mental chaos. The Breem have placed themselves in our way so we would not stumble into what they call the Emptyspace and be destroyed by a thing living there. They have no other aid to offer.

"BY DUMPF, a small thing to know. Some DUMPFING monster lives out there. HUMPF! Would they like us to get rid of it for them?"

I asked. They would like that. If we succeed they will give us a treasure, a long crystal rod kept in a high cave. This thing keeps them from their treasure.

"Then, BY DUMPF, it must be this rod we seek."

"Certainly," added Sorrowful. "I firmly agree. It must be this rod, the thing in my night thought, called the Key of Time."

"Then, BY DUMPF, we can see to it in the morning. It is too dark to fix a meal. Good night."

Heavy rustling and mumbling came from the dark, followed by heavy breathing.

"Well," said Sorrowful, "that is the only thing to do."

One by one the purple eye glows winked out.

"Smoke?"

Sleep. I will watch.

"Umm. Yes." Sorrowful rummaged through his pack and made his bed and asked, "Ah, Smoke?"

Yes?

"What is that thing out there?"

Some sort of rock creature.

Warm fur brushed against him.

"Aaaaargh, what? What?" He lurched to his feet.

Sleep with me, Sorrowful.

"OH." Sorrowful sat down and relaxed.

"It is you. Why thank you, Smoke. That thing is the horror of my night thought."

Yes, I know. Come. Sleep.

Sorrowful lay back in the soft thick fur, his night thought kept away by the deep thrumming coming from Smoke.

He opened his eyes and rolled his head.

Sunlight streamed through the vegetation and illuminated a strange scene. The entire company was awash in small furry creatures, standing, moving, gazing at them. Wide staring eyes. Soft fingers patted over them, brushing, touching.

Sorrowful stood up and yawned.

Smoke sat up, stretching and yawning, great canines gleaming in the sunlight.

The Breem appeared to take no notice of them.

The Company quickly found that they could walk without stepping upon the Breem. The jostling throng parted, slipped aside just before a foot could trample their toes.

Suddenly a large cluster of Breem began to rise into the air and slide tumbling, a torrent into a heap, lightly landing on their feet to stand and peer.

"BY DUMPF, so this is what they look like in the

light."

Mountain shed sleeping bag, blankets, and more Breem.

"Certainly small pebble folk. What is for breakfast?" His stomach rumbled loudly. A few of The Breem peered at him.

"The Guard are working on it," stated Sorrowful.

"Good!" Mountain shoved everything back into his pack, gently picking out a few of the Breem that somehow had become wrapped in his blanket.

"This meal will not be like the last one," explained Sorrowful.

Mountain frowned at him..

"HUMPF! It appears the civilizing influence of my presence didn't last very long."

Smoke, who had been padding toward them, suddenly stopped and stared at one of The Breem.

"Smoke?" asked Sorrowful.

Sorrowful, that thing has become more aware of our presence. We should hurry to the Emptyspace.

"Yes, you are correct. Sergeant."

"SAH!"

"Let's get everything fixed and over as fast as possible, we must hurry."

"SAH!"

The Sergeant spun on his heels, shouting orders.

In moments the camp was hurrying through breakfast, then packing and preparing to move out, surrounded by jostling Breem who seemed to be in and around everything.

"Smoke, are they coming with us?"

Part of the way. They will not enter the Emptyspace.

"Sergeant."

"SAH!"

"Send an advance party as fast as possible into this Emptyspace and watch for this thing, what ever it may be. Smoke will go with you and keep us informed."

No need. The Breem have watchers. Look up.

Sorrowful did.

High overhead a number of winged creatures circled lazily in the thermal currents, soaring in great widening arcs. A long line of them stretched into the distance.

The advance party of The Guard trotted down the trail. The remainder spread themselves around the edges of the camp group.

"Sergeant."

"SAH!"

"Be very careful. This thing is very dangerous."

"SAH!"

The Sergeant ran to catch up with his advance party.

The Company headed down the trail after them surrounded by a milling turmoil of Breem.

"BY DUMPF," grumbled Mountain, "these are strange folk."

"No stranger than something that would eat everything in sight," observed Sorrowful.

"HUMPF!"

It was late in the day.

The space they now walked into was sparse with a scatter of brush clumps and thickets. In between sandy covered patches. The trail took them around a low hill.

"BY ALL THE ROCKS AND STONES! A sand sea."

The Emptyspace.

A vast glaring white empty space of dunes and rills. Jabbing up toward the sky, a vertical tower of rock. Small specks circled high over the top. The watchers.

The Breem scattered into the nearest large thicket.

Our destination.

"That spire of stone?" Sorrowful pointed.

Yes. It is where the crystal rod is kept. And it is where that thing lives.

Smoke padded out onto the white surface.

Firm. Very firm.

"Good news, BY DUMPF! Wallowing through soft sand is slow going."

Mountain walked out into the white, stepping carefully, stomping one foot then the other.

"Firm enough. Firm enough for me, firm enough for all of us." He peered down and rumbled, "I can just see the marks made by the advance party."

"Really and truly?"

"RUMPF! I said so, did I not?"

"Well, yes."

"Well then, BY DUMPF, it is so. The Guard leave an easy track to follow for those that can see."

Slowly carefully they followed the advance party out into the Emptyspace.

The Breem watched them fade into small specks and puzzled over these strange creatures. And watched them from on high. And discussed them.

Mountain led the way, headed directly toward the rock tower, the way The Guard had gone.

From the top of a high dune they saw the advance party, a long line slowly advancing.

WAIT!

Smoke's command jolted Sorrowful and Mountain to a halt.

She fed them the view as seen by the circling watchers. A large shape had disconnected itself from the face of the rock tower and moved toward the advance party.

The advance party halted and drew their swords.

The Sergeant ran back a dozen paces and spun around, ready to shout directions as needed. It saved his life.

The sand parted and the center of the line collapsed, swallowing two of The Guard.

The rest leaped back, seeking firm ground, backing away from the rapidly softening sand.

Finding it, they spun back to face their opponent.

It seemed to be content to wait and watch.

Their vision snapped back to normal.

"BY DUMPF, we had better hurry."

"Correct. It appears we are all needed"

"DUMPF!"

Mountain trotted ahead, Sorrowful running at his side. Behind them, The Guard stretched out into a wide line. Smoke galloped off to one side.

"Where is she going?"

"I am sure we will find out in good time," suggested Sorrowful.

Joining the advance party they stood and stared down the long slope at the thing.

It was gigantic, many times the size of Mountain. It had stepped back against the rock tower, blending into the craggy surface.

The Sergeant ran up to Sorrowful to report.

"Lords, we have lost two men."

Sorrowful nodded. "Yes, we saw. Gather the others and let us try and find a way around that soft sand. We do not want to lose any others."

"Lord, that sand was firm. Then suddenly it did go soft."

"HUMPF! How far were you from that thing?" Mountain pointed at the creature watching them.

"Lord, one hundred feet."

"Then we shall stay that far away."

The group started forward, carefully watching their opponent. It remained against the rock.

"Mountain, can you still see it?"

Mountain nodded. "Yes. I can see the crack where it joins. And there are color and texture differences. This is an ambushing creature. Close enough!"

They stopped and stared.

Mountain stomped heavily. "Hard enough now. I shall give it a small tap, knock a piece from the old matrix, BY DUMPF!"

He unhooked the great cudgel from his belt and waggled it, settling his grip.

Sorrowful shook his head. "I do not like that idea."

Mountain sat with a thud next to him and looked

into his face.

"ROCKS AND STONES, Tale Teller, this is my kind of place. Who else should proceed?"

Sorrowful twisted his lips and frowned at him.

"Well, I just do not like it. Do be careful."

Mountain lurched to his feet. "HUMPF, am I ever anything else?" He whirled the arm holding the cudgel and announced, "Now, BY ALL THE SANDS AND RILLS, let us see what type of stone we face here."

He stepped forward, carefully scanning the surface before him, placing each foot just so. Until he stood next to the thing.

It hadn't moved.

Carefully Mountain looked it over, carefully searching its craggy surface, seeking those signs of weakness and stress he could see in any stone. Then he jumped back, whirled around and struck it. The club bounced high in the air and back over his shoulder.

Sorrowful heard the sharp *CRACK* and saw the puff of dust where the cudgel had hit.

Pieces of rock tumbled across Mountain's feet. He danced lightly away.

The thing shuddered and slid forward, sand softening under Mountain's feet.

He skipped sideways to a firm spot and trotted back to Sorrowful.

"Well, BY DUMPF, was not that a surprise?"

Sorrowful smiled at him. "Most assuredly. What happened?"

Mountain looked back over his shoulder.

"It must have been sleeping, or whatever it does. I could see a number of fault lines crisscrossing its surface."

He beamed happily.

"So, with a RIGHT-RUMPFING blow, I struck it. Just to test the structure, you see." Then he whispered, "Never saw a rock like that before."

And laughed loudly, "HEH, HEH! But, BY ALL THE BOULDERS, it shattered none-the-less."

Sorrowful's grave expression and question stopped Mountain's joy. "Now what?"

"HUMPF. How should I know?"

"We have learned two things."

"What may they be?"

Sorrowful held up one finger and stated, "We know it can be injured. Or broken." A second finger joined the first. "And I think we may safely say that it will only come out so far." He pointed. "See, it always stays a certain distance from the rock tower. It must be guarding it."

We know three things.

"What?" asked Sorrowful.

It is a creature of Dram's. I can smell the foulness oozing from it.

"Oh dear, oh dear, oh dear."

Sorrowful shook his head back and forth.

Mountain stared at him. "What, what, what? If you tell me that you had another of those night thought stuffs, I will feed you to that HUMPF out there."

Sorrowful glared up at him and stated firmly, "It is not that. Do you not see?"

"HUMPF AND BUMPF! NO. I do not see. What?"

"This creature is a thing of Dram's, therefore . . ?"

"Therefore, what?"

"SOTHEREFORE, IFYOUWILLLETMEFINISH! This must be part of John Tinker's quest. Which means that we will have to get rid of it."

Mountain slowly settled to the ground next to Sorrowful as Smoke silently padded up to them.

"BY DUMPF, I do not see how we will do that. That walking hill will not stand still while I pound it into gravel and dusty dust."

Sorrowful sat down and placed one hand on Mountain's ankle. "You are correct. Probably."

It has moved forward.

Mountain leaped to his feet. "BY DUMPF, it has."

Sorrowful scrambled on hands and knees to escape. Then he stood and stared. "It has. But it has stopped. Has it not?"

"BY DUMPF! Correct. So much for your idea of distance."

"I still think if we stay a certain distance back, it will stay put."

Behind them they heard a deep, grinding roar as geyser of sand shot into the air and rapidly traced a great arc and poured back down. A deep crevice had yawned open, encircling them, running from stone bluff to stone bluff.

One of The Guard charged up. "My Lords, tis a great fissure, wider than a man can leap."

Mountain looked down at Sorrowful.

"HUMPF! There goes another of your ideas. That RUMPFING rock pile has trapped us."

With a soft whump, a section of sand sloughed away, the edge moving closer to them. Dust drifted across the sand mouth gaping at them.

"BY ALL THE STONES THAT BE, we are not only trapped, but are losing ground."

Sorrowful kicked him on the side of the boot.

"Really an inopportune joke."

"Joke? What joke?" Mountain pointed. "See, there it goes again."

Another section fell, then another.

Mountain frowned. "We will be forced to face that slag heap in short order."

Sorrowful shuddered. "It is my night thought turned into reality."

"And what did this night thought stuff of your's show us?"

Sorrowful stared down at the white sand surface and stated, "Only that we can not defeat it with any of our weapons."

Mountain stepped in front of him and hefted his cudgel. "Well, we will TRUMPFING see about that."

He stomped out toward the creature grumbling, "RUMPFING ROCK PILE!"

Sorrowful ran after him, yanking at Mountain's pant leg. "STOP! STOP!"

Mountain stopped and looked down. "Why?"

Sorrowful kicked one leg. "You could be killed."

Behind them another section of sand fell into the ever widening crack.

"ROCKS AND STONE, SAND AND GRAVEL, Sorrowful, make your choice of deaths." Mountain pointed. "That hole. Or this thing."

He waggled his club at the creature. "No rock has ever defeated one of Stumpf, animated or not. You stay here and watch."

Mountain strode forward, covering the ground quickly.

The creature quivered but remained where it was.

Mountain reached and swung.

CRACK!

He jumped back as a shower of rock thumped onto the sand.

He ran to the opposite side and struck again, dislodging more pieces. Then he stepped in front of the thing and drew his arm back and down. They could hear him bellow, "DUMPFING DUMB ROCK HEAP!"

He swung.

The sand opened up. He plunged out of sight. The swirling sand quickly covered the spot and smoothed over.

"NNNNNOOOOOOOOOO!"

Sorrowful hurtled forward, his hand grabbing for his weaponkin.

One of The Guard clenched him by the upper arm and almost yanked him from his feet.

"Stay back, My Lord, tis not safe."

Sorrowful thrashed back and forth in The Guard's grip. "**NOT SAFE, NOT SAFE!**" he screamed. "**NOT SAFE, NOT . . .** "

His words were wiped away by a roaring fountain of sand that erupted in front of them. Bursting upward, ripping the air into whirling maelstrom of sound and crystal particles. Piercing the screeching tortured air they heard a jubilant cry as the sand twirled faster and faster.

"FRRREEEEEEEEEE . . . "

The wind sucked more and more sand into the rapidly forming cloud. The white began to darken as a deep stain spread through it, seeping outward from the center.

The wind stopped. The sand settled, forming a great dune in front of them. It was purple. From inside they heard a silken voice sing a haunting melody.

"We see you, Mountain . . . Mountain, Mountain. We see you . . . Come and dance with me, Mountain . . . Mountain, Mountain."

Smoke slipped up beside Sorrowful and sat.

One of The Guard spoke, "My Lord, what manner of thing be this?"

Sorrowful started to speak.

The sand blew up in front of them as a large shape surged to the surface.

Mountain sat up and began to knock sand particles from his clothes. He was covered with purple grains of sand. He stood and patted himself clean.

"Madame." He made a stiff bow toward the sand dune. "Many, many, many thanks. It was a timely arrival, BY DUMPF!"

"We see you, Mountain . . . Mountain, Mountain. We see you . . . And we thank you for our freedom, Mountain . . . Mountain, Mountain."

The sand swelled and rose directly in the center of the dune. And poured aside. A young woman dressed in purple stood and smiled down at them from the top.

"You have taken us far, Mountain . . . Mountain, Mountain. The sand-trells cried at my departure. But the Gett are wise. You celebrated my birth Mountain . . . Mountain, Mountain. And you danced with us. Now celebrate my rebirth in this, my new home, a new place for the Sand-Trells."

Mountain reached up and touched the chain around his neck. The small vial was shattered and broken.

"BY ALL THE ROCK THAT FALLS, I must have broken it when I fell. She has been with us all along."

"Stand and watch, Mountain, Mountain . . . Mountain. Stand and watch . . . "

She sank from sight as the wind began to answer her call. It swirled, harder and harder, a whirlwind sucking sand into its center and up and out. Higher and higher it rose.

The storm stretched from stone to stone, singing and whistling, drifting toward the rock tower, widening, widening.

They stood in the eye of the storm, surrounded by blasting sand. All they could see was a purple wall roaring sand. All they could hear was that wind.

It stopped. The sand dropped, pouring down, resettling into a great, purple dune with a low center.

A soft voice sang sweetly, "Goodby Mountain, Mountain, Mountain. Come and dance with us again . . . it is time to settle and rest . . . goodbye, Mountain . . . Mountain, Mountain. Goodbye."

Mountain wiped at his face with his sleeve.

Sorrowful tugged at his pant leg. "Do you see that rock creature?"

Mountain looked up and shook his head. "No, BY DUMPF, I do not. It has been ground into dusty dust.
Look there." He pointed at the rock tower.

A deep gouge had been carved into the face of the rock tower. It rose glistening, polished, straight up, finally curving outward to rejoin the original surface. The stone mirror glistened in the sunlight, reflecting earth and sky.

Sorrowful pointed up at a small opening just where the curve began to flare outward. "That is the cave where The Breem keep the crystal rod. Now we will not be able to get it. Who could climb such a smooth surface?"

Mountain walked closer to peer up and squint. Then he turned back to Sorrowful.

"Well, Little Fly, it will be a HUMPFING HARD climb up the backside, over the top, then down and under, but it can be done." He patted Sorrowful gently on the shoulder, wobbling him badly.

"That ought to give you enough adventure for two or three tales, BY DOUBLE-DUMPF!"

"Adventure?"

"I will take you up and over. And then I will give you instructions on how to creep upside down into that cave." Mountain gestured grandly. "Come, let us start."

No need.

"What?"

"UMPF?"

The Breem are doing it. Look up.

Mountain and Sorrowful did, scanning the sky.

"There, there!" Sorrowful pointed at a black

speck circling down.

"RUMPFING SHARP eyes," grumbled Mountain.

A leather-winged watcher drifted down and down and then floated effortlessly under the rock overhang and into the cave.

"BY DUMPF, made it look easy." Mountain stared at the cave mouth.

"UMPF, here it comes."

The flier hopped from the cave lip and dropped sharply, popping open great wings and gliding steeply downward to land lightly in front of Sorrowful. It took one hop, dropped something, and was airborne again.

The crystal rod lay gleaming in the sunlight.

Sorrowful bent over and picked it up.

"It is The Rod of Time!"

"MY LORDS!"

The Sergeant's call turned their heads. He was pointing to one side of the dune.

The portal waited for them, fire-snakes roiling and hissing. The heat haze was so intense over its surface that they could not see what lay on the other side.

"BY DUMPF, it must be time to go. Let us say our farewells."

Mountain stomped away to stand high on the purple dune, Sorrowful at his side.

"Farewell, Great Lady, we are forever in your debt." Mountain made a stiff bow.

Sorrowful made a more courtly sweep with hands and arms.

A section of the dune slipped and covered their

feet, hissing softly.

Mountain stared downward, then twisted away.

"Don't stand great lump, DUMPF IT ALL, let us go." And stomped off.

Sorrowful trotted after him, calling, "Sergeant, are we ready? Smoke?"

"All ready, Lords."

Ready.

Sorrowful waved both arms. "Then through the portal Sergeant. After that Smoke. Mountain will follow me."

He patted sand from his clothes. And made sure that the rod was safely tucked away.

The Guard trooped through, then Smoke and Sorrowful.

Mountain stood and cast one final glance backward at the great mound of sand. And stepped through.

A soft voice that rang with the tinkle of crystal whispered gently into the silence.

"Farewell, Mountain . . . Mountain, Mountain. Farewell."

Magic, Magic, Magic

Clear Bandler.

Sunlight streamed through the large window. On the floor, the quilt mass stirred. And violently erupted.

Tinker's head and one shoulder popped out, a whale broaching the surface. He stared blankly around the room, remembered where he was, and said, "Bathroom."

A door in one wall swung open. He stood and lurched in that direction. Moments later he returned, and began to prod here and there with his feet.

"Rise and shine, rise and shine."

One foot bumped into something. "Ha, there you are." He jiggled it. "Come and see what I have found."

He turned and headed back into the bathroom and stood staring at the floor.

A sleepy voice breathed in his ear, "Tis mere tub empty, My Lord."

"Right."

Chicken pushed past him, one hand trailing over his ribs and stepped down into it, laying back. She looked up at him, her voice echoing hollowly.

"Tis dry. Wouldst make fane bath."

"Have you forgotten what we were told by our host?"

She nodded. "Seems so, LordLove."

"Ready?"

"As ever."

"Then, ask and ye shall receive. Room, fill it up. Pronto."

Instantly the tub was full. Chicken reared straight up, flinging water in all directions. She wiped her face and glared at him.

"T'was most foul a'deed indeed done, Our Verra Own Sweet Prince. Step thee hither."

"I don't like the look in your eyes, Princess."

She batted her eyes at him and murmured, "Noble Sir, would this, thy most pliant of servants, ever bring thee harm?" She turned her back and slipped deeper into the water, mumbling quietly, "Praps some small bruise but nothing fatal."

Much later, wrapped in voluminous towels, they returned to the first room.

Tinker reached over her shoulders and tugged at the towel edge. "Order us some breakfast, wench, while I try and find our clothes."

He turned around and began to kick around in the quilting.

Chicken cast a wary eye around the room and cleared her throat. "Ahem, sweet room? Some suitable repast for Our Lord and Our Own self . . . please?"

A portion of the wall beneath the window deformed and reshaped itself. A table and two chairs appeared. The top of the table was covered with steaming platters.

Tinker finally found what he was looking for.

"I wonder if this room does laundry."

He carefully placed the clothes in a spot and stepped back.

"Hey there, room. How about cleaning our clothes. That last place was rather filthy."

There was a slight twang and the clothes were stacked in two neat piles, clean and crisp.

"My Lord, breakfast does await. Tis most delicious."

He turned. "You started without me? Do you smell flowers?"

She smiled. "Indeed, Sweet Prince we do start some. And we do just a small nibble partake for to see that all be most correct for thy most Noble Self."

"Ha, I bet?"

"What be thy wager?"

He stepped up behind her, leaned over and whispered in her ear, and tugged her towel loose.

A Small Bit of Cultural Data.

The Garden Gnomes are a small folk, perhaps the smallest of all the folk. As their name implies they are fascinated by gardening and frequently visit those gardens that they recognize as being above the average in terms of arrangement and care, whether ornamental or functional.

At some point, in their past, one of them had been seen while visiting a particularly well designed ornamental garden. This kind of happening was not something that they liked to happen nor did they like to talk about it.

This garden, as things seem to happen to this folk or that folk over their histories, happened to belong to a sculptress of some skill and very fast eyes. She made a statue of what her eyes saw as just a fleeting glance and sit this statue in and among an artfully organized patch of flowers.

And as things so often happen a visitor saw this statue and asked the owner to make one for him. And so it went.

And so it went.

Much to the consternation of the
Garden Gnomes.

And eventually an entire industry sprang up around these statues and their production. People even wrote fanciful books about the culture of these things. They were all wrong, of course. None of the authors had ever talked with one of these small folk or had ever visited a Garden Gnome village.

The end result of all this was that the Garden Gnomes retreated deeper and deeper into areas where they would not, or could not, be observed.

Young Garden Gnomes, every one in awhile, on a dark, a particularly dark night, would steal one of these statues and hide them away.

Of course, it had no effect on the overall population of these fake garden gnomes. The industry was to well intrenched.

Clear Bandler.

They were sitting at the table, dressed, and sipping coffee when the wall opened and Toucan and Goose strolled in. Goose was dazzling white. He spun around, smiled, and asked, "What think you, Sire? Rah'ther clean, what?"

"Cleaner than clean.'

Two chairs appeared. Toucan and Goose sat. Goose smiled at them.

"Strange wall would us not let in till thee were done with thy meal!"

Chicken pinched Tinker's thigh.

"Did you eat?"

"Deed we did. But, praps some small morsel or two. $1.98 does set himself fine table."

Goose served himself a thing or two, smiling broadly.

"I think that we might go outside and look around," suggested Tinker.

Goose hastily swallowed. "Aye, Sire."

Toucan nodded.

Tinker looked at the window and spoke to the room, "We'd like to go outside."

A door opened in the wall near the corner of the room.

Outside, they stood on a spacious lawn dotted with shrubs and trees. The house reared upward and sideways, sprawling aimlessly across the landscape.

Tinker smiled at the scene.

"I'd say our host has rather large tastes." And wondered where the flowers were, the ones that he had smelt.

Chicken nodded. "Indeed. Do pear a'me most castle-like."

A door appeared on the side of the nearest tree, and swung open.

$1.98 stepped out.

"Good morning, Lords and Lady. Did you sleep well? Did you get everything you desired?"

Chicken snaked an arm around Tinker's waist and patted him on the hip.

Everyone nodded.

Tinker waved his hand. "This is quite a place you have."

$1.98 beamed at him.

"Do you really think so? It isn't really all that much, you know. I am just a small magician." He held up one hand, thumb and forefinger almost touching. "You should meet some of the others."

"Others? Here?"

$1.98 looked at Tinker, very puzzled.

"Of course. It is an honorable profession. But hard to get into. Quite small in number. Hard to become one, lengthy training, few teachers. But there are others. Let's see, how many, ummmm?"

He reached up into nowhere and extracted a small crystal ball which he peered into with one eye.

"Right! One, two, three, four. Ummmm, ummmm, ummmm." He pushed the ball away. It disappeared.

"Not that many, I suppose. But enough. Eleven in all. Seems quite enough to me."

Tinker smiled. "You are the twelfth one?"

$1.98 nodded. "I am the twelfth. The last one, so far, to join the ranks."

"All trained by Big Red?"

The magician vigorously shook his head.

"Oh no! I am the only one trained that way. I don't know who trained the others, trade secret you see."

He bent toward and whispered, "You never tell

where you got your training, you just demonstrate it. But I know I am the only one here, he told me."

Tinker decided that this was the time to get down to the case at hand.

"Did Big Red tell you who we are? Or why we are here? Or what it is that we are about?"

$1.98 waggled his head. "No, no, no! He just said that I was to expect you, help as much as possible, things like that. Provide food and lodging."

He reached out and lightly touched Tinker's arm.

"You must be a mighty magician to have Big Red do your bidding."

Goose giggled.

Toucan tried to hide his smile.

Tinker did laugh. Then he draped his arm around the magician's shoulders and led him off, away from the others.

"How about we find a seat somewhere and I will tell you a little tale about that. O.K.?"

$1.98 pointed to a long park bench that had just appeared. "How about there?"

"That will be fine." Tinker let him go and sat down and suggested, "You better sit. This is a long story. And I think you should hear the whole thing."

"Certainly, whatever you wish."

Chicken sat on the ground on the thick grass next to Tinker's legs and leaned against them. Toucan and Goose wandered off to inspect the grounds.

Tinker took a deep breath and exhaled slowly.

"O.K. It started this way. One morning I was just sitting in my favorite chair, sipping coffee, and watching the morning star hanging over a nearby ridge.

The next thing I knew . . . "

Tinker's voice droned on and on, covering all his adventures, how he met his various companions, and of Big Red and Dram. And all the events since.

" . . . and so here we are. And there you are. And that is that. Any questions?"

$1.98 sat and stared at him. Tinker stared back. Chicken turned her head up and around, wondering why the magician was being so silent.

Suddenly $1.98 leaped away and fell to his knees facing them, throwing his arms wide, and stated, "Anything that I may do, command me."

Tinker started to rise. Chicken grabbed his ankles and shoved on his thighs, forcing him back into his seat.

"OOOOF!"

$1.98, still on his knees, had started to scrabble backward, away from the rising Tinker, his eyes growing wider and wider.

Tinker shook his head and said, more or less calmly, "STOP THAT! Will you stop doing that. Stop cringing, or whatever that is."

$1.98 stopped. "Of course, Mighty Warrior."

Tinker sighed, loudly, and stated, "And we are not mighty warriors or anything like that. We are just poor mortals that have gotten sucked into this." He frowned at Chicken. "Again."

Then he looked back at $1.98 who had stopped backing up.

"And if you are supposed to be helping us, you can't do it crawling around on the ground on your knees."

Chicken stood and sat down next to Tinker and

slowly toppled him over so that she was leaning across him. He ignored her and continued to speak to $1.98. "And," he said, waggling his finger at the magician, who cringed. "We don't go around slaying dragons."

Chicken laughed and kissed his ear. "My Lord, we do be a'kill one, have we not?" She sat up.

"Yep. Right." Tinker sat up. "That is not what I meant. And you know it."

Chicken stuck her tongue out at him. "Indeed We do, Me'Lord." It was her soft, demure voice.

But thee do be a'frightening poor $1.98.

"I am?" He looked at $1.98 and smiled. *Want to buy a good, used car?*

Chicken banged him in the ribs with her elbow. He grunted. And glared at her.

"You are supposed to help us, correct?" He looked again at $1.98.

$1.98 nodded vigorously. "Yes, yes. I am."

"Well, then, and do what we tell you, correct?"

More vigorous nodding. "Yes, yes."

Tinker patted the empty space next to him and suggested, "Then come and sit down. And try and relax, will you?"

$1.98 cautiously stood, walked over and sat down, not too close to Tinker. He leaned forward and looked him around at Chicken. She smiled.

"I will try," said the magician. "But you must realize that I have never heard of anyone, not even in the greatest legends, who has done all the things you have just related. Not even any of the other magicians." He tried a tentative smile.

"If it had been anyone else, I would not have

believed them, not at all. But Big Red said so, so that is another matter all together." $1.98 tried another smile.

"I would have figured anyone else to be quite mad, as zorky as a zeebeast, in fact."

Tinker smiled. "Well, we, are not that. I don't think."

He saw Goose and Toucan coming back toward them. "Although Goose does get a bit silly at times."

Goose laughed and tried to look innocent. "Me, Sire?" He settled to the ground facing them. So did Toucan.

Toucan spoke first. "Highness?"

"Yes?"

"Did thee find why we be here?"

Tinker shook his head. "Nope. Not a clue. He doesn't seem to know any more than we do. The answer lies out there, somewhere. Or perhaps this is just another Big Red joke. But I suspect it is a Big Red maneuver."

$1.98 shook his head. "I do not think that it is a Big Red joke, John . . . ah, Lord Tinker."

"Just call me John, or Tinker, please. These three won't give up, but you don't have to."

A disembodied voice spoke to them. "May I enter?"

$1.98 looked up and smiled. "Of course, of course. Please join us."

A smiling round individual began to appear, standing in front of them. He was dressed in flowing robes. Around his neck he wore a bright green scarf. When he was totally solid, he bounced over to them.

$1.98 jumped to his feet and disappeared, almost,

inside the others voluminous embrace. They could hear $1.98's muffled voice. "It is good to see you. Come meet my guests."

$1.98 was released, and arm in arm, the two men walked back to the bench.

"John Tinker, this is my good friend, Orotundy. Orotundy, this is the Princess Chicken and her brothers, Prince Toucan and Prince Goose. And this is their mas, ah, leader, Lor . . . ah, John Tinker." $1.98 was getting nervous again.

Orotundy beamed at them. "Then you are friends of mine if you are friends of $1.98's." He turned toward $1.98 and stated, "They are not totally unknown to me." Everyone looked at him in surprise.

$1.98 sat down with a noticeably thump. "They are not?"

Orotundy chuckled, a liquid gurgling sound.

"No. In fact, I heard of them from Drimwhistle, that old gossip."

"How?" asked $1.98 and Tinker at the same time.

Orotundy rolled his eyes at the bench. "I will tell you, if you make room for me on the trim."

Tinker and $1.98 sidled sideways. Tinker pressed against Chicken. She wiggled gently.

Orotundy settled his bulk with a nervous motion.

Do seem most like fair chicken settling on fair eggs, LordLove.

Tinker smiled.

Orotundy beamed back at him, enjoying his audience, taking his time. Then his smile faded as he stated, "I am one who bears a wrong message. But I thought someone should do it. None of the others would. You know how stand-offish that bunch can get." He directed this last comment at $1.98.

The magician nodded slowly. "They can be that. What is this unwelcome thing you bear to my place?"

One pudgy finger waggled at $1.98 as he said, "First we must explain how I knew of your guests. Beady eyes see all, you know."

$1.98 nodded. "Yes. Go on."

Orotundy sighed. "Well, anything. A black, magical spot ate Tringledong. One moment he was standing there, showing off his fire display." He waggled one finger.

"You remember that one, gaudy and all bright orange and green. And the next happen, this black lump just thudded down out of somewhere and swallowed him." The fat finger dropped into a fat lap as he explained, "Well, as you can imagine, the flames got out of control and consumed half of Big-Im-Trim. Half the place. Smoking ruins on the mountain side. Rather poetic. Gamble just happened to be passing. He passed in, took a peek, and the good folk almost mobbed him. Blamed him for all the destruction." He smiled at Tinker.

"Serves him right, trying to grab a secret. So, anytime, after a good struggle, he got it right, and skipped out. Just as this great black lump tried to snatch him. He swears that it rasped *Tinkermeat* just as he popped in."

Chicken, Goose and Toucan leaped to their feet, hands flying to sword hilts. They faced three different directions.

$1.98 lurched away, banging into Orotundy. It

was a soft thud. Then he leaped to his feet. "WAIT!"

"What?" demanded Tinker.

"Nothing may enter here without my permission."

"What about that black thing?"

"My guardness is a thing given by Big Red."

Chicken swirled around, slamming her sword back into its scabbard. "Big Red?"

$1.98 nodded, more vigorously than ever before.

"Yes, yes, yes. And thus I have no fear of anything outside. Do you qurib?"

Tinker spoke for them all. "Yes, we do, ah, qurib."

He turned toward Orotundy, who sat quite unmoved by all the sudden commotion, and asked, "What else do you know of this black thing that eats magicians and searches for us?"

Orotundy shook his head slowly from side to side. A feat which seemed to send several waves down through his several layers.

"Dimlittle, it does. Brib The Mighty shot for it and lost all the fingers on his left hand. Clear up the ranbangle. So the rest, myself with the group, of course, thought to leave a srib of that stuff niddly. Wouldn't want to lose my digits." He waggled plump sausages in the air. "Can't top without them, you see."

$1.98 forced a place between Tinker and Orotundy, who seemed to have flattened sideways into all available space. "Is that the news?"

"Brangto!"

"I see." $1.98 frowned.

"Well, I don't." Tinker rose and began to walk

back and forth. A faint humming seemed to come from his back. He could feel the vibration of his weaponkin where it nestled diagonally across his shoulder blade.

$1.98 started. "What is that noise?"

Tinker pointed up and over his left shoulder.

"Just Slayer. It must sense action. Or something."

The small magician hurtled to his feet and looked in all directions at once.

"Here? NEVER." He fumbled in the air and ripped out a long ebony wand and began to jab it this way and that.

Orotundy heaved himself to his feet, gesturing wildly at $1.98.

"Hold, hold! If you are going to fliber with that, I would just rather be upon my way. First. The last time you took the top out of Mount Nifle. And ruined the Tower of Fimmly. Also."

Begrudgingly $1.98 shoved the wand up his left sleeve and mumbled, "Perhaps you are right. But I will just keep it handy for now."

Orotundy lowered himself back onto the bench which creaked loudly, sagged and rebounded. He sighed, "Ahhhhh, that is that."

Tinker stared at both of them and suggested, "If you two are done doing what ever it was that you were doing, perhaps you-all could tell us mere, unmagical mortals what all the fuss is about?"

$1.98's mouth fell open and snapped shut.

Orotundy spoke quickly into the silence, "Fimble! The Magician's Guild decided that this foul, black, lumpish thing is not to be interfered with. Did not want to reduce our exalted ranks any further. We have enough work to do as it is. Besides the beside, it appears that we really can not do much about it anyway." He looked at Tinker and the rest. "And you are guests of $1.98. So, that put it with him, does it not?"

Tinker looked at Orotundy, then at $1.98, and asked, "Does it?"

$1.98 nodded sadly. "It does."

He looked at Orotundy. "I could use some help."

"That would make it a rimble."

"A rimble it is."

"Finegoodly!" Orotundy beamed. It was a great bargain. "What would you?"

"Well."

$1.98 leaned over and began to whisper into Orotundy's ear. Orotundy's eyes grew wider and wider.

"All that?"

$1.98 nodded.

"All of course!" agreed Orotundy.

Orotundy reached through his robes and plunged his arm up to his elbow into his stomach and stated, "All that stuff is in here somewhere." He smiled at Tinker, who stared, wide-eyed, at him, and said, "Just a matter of finding it."

Orotundy continued to fish around, muttering to himself.

Tinker and the rest watched the performance in astonishment. $1.98 just waited patiently.

Finally Orotundy began to yank out items and hand them to $1.98. "Here you are, as requested."

Finished, Orotundy stood and fluffed his clothes back into order. Then he turned and laid a heavy hand on $1.98's shoulder. "If there is anything else, give a call, will you. I have to go now. Small show in Valevin."

He waved goodbye as he began to fade. "Farewell . . . "

Goose stared at the empty space and giggled, "Jolly good show, jolly good."

Tinker clapped his hands together just to get their attention. "That answers that," he stated.

"What, My Lord?" Chicken stepped closer to him.

"Now we know what we are after."

She still looked puzzled.

"The black stuff, Sire?" asked Goose.

"Right. The black stuff."

"Ah, Highness?"

"What, Toucan?"

"How find we ourselves this stuff?"

Tinker spun on his heels and patted $1.98 gently on the back.

"With our host, of course. He should be able to lead us to it, I would think. Right?"

$1.98 straightened his shoulders, a look of determination spreading across his face.

"I will do it. But I hope this will be as Big Red said it would."

"What did he say?"

$1.98 smiled, a small smile. "His exact words, John, were this. Have a good time. Do you think we will?"

Tinker laughed. "I don't know about that, but it will probably be interesting. If we survive, that is."

$1.98 quickly checked the faces of the rest to

identify the joke. No one smiled.

Tinker stepped away and smiled. "Take us away. You can find this place, can't you?"

The magician nodded. "Yes, really the simplest thing to do. Just follow me around the tree."

He walked around the tree and disappeared.

Tinker looked at the others. "Everyone ready?"

All nodded.

He took Chicken's hand and tugged her toward the tree. "Let's go, then."

Goose and Toucan followed them.

And they stood and looked around at what appeared to be a small town square. A large portion of the town was a mass of blackened ruins, smoke was still seeping up from the shattered and tumbled structures. Orotundy hadn't been exaggerating at all, the place was a mess. A crowd of irate citizens gathered around instantly and began to chant.

"Big-Im-Trim, YES! Magicians, NO!
Magicians go home."

"Boy, does that sound familiar," mumbled Tinker.

One of the crowd, a thick-set, angry individual, screamed at them, "MAGICIANS, YOU DIE!"

Goose, Toucan, and Chicken reached for their swords.

Tinker hissed at them, "Hold on, gang. We don't want to trigger a reaction. So far, it is just noise."

"But Sire," sputtered Goose. "They all do be

a'carryin' stones."

"They haven't thrown them, have they?"

"Nay, they have not . . . DUCK!"

The last chanter had hurled his missile at $1.98, who stood unblinking at the sudden action.

The stone shot at his face, took a graceful up curving path around his head, and swooped around and back toward its owner. It stopped in front of the chanter's face, hovered for a moment, then struck him with a loud *thunk.* The smack was detectable over the crowd noise. It quieted them down instantly. The chanter grabbed his face and yowled, dancing around, mashing a large handkerchief to his face. It rapidly became a red color.

$1.98 looked at Tinker. "He should have known better." He shrugged his shoulders.

"A bloody nose and two black eyes will make for a dramatic story later on. Come, we must go this way." He pointed.

"The thing we seek went that way."

He started to walk in the direction he had pointed. Tinker and the rest followed him.

The silent crowd watched them depart the town square.

"Do not worry about them," said $1.98 over his shoulder. "I think they will behave. Now."

Behind them, they heard the sharp clatter of rocks dropping to the pavement as the carriers of these primitive missiles got rid of their burdens, trying to not be noticed by the magician. The crowd filtered back toward their homes leaving a trail of litter behind them.

"Ahhh, $1.98?"

"Yes, John?"

"Where did they learn those phrases?"

"What phrases?"

"The ones that they were chanting."

"Those? Tradition. Those chants are part of the oral tradition of this region. The chant structure has been handed down over the generations. The origins of those folk-speaks are lost in the mists of time. Why?"

"Ah, just curiosity."

They wandered through the rubble and debris and stopped. They had reached an area where the houses were untouched.

"Him, hem," mumbled $1.98, "it seems to have gone somewhere."

"Can you follow it?" $1.98 shrugged a shoulder.

"Just have to see. Wait here, I will try to find its trace."

The magician began to walk in ever widening circles, singing to himself. He wandered in and out and around the standing houses. Then he trotted back to them.

"It is on the road to MarKaton."

"MarKaton?"

"A dark and wild place. Just a short hop from here. This way."

He spun and hopped. And was gone.

"Hop, hop," giggled Goose. And hopped.

They all did.

Growing Green.

The Garden Gnomes were holding a meeting. This time they were not discussing flowering plants or trees or shrubs or even ornamental horticulture, a favorite topic, or who had the best flower bed last week.

They were discussing tales of strange events that wandered across any number of elseplaces before coming to the attention of their somewhat pointed ears.

Phineas Grass scowled at an errant weed in the meeting grounds emerald grass and grunted.

"This strange organism in not a threat to us," he stated as he bent to remove the plant that belonged in another area.

"Absolutely," agreed Hiram Toadstool. "We are only innocent gnomes."

"Not so innocent," purred Franny Waxflower, smiling softly at him.

"To non-gnomes," grumbled Franelkan Vetch. "And what do we really know?"

"The things has caused no small amount of chaos. And destruction," stated Phineas.

"Not to," Hiram glanced at Franny, ". . . to innocent gnomes."

She winked at him. "Perhaps we ought to sent an emissary to explain our innocence to this thing?"

"We do not know where it is," stated Franelkan.

"I heard," pipped up Tiny Rosebud, "that it is hanging around that elseplace where that unpleasant witch lives."

"Which unpleasant witch?" Hiram stared at the others. "They are all unpleasant."

"Correct," shrugged Tiny.

"So?" growled Hiram.

"I will write the name on a piece of bark and pass it around. I do not want to say that name out loud!"

Tiny peered at the surrounding trees and shrubs. "She might hear."

Franny took the bark and read the name. And gasped. "OH! That one!"

"Urk," gasped Hiram, hastily shoving the bark away.

When all had a chance to read the name, the bark was crumbled into powder and carefully scattered under a flowering *Agalean* shrub.

"I will go," said Tiny.

"Very brave," stated Hiram.

"I am also the smallest," explained Tiny. "There was nothing said that this thing picked on really small people."

"You are not people." Franny patted her on the shoulder.

"Erm, little gnomes," amended Tiny.

"Well, safe trip," offered Phineas.

They all nodded and watched her stroll away, off through the hedges. And hoped that she was correct about little gnomes being safe.

MarKaton.

The road where they were standing was made of large, rough blocks of stone. The walking surface had been polished by the passage of many, many feet. The road sparkled blue in the soft light filtering down from the grey sky. The road ran arrow-straight toward a large plateau that stretched from side to side in front of them. Built onto the near vertical cliffs was a squat, lumpish collection of structures, all hugging each other and the cracks and crevices that gave the town purchase in its precarious position.

$1.98 pointed at it.

"That is MarKaton, a rather blighted community living in a rather blighted place. From here we have to walk, it is not far."

Goose smiled, and asked, "May we hop?"

$1.98 shook his head.

"No. Rules of the place take precedence."

Goose and Toucan exchanged glances and followed after Tinker and Chicken and the hurrying magician. They could see something stirring at the base of the plateau wall.

It humped and bumped.

It grunted at them.

They stopped.

"Sire," hissed Goose, yanking his sword free. "I do believe we do find spot correct." He stepped to one side as Toucan and Chicken swung their blades in wide arcs.

"$1.98," called Tinker, "perhaps we could just stand here and see what that stuff is going to do?"

The magician swung around and walked back to the waiting group and nodded. "Ummmm, yes, perhaps you are right." He appeared deeply distracted.

Tinker stared at him. "Something wrong?"

"Wrong? Ahhhh, no. There is nothing wrong. Why do you ask?"

"Well . . . you looked sorta preoccupied for a moment. Not something to be doing just now, I would think."

"Oh, that." $1.98 smiled as he explained, "I was trying to decide what sort of magical thing to try on this spot as well as trying to remember the activating spells for the materials Orotundy gave me."

"He didn't tell them to you?"

"No. I guess he just figured that I would know them." $1.98 stared into space and mumbled, mostly to himself, "He is most likely correct. It is just a matter of remembering where I have placed those things, that is all. AH, HA!"

He reached into the air and retrieved a small, leather-bound book and began to rapidly page through it murmuring softly, "Everything is in here. Somewhere."

Tinker spoke gently, "I think you had better hurry. It is coming this way."He pointed.

A great, flat blackness was humping toward them, rapidly closing the distance between them and it. IT was at least one hundred feet from side to side and from front to back. It didn't appear to be very thick. To Tinker, it resembled a very large, very ugly pancake.

The thing grunted each time it bumped forward. There was another sound coming from it. It grew louder and louder as the creature edged closer. It sounded like dozens of teeth grinding together.

Tinker reached up and swung his weaponkin free. The blade hummed and vibrated gently.

$1.98 continued to page back and forth in the small volume of spells and began to mumble to himself.

Tinker waved his companions forward. "Well, here we go."

One of $1.98's hand shot into the air, halting them as he ordered, "WAIT. I've found it. Ummm, one of the things I was searching for, at least."

They stepped to one side and watched him.

The magician reached into one of his pockets and yanked something free. The book floated where he had left it.

Uncorking the small bottle, $1.98 mumbled something at it and threw the container high into the air, directly at the approaching monster.

"What was that?"

"Spot remover, John."

"Spot remover?"

"One of the items Orotundy gave me."

The bottle bounced off the upper surface of the creature, spilling its contents widely.

They waited for something to happen.

Nothing happened.

"Oh dear," said $1.98.

"What?" asked Tinker.

"It appears that it is not a spot."

"Wonderful," grumbled Tinker as he looked at his companions. They nodded. They all started forward again.

"WAIT!" $1.98 held up his hand, again.

"Now what?"

The magician burbled something and threw a small wad of white stuff at the creature. As the wad flew through the air it rapidly expanded and dropped with an audible *thump* on the flat surface. The stuff continued to expand.

"By George!" gasped Goose. "What manner do be such a'stuff?"

"That, Prince Goose, is gap filler."

"Gap filler?" Tinker was having trouble keeping his voice steady. "From Orotundy, I suppose?"

$1.98 nodded his head.

The white material had completely covered the black monster and was beginning to drip over the outer edges of the creature. Slowly the edges of the thing began to rise. In a sudden motion, the creature turned itself inside out and resettled to the ground. It made a loud grunt.

"I think it just ate the gap filler," observed Tinker.

"Ummm, so it has, so it has."

$1.98 smiled at him and stated firmly, "At least we know something."

"What's that?"

"It is neither a spot nor a gap."

"Whoopee," replied Tinker.

"Ummmm, yes."

"Now what?"

$1.98 stared at Tinker. "Now what?"

Tinker nodded. "Yep."

"I think that it is time for me to take more drastic measures."

"Fire when ready, Gridley."

$1.98 looked puzzled, then he turned and whipped the long, black wand from his left sleeve, slashing it back and forth in front of him.

"A few practice strokes," he explained. The wind whistled as he did so. It sounded just like someone fly fishing.

Tinker looked at the wand. "Is that the same one

that Orotundy shied away from back there?"

The magician beamed at him. "The very same one. I will just have to use it if we wish to get rid of that thing."

"Better hurry before we become hors-d'oeuvres."

Tinker waved the others back behind $1.98 and asked, "You don't mind if we stand back here, out of the line of fire, do you?"

"What? Oh no, go right ahead. Perfectly safe, though, perfectly safe."

$1.98 shook the wand one more time. It appeared to be growing longer and longer. He said something.

A section of the plateau in front of them sheared away. The torrent of rock ripped away one edge of the town.

"**OOOOPS!**"

He jabbed the wand at the still advancing monster. Far to the left, the cliff face exploded. Some of the rock pattered down close by. The explosion left a gaping crater which glowed red.

"Himmmmmmm, hem?" $1.98 danced from side to side, the wand jerking and twitching here and there and stated, "Slash! Jab! Poke!"

Rock, debris, dirt and dust showered, pattered, and billowed in all directions The noise numbed their ears. In the dim, dust filled cloud, they could just see $1.98 make a great downward stroke.

The ground heaved straight up and split open. The fissure ripped toward them.

Tinker leaped to one side as the crack rumbled past.

"MY LORD!" screamed Chicken.

"Safe, Princess, safe."

$1.98 shoved the wand back into his sleeve and leaned forward, peering into the rapidly settling dust cloud swirling around them.

As the air cleared they all could see the transformed environment. The towering plateau was now a mass of shattered rock. Steam billowed up from newly created vents as lava ran thick down one side and streamed into the valley. Ash plumes billowed upward, darkening the already dark sky. Rock lay mounded in haphazard heaps. The roadway was gone. Nothing stirred.

The ground shuddered as the black thing lifted to the surface.

"Oh dear, oh dear." $1.98 stepped back. Then he leaped to one side. "**HORRORS!**" His hand flew up his left sleeve.

Tinker jumped to his side and grabbed his arms.

"Hold it, sport, that belongs to us."

The portal stood in front of them. It surface shimmered with the heat haze. The fire snakes roiled and hissed at them as a gigantic form stepped out.

"BY DUMPF, an ugly spot."

"Mountain!"

The huge man nodded at him. "BY DUMPF, I am. Where are the others?"

"What others?"

"The rest. I stepped in last."

Tinker smiled. "It seems, Mountain, that the last shall be first."

"What?"

"Nothing."

The black creature humped closer and reached for the portal.

Mountain scrabbled to one side, yanking his cudgel free.

"ROCKS AND STONES, what is that thing?"

Tinker ran around him, swinging his sword, attacking.

A fire snake snapped past his face and struck the monster. Steam jetted up as the fangs sank deep. The flash blinded them all. The explosion tumbled everyone through the settling clouds of dust. They heard the portal faintly through roar.

Bing-bong.

They struggled to their feet, wiping eyes and faces, staring into the clearing air.

The creature had recoiled backward. A large section of it was missing. All along the rip, tattered shreds hung loosely. Almost one-quarter of the creature was gone.

"By George, Sire!" said Goose.

"You can say that again."

"By George, Sire."

Tinker sighed and shot him a quick glance.

Goose was staring at the monster's wound. So was Toucan.

"Highness, it do seem for to be a'fading."

"What?"

Tinker turned to looked at the thing. Toucan was correct. It was now a light grey color turning into a thin, Wispy smudge. Then nothing.

$1.98 ran to where the monster had been, spinning and searching.

"Is it gone?"

$1.98 shook his head. "Not gone. Changed locations." He spun around and around and around.

"Do you know where it went?"

The magician gasped and ran up to Tinker, yanking at his arm.

"Quickly. We must hurry. It is headed for *Tripple* and Plum Duff!"

He spun away and ran down the road behind them, leaped over a large stone. And disappeared.

"That way, gang, that way!"

Tinker ran after the magician, the rest on his heels.

"But, My Lord, thy portal?" cried Chicken.

Tinker stopped. "Forgot." And looked around.

It was gone. "Now what?"

"This way," called $1.98.

"RIGHT!" shouted Tinker, grabbing Chicken's wrist and tugging her toward the voice.

One by one they leaped over the large boulder.

Mountain stood and stared. Then he stepped past and looked around. There was no one there. A voice spoke from the air.

"Try it again. Only this time jump . . . over that boulder."

Mountain frowned, walked back, and jumped.

He thumped heavily down. Now he was standing on the edge of a green valley completely enclosed by towering crags.

Goose banged him on the side of the leg. "Well done, old chap."

"RUMPF! Strange way to move about."

Stabbing straight up from the middle of the valley were three sharp spires of rock, a soaring trio. Suspended from the three peaks, seeming to float in space, a light, film structure, gossamer dream anchored by spider-thin threads.

$1.98 pointed at the structure and explained, "That is *Tripple,* the home of Plum Duff."

He waved one arm and jabbed a finger frantically. "See there, see there."

A black stain was inching up one of the rock spires.

Tinker spoke. "How do we get up there?"

"We will have to ask permission," said $1.98.

He strolled out into the meadow and yanked the tallest flower from the ground. It resembled nothing so much as an oversized poppy. Poking his face into the blossom, $1.98 asked, "Hello, hello, anyone home? Hello, hello?"

The flower spoke back, angrily, "Yes. There is. Who wants to know?"

Clenching the flower tightly just beneath the blossom, $1.98 shook it violently.

"Don't be such a rimmel. We are here to help you. Look to your slope. You need us. Let us in. **NOW!**"

A honeyed voice cooed back, "Oh, it is you, $1.98. Why didn't you say so. Come on in."

They stood in a fairyland structure of billowing walls and streaming sunshine.

A very small, very feminine figure reclined upon

a very large couch. She smiled warmly at $1.98. And purred at him, "It has been some time since last you visited. You should come by more often."

The magician's face turned bright red as she turned her gaze upon the others.

"And this must be the John Tinker and his companions of whom I have been hearing so much." She pointed behind Tinker and demanded, "What is that?"

Mountain frowned at her. "RUMPF!"

Tinker cleared his throat and told her, "That is Mountain. Also one of my companions. He just arrived."

"DOUBLE-DUMPF!" rumbled Mountain.

The woman bestowed a radiant smile upon one and all.

"I see. Then, you are most welcome. But how do you propose to defend me from that stuff out there?"

She waved one hand airily in the direction of a large window.

$1.98 fumbled with his sleeve. "Yes, good question. Ah, I think, that is . . . ummmm, it seems to me, that. Well." He looked over at Tinker and stated, "I really do not know. For sure." Then he shot one finger into the air, a determined expression now on his face. "BUT, I am sure we are here to get rid of it."

He looked at Plum Duff, a very confused expression flowing across his face. She gave him a slow smile that said much. His face flashed crimson. Again.

Tinker told her of their quest. And waited.

She stared at him and nodded. "I see. You are the key. What do you suggest?"

Tinker shrugged. "To tell the truth. I don't know either."

He looked at $1.98. "It usually takes us awhile for the solution to come by." Then he pointed at the magician.

"But he does have a rather powerful wand up his sleeve."

"WHAT?"

Plum Duff leaped to her feet and with one bounce was standing on the couch glaring at $1.98 as she snarled, "You brought that thing, the Black Snake, here. How . . . dare . . . you?"

Thunder rumbled from the surrounding walls, over, and under their feet. Something awful was approaching.

$1.98 leaned forward and stared into her eyes and spoke quietly to her, "I forgot about it in all the rush to get here. Ummmmm, I was afraid that thing would eat you if we did not hurry. I am sorry."

She purred, the rumbling died away. "You were really worried, weren't you?"

He nodded.

She gave him a quick kiss.

He turned red again.

She smiled and did it again and suggested, "We will really have to do something about that blush of your's, ummmmmm, one of these days."

Plum Duff dropped lightly to the floor and walked over to Tinker and looked up at him. She was as short as Sorrowful. "What do you suggest, Lord Tinker?"

"I think he might as well use that wand again."

Her head snapped toward $1.98. "Again?"

$1.98 and Tinker both nodded their heads.

Tinker spoke first. "It didn't seem to work very well although he did manage to tear up the countryside pretty good."

Plum Duff smiled knowingly, and nodded. "Yes, I know about that. He really does not have very good control. With a few pleasant exceptions."

$1.98 blushed again.

She laughed. "There are times when I really think he should have stuck to making sauces. But then, if he had, we would not have met." She winked at the ever-glowing magician.

Tinker thought that the room had grown noticeably brighter.

Plum Duff strode over and dragged $1.98 to one side of the room and told him, "Here dear. Now aim that wand over there and let us see whether you can hit that thing. I will stand here, right by your elbow. Shall we give it a try?"

$1.98 nodded and fumbled the wand from his sleeve. It slithered out with a dramatic flourish. And promptly blew a hole in the ceiling.

Plum Duff yanked his arm down and shoved his hand in the correct direction.

"Over there, over there!"

In the midst of blushing and stammering, he fired off a blast. The top of a far mountain disappeared.

Plum Duff stood on tip toe and whispered, "Just a little lower, sweet frimp."

The blast ripped through the middle of the monster. It quivered and continued to crawl toward them.

She frowned. "That does not seem to work. Put that thing away, my dear. We need something more powerful."

She turned slowly away, deep in thought. And recoiled, eyes popping wide. "**A TRUE HORROR!**"

Plum Duff grabbed something from nowhere and whipped her hand back, preparing to throw.

$1.98 clamped her hand in his fist as she did. The jolt yanked her off her feet and back against him.

Tinker whirled around, reaching for his weaponkin.

The portal stood in the middle of the room, fire snakes roiling and hissing at everything.

Sorrowful stepped out followed by Smoke and The Guard. They pushed around Tinker. The room was getting crowded.

The shock of their joining, rejoining, Smoke, Chicken, and himself, rocked Tinker back on his heels. Chicken gasped and clutched his arm.

He smiled a rather weak smile at her. "I am all right. Now." And sagged sideways.

Plum Duff squirmed from $1.98 arms and stalked over to glare at one and all and demanded, "Who are these folk. And what is that thing?"

She pointed at the portal. "And what is this monster?" She jabbed a finger at Smoke.

Tinker lurched upright, shoved himself between their angry hostess and the rest.

The portal vanished.

It made no sound at all.

"All part of the group," he explained. "That was

the portal. Certainly coming and going a lot."

He pointed to the rest, one by one.

"This is Sorrowful Mistidings and The Guard. And this is Smoke of the Velvetmist. Although there appears to be fewer of The Guard than when we started. What's going on Sorrowful?"

Sorrowful looked around at his new surroundings and suggested, "Perhaps that can wait until we have time. It is a rather large tale."

Tinker nodded.

Goose began to inspect The Guard, speaking in low tones with The Sergeant. Chicken, Toucan, and Mountain huddled together.

Tinker shouted into the milling crowd, "**All right, all right, that can wait!**" As faces and eyes snapped in his direction. "Right now we have a major problem to solve." He pointed out the window.

The black spot was oozing up the spire almost to one of the gossamer threads supporting the structure.

"Any suggestions on how we can get rid of that thing?"

Sorrowful ran over to the window to take a closer look, casting an appreciative glance at Plum Duff as he passed by. She winked at him.

$1.98 frowned and turned red.

She patted his hand. "Just kidding, dear."

Sorrowful spun around.

"What is it?"

"Probably a thing of Dram's," answered Tinker. "Any more weapons? Anyone?"

"Oh," said Sorrowful.

Chicken slipped an arm under Tinker's and

nudged him with a hip. "My Lord, there do be one weapon still unused."

"What?"

"Strange wand young Silly do gift thee."

Tinker smiled and fished the small wand from his pocket. "Yep, there it is."

He looked over at Plum Duff and $1.98. "Maybe one of you two can work it. What do you think ?"

They walked over. Plum Duff reached for the wand. "OUCH!" Her hand snapped back. "It is protected."

"Protected?"

"Yes. It has a protect spell locked to it. There is no way that I can handle it. Whose wand was it?"

"Big Red's," said Chicken.

"Maybe $1.98 can handle it," suggested Plum Duff. "He was his student." She nudged the magician.

"Give it a try, dear. It will not hurt . . . much."

Gingerly $1.98 reached out and lightly touched the wand with the tip of one finger.

"It tingles."

"Take it dear."

He did.

She gave him another shove. "Over to the window."

$1.98 stepped over to the window and looked out. As he walked he changed. His hesitation fell away. He seemed to grow taller, larger. Energy poured from him. He squared his shoulders and began to speak softly to the wand. It glowed and began to pulsate. One tip began to sparkle.

Plum Duff spun and began to push and shove

everyone backward and ordered, "Stand back. Stand back, I say. He is dangerous. Back, back!"

$1.98 turned to look at them.

Chicken gasped.

The magician's eyes were two red glowing pits, crackling fire. Electric arcs crackled over his robe.

"She is quite right, John," said $1.98. "This is a mighty thing you have been carrying in your pocket. And I am quite dangerous."

He smiled. Small curls of smoke drifted from the corners of his mouth.

"Duff, please take them away from here." He turned back to the window.

Plum Duff turned and pointed down.

They were standing deep in the valley. Far above, to one side, they could see her house. The monster was now creeping along one of the strands anchoring the house.

Goose squinted. "Sire, I do see some slight motion at gaping window."

An arc of lightening flashed from the window, impaling the monster. It exploded.

The flash hid everything, house, spires, sky. The shock wave echoed off the stone walls surrounding the valley and blew them rolling over the ground. Lightning crackled and roared from lowering clouds, striking all around them, blasting deep holes in the meadow, hurtling dirt and grass and flowers in all directions. Through all the noise and confusion they heard a soft thump, a muffled cry.

As they struggled to sit up, a figure stumbled through the gloom toward them, fell on his knees and crumpled forward, a small object falling from loose fingers.

Tinker lurched up and started forward.

A small figure flashed past, shouting, "Get away, get away. I will take care of him. GET AWAY!"

Tinker reached down and picked up the small stick. It was the wand, still hot to the touch. He put it back into his pocket.

Plum Duff sat and cradled $1.98's head in her lap, stroking his forehead, speaking softly to him.

They gathered around, wanting to help, not knowing what to do. She glared at them, tears running down her cheeks.

Behind them they heard it, crackling.

Bing . . . BONG!

It was the portal, calling them onward.

Tinker waved them toward it and turned back to Plum Duff and $1.98 and asked, "Is there anything we can do?"

She shook her head. "NO!"

"Is he alive?"

"Barely."

Tinker hesitated. "We have to go, you see . . . "

Plum Duff looked up. "I see. Go!"

Tinker nodded and turned toward the portal. The group slipped through. Then Smoke slipped through. Tinker grabbed Chicken's hand and followed.

Behind him, he heard Plum Duff's anguished scream, "**AND LEAVE US ALONE! JUST LEAVE US ALONE!**"

The portal winked out just as a great flash of lightning blasted the spot where it had been standing.

I Will Uncover For You A Hidden Thing

The End Of Time (?)

Tinker and Chicken stepped from the portal to face a waiting audience.

The entire company.

Sorrowful could hardly contain himself in his need to hear everything. He bounced on his toes.

"So, John Tinker, what was that all about? We had hardly arrived and we are off again. To here." He gestured at their surroundings.

"Where ever here might be."

"BY DUMPF, Most correct. What kind of place was that? And what sort of folk were those? RUMPLING UNCIVILIZED! Never even offered us a meal."

Tinker laughed at the uproar and tugged Chicken sideways, looking for a spot to sit down.

"All right, all right. Let's just sit down and relax. And then we can talk. O.K.?" He sat, Chicken by his side.

BING-BONG! TA-BONG!

The portal winked out.

"Oh, oh!"

Chicken grasped his forearm.

"My Lord, why hast thee of a sudden gone so dower in mein?"

Tinker slipped an arm over her shoulders and tugged her against his side.

"That racket just told us something. Unpleasant. Bad news. Very bad news."

The Company settled around them.

Smoke sprawled along Tinker's free side basking in their completeness. Then Tinker told them everything that had happened on $1.98's world.

Sorrowful told them of The Breem and then asked, "So where are we now, John Tinker? And why did you get so pale when the portal disappeared?"

Tinker turned and asked him, "You remember the noise the portal just made?"

Sorrowful nodded and stated, "Yes. of course. It went BING BONG, TA-BONG." It was a very accurate imitation. "Why?"

"When was the last time you heard the portal making noise?"

Sorrowful's face drained of color, his eyes darted around.

"I see that you remembered."

Sorrowful nodded and then cleared his throat, "Ahem. I did. This is a place of Dram's is it not?"

"I would bet on it."

"BY DUMPF!" Mountain surged to his feet, cupped one hand over his eyes and peered dramatically here and there.

"So THIS is the End of time? DUMPF . . . perhaps

it is."

They were gathered on the wide, flat near one of its edges. The soil, what there was of it, was gray-black, dusty. Dry. Gritty. No green things grew here. Nothing grew here at all. The sky was the same color as the air, sorta grey, sorta dark.

Clouds surged and billowed over their heads. As far as they could see, the landscape was ragged, ripped, a series of plateaus jutting up from the deep canyons, dark and mist filled.

The top of every plateau was the same height as all the others.

No wind. No sound.

Silence.

A dead place.

"Sire?"

"Goose?"

"This do most proper look a'place for Dram, if I do say so."

"How now, Higness?" asked Toucan.

"Now we have to figure out where the phoenix nest is located, get to it, have Mountain lay his egg. Then we are done."

"Ahhhh, John Tinker?"

"Sorrowful?"

"What do I do with this?" Sorrowful held out a crystal rod.

"This the object which we recovered from the land of the Breem. It is called The *Rod Of Time,* I think."

Tinker rummaged through his pack a pulled out a small crystalline square and held it out.

"We got this souvenir from the planet Rinn, the

city Rinn. It is called *The Heart of Time.*" He poked a finger into the small opening. "I will bet that rod fits in here." He held out his hand for the rod. "Let me have it and we will see."

Sorrowful leaned forward and started to pass it to him.

Toucan leaped between them and snatched the rod from Sorrowful's hand and ordered, "WAIT!"

Tinker lunged backward. "What?"

"Thy pardon, Highness, but one small suggestion if I may do so?"

"Sure. Go ahead."

"Highness, we know not what manner of event do happen when things magical do be brought one a'one."

"O. K.?"

"Then, as thee do be our focus and focus of all things a'happening, it do pear a'mine own self t'would proper nay be for thy Most Royal Self do be a'plunging one rod into one heart."

"Ummmmm?"

Mountain stomped over, leaned, and peered down at them.

"DOUBLE-DUMPFING, RAR-RUMPFING ALL, John Tinker, these unknown devices might produce horrible results. And I think we should not allow you to be lost." He shoved one great hand between them.

"BY ALL THE ROCKS AND STONES, SAND AND PEBBLES, HAND IT OVER! I will shove that rod in."

Toucan spun away and to his feet and shook his head. "Nay, nay, great friend, t'will not do. Your great strength may be needed still. I do be most logical choice. Unhand box, Highness."

"Why you?" asked Tinker.

"Most simple and straight forward. Goose do lead The Guard. Lord Sorrowful do record all. Smoke and mine own Noble Sister with thee do be but one unit. Lord Mountain do carry The Egg. Thus and thus, tis a'me!"

Twin flashes of fire sparkled from Tinker's neck.

"My Lord," gasped Chicken, "it do return."

"What?"

"Thy amulet dragon pendant."

Tinker reached up and felt the thin chain and smiled. "Sho nuff, it is."

Goose ran up and peered closely at it. "Tis true, Sire, it do be one and same." He sighed and said, "The Golden Dragon of the House of Chen." He smiled at the gathering. "Jolly good news." And beamed at Tinker.

"Do call her forth."

"Huh?"

"Do call the Lady Chen forth," Goose urged.

Tinker slowly shook his head.

"I can't do that. Goose. I do not know how. She just appeared the last time. It is just like every thing else. I don't have any control at all."

Goose lost his smile and wandered back to The Guard.

A soft, musical voice spoke from just behind him. It sounded like tinkling bells.

"And why does the Mighty White Warrior plod so slowly? Have we lost the battle already?"

Tinker lurched sideways into Chicken who was

trying to twist around to stare at his neck.

Goose spun around, grabbed the shorter figure, and twirled her up around and around in the air.

"Lady Chen, Lady Chen, you have returned. Hip, hip. Hooray."

"BAOFEGYOO! Put me down!"

"At once, Mightiest of Dragons."

Goose spun to a halt and gently set her on her feet next to Tinker who was staring at them.

Goose bowed to her. "Your humblest of servants. Me'Lady Chen." He made another, more courtly bow, sweeping his arms grandly. Then he strode off, shouting orders to the Guard.

"All right, all right, all right! SERGEANT!"

"SAH!"

"Do let us get this mob in order, shall we? Do this be military organization or rabble? On the double, man, on the double."

"SAH!"

Tinker looked at Chen, now standing close by, his hand touched his neck.

"You have returned."

She smiled at the obvious and said softly, "To serve you in what little way this humble female might, Great Lord and Master." Hands tucked in long sleeves, she bowed to him, three times.

"How may this lowly woman aid you now? Mighty Leader and Savior of the Universesss?"

Tinker waved his arms in frustration and snarled at Chicken, "You talk to her, Princess."

Stalking away, he bellowed, "Toucan! Goose! Sorrowful! Strategy time."

Smoke flowed over and stood by Chicken and Chen.

She certainly stroked his fur backwards.

Chicken laughed at Smoke's observation and asked, "Lady Chen, know you where we do be?"

"Yesss. Thisss isss where all start and end, the place of chaosss from which the yin and yang are formed. We must be gone before the beginning-end or our existence will never be. This iss shengfu." Chen looked over at Tinker and the rest in deep conversation.

"The Great One will require all the strength we can provide. In thisss place the linesss of magic run in all directionsss, the threadsss are tangled. Come, he isss settled."

The three of them walked over to join Tinker and the rest, standing in relaxed conversation.

Chicken jabbed Tinker in the ribs, lightly, with an elbow and asked as demurely as she could, "My Lord, may we but join thee?"

"Ooof! Easy there. Of course. We have a problem."

"What be that, My Lord?"

"How to find the end point." He rubbed his ribs.

"Toucan insists that he is the one to try the crystal rod and cube. He is not willing to be dissuaded."

"Brother," she hissed, all Royal Command, "do hand Our Lord those things which do be most rightly his. Thee do presume too much."

"Sister," snapped Toucan, "tis place of danger great that we do be in. Our primary duty, primary I say, is to protect Our Lord! First, above all else! All else. Say thou nay pon this fact plain and simple?"

Chicken's hand slid toward her sword hilt.

"HOLD AND DESIST!" Goose stepped between them, shoved them apart. His sword sprang into his hand as he danced back, the blade flashing in the space between his brother and his sister.

Chicken's blade hissed into the air and lightly tapped, shining blade resting upon shining blade.

"Do most kindly aside step, Brother Goose," she purred.

Tinker barreled into the middle of the glowering trio.

"What do you three think you are doing? This is nonsense. STOP IT! Or I will punch the daylights out of all of you."

Toucan was suddenly lifted into the air.

"BY DUMPF, John Tinker, NOT BY ALL THE ROCKS AND STONES WILL THAT BE NECESSARY!"

Mountain set Toucan away from the group.

A soft cloud swirled around them, enveloping them in a dense fogmist.

"Now what is going, on?," snarled Tinker as he spun around and around, seeking whatever this new thing was.

A silky voice spoke into his ear, "Thisss isss my doing, Master Of All. It will calm everyone down."

"Calm them down?"

"They are infected by thisss place. Chaosss wasss taking hold."

The mist thinned and disappeared. The small group stood and stared at each other, very puzzled and somewhat confused.

Chicken stepped to Tinker's side. "My Lord,

what do happen just enow for we do be most angry and confused, one t'other"

"Not to worry Princess, just some of Dram's merry pranks, I suspect. But Chen took care of that."

Chen was far to one side, standing close to Goose, holding an intense conversation.

"Now, where were we?" Tinker asked as he looked at them.

"Oh, yes. Toucan let me have the box and rod."

"Certainly."

Toucan handed over the two sparkling objects.

Tinker slowly turned the cube around until he located the small hole and them set the end of the rod next to it.

"Certainly looks like it should slide right in."

"Indeed," agreed Sorrowful.

Toucan, gather every one in," said Tinker, "then I think we will just try out this gadget and see what it does."

Toucan hurried away and began calling the rest of The Company together.

"Will endeavor such be safe, My Prince?"

Chicken peered at the things that he held.

Holding the rod and crystal cube in one hand, he pulled her close with the other.

"Has anything on this trip been safe, Princess? Smoke?"

Behind you.

A long tongue licked the back of Tinker's neck.

His head jerked forward. "Stop that! It tickles."

Leaning her head on his shoulder, the one opposite to Chicken, Smoke puffed air through her lips.

I know that.

As everyone gathered close, he looked around and said, "Guess everyone is ready. Hold tight."

Chicken grabbed him by the belt as Smoke's tail curled around them both. He held the rod in one hand, the cube in the other.

Then he shoved the rod into the opening. The rod slid smoothly in and touched bottom.

The sky flickered . . .

They stood . . .

And waited . . .

And waited . . .

And waited . . .

"HUMPF!" rumbled Mountain, "those things weren't worth the DUMPFING trouble to get!"

Chen spoke to Tinker, "Great Master, we have moved. This is no longer the place where once we stood."

"Oh my," gasped Sorrowful as he looked around them.

"BY DUMPF!" added Mountain.

They were on a different plateau.

This one had a long finger, a long ridge that stretched away, curving into the distance, out and around a broken tower of rock. All colors here were darker. Greyer. Almost black. The clouds hung lower, dirty, black edged.

Tinker shook his head and looked around, tearing his eyes from the swirling mass overhead. He had felt as if he had been falling upward. Up into nothingness.

"Goose."

"Sire?"

"Let us take a careful look and see where this ridge leads."

"Right, Sire." Goose trotted away. "Sergeant!"

"SAH!"

"Double skirmish line."

"SAH!"

The Guard formed up and started toward the far end, Goose and the Sergeant in the center.

Sorrowful ran to catch up with them and called, "May I join you?"

Goose waved him forward. "My Pleasure, Lord."

Tinker waited until the advance party was a good distance ahead, then started forward, taking Chicken's hand, touching Smoke with his free hand.

"Stick close," he told them, "I feel the need for your comforting presences."

"Yin and Yang," observed Chen from behind them.

"What?"

"Yin and Yang. The two principles that rose from chaos as the universe was created. Often seen as male and female. Together they form a unity."

Tinker nodded. "Right." Then he quickened his pace.

Chicken bumped him with her hip and

murmured, "Where err thee chose for to lead, Our Own."

Chen stood and watched them, waiting until Toucan and Mountain passed her.

Then she followed.

The long land-thrust slowly dipped downward. In the far distance it rose again, curving to the right. It was a spiral twisting around heaped up rock piercing the clouds.

The edges fell straight down into dark swirling mist. Distance in this place turned out to a very deceptive visual problem.

The far end was no closer hours later. Only the edges on either side seemed closer. The walkway was getting more and more narrow.

Tinker had watched carefully, not trusting his eyes. But the spaces between The Guard had shrunk. At first there had been big openings between them as the line passed forward. Now they were almost touching shoulders.

Goose stopped and waited for Tinker to approach.

"What's up, Goose?"

Goose pointed into the distance.

"Yonder do be somethin' a'walkin' this self same path, a'comin' toward us. It do pear a'me some goodly crowd."

Toucan cupped his hands around his eyes and stared where Goose pointed.

"Indeed, Highness," he agreed, "we do be about meeting with something."

"Something?"

"Indeed. What err do approach do move not as we ourselves."

Mountain, listening to their conversation, yanked his cudgel from his belt.

"BY DUMPF! This will be Dram's doings no doubt. We are near the end, so it is time that they show their misshaped selves."

Tinker turned and looked up at him.

"I don't want you getting involved in what ever this is!"

"BY DOUBLE DUMPF, John Tinker, I can take care of myself."

Tinker sighed.

"I am sure that you can. But, you are carrying The Egg of Time. Above all else, it must be protected. And that is your job, not getting embroiled in some mob scene. So stay in the back. Out of trouble."

"HUMPF! AND DUMPF!"

Tinker smiled at him and suggested, "Of course, if they get through our ranks then you may do what ever you wish."

"And how am I to get home if you let that happen?"

Tinker shrugged his shoulders.

"DOUBLE DUMPFING DUMPF! How did I let myself get into this?"

Tinker laughed and said, "That is the question all us victims ask."

"WHAT DUMPFING QUESTION?"

"Why me?" laughed Tinker, "why me?"

Chicken slipped her arm around Tinker's waist.

"Thee peer most jolly for such a'place as this?"

He kissed the tip of her nose. "Just relief I think."

"Relief?"

"Right! This trip has been more confusing that the last one. We have neither help nor devices, magical or otherwise, to help us. But we have made it to the end. So. It is a relief. That is all."

Toucan pointed.

Goose was arranging The Guard.

"We have but time small, Highness," stated Toucan.

They walked slowly toward the advance party.

"A vast crowd. Thrice our number," observed Toucan as he peered into the distance. "Most strange a'silence."

"Smoke?" asked Tinker.

Dram's. Driven by one mind.

"Might have known."

Evil, evil, evil.

Tinker kissed Chicken hand and released it.

She pulled her sword free and danced away as his great blade swung down and out.

Tinker could feel the tingle as the weaponkin hummed to itself, ready to kill things.

Goose urged The Guard forward, "Sergeant!"

"SAH!"

"Hold the center and push on. We do have some distance yet to travel."

"SAH!"

The black mass surged toward them.

Now they could see individual shapes and forms. The things gibbered and chirped, jumping, sliding, oozing forward. Fangs clattered, eyes glared. The jostling mob surged and billowed, filling the narrow causeway from side to side. And stopped. And waited for Tinker and his small group to approach.

The Guard yanked their great two-handed swords free and stopped, waiting for Goose to command them into action.

As Tinker approached their backs, Goose called out, "Sergeant!"

"SAH!"

"Scatter this rabble."

"SAH! All right lads, on my signal."

A deep voice boomed from the black mass of creatures, "Stay your hands, Noble Sirs. We are not here to fight. We are your escort."

Tinker stepped to the side of Goose and called, "WHAT?"

Five of the creatures huddled together. And shuddered. And fused into a single mass.

It surged upward, high above all heads and stated, "I am the Hand of Dram." Eyes glared red fire.

"You will follow us into Chaos. The End of Time."

Tinker nodded. "O.K. sport. Lead on."

The Hand of Dram turned and pressed back through the jumbled mass, crushing those who weren't quick enough to clear a path.

Chicken and Smoke joined Tinker as the giant figure led the squealing horrors away.

"My Lord," gasped Chicken, "do we follow such as that?"

"Sure we do. They are going our way. And for the moment, behaving."

She tapped the tip of her sword against the end of one of her boots. "We trust them not, LordLove."

"Nor do I, my dear, nor do I."

It was Tinker being W.C. Fields and said, "Come, my dear, a little stroll, a little promenade, after yon motley crew."

Smoke, watch that mob closely.

"We don't want any surprises," added Tinker.

Yes. Far ahead, at the edge my sensenet, something lurks.

"Goose, let's go!"

"Righto, Sire. Straight ahead, Sergeant."

"YES . . . SAH!"

"Not too fast, Goose. Leave leave lots of room between them and us."

The Guard waited.

Then started forward.

Tinker swung his weaponkin up and back, taking Chicken's arm after she had slipped her sword back into its scabbard.

As they strolled arm in arm he leaned close and whispered into her ear, "We need not be as relaxed as we appear. This is all show for Dram who I am sure is watching very closely."

She whispered back, "Oh aye, Me'Lord." And smiled happily.

MindMates.

What?

There is a great herd bearing down upon us. They are just behind this tower and are about meet our escort. And.

And what?

Dram is with them.

"Oh, oh."

"Highness?"

"Toucan, spread the word, as casually as possible. Another group is approaching with the Head Tiger."

"Tiger?"

"Ah . . . Dram himself."

"Oh, I do see. Very well. Highness."

Toucan wandered off through their ranks as Tinker drifted back to speak with Mountain.

"How goes the walk?"

"BY DUMPF, easy as is easy. RUMPFING DULL!"

"Not much longer. We about to meet up with Dram. He thinks he is surprising us. Look surprised. And be ready."

Mountain hitched his pack higher on his shoulders. "BY DUMPF, I am."

Chen had listened to all that was said and nodded.

Tinker hurried back to Chicken's side and wondered what it would be this time.

Then he heard it.

Screaming. Yowling.

In the distance.

Getting closer.

And closer.

"**ALL RIGHT**," called Tinker, "**ENOUGH PRETENSE. EVERYONE, READY. HERE THEY COME!**"

The great, black, surging mass bore down upon them. Their so-called escort parted and danced and sang as the horde poured through their ranks. The mass surged across the causeway, blocking forward progress. And stopped. Waiting, a safe distance from the front rank of The Guard.

As the Company stood and watched their foe, a slight figure dressed entirely in white sidled from the packed ranks, and stepped into the space separating the two groups.

He smiled at them and said, "Well, well, well, John Tinker. So we meet again. Heh?"

It was Dram. His glance oozed from individual to individual. Chicken felt a chill.

Dram smiled, and rolled his eyes and stated, "Same old gang, eh?" Then he shook his head. "Oh, I see, not quite the same old gang, is it? This time you have another bit of exotic stuff with you, heh? So, one comely wench wasn't enough, you old letcher you? My, my, my."

Dram winked at Tinker and ogled Chen and whispered, a loud stage whisper, "A very tasty morsel, indeed. Yes, indeed. It is."He leered at Tinker, a slow smile creasing his face and said, "There might he hope for you after all, John. Heh?"

Suddenly Dram straightened up and snapped his fingers, his eyes dancing from spot to spot.

"Wait a minute, wait just one minute now. You are not the same old gang after all, not at all."He waggled a finger at Tinker, and wondered, "Ah, ah, ah, you are missing some. Now where is that purple lizard creature and those rolling computers of your's John?

Heh?"

Tinker smiled back at him. "As you can see, not here."

"Uumm, yessssss. But where are they, John, where are they?"

"Gone, Dram, gone. Two-Byte went up in a puff of smoke and I traded Tai away, back there in the universe of times and places."

"Tooooo bad." Dram wiped at one eye with a finger and sniffed dramatically and he sighed, "It is always sooooo sad to lose good friends, or creatures. Sooooo sad."

He looked up and clapped his hands together.

"Well, enough of this chit-chat, time, in a manner of speaking, is a'wasting away. What little there is left of it. Heh, heh."

Dram shot a smile at Tinker. On. Off. And did it again.

"So, John Tinker, it is the same old question, even if it isn't the same old bunch. This is different. As you can see."

He gestured broadly. Tightly packed black masses chattered, their eyes glaring.

Hungry.

Rapacious.

Ready to kill.

"So, John. Will you join with me? Or will you die?" Another quick smile. On. Off. "Heh?"

Tinker stared back. And waited patiently.

Dram swung his arms back and forth. Back and forth. And sighed, "Come on, Johnny, you know you can't beat ol'Dram. As you can see, I am still around, in spite of past efforts. And this time," he waggled a finger at them and stated, "you don't have any of those fancy magical rings, heh? Nor do you have any of those deceptive necklaces."

Dram rubbed his neck and glared over Tinker's head. "Do you, Mountain?"

Mountain glared back and fingered his cudgel.

A slow smile crept across Dram's face.

"So you see, this time you are unarmed. Left in the lurch by that meddling fat, red rooster, Big Red. Naked to thine enemies, so to speak, heh? Of course we could work something out, don't you think?"

"Nope," replied Tinker.

"Nope?" gasped Dram, "why not, if I may he so bold as to ask?"

"Because, Dram old buddie-buddie. We are not interested in letting you end the cycle of the universes. Wouldn't be any thing for us to work with if you did. So, no deal!"

Tinker waved one arm. "Stand aside and let us pass. We have work to do."

Dram stamped his feet in a rapid tattoo and cried, "I won't. I just won't!"

He turned, flounced to one side and cast a coy look over one shoulder at Tinker. "So there!"

Then he spun around and snarled, "Die, John Tinker, DIE!"

The stirring black masses parted to let Dram slip back through their ranks, shifting their feet, anxious to be about their terrible work, impatient to be set free.

From far in the rear came a strangled cry, "NOW!"

The demonic horde surged forward.

Tinker heard swords snickering free all around him.

"**HOLD!**"

Two blinding flashes of blue light arced past The Company. Where they touched the demon masses, steam ripped into the air and destruction reigned. Bits and pieces rained down as rivers of gore flowed from the twin gashes ripped through the packed ranks.

Tinker whirled around checking whatever it was that was now behind them.

An enormous black sphere sat there, perched upon heavy struts. The outer skin ticked quietly. A familiar figure was rolling down the landing ramp. He laughed happily.

And fired both weapons again, enjoying the carnage being created before him.

"HO! Ho, ho, ho! It does seem that we are forever meeting in strange and far away places, John Tinker. And that I am forever getting you out of tight spots."

"Macabre!"

The round belly shook with laughter. "Who else?" he asked.

He stepped lightly to the ground, pointed one weapon at the surging mass pressing toward The Guard and shouted, "Go get , em, fellows."

Eight small blurs shot past his legs, buzzing wildly, followed closely by two glittering creatures. They hurtled into the demonic horde.

Even as Tinker remembered what those things were, he could see the screaming ranks thinning. Bodies and body parts were falling to all sides. Demons were disappearing in masses and pockets. The still living monsters began to edge away and turn and run.

Unseen scythes cut them down, flashing bursts of light blazed from the throng.

And then.

Sudden silence.

Far into the distance ran the survivors. Up close only the dead remained. And a single, solitary figure dressed in white picking his way toward them, stepping carefully over and around the slaughtered. Then he stopped and stared at the rotund, smiling figure, and asked, "Who are you?"

"Macabre."

"You are dead!"

"HO! Ho, ho, ho, ho, ho. You confuse pere for fils." Macabre fired both weapons.

Dram disappeared.

"Missed," hissed Macabre.

"Missed?"

"Yes, John, missed. I saw him disappear just as I fired. He is quicker than he looks. Come on, let us go and get him."

Macabre started walking into the mess he had made and said to Tinker, "You can tell me what you have been up to since last we met. Gyreship will come along in her own good time."

"What?"

"Don't look so confused, John. We have changed much since last we parted. Both have gotten larger."

Macabre holstered his weapons, patted his stomach, leaned over and whispered softly, anxious that only Tinker could hear his words, "There are times, now, when I am not sure who is running whom. Me or Gyreship."

They walked out the far side onto clean rock.

Chicken took a place on the other side of Tinker and watched Macabre carefully as he strolled along, beaming happily.

Macabre nodded at her and smiled and nodded as he said, "Fair Princess, I see that you are as fierce as ever."

As Chicken started to make a retort, Tinker grabbed her arm. "Let's save our energies for Dram when we finally catch up with him."

"HO! Ho, ho, ho, ho, ho, ho. Well put, John, well put."

Macabre bobbled his head up and down and popped his hands together.

"Then tell me, what have you been doing since last we met?" He smiled slightly and stroked his hair, touching the grey streaks.

"It has been, for me, quite a long time. But you seem quite unchanged and untouched by the passage of so much time."

Sorrowful tapped Tinker lightly on the elbow. "May I?"

Tinker smiled. "Certainly."

Sorrowful beamed and sucked in a great breath. And paused, just the correct amount of time.

"SO! In a time and at a time . . . "

They all walked in their chosen direction as Sorrowful narrated the tale of their adventures up to this point.

The tale ended and they were standing at the edge of a flat, open space. Far out, in the center, forms scurried back and forth.

Toucan spoke first, "It do appear, Highness, that we have, once again, met with Dram and company most vile."

Sorrowful pointed. "It appears we have come to the end of our journey."

Tinker nodded and asked, "Yep. Macabre, can you keep those creatures of your's under control?"

Macabre rubbed his hands together, a dry, rasping sound.

"Nothing will move without my command. I waited long and long to meet up with Dram. A certain personal matter, as you may recall."

"We will have to work together to take care of him."

Macabre looked at Tinker, a flat, stone carved expression and nodded. "Of course, of course."

Three figures appeared at one side and hurried toward them.

The central one appeared to be supported by the outside two. He was stumbling more than he was walking. Those assisting him wore brown robes. The shambling man in the middle wore a robe of many colors, a badly tattered robe of many colors.

Chicken clenched Tinker's arm.

"My Lord, he do pear most familiar in pace and stance."

Tinker looked to one side.

Smoke?

Help, MindMate.

Who?

Look.

He did and stared and said, "It is $1.98."

"Tis most true, My Lord," agreed Chicken.

The Guard opened a way for the lurching magician and his robe helpers.

Tinker waited and asked, "What are you doing here? In that condition?"

"You need my help John Tinker."

$1.98 gave him a wan smile. And lurched sideways.

"Such as it is," he added. The thin magician glanced around at The Company and nodded to himself.

"They are all gathered together, are they not?"

"Yep."

$1.98 stared at Macabre's pets, The Sparkling Tigers and The Vipers. And nodded again to himself.

"I am just more help. And I think I will be needed."

He shrugged his shoulders and sagged toward one side. The robes clenched his arms and held him up. The magician looked at Tinker.

"Still recuperating from my last performance. I may be tattered, but I am not torn. Just a little bit wobbly, that is all."

He started to fall backwards. The robes thrust him upright, he smiled. "Good thing I brought them along." Then he held one hand out. "You still have that wand from Big Red? Give it to me. Please?"

Tinker reached into his jacket pocket, asked,

"You really sure you want it?"

$1.98 nodded, carefully. "Yes. Wouldn't make it from here to there without it." He gestured over his shoulder toward Dram's gathering.

Tinker placed the wand in the outstretched palm.

$1.98's fingers curled around it.

The robes collapsed into a heap.

The magician stretched and smiled and sighed, "Ahhhhhhhhhhh, that feels so good."

He bent over and made two small bundles of his helpers and stuffed them into one of his pockets, and asked, "Now, shall we see to that pestilence over there?"

He smiled sheepishly at Tinker and Chicken.

"We have to hurry, this, urm, will not last long. And if you should happen to come for a visit, please do not mention this to Duff, will you? She would get rather, ah, over-excited."

"Sure. Let's go, Goose." Tinker waved them forward.

Goose laughed and waved his sword over his head in a great circle. "Tally ho. Sire. TALLY HO!"

Goose and the Guard began to trot toward the enemy.

Dram scattered his black, gibbering things across their path.

Tinker reached up and yanked his weaponkin free. It fell heavily in his grasp and hit the stone with a dull *clank*.

"What the?"

Tinker hefted the weapon and turned it over in his hands He couldn't feel a thing. It was just an inert piece of metal. He spun and yelled at Mountain and Sorrowful, **"WEAPONKINS! HOW ARE YOUR WEAPONKINS?"**

Sorrowful ran up to him. "It seems to be dead."

Mountain thumped up to them.

"BY DUMPF, it is true. Nothing but unfeeling wood."

Sorrowful's brows furrowed and asked Tinker, "What does this mean?"

"It means . . . "

"IT MEANS JOHN!"

Dram's voice sailed over the distance separating them.

"THAT YOU HAVE NO TRICKS HERE, NO TRICKS AT ALL!"

BONG!

"Highness, the portal."

"What?"

"My Lord, it did just appear. To thy left."

Tinker looked.

The portal stood there, the fire snakes roiling and hissing.

Toucan looked at Tinker. "What do this mean this, Highness?"

"I do not know. We haven't done anything yet."

BONG!

"BY DOUBLE DUMPF!" rumbled Mountain, "three of them."

Two portals stood there. One on either side of the first. It had replicated itself.

BONG!

BONG!

BONG!

Portals flashed into existence, rapidly encircling them all.

"**MOUNTAIN!**" called Tinker, "**LIFT ME AS HIGH AS YOU CAN.**"

Two great hands caught Tinker under the armpits and yanked him upward. Tinker could see that the portals had almost enclosed them and were almost on the point of meeting.

Goose, the Guard, everyone, everything, stopped to watch and to look.

"All right. Set me down."

"BY ALL THE ROCKS AND STONES, what did you see?"

"The portals are making an enclosure. We and Dram are inside a big cage, all of us."

"Then," announced Mountain, "it is time to stomp this place clean."

He banged his cudgel on the rock surface. "Even if this is only dumb wood."

"Into the fray, Sire?"

"Into the fray, Goose."

"SERGEANT!"

"SAH!"

"CHARGE! No quarter asked for, no quarter given!"

Goose and The Guard hurtled themselves at the demonic hordes.

Macabre stepped past Tinker, touched his forehead with a finger and casually strolled into the roiling mass, firing to either side.

The Vipers whirled through gore filled tunnels while the Sparkling Tigers shattered everything within reach as they remained by Macabre's sides.

They could hear his laughter as he disappeared into the battle.

HO! Ho, ho, ho, ho, ho, ho. Death and destruction. I love it. HO! Ho, ho, ho, ho, ho, ho."

The conflict roared around Tinker and his companions.

Chicken, Smoke and Toucan held the surging monsters away from him and $1.98.

Mountain swept a constant clearing around himself and Sorrowful.

And then, ever so slowly, they became aware of a gradually thinning in the ranks of Dram's malevolent troops.

A great explosion blew away the entire center of the battle.

Macabre stood there, dripping green and blue-purple stuff.

"There dam'me, that does for that. To me, Vipers, to me."

He trundled forward into the remaining ranks of Dram's creatures, the buzzing things whirling around him.

"HO! Ho, ho, ho, ho, ho."

And then there was . . .

. . . silence.

It was a silence so thick that ears and minds couldn't recognize it.

Weary figures began stumbling toward Tinker and his immediate companions. They waded through a sea of carnage, a tide of mangled horrors.

To one side, on a small knoll, stood Dram. He was turning slowly around and around, staring in disbelief at what had been his army.

Macabre called, "**DRAM!**"

Dram stopped turning and waved a languid hand at him.

"Why Mister Macabre, how kind of you to drop in."

"**DIE!**" bellowed Macabre.

Two brilliant beams flashed and struck. And arced high into the overhead greyness.

Dram laughed. "You can not touch me. Nor can any of the others of this dismal gathering. It is too late, much too late."

He pointed to one side. Large white shards glistened in the soft light. He laughed again.

"The Egg of Time is broken. No phoenix will ever arise again. The endless cycle is finally over."

Dram waved his arms in a victory gesture, looking much like any number of politicians Tinker had seen.

"NOW! You there," he pointed at them, "bow down, bow down to the new hand of the universes.

"MEEEEEE!"

Beginnings. Endings. It Is All The Same Thing

The End of Time (?)

Everyone looked at Tinker.

Dram's laughter bounced and echoed from the surrounding portal wall.

Tinker smiled and walked toward Dram and said, "Not so fast, fellar. This game isn't ended just yet."

Dram watched him approach and winked, a slow languorous wink.

"I do admire your steadfast nature, John, I really do. Never say die, heh? Sorry to say it, John. But it is over this time. Ces't finis. Heh."

"Nope."

Tinker continued to walk toward him.

Dram took one step backward. "I do not like the look in your eyes. Stay away. Your weapon is dead. You can't touch me."

Tinker stopped and turned to Chicken who had rushed to his side.

"Here, Princess, hold this for me. Do not lose it." He placed his weaponkin in her hands. Then he turned back toward Dram.

"BACK!" shouted Dram. "Go away. You can't touch me."

Tinker stepped up and close to him and smiled.

"Yes, I can." And launched a killing blow.

Dram rolled his head away from the blow.

Tinker's knuckles ripped across Dram's cheek. As he felt his fist slide by, Tinker shifted and twisted. His elbow smashed into Dram's jaw, knocking him stumbling to one side.

Tinker slid toward him. "See?"

Dram stared at Tinker as he approached, frowning, rubbing his jaw.

Tinker flicked a left hand strike and a low kick. The hand strike misdirected Dram. The kick thudded into Dram's thigh driving him lurching the other way.

"Guess what?" asked Tinker. He stepped closer. "This is the end of the line."

"Not yet, not yet!"

Dram seemed to grow and swell. Faint lines of energy rippled over his clothes. He jabbed an index finger at Tinker. The blast hurtled him backward.

"Not just yet."

"**JOHN TINKER, TURN AND FACE ME!**"

The words of command boomed from $1.98. Tinker carefully turned, watching Dram from the corners of his eyes, and looked at the magician.

$1.98 pointed the wand in his hand at Tinker and chanted.

"All . . . the . . . power . . . is . . . you!"

The wand snapped through the air and buried itself in Tinker's chest.

Tinker exploded.

Chicken's screams echoed in his ears as he felt himself rip apart.

He was aware.

All the particles that had been himself were spun hurtling outward, an ever expanding sphere of energy.

Wisps of cosmic dust. Spinning, spinning, spinning.

He was aware.

Stars.

Planets.

All the debris of the universes flashed past.

He was everywhere. And nowhere at all.

He was filling the universes of time and place.

Bits and pieces.

Spinning and twisting.

Floating . . . floating . . . floating . . .

He was aware.

And then.

Slowly . . .

Ever so slowly . . .

He stopped.

And fell.

Nightmare endless falling.

Bottomless.

Forever.

Falling . . . falling . . . falling . . .

He was aware.

He was back!

$1.98 was dragging a wildly struggling, screaming, cursing Chicken backward, barely managing to avoid being slashed to ribbons by her sword.

Tinker turned and looked at Dram.

"Now it is really time to finish this."

Two great hands slid under his arms, four great talons under his armpits while the fifth curved over his shoulders, holding him.

"Not so fast, Great Master. Grandfather Chen would he sorely vexed with thisss worthlesss female if I let you proceed improperly prepared."

"Chen?"

"It iss so. A final gift. Grandfather Chen trained you in the dragon style martial art. The small magician has given you special magic. Now I give you the strength of the dragon, one of the elemental forces of the universess. Great Master, these giftsss are transient. Physical strength fadesss. Only knowledge survives. Ready?"

"As I will ever be."

"DEATH TO OUR ENEMY!"

"DEATH IT IS."

He nodded.

Her talons snapped open, releasing him.

Tinker strode toward Dram, stalking him, focusing all his energies on one place.

Each step he took boomed, the ground rolled under his heavy tread. Light poured from his eyes causing Dram to shield his own.

Tinker paused and looked around the enclosure. As his gaze passed over the carnage, it steamed and faded. The dust swirled away. He glanced at his companions.

They grimaced, shielded their faces with their hands, and recoiled from him.

Princess? Smoke?

Chicken screamed and started to collapse.

Tinker's face contorted with anguish.

What have they done to meeeeee?

Toucan and Goose leaped to Chicken's side, grabbing her, lifting her to her feet.

He felt a closeness swirl around Chicken and Smoke.

MindMate, do not speak to us. My mindshield cannot stand against you. It is Dram you seek, not us.

Tinker whirled around, rage churning up from the dark center, from the dark places of the soul, confusion still painting his face.

Dram watched the group and began to laugh and dance.

"Too bad, Johnny Cakes, toooo bad. Someone has selected the wrong hero, this time, heh? To bad."

He leaped and stomped upon the shards of the Egg of Time, stamping them into smaller and smaller bits.

"I knew, I knew it. I KNEW IT!"

Dram's words boomed, and echoed back, ". . . knew it . . . "

Tinker's blow hurtled him out of the nest, stumbling, falling to the base of the mound.

Dram rolled frantically away as Tinker's hand struck the ground where Dram's neck had been.

Rock and dust blasted in all directions.

Leaping to his feet, Dram staggered away,

lightening flashing and crackling around him as he called in protection and strength.

Leaping forward, Tinker's hands flew in a blurred tattoo as he sought some small crack in Dram's defenses.

Pounding.

Pounding.

Pounding.

Slowly Dram was forced backward, further and further to one side of the clearing. Back toward the surrounding wall of portals.

Sorrowful kicked Mountain on the side of one boot and tugged at his pant leg and suggested to him, "It would seem to me that this is a most opportune time for us to place The Egg of Time in its nest."

Mountain stared down his nose at his tiny helper, jerking his eyes away front the violent combat on the far side of the open space.

"BY DUMPF, you are correct in that. Let us put this burden where it rightly belongs."

Shrugging his shoulders, he slipped the pack gently to the ground, bent and carefully unfolded the packing material he had wrapped around the egg. Cradling it in both hands, he straightened up.

"Don't just stand there, Sorrowful, let us get this RAR-RUMPFING thing into its home and be done with it."

"And over."

"BY ALL THE ROCKS AND STONES, over it is."

Mountain stomped heavily over to the mound and peered down into the shallow depression."

HUMPF, looks just like a nest. Shove all those

bits and pieces aside. Then I will set this treasure in its box. Hurry, will you. I do not think we want Dram to notice what it is we are doing."

"Most certainly."

Sorrowful scampered into the depression and began shoveling shards of egg shell in all directions.

"Pretty thick stuff this is," he observed as he held a piece up for Mountain's inspection.

"BY DUMPF, take some home with you. Look at it later."

Sorrowful beamed and carefully stuffed a small fragment into a pocket. Then he stood and dusted his hands smartly.

"There you are. All clean. All set."

He smiled up at Mountain.

"You may lay your egg now . . . Madame." He made a low bow and leaped out and to one side.

Mountain frowned, glared, bent low and gently eased his burden into the middle of the nest.

"ROW-RUMPFING, DUR-DUMPFING time for joking, if you ask me. HUMPF! These tiny folk have BUMPFING-BENT minds."

With a slight thump, the egg was settled into place.

Mountain straightened up and stepped back.

"BY DUMPF, that is that. The last stone has been set as my twice grandfather did often speak. DUMPFING well done, I would say."

Sorrowful bent and wiped small specks of dust from the flat white surface with his hand, stopped, and peered up at his large companion, a very worried expression on his face.

"AHHH, MOUNTAIN?"

"Yes, my talking small bit."

Sorrowful began fidgeting, here and there.

"It would seem to me, it would, that we should, ahhhhh, that we ought, to urge the rest of The Company to head for the closest portal and hope that they will let us go somewhere else."

"Nervous midget, we are done."

"Do you not feel it?"

"What?"

"The heat?"

"What HUMPFING HEAT?"

"From there." Sorrowful pointed at the egg.

Mountain frowned, bent over and gently placed the palm of one hand on the upper surface, and snapped upright.

"BY DUMPF. It is heating up."

"And that means?" prompted Sorrowful.

"What?"

"The restart of the universes. In one big bang!"

Mountain scooped Sorrowful up with one hand and starting running as hard as he could toward the nearest portal.

"You are RUMPFING RIGHT! Time to leave."

Tinker parried and shot a hammer fist down, then he punched straight ahead.

It took Dram on the chest. Bone cracked. Dram sagged to his knees and struggled to rise.

Suddenly Tinker realized that they were normal again. He kicked down and sideways, his full leg strength and body weight behind the stomping kick. He heard Drams knee joint snap

BONG.

BONG

BONG. BONG. BONG. BONG.

BONG.

BONG. BONG.

The portals were clanging all around the perimeter. Their surfaces were flashing from color to color to color to color to color.

Tinker spun and stared.

His companions were running in all directions.

He ran to the top of the mound and peered down at The Egg of Time. The egg was shuddering.

Faint lines were starting to appear across the pale surface.

Leaping to the base of the mound, he ran as hard as he had ever ran, screaming., "**RUN FOR YOUR LIVES, THE EGG IS HATCHING!**"

Smoke and Chicken stood, waiting for him. Nearby loomed the great Chinese dragon.

"Nooooooo." Dram was dragging his wrecked body toward the mound.

As Tinker hurtled up to them, Smoke spun and leaped.

This way, MindMates.

Tinker grabbed Chicken's hand and yanked her after himself and Smoke. As they entered the portal, Chicken twisted to look back. And crashed into his back, spinning them down into darkness, into nothingness.

The portal winked out, pinching off the brilliant flash of light and energy behind them.

Home Is Never The Same Place. Twice.

Grandeville. Tinker's Place.

Tinker struggled to wake up. And looked. At what?

It was a ceiling. Miles and miles away. And slightly out of focus. A blob moved into his field of vision. It seemed to him to be much closer than the far away ceiling.

It spoke to him, did this blob, "My Lord, do be thee alive?"

He managed a small croak of an answer, "Princess? You here?"

Squinting horribly, he managed to get his eyes to focus. Her face smiled down at him.

"Oh aye, Our Verra Own Bonny Prince. At thy side, as always. Canst thee sit up? We do be a'home."

"How come it is always such a traumatic event getting back?" he mumbled to himself. He struggled and managed with some help to get into a sitting position.

"Well, I think with your strong arms and lots of TLC that I will make it."

He flopped back onto the rug. And admired the ceiling. It wasn't all that far away now.

"TLC?"

"Tender loving care. Give me a little help and we will try that again."

She did.

He sat up.

"Well, all better, sitting up," he grumbled. And sniffed loudly. "Is that coffee I smell?"

"Oh aye, My Lord, tis that. Master Chen do say that thou wert most alive and do leave the body where it do lay. Then he do go kitchen way for to start pot of coffee a'brewing."

He nodded. "Good. I can use a cup."

"Would thee prefer to drink there or praps rise toward comfortable chair or couch?"

"The comfort of the soft couch would be fine."

"Be thee able to stand?"

"We'll see."

Soft but strong hands reached down from behind him, slid under his armpits and lifted him gently upward, setting him lightly on his feet. A soft voice purred as lips brushed his ear, "Perhaps we could all sit on the couch?"

Tinker took two halting steps forward and carefully hitched his aching body around.

A woman dressed in dark clothes, smiled at him. Her shoulders were wide, her hips narrow. She had olive-brown skin, jet-black hair cascaded down over one shoulder.

She was beautifu1. She was slightly taller than he was. She wore dark sunglasses.

Chicken grabbed his arm as he sagged to one side. Her action reminded him of $1.98 and his two robe helpers. He smiled at the thought.

"I feel like a certain magician. Who are you?"

She smiled, white glistening teeth, and said, "You do not recognize me?"

"Fraid not."

He looked at Chicken and asked her, "Princess, who is this? I feel much too battered and too tired for guessing games just now."

Chicken laughed, a soft deep-in-the-throat laugh, as she replied, "JohnLove, praps thee remembers not most solemn promise of the Red Magician."

The stranger reached out and lightly touched the tip of his nose with one finger while she removed her sunglasses with her other hand. Gold-yellow eyes twinkled at him.

"Smoke!" he gasped.

"In the flesh, MindMate. With you and The Princess as you wished me to be. Big Red and I saw your deep thoughts also, MindMate."

She turned around very slowly and blinked those great, seeming-to-glow, eyes at him over one shoulder, arching her back and purred, "Am I still as beautiful as I was before?"

Tinker hastily cleared his throat. "An absolute dazzler," he croaked. "But all I wanted was for us to not be separated again."

Chicken poked him gently in the ribs and wondered at him, "Do We be a'dazzler, My Lord?"

He nodded at them. "Right. A pair of dazzlers. Two beauties."

Smoke turned back and frowned at him. "But I lost my beautiful tail."

Tinker grinned a crooked smile at her. "Smoke,

you still have a beautiful tail. Believe me, all the males you pass will admire it."

Smoke stepped to his side, Chicken nodded. They lifted him and carried him to the couch where they crashed down into a disorderly heap.

"OUCH! OUCH! Careful ladies, I think my frame is bent."

"OH, MY LORD!" gasped Chicken, thrusting herself into a sitting position, her eyes round with fear.

He struggled upright. "Just a saying, Princess, nothing more."

He carefully slid one arm around each waist and tugged them close. "So, Big Red kept his promise after all. We are together. And now you are human, big cat."

"More or less, MindMate."

They both leaned heavily against him.

He smiled and said, "Although it seems he has had one last joke."

What manner of jest be this, My Lord?

Both can still do that, huh?

Yes, they answered in unison.

All three of us?

Of course, MindMate. LordLove.

Tinker started to laugh, then quickly stopped. His ribs hurt.

"The joke is in your eyes, Smoke."

"My eyes?"

"Right. Big Red left them the way they were."

"Why not? They are beautiful."

"Well, that's true, but . . . "

"But what?"

"But here, in my elseplace, people do not have

vertical pupils set in gold-yellow eyes. I guess you will just have to wear those shades whenever we go outside the house."

"Shades?"

"Those things you were wearing on your nose."

"Oh."

Then the awareness dawned upon him. The house was quiet. All he could hear was Chen in the kitchen, nothing else.

His head flopped back against the couch.

"Where are the rest of them? All I remember was everyone running every which way. And us jumping through the portal after Smoke. And my yanking Chicken with me. Then not much more. Something crashed into my back."

Chicken gently stroked the hand she held. "Great weight twas Us, Me'Lord. We do turn for to watch. Lady Chen's great tail do Us thrust swiftly after thee."

"The Golden Dragon. She died? With the rest?"

Chicken shook her head. "Praps not. It do, in quick glance, seem a'Us that We do see fierce dragon through near portal lurch in with front claws a'clenching the Goose."

Tinker smiled. "Good, at least they made it, together. Did you see anything else?"

"Little. The Guard do be a'fighting many new monsters just made by Dram."

She threw both hands over her face and sobbed, "They do burst into martyr flames. We do naught else see. "

They sat silently for long moments, then Smoke cleared her throat.

"MindMate, just as I leaped through the portal I think I saw Mountain lunge headfirst through one on the far side. It looked like he was carrying someone cradled in one arm. Sorrowful perhaps."

Chicken wiped her eyes as Smoke continued.

"I know that I saw the Sergeant and some of The Guard pelting toward a portal. Others of The Guard were leaping between them and the advancing monsters of Dram's."

Tinker turned to look deep into those golden eyes. "What about $1.98 and Macabre?"

Smoke shook her head. "They were in a different part of the arena."

Tinker slumped and sighed, "A terrible price, we paid a terrible price to do what we did."

Master Chen entered the living room carrying a tray laden with coffeepot, cups, and a plate of cookies.

"Nephew," he observed, "it would appear that you have recovered nicely." He made a small bow to Chicken. "Princess, would you pour?" He shot Tinker a hard look. "That is, if my unworthy nephew could stop fondling you long enough for you to do that."

Chicken sat up, leaned forward and poured each cup full as soon as Chen had set the tray down on the small table he had shoved in front of them. Then Chen took a cup, sat in Tinker's favorite chair, and beamed at them, and stated, "Now, perhaps you might leave the other young woman alone and introduce us." It was a soft but stern command.

Tinker struggled and sat up. "Master Chen, this is Smoke. You have already met her."

"The giant cat thing?"

"I am no longer that, Uncle. I have been Big Red transformed. And never a thing." Smoke flowed to her feet, smiled at him, and made a proper bow.

Chen nodded. "So it seems. And very well mannered also. Unlike some."

He looked at Tinker. Then he stared harder. "You have lost my dragon?"

Tinker ducked his head. "Your dragon has a mind of her own. I don't know where she went."

Chen nodded at Smoke as she reseated herself. "Did I hear someone say that she was clenching Prince Goose in her arms as she departed?"

"Yes, Uncle."

"Ummmmmmm." Master Chen smiled slyly. "She has always been noted for having a roving eye." He shrugged. "However, she always returns to the House of Chen."

He leaned forward and patted Tinker's knee. "So, Nephew, tell me of your adventures."

"I'd rather do that tomorrow. After a good night's sleep. It has been a long and hard time for all of us, especially at the end."

Tinker rose unsteadily to his feet and looked from Smoke to Chicken. "Shall we?"

"Indeed My Lord."

Smoke stood. "Will we sleep in this water bed thing that Chicken told me about?"

"Sure. Room for all ."

"But Nephew," protested Master Chen. "It is only just past dinnertime."

"We are still bone weary."

Tinker tugged at Chicken and Smoke. "Come

along beauties, we can talk to Chen in the morning. If you would each take an arm I think I will be able to manage getting that far without collapsing."

Tinker smiled at Chen. "Good night. We will have a long talk tomorrow."

Chen waggled one hand at him.

"What's the matter, Chen?"

"A strange business, Nephew, very strange business. Even knowing what you told me before, it is still a very strange business."

"How so?"

"You only left this morning."

Individuals Of Note

Grandeville

John Tinker – the individual utilized as an intermediary by Big Red in his ongoing activities to maintain the balance of forces in the universes. Tinker is now merged telepathically into a single mental entity with Chicken and Smoke following the cultural value's of Smoke's people.

Smoke of the Velvetmist – once physically a gigantic telepathic carnivore, now transformed into a human appearing female by Big Red.

Princess Chicken – once physically a fluffy Easter basket toy, transformed by Big Red into a human.

Prince Goose – a windup, plastic toy transformed by Big Red into a human. Goose commands The Guard, a number of wooden soldiers also transformed into human appearing soldiers.

Prince Toucan – a windup, plastic toy transformed by Big Red into a human being. He is the brother of Goose and Chicken.

Adam Lieu Chen – Master Chen owns and operates *Chen's Chinese,* a restaurant in downtown Grandeville. He trained, and trains, Tinker in the martial arts.

Chen Gum Lung - *The Golden Dragon of The House of Chen,* a amulet gifted to Tinker by Master Chen.

Kappa "Doc" Heckmann – anthropologist and adventurer. A friend of neighbor of Tinker's.

J. C. Smith – a friend of Tinker's who works for Doc in many capabilities.

Membrane – one of Doc's "associates," who runs Doc's business, *Cactus Spine,* which specializes in cacti and succulents.

Badnews Treefalls – one of Doc's "associates," who is his constant companion.

Paradise

Big Red – a pure force of magic personified, primarily concerned with maintaining the balance of the universes, and at times, involved with Tinker and companions in doing that.

Various Places

Dram – once a magician-in-training, now one of the pure forces personified. Often called *The Evil One* due to his ambitions and activities.

Stumpf

The-Mountain-That-Walks – usually just called *Mountain* and sometime companion of Tinker et al.

A Place Unnamed

Macabre – who specializes in killing things.

The Six Lands

Sorrowful Mistidings – A professional *Teller Of Tales,* an honored profession among his folk.

Clear Bandler

The $1.98Magician – trained by Big Red and told to aid Tinker in whatever manner that he could.

Plum Duff – magician and consort of $1.98.

About the Author

George R. Mead began to study anthropology in 1962 after being discharged (honorably) from the U. S. Army, Combat Engineers. He eventually received a B.A., M. A., and Ph. D. in his chosen field, before that an A.A. in Engineering. And many years later an M. S. W. in Clinical Social Work. He has worked in aerospace, taught at the college and university levels, worked in a community action agency, ran a restaurant, been unemployed, and worked for the U. S. Forest Service. He is now retired from the work-a-day world but does a certain amount of consulting, writing, and research. He lives seven miles outside of the small town of La Grande, Oregon, with his wife, two cats, and one dog, Jettz (all lab).

About the Author

George R. Mead began to study anthropology in 1962 after being discharged (honorably) from the U. S. Army, Combat Engineers. He eventually received a B.A., M. A., and Ph. D. in his chosen field, before that an A.A. in Engineering. And many years later an M.S.W. in Clinical Social Work. He has worked in aerospace, taught at the college and university levels, worked in a community action agency, ran a restaurant, been unemployed, and worked for the U. S. Forest Service. He is now retired from the work-a-day world but does a certain amount of consulting, writing, and research. He lives seven miles outside of the small town of La Grande, Oregon, with his wife, two cats, and one dog named Jettz (all Lab).

www.ingramcontent.com/pod-product-compliance
Lightning Source LLC
Chambersburg PA
CBHW052337020726
47503CB00001B/8

* 9 7 8 0 9 8 9 0 9 2 7 5 3 *